NIGHT OF THE VAMPIRE

She stared at the movement of curtain in the breeze, the easy fluttering of ghostly white against the wall.

Somebody was sucking on something. She heard the faint smack of lips—a quiet intake of liquid.

She went into the hall.

She could see through the open door of Paddy's room, and in the dim light, she saw a huge, black blob hovering over the bed. Like something from another world, it had no definite shape, though she could see the droop of a long wing and at the end of the wing, claws, one or two, curled.

She screamed, and the thing lifted its head and looked at her. Its head was small and hunched between the sharp, bony rise of folded wings. It had a wide mouth and teeth that gleamed in the dim light. Two long fangs dripped blood, one drop from each fang. She saw the blood clearly as it fell to the white sheet folded a few inches over the light blanket on Paddy's bed.

She rushed toward the bed, then whirled back and turned on the ceiling light. When she turned again, the terrible bat-like creature was gone. Paddy was sprawled and pale, and she realized he was dead.

VAMPIRE CHILD

RUBY JEAN JENSEN

ZEBRA BOOKS
KENSINGTON PUBLISHING CORP.

ZEBRA BOOKS

are published by

Kensington Publishing Corp.
475 Park Avenue South
New York, NY 10016

First printing: January, 1990

Printed in the United States of America

PROLOGUE:

Black wings.

Black wings beating against his window pane.

Big, big black wings that stretched from one side of the window to the other. Not smooth, silky wings with feathers, like birds, but something else, something that came in the night.

A terrible face.

Shrunken, wrinkled, with a wide mouth and long, sharp fangs.

A slit mouth that reached from one side of the head to the other, with sharp, pointed fangs in front, jutting out toward him, striking the glass of the window pane.

The eyes were gone. There were only holes where eyes had been. Rotted holes. Deep and empty.

He screamed, and the light came on, and the window pane reflected the room, his bed, his mother coming in the door.

"What is it, Paddy?" she asked, taking him into the safety of her arms, holding him tightly against her, pressing his face to her bosom.

But he couldn't say. He couldn't describe what he had seen. "Wings," he wept, clinging to her, trembling. But the word told nothing of what he had seen.

"Night terrors," she said. "Bad dreams. Go to sleep, Paddy, it'll be all right."

But he was afraid. The bad thing with the sharp fangs and the wings wanted him, was coming for him.

One night it would get into the house. Or it would find him playing in the yard. It would get him.

And he would never be Paddy anymore.

5

Chapter One

Babette woke, trembling, listening.

The blind in her small bedroom was drawn to close out the weird, dancing figures created by a street light shining through the leaves and limbs of a tree. At first she thought the blind had snapped up, as it sometimes did, scaring her, waking her, making her too conscious that she was alone in the house half the night with her two-and-a-half-year-old baby brother, Danny. The noise making him cry in his room, next to hers. But her room was dark, and the gyrating figures played in silence beyond her blind.

She turned her head slowly, breath held, and looked into the hall. The night light in her baby brother's room glowed like a strange, dim, white moonlight in the hall. She thought of the downstairs, and the bars on the windows. All the houses in this older part of South Dallas had bars on the downstairs windows. It made her feel safer, in the evening after Mama had gone to work, and there was no one in the house but herself and Danny. It helped her mom feel better too, she knew, though Ketti still cautioned her every day to never open the door to anyone, and never leave the house.

She heard the sound, something that could have been part of the old house drying in the summer heat, but it was inside, close, the quiet movement of someone. It sounded like Mama walking in her room, or in the hall near Danny's room. She must be coming to check on Danny, as she always did when she came home from work.

Babette drew a breath of relief. They were no longer alone. She turned over onto her right side and felt the lifting of the burden. It was always that way when Mama came, and the baby was no longer Babette's full responsibility.

Ketti walked through the room from the one-car garage to the backdoor of the house, feeling that someone was right behind her, as she did every night when she walked these few dark feet. Her key was in her hand, but already she was wondering, wary, half angry at Babs. The light in the kitchen was out. Hadn't she always told Babs not to turn out the damned kitchen light? There was no backyard light in this old dump, never had been, and never would be, according to the stingy landlord. She had lived here almost three years—two years and seven months, to be exact—and for the past two she had been coming home from work at two-thirty, the middle of the damned night. And all that time, the only light she had at the back of the house was the kitchen light. Babs kept turning it out, and Ketti kept telling her not to. Finally, Babs seemed to be getting her head straight and remembering; but now the light was out again. She expected more from a girl of fourteen.

She had to be angry, to keep from being frightened.

The darkness moved around her. The tiny backyard was filled with black shapes that swelled toward her. She imagined dark, hooded men who crept to backdoors and waited. Some didn't wait, but went on in, only slightly deterred by a locked backdoor. She didn't try to use the front door, ever, because it had a bolt, and she wanted her kids to be as safe as possible while she was at the bar serving drinks for eight hours.

But it wasn't the possibility of burglars that scared her deep down, filling her with a cringing, withdrawing fear that could turn into helpless panic, into a crushing world of nightmarish terror. Burglars sneaked in, took what they could find, and left. In this house, there was nothing to take. There was one TV, black and white with a plastic exterior and scratched face, and a volume knob that came off in your fingers. She had bought it two years ago at a garage sale for ten dollars. Who would break in for that? The blankets,

7

sheets and dishes were worth nothing. It all came from Goodwill. No it wasn't burglars who scared her.

He was here, somewhere. The child she had called Paddy with love, once upon a time. She sensed his presence. For several days now she had been afraid that he had found them, somehow, even though when she sent him to live with his father three years ago—after he had killed Billy—she had taken Babette, who was eleven then, and moved without leaving a forwarding address. There was no one in the world she had contacted. With her daughter and another child on the way in a few months, she had moved to Dallas, halfway across the country from her home in the northwest. She had rented this house with bars on the windows, tucked in among other houses, shopping centers, businesses, and tall, mirrored buildings that formed the Dallas skyline.

She had tried to lose herself and her surviving children among the people on the street. Dark-skinned, as if they had been in the hot sun from birth, they spoke a language that was foreign to her much of the time. No one knew her. She'd had only one purpose in life: protecting the children she had left.

Danny was born here, one night at midnight, with only Babette as an attendant. But even in the throes of her misery, she hadn't wanted anyone else. A local doctor had come in just long enough to make out a birth certificate for Danny. And then Ketti had gone back to work, and Babette was left to babysit from six-thirty in the evening until two-thirty in the morning. Fortunately, Danny had been a good baby and had slept like a little log from six o'clock on.

"That's what natural childbirth does," the old doctor had said when she took the baby for a checkup, as if the natural birth was something Ketti had chosen, instead of something she had been forced into by circumstances. "Makes a contented baby."

Working in the darkness, her fingers found the keyhole in the doorknob and inserted the key. The lock turned with difficulty, as it always had. Ketti began to breathe again. At least no one had broken in the backdoor. Babette had just forgotten the light again, that was all.

She felt inside for the light switch and the darkness was

suddenly dispelled. The naked bulb shone down on the kitchen's spare furnishings—the row of dark cabinets, the old, chipped sink, the stove against the wall, the round, plastic-covered table.

Babette had left the kitchen clean, as she always did.

Ketti stooped and took off her shoes, but her eyes were searching the dark hall that led to the front room, the extra room in the middle of the house that had no furniture, and the stairway up to the three bedrooms. She could see the light reflecting on the glass of the front door with its protective bars.

She listened, all her senses alert.

Paddy. Patrick. Would she know him now, at age thirteen? At age ten, when she had last seen him, he was deceptively sweet-faced, as perfect as a flower. No one had known her fears as she watched him growing, becoming something that terrified her.

It wasn't possible that he could have found them.

She'd been having the jitters, that was all. She'd go upstairs and look in on Danny, just as she always did, and then Babs, and find them both sleeping, just like always.

She picked up her shoes and carried them with her, leaving the kitchen dark. The floorboards creaked softly in places along the hall and up the stairs. She didn't turn on a light. The dim night light in the baby's room made a dreamlike glow in the hall, and she was led by it, comforted by it, as she climbed the stairs.

On the landing she stopped.

An eerie sound sent chills deep into her being, to the depths of her soul, resurrecting terrors that lived in her nightmares. It was the same sound she had heard three years ago, and once before that, when Paddy was five. The soft, almost soundless sucking, the pulling of life's blood.

She dropped her shoes. Her ears thundered with rushing fear as she ran to Danny's door. The night light plugged at the foot of his narrow bed revealed a dark figure hunched over the body of her small, helpless son. She wanted to scream, and her mouth opened. But there was silence except for the sucking of her baby's blood.

9

Her hand sought the light switch, and a yellow glow, only slightly brighter than the night light, opened up the scene.

The figure leaning over the bed reared and looked toward her. His face was much the same, but older, more handsome. Dark blond hair fell in loose curls on one side of his forehead. His cheeks were thinner. His lips full and red. His chin stained.

From the corners of his mouth blood ran, trickling in two lines down to his chin, making him look like a puppet with a hinged jaw.

The scream in Ketti's throat was no more than a cry of fury and terror as she plunged toward the figure on the bed. Hands out, fingers curled, she intended to kill him with her bare hands, to destroy him as she should have years ago.

Babette was shocked awake by the sounds of fighting, the bumping of bodies against the walls and floor. She heard someone trying to scream, or cry out, as if they were being strangled, or in a nightmare and unable to voice their fears. Before she was fully awake, Babette was out of her bed and running toward the door, even as her instinct urged her to turn back, hide, cover herself. But Danny was in there—closer to the fighting. Why wasn't he crying? Disturbed by the sounds? Sleeping . . . he was still sleeping . . . thank God.

Entering the hall, she saw two bodies struggling in the streak of light from Danny's bedroom. She had a brief, flaring realization—the sounds she had heard earlier, the sounds she had thought were made by Mama, had been made by an intruder after all. Someone had broken into the house. And now there were two bodies locked in a struggle, and she wasn't sure if one of them was her mother.

She saw blood shining red, glistening in the darting tracks of light as the figures turned, edging closer to the banister, bending against the sound of cracking wood. She saw blood on hands and faces she didn't recognize. The fighting figures didn't see her. Screams burst incoherent from one of them, and words bubbled as if drowning in blood. *"I'll—kill you."* It was a woman's voice, but Babette wasn't sure

10

if it was Ketti's. There were more words, words that sounded like *you can't do this to me—why are you doing this to me*. But they were mixed with other sounds, the cracking of the banister, of feet against the floor, of grunting so fierce it could have come from animals fighting in a pen.

Her back against the wall, Babette slid past them. When she reached the opening to Danny's room, she turned and ran onward to the top of the stairs and headed down, falling partway, rolling helplessly over the sharp edges of the risers before she managed to grab the banister and pull herself to her feet again. Numb to her bruises, she ran to the front door and began fumbling with the locks. Light from the upstairs bedroom hardly penetrated this shadowed area. Beneath the stairway was blackness, like a dungeon, and into that blackness one of the bodies fell screaming, the cry ending abruptly as the figure struck the floor.

Under the street light on the corner stood a group of Chicanos, young men mostly, at least half a dozen. Ordinarily Babette would have been wary and would have crossed the street to avoid them. "They carry knives," her mother had warned. "Be careful." But now she ran screaming toward the men and they seemed to understand her need without her voicing a coherent sentence. Several came running toward her, and the others turned to the pay phone under the light.

Babette whirled back toward her house. "My mother—! Someone is hurting my mother!"

They went ahead of her into the house. Stumbling over the threshold, she saw the light had been turned on in the entry and one of the guys was bending over the figure on the floor, offering a helping hand.

Babette saw Ketti leaning against the man who bent over her. With the back of one hand, Ketti was brushing her hair off her forehead. Babette stared at Ketti's hand. It was red with blood. Blood stained the fingernails, the long, carefully tended nails. It stained the palm and slid in slow rivulets down her wrist. Yet there was no blood anywhere else except the front of her blouse, as if she had brushed her hand there.

Ketti was helped to her feet by the man.

Babette saw movement on the stairs and looked up. For a moment, she didn't recognize the figure coming down. His face was covered in blood. Blood was smeared across his chin and ran from long cuts and scratches on his cheeks. He came down the stairs slowly and stopped at the bottom, and all the while, his eyes were on Babette.

He stood within six feet of her, and she looked into light gray eyes that were strange, yet in some way vaguely familiar. Then he spoke, his voice calm, as if he was in shock.

"Mama tried to kill me," he said.

Babette stared. *"Paddy?"* she said, incredulous, disbelieving. *"Patrick?"*

"Mama tried to kill me," he said again, and he began to cry.

Chapter Two

The scene in the living room unrolled before Babette with a kind of slow motion horror. Her vision torn between her mother and her brother, her delight in seeing Paddy for the first time in three years was turning into a nightmarish unreality. His cheeks, forehead, and chin were furrowed with bloody gashes. Yet he was her brother—she felt sure the boy was Paddy.

He had changed.

This tall, blond, handsome boy had lost none of the baby softness she remembered. But she would have known him anywhere, had she really looked at him. He was so much taller, though, so much older, that she wouldn't have looked at him if she had been searching for her little brother. The boy began crying, and his tears smeared the blood on his face. Babette wanted to run to him, just as she always had when he was little, and comfort him, and say to him, *"Mama didn't mean it."* But she was frozen.

Ketti was pushing away the man who was making an effort to lift her off the floor. He kept holding one of her arms.

"Ma'am, are you hurt? Ma'am, are you hurt? What happened? Did you fall?"

Fall? Babette had almost forgotten. The banister was broken, its splintered parts littering the living room floor around Ketti. Babette wanted to go to Ketti, too, to ask her if she was hurt. But Babette couldn't move. She stood observing the dreamlike movement of people around her as if she was the emotional nucleus.

Ketti was limping, making a kind of hurt animal sound as she went toward the foot of the stairs. She passed Paddy without looking at him, and by the time she turned the corner by the newel post she was running up the stairs and calling, "Danny, Danny Boy? *Danny!*" Her voice rose in intensity so that it had reached a scream by the time she limped out of sight into Danny's bedroom.

Her scream turned into a wordless cry that went on and on like the ambulance and police sirens that swelled in the night.

Babette found herself moving. She held her arms out, and Paddy came into them. She held him, her cheek pressed to his. They were the same height now, and it seemed so strange—she used to be able to press his head beneath her chin. He had been so little and so skinny most of his life.

Sounds of her mother's screams upstairs and the footsteps of the people from the police cars and ambulance thundered in her ears as Babette cried, "Paddy . . . oh, Paddy. . . ." But then her voice choked. She felt the shaking of her body. It was going out of control. She wanted to go upstairs to her mother and Danny, but she couldn't move. She was reliving a scene from her past, a scene that she tried to forget, but one which returned to her often in her nightmares.

Then too, Ketti's screams had seemed to be the only world, the total reality. And then too Babette had run into the hall, in another house, to see Paddy with blood on his

13

face, and terror in his wide, pale eyes. And then—a baby brother was dead.

Then. Three years ago.

She had asked Paddy—whose real name was Patrick, a name she sometimes used especially if she was talking to other people about him—that terrible night three years ago what had happened. But he hadn't been able to answer. Babette had never even learned what Mama had done to him to make the blood on his face. Had she slapped him? Made his nose bleed? But Mama never hit Paddy. Never in all his life had Mama slapped or even spanked Paddy, not that Babette knew of. But all Paddy had said was, "Mama hurt me."

Tonight the scene had been repeated, but with a stronger, harsher accusation. *Mama tried to kill me.*

Babette held him, felt his arms hanging loosely around her waist. His head had lowered to her shoulder.

She saw men going upstairs, two wore uniforms, the other white. A second person in white, a woman, put her hand on Paddy's shoulders and said, "Let's take a look at you."

Babette released him. She could feel his blood smear on her face and she instinctively reached up and wiped it with the back of her hand. Seeing the blood on her hand, she wiped it on her pajamas.

"What happened to you?" the paramedic asked.

"My mother tried to kill me."

Babette stared at Paddy. She was surprised he had said that, and in such an odd, flat tone of voice. *My mother*—it sounded so distant, somehow, so impersonal. She had never heard him call Ketti anything but Mama or Mommy, and he had always referred to her as *my mama.*

"Well, my goodness," the person said with an odd joviality that seemed to clash with the night's events. "You've certainly got some deep scratches. Why don't you come over here and let me cleanse these and put something on them? Hey, Jim, don't you think we ought to get this boy to the hospital?"

The screaming had stopped, Babette realized suddenly. Sometime during the time that Paddy had separated from Babette, Ketti had stopped screaming.

14

Babette started upstairs. She squeezed between a couple of the men who had come in off the street to help her, and had her hand on the newel post when she was stopped by a man wearing a uniform.

"I need to get some information. Can you help me?"

Babette stopped and stared up into a man's face. He was tall, and his head was haloed by the blinding light of the naked bulb in the ceiling of the living room. The glass globe that fit around the bulb had one day just turned loose and fallen, scaring her and Danny nearly to death as it exploded on the floor behind them while they were watching television. There was no money to replace it, so most of the time the ceiling light was never turned on. They had started using only the two table lamps.

She stepped to one side to get out of the way of someone going up the stairs, and to put the patrolman's head against a less blinding background.

"Do you live here?"

"Yes." Her voice sounded almost normal to her ears, but she wasn't able to go on and tell him the things she knew he would want to know. It was just like the last time—three years ago. The police, the ambulance attendants, the questions . . . Billy. *Danny.*

Oh God, Danny.

"My brother . . ." she managed. "My baby brother . . . ?"

"How many people live here?"

Just like last time . . . Billy . . . Danny . . . Paddy . . . blood . . . Mama fighting with Paddy. . . .

Babette whirled away from the officer and started up the stairs again, but stopped, frozen, staring upward. A man was holding up Ketti, supporting her at the top of the stairs. She stood in silence, her head hanging down. She looked as if she would have fallen if the man hadn't been holding her.

Two men were coming with a stretcher that held a small body, covered, and Babette knew it was Danny. She felt a scream in her throat—a rejection of Danny being taken out just as Billy had been—but it never erupted. Someone gently pushed her against the wall, and she stood there, hands flattened against the rough surface of the plaster, as the stretcher with the small, still body went by.

15

Ketti went past her then, the man's arm still supporting her. She didn't lift her head.

Babette looked for Paddy, and saw he too was gone. She was alone now with the few strangers remaining in the house.

The officer said, "We'll need to take you down to the station, Miss. Your—mother—won't be coming back for awhile. We can't have you alone."

Babette went with him, pausing on the threshold to look back into the living room. It wasn't big, it didn't have much furniture, and none of that matched. The old television's face was dark and still, but for a moment she saw a scene. She and Danny were sitting together on the floor in front of the television, sharing a bowl of popcorn. It was a scene that had been played out in this living room since Danny was old enough to sit up, to gum around in his toothless little mouth the soft parts of a piece of popcorn. He had been so eager for those little tidbits, so eager he would lean forward and make funny little half-crying sounds, reaching out chubby little fingers, and later, digging his hands into the bowl and trying to put it all into his mouth. Babette, laughing . . . then. . . .

She began to cry. The outside world blurred as she walked into it.

He had lost his chance to run away. The minute he saw the men thundering into the house like a bunch of bulls, he knew he ought to climb out the window, drop to the ground and just split. But she had hurt him, really hurt him, this time, her long fingernails, hard as metal, digging, digging at his face. It was like she was trying to dig out his eyes. She would like that, wouldn't she? Blind him. If she couldn't get rid of him by sending him to his old man, or if she couldn't kill him with her bare hands, then she would dig out his eyes and blind him.

All this time, he had wondered where they'd gone, Mama and Babette. He had never expected a card from his sister to come in the mail, telling him their address.

He lifted his hand and rubbed the back of it against his

16

mouth. Even though the nurses had cleansed and doctored his face, it didn't help the taste in his mouth. He wanted to gag. Blood. Why did he always taste blood?

His face stung as the nurse put more gunk on it. He jerked away again. The bright lights in the hospital emergency room hurt his eyes.

He should have split while he had a chance.

"We need some information," a dark-haired, smiling man in a suit said to the nurse who was still dabbing at Paddy's face. "Is he up to it?"

"Sure, I don't see why not. His injuries aren't as serious as it seemed at first. There was a lot of blood, but the scratches aren't deep. No deep cuts or anything like that."

"Okay, son."

I'm not your son.

The nurse had backed off, saying something about sitting down. Paddy knew she was talking to him, but that part of him that wasn't *him*—the dark, winged horror that had left part of itself in his brain, burrowed in like maggots—ignored her. That part of him detested people, especially adults. And Paddy was helpless against it at times. He stood tall and straight, his arms at his side. *I don't want to sit. I want to leave here.*

It was getting harder and harder to tell which of the thoughts that went through his mind were his own.

"What's your name?"

"Patrick Skein."

"How old are you?"

"Thirteen."

"That lady was your mother?"

"Yes. She tried to kill me."

"Why?"

Paddy looked beyond the detective's head. He noticed the man's ears stuck out a bit against the background of the peach-colored wall. Emergency rooms weren't white in most hospitals and clinics, they were something else—pink, blue, rose, peach. . . . He'd been in a couple.

"Can you tell us why?" the man asked, his voice softer.

"I don't know why." That wouldn't do, he thought. What would Ketti tell? And Babette? He trusted Babs more. She'd

17

always stood between him and Mama, or his stepfather, or the school, or anyone else that picked on him. "Maybe it was because . . ." He had been going to say because she didn't know who he was. He had been going to tell the detective that he had come in without her expecting him, through an upstairs window, and she had jumped him. But that would excuse her from what she had done, and something within him, the other part, didn't want that. He ended by shrugging, dropping his chin so his head hung in dejection. The nurse patted his shoulder in sympathy.

Detective Sergeant Mark Ford had been put on the case because of the death of the child, and because of his ability to find hidden meanings in cases that seemed open and clear. He watched the boy. His face had been viciously gouged from forehead to chin. Several long, thin paths had been treated with a clear ointment that left them looking pink and raw. His lower lip had been cut slightly and was swollen. He was a mess. Still, he was a handsome kid.

Mark thought of the two-year-old. So far the cause of death seemed to be SID, or crib death. The medical report wasn't complete enough to rule out everything else. But the strange thing to Mark was that this kid had shown no interest in the condition of the baby. According to the mother, and the statement he had given to the police officers, the boy was her son. The statement was so brief it was almost worthless. One woman, divorced; two sons, one two-and-a-half years old, the other thirteen. One daughter, Babette, fourteen. Nothing more.

"The baby," Mark said, watching for any change in the boy's expression or position of his body. "What was the baby's name? Your little brother."

For a long moment Patrick said nothing. Then he lifted his shoulders slightly and let them fall again.

"I don't know."

Mark frowned. "You don't know?"

Patrick lifted his head, but his eyes stared at the wall behind Mark, as if he was looking at a distant horizon. His eyes were odd but beautiful, a very pale color, not blue nor green. Gray, Mark decided. Very pale, luminous gray. His lashes were long and thick and curled up at the ends, a rich golden brown, darker than his hair. On his chin was a pale golden fuzz, this boy, and his upper lip was coated with the same fuzz. This boy, at thirteen, was precociously mature. He looked more like a sixteen-year-old. But his voice had not changed, he still had a little-boy voice. And his body was slim and young, with none of the developing muscle of an older boy. None, at least, that was visible beneath the loose, dirty shirt he was wearing. He looked as if he hadn't changed clothes in a week. The ragged holes in his jeans had not been put there by fashion, they were worn. The material was thin for several inches around the holes at his knees, unlike fashionably torn jeans.

"I didn't live with my mom," he said. "I didn't even know she had another baby. I haven't seen my mom in three years. She didn't even send me a birthday card, or a Christmas card. She just dumped me and left—her and Babette. They even left my stepfather."

Jesus, Mark thought, the messes some families could get into.

"So now you came to live with her again?"

He shrugged. "I came to—to visit, I guess. I don't know. I just came. And she tried to kill me."

The boy looked at the floor.

Puzzled, Mark watched him. He sensed something, something that had no face.

"Were you with your father?" The divorce rate of recent years had created many odd family circumstances, but it didn't explain this mother's treatment of her son. He'd have to talk to her.

"Yeah."

"What's his name?"

"Justin. Skein."

"And the address?"

"Post Office Box forty-two. Springville, Washington."

"No street number?"

"No. We lived out in the country."

"Telephone?"

"No."

"He gave you permission to come here? Put you on a plane or something?"

The boy moved. His eyes lowered so that Mark could no longer see their expression. He was almost squirming, his movements quick, without direction. He had nowhere to go. But Mark had a feeling the boy was looking for a way out.

"Well, we'll need to contact your father." Mark slipped the small tape recorder he always carried on investigations back into his pocket and pressed the off button. A runaway, he thought as he headed for the door.

"He's not there," the boy said suddenly.

Mark stopped. This was always a puzzle on the few occasions when he got involved in a child abuse case. What to do with the child? At that point he usually bowed out and someone from Child Services was called in.

"Where is he?"

"I don't know. He went away."

"He left you alone?"

"Yeah. He left me alone."

The nurse made a sound of sympathy for the boy. Mark watched him. Why had he waited so long to give that information? The boy's eyes were searching the room, then they settled on the nurse. But not on her face. He seemed to be looking at her throat. He was staring at it intently, not blinking. Mark quickly surveyed the nurse, taking in her total appearance: middle-aged, maybe more, plump verging on obese. He decided that the woman's neck was just a convenient spot for the boy to pin his stare.

Mark looked at his watch. Almost four-thirty in the morning. Had the kid had any sleep tonight? No wonder he was falling into a state of mindless staring.

"Got a place to put this boy to bed?" he asked. "Child Services is probably around somewhere, if you don't."

"We'll take care of him, don't worry." The motherly nurse put her arm around Patrick and patted him on the shoulder.

Mark went down the hospital hall toward the exit. A few nurses were at the desks. The emergency room receptionist

20

was reading something that looked suspiciously like a novel. The waiting room was empty. Not much was going on at this time of day. One woman looked as if she was waiting for someone. She carried an attaché case and was carefully, though not elaborately, groomed. Child Services, he thought, and nodded a greeting at her. The abused boy's problems could be turned over to her for the time being.

But the detective carried the burden with him as he went out into the street. In the east, the sun was sending a glow into this part of the world. Another night was coming to its end.

Why, he wondered, would a mother leave one of her children, and not even send him a Christmas or birthday card?

Chapter Three

Mark watched the young woman come into the interrogation room, his curiosity alert. What kind of woman was Ketti Graham? He had a few basic statistics: divorced, age thirty-three, mother of three children, one of them now in the county medical examiner's possession.

Ketti was still dressed in the clothes she had been brought to jail in, jeans and a pullover knit shirt. She was medium sized, about five feet four and one hundred ten or fifteen pounds, well-built with a small waist and well-developed bust and hips. She had dark blond hair that didn't look as if it had been touched with any kind of artificial color. It was styled loosely, as if all she did was wash it, cut the bangs and let it hang. If she had been wearing makeup, it was gone now. She was attractive, but she was drooping, with exhaustion partly, and surely with a lot of emotions—though it was hard to tell with women who chose to abuse their children.

Mark stood up and put out his hand. "I'm Sergeant Mark Ford, Mrs. Graham. Is it all right if I call you Ketti?"

"Sure." She nodded as she spoke, and put her hand in his. It was cold and thin. She didn't smile, or even look at him as she sat down at the table. She clasped her hands and rested them on the table top, her eyes seeking something in the corner.

"You haven't had much rest, I guess," he said as he placed the recorder on the table between them. She shook her head without speaking, and he didn't bother to tell her she'd have to talk. Nothing important had been said yet, no questions. He looked at her, wondering just where to start. He was not liking this case very well. He was used to shootings, knifings, and even a poisoning once in awhile. His cases were usually clear-cut, nothing mysterious, not this kind of thing where it seemed the crime was something subtle and hidden.

Suddenly she said, "My baby." Her eyes came to his, hitting him in a way he wasn't prepared for. They were nakedly desperate, pleading. These were the eyes of an unloving, abusive mother? At that moment he didn't believe it. "Is he—could it be that he—he's not—is he . . . ?"

She stopped, her lips pressed together but trembling in spite of the pressure she put on them. Tears brightened her eyes.

"I'm sorry, Ketti. The baby is dead."

She moaned faintly and lowered her head. He was reminded of the way Patrick had lowered his. Her hands clasped together so tightly it seemed he would soon hear the crushing of her fragile bones.

"The medical examiner is doing an autopsy. It's the law in sudden or accidental deaths. It's the only way the cause can be determined," he said. "Haven't you been told?" He answered himself. "Obviously not."

He waited, expecting her to ask what had been wrong with the baby. That was one of the things grieving parents always wanted to know. What happened? What caused the death? What has the medical examiner found out?

She didn't ask.

He said, "The medical examiner's report should be in soon. You'll be notified."

She squeezed her eyes shut. Then she said, "Instant death. Crib death. Whatever. With a strange lack of blood in the body. Anemia, or something. Just a—a stopping of the heart."

He frowned. Yes, that was the consensus so far. How could she know this? But of course someone must have told her. She hadn't actually said that she didn't know the baby was dead, or what the reason for his death might be. He had only surmised by her attitude that she didn't know.

He looked at his watch. It was getting on toward morning, and he had the girl, Babette, to question. This first questioning process was needed mainly to establish relationships, and what happened. If a second was needed, he hoped the less obvious facts might be brought out-if there were any.

"Would you like to tell me what happened tonight, Ketti?"

She shrugged, and her movements reminded him of her son's. Both reluctant to talk. She shook her head, turning it so that her profile was toward him. Her eyes were downcast, staring at the floor. There were no tears, but the slump of her body spoke of her lack of hope.

"I worked," she said. "I went to work like always in the evening. I work as a waitress in a bar a few blocks from home. I drive. I have an old car." She stopped. He waited, expecting her to go on, but she didn't.

"Was the baby all right when you left? Or had he been sick lately?"

"He was awake when I left. He was fine. He hadn't been sick."

"Do you have a babysitter?"

"Babette. My daughter. She's fourteen."

"She was with him, then."

"Yes."

"And your other son, Patrick? Does he live with you?"

"No."

"You attacked him, so we understand. He feels you tried to kill him. Why, Ketti?"

For a long moment she said nothing. Her eyes stared steadily at the floor. "He—I didn't know he was there. He had come in while I was gone."

"Didn't you want him there?"

"He's supposed to be with his dad."

"What's his dad's name?"

"Justin Skein."

"Where does he live?" Sometimes in cases like this, information didn't match. He would ask this same question of not only Ketti and Patrick, but Babette, too. Where was this elusive father? He had put a call in to the small town where Patrick said he lived, but no answer had come back yet.

She gave the name of the town, and it was the same as Patrick had given. But she added, "I don't know his address. When we separated, he moved to another house, or maybe to a trailer. Then I took Babette and Paddy and moved to another town."

Paddy? It was a soft and loving nickname for a little boy whose name was Patrick.

"Out of state?"

"No, not then. Just a few miles away." She shifted her position, turning her face so that he had a full view of it. Her eyes focused on her hands clasped on the table in front of her. "I married, and Paddy went to live with his dad, his own dad, after—two years after I married."

"But you're divorced now?"

"Yes. He was my second husband. I wasn't married to Justin. My first, Babette's father, died. His name was Roger, and we were high school sweethearts. . . ."

Her voice had grown soft and dreamy while she talked. He could almost feel her relief at being back, for a moment, in a better time. But then he saw pain fill every movement of her face.

"He was killed. A car. The usual. He was a fast driver, and didn't make a curve on the mountain road. Baby Babs, which is what he called her, was just a few weeks old."

"You married again—how long afterwards?"

24

"Well, not as soon as it might seem. I met this guy. I was alone. Except for Baby Babs. I didn't have anyone to turn to, no folks to speak of. I mean my mom was still alive then, but she had a husband and other kids. I didn't know where my dad was, and still don't. He may be dead, too. Anyway, I met this guy, Justin, and he was okay. So he moved in with me. We never really got married. We lived together just a few months, but he always kept in touch with Paddy."

The frozen, withdrawn, almost catatonic look came over her face again, and the flow of information stopped. Mark watched her, waiting, and saw there would be no more voluntary information.

"So how did you come to move here, so far away from your home state?"

"Job opportunities. And—I wanted to start a new life."

"You, your husband, and daughter?"

"No. Just me, and Baby Babs. Babette."

"Danny, the baby? How old was he?"

"When we moved here he hadn't been born yet."

"You were divorced before he was born?"

She hesitated. "I'm—I never got a divorce."

"Where is his father? He has to be notified."

"Edward Graham. The last I heard of him, he was living in the same town where I lived with him. Back in Washington."

"Didn't he know about Danny?"

"No, he never knew."

Incredulous, Mark watched the woman. "Why?"

He had a feeling there was a lot he wasn't hearing. This woman's relationship with her first husband apparently had been very good. But after that, nothing went right. Was this a case of a one-man woman who, in the depths of her heart, was unable to commit herself to another man? Or did it have something to do with the children? The second man evidently had taken the son, Patrick, to raise. Was that the reason she didn't want Danny's father to know about him?

"Were you afraid Danny's father would take him away from you, the way Patrick's father took him?"

The way Ketti looked at Mark—with a sharp, darting

stare as swift and piercing as a bullet—before she lowered her eyes again, told him plainer than words that he couldn't have been more wrong.

He sighed. Getting information out of some of these people was like pulling one's own teeth. He was tired, too, and getting hungry, and wanted to go home, where the atmosphere was paradise compared to this. His wife, Janice was a top-notch mother and he loved her for it. Their two kids, Sammy, age five, and the baby, Sarah, three, didn't know what it was to be pushed aside. Thank God. He recoiled at the thought of someone ever scratching Sammy's face the way this woman had gouged the face of her son, Patrick.

"You know why you're here, don't you, Ketti?"

She nodded, then shrugged again.

"Your son, Patrick, says you tried to kill him."

She said nothing. Mark had no clear picture of what had happened tonight at her house. She had come home from work as usual. Patrick was there. She hadn't been expecting him. He was supposed to be with his dad, a thousand or more miles away. She had attacked him. Then, or perhaps before, the baby had died—simply gone to sleep in his bed and passed away.

It was a hell of a picture, murky and swirling, like the waters of a flooding river whose currents are going in all directions.

He gathered up his notebook and tape recorder. "Why don't you get some rest, Ketti? I'll be back later."

At the door he turned back. She had risen, but was still standing at the table.

"I'm sorry about your son, Danny, Ketti."

Tears filled her eyes. She let them overflow without raising a hand to her face. She nodded, but said nothing. It wasn't the time, he felt, to ask her the question he had really turned back for. *Why did you hurt your son, Patrick?*

Babette had never known time to drag so miserably. She had been given a bunk in a tiny, empty cell for a couple of hours, but hadn't been able to sleep. She wasn't in jail, the lady in uniform had told her, they were just letting her stay

26

in this small cell for a rest while other things were being handled. Then, while it was still very early, she was taken into another room that had a table and a desk, and given breakfast. Whenever she asked to see her mother or brother, she was told nothing. It wasn't like no one was hearing her, it was more like none of them had the time to do anything about it. She felt at times as if she was going to start screaming.

The first familiar face she saw was one she had seen somewhere else earlier. She couldn't remember where now, but she thought it might have been at her house, or just after she was brought to the police station. She stared up at the familiar man, almost afraid to hope. He wasn't old, nor was he young. He had dark hair and a tanned complexion, and his eyes were brown and kind. He was smiling at her as he sat down on the bench. His hand covered hers for a moment. She'd been alternately leaning on her hands and sitting back with them clasped on her elbows, waiting, for days it seemed. The horror of the past few hours was unreal, as if at any minute she would wake up and find it had been just a nightmare after all. Danny would be upstairs in his bed, sleeping. Mama would be at home. And Paddy . . . ?

"Babette?" the man said. "I'm Mark Ford. Sergeant Ford. How are you doing?"

"Okay, I guess. But—why am I here? Why can't I go home?" She wanted to ask more—about Danny, about Paddy, and Mom. But with a smile, the man put a small tape recorder between them and began to talk.

"This is a recorder. It makes a more accurate system of keeping track of what people say. First, we have to go through a bunch of basic questions. I hope you don't mind."

She nodded, and answered the questions as they came, tensely waiting for the moment when he would answer her questions. She told him how old she was, how long she had lived in Dallas, and where she had lived before that. She told him she didn't know any relatives. There were no close ones that she knew of except Paddy, and Mama, and . . . Danny.

"They told me Danny is dead," she intercepted. "He's really not, is he?"

"Yes, he is. I'm sorry. It was a crib death."

She stared at a spot on the wall, hurting, wanting to cry to relieve the torment of her grief. "It was just like the night Billy died," she said in a hoarse, whisper-like voice.

"Billy?"

"Yes. He was my other baby brother."

"I haven't heard about him. When was that? Tell me about him."

She drew a deep breath and told him how Billy had been so sweet, and how he had gotten weaker and weaker, and finally one night he had gone to sleep and had not awakened.

"It was just like tonight. Last night. I heard Mama screaming, and I ran into the hall and there was Paddy—and Mama—and—and—" She stopped, feeling an instinctive need to be careful of what she said. Others might not understand. She didn't understand. Had Mama hit Paddy then, too? She hadn't known then, and she didn't know now. But if Ketti had, why, why would she when she had never hit him any other time?

"And?" he asked.

"And . . . the baby was dead."

"How long ago was this?"

"It was three years ago. Billy was just thirteen months old."

"This was when you were living in Washington? And your stepfather—what was his name?"

"Ed Graham."

"He was with you then?"

"Yes."

"But after that?"

"After Billy died, Paddy went to live with his dad, and Mama and I came here."

"Alone? Just the two of you?"

"Yes."

"What about your stepfather, Ed?"

"I don't know. We left him there. At the house. He didn't try to stop us from leaving. He just sat there with his head in his hands. He loved Billy a lot. But Mama wanted to leave. She didn't even tell me we were going until we were in the car."

She had been afraid, she remembered, that Ketti was going to take her somewhere and leave her, too, the way she had left Paddy. She had cried, and pleaded. *Mama, don't leave me somewhere.* And Ketti had taken her hand, and squeezed it so hard it hurt. *I'll never leave you, Baby Babs. I want to make sure nothing happens to you. I want you to be safe.*

She had never understood what her mother meant. Weren't they safe at home? With Ed?

"But your mother must have been pregnant at that time?"

"I guess she was. I didn't know for several months." Babette felt a bittersweet rush in her heart. "It was like having Billy back again, with a different baby added, because Danny was a lot like Billy. And yet, he was Danny, too. Danny was smaller than Billy. He was never really as chubby and big as Billy. Mama made me stay with him constantly when she was at work, she was so worried about him all the time. But I would have stayed with him anyway, because I had taken care of Billy a lot, and I didn't want anything to happen to Danny." The tears came for the first time since she had been brought to the jail. She sat with her palms flat on the bench on each side of her and simply let her tears drop onto her jeans. After a moment, she used the back of her hand to wipe the wetness off her cheeks, and shook her head at the handkerchief the man offered.

"Somebody brought me my clothes tonight," she said. "I don't know who. I had to come here in my pajamas, and I stayed here in them about an hour, then someone handed me a sack and it had a pair of my own jeans and a shirt. Is Mama . . . ? Did Mama go home? Why am I still here? Can I see Paddy?"

"Tell me about Paddy," he said. "How long has it been since you last saw him?"

"Three years. Not since the day of Billy's funeral."

"What happened then?"

"After the funeral? Mama packed Paddy's clothes . . ."

I'm not going, you can't make me. But their mother had worked with her lips pressed into a hard line, puckers in her chin. At the funeral Paddy had sat with Babette and she had held his hand. Sometimes she looked at him and he looked just like he always did, except for a strange kind of anger on his face. She knew anger in Paddy, because it had come so often. There would be a sharpening of his cheekbones, somehow, even when his cheeks were still round and babyish. And his eyes would become smaller and the color more intensified, not darker, but brighter. And he would look at her as if he hated her. At those times she felt confused around Paddy because he never said he was angry, or that he hated her, or anyone. It was just something she knew. *You hate me*, Paddy had yelled at their mother. *Who's going to take care of me?* And Babette herself had run after Ketti, pulling at her arm when she threw the overstuffed suitcase into the back seat of the car. Ketti was still wearing the new dress she had gotten especially for Billy's funeral, and she was beautiful in it. Even Ed had walked out to the car, his face puzzled and worried, and he asked her what she was going to do. Ketti hadn't answered. Rain started to fall from the heavy clouds, and Ketti's beauty shop hairdo was getting wet. Her long, blond hair had started to fall into the style she usually wore, and little drops of rain ran down her cheeks, like tears—the tears nobody but Babette had shed at the funeral. Ketti hadn't even answered Ed. She had thrown the suitcase into the car, then reached for Paddy, and grabbing him by the arm, almost threw him into the back seat, too.

Babette stood by the road crying as the car disappeared behind the tall fir trees in the bend of the road. At her side stood her big, husky stepfather looking as helpless as she felt.

"Babette?" the man with the tape recorder said gently.

Babette returned to the moment. "She took him away. For a long time, she wouldn't even tell me where she had taken him, then she said he had gone to live with his father, whose name was Justin. I guess he used to be my stepfather, but maybe not. I didn't know him very well. A couple of times he came after Paddy. But Paddy never wanted to go, so his dad didn't come often."

"Did you communicate with Paddy after you came to Dallas?"

"No. Mama wouldn't let me."

"Why?"

"I don't know."

"How did he find you if he didn't know where you were?"

"Well." Babette clasped her hands in her lap. She had polished her fingernails and it was flaking off. She began to pick at the flakes. "I did it. Without her permission. It was his birthday last month, so I sent him a card. The town where his dad lives, where we lived with him, isn't very big, so all I had to do was send it to the post office, and I knew Paddy would get it if he still lived there."

"Did he answer?"

"No."

"So last night he just showed up and knocked on your door?"

She lifted her head. On this point she felt confused, as if Paddy had somehow just walked out of her dream. She had been dreaming, she suddenly recalled, that he and she were playing with Billy and Danny. It was a strange dream with scary overtones that threatened to turn into a nightmare.

"No, it wasn't like that. I didn't even know he was there until I heard Mama screaming." She frowned. She didn't understand.

"Tell me about it," Mark encouraged. "Tell me everything you remember about what happened from then until the police came."

"I heard the screaming. I ran into the hall and I saw Mama fighting with someone. I thought it was a burglar. She fell through the banister—or someone did. I don't think I knew who it was then. I ran out of the house and to the corner where a bunch of guys were hanging out, and they came back to the house with me, and one of them turned on the lights, and there was Mama. She had fallen—and there was Paddy and he had blood all over his face." She shifted uncomfortably on the bench, something inside her memory trying to make sense of this past night. "It was like—it was like the night Billy died. Mama had been

31

screaming then, too, and Paddy—Paddy had blood on his face."

"He had been struck?"

"I guess so. Maybe his nose had bled, because his face wasn't cut or anything like that. Then." She looked at her hands. He was still waiting, and she realized she hadn't finished the story. "Then the police came, tonight, I mean. And ambulances. One, maybe more. And someone said the baby was dead. They brought him down. No one let me see him. And then I was brought here. Mama was taken away before I was, and so was Paddy. I don't understand why they don't let me go home. I want to see my mother and brother. I want to see Danny, too."

Mark patted her shoulder. "I'll see if I can get you in to see your mother, but I think your brother, Paddy, was taken to the hospital."

"Where is my mother?"

"She's in jail, Babette, for child abuse."

Babette stared at him, unable to assimilate this information. She almost laughed, it sounded so ludicrous. Ketti, a child abuser? Ketti, the affectionate, loving mother she'd always known? But then Babette remembered again the day Ketti had made Paddy go live with his father, and all the years since when she wouldn't even let Babette talk about him. Once Babette had accused her of not liking Paddy, and Ketti had said after a long, thoughtful silence, "Don't like Paddy? My firstborn son? Babette, you've no idea how much I loved Paddy. I loved him so much it still breaks my heart."

Chapter Four

Babette was ill at ease in the strange, bare room. A long table, like a banquet table, was in the center of the room, with four chairs on one side and four on the other. There was no other furniture. The walls were painted white, as were all the walls she had seen in this police station. A uniformed policewoman had brought her here and then gone away, and Babette wished now she hadn't come. "I want to see Mama," she had told Sergeant Mark Ford, and he had told her, yes, he'd see that she did. A lot of long, dragging minutes passed, and then she had been brought here.

When she crossed the room to the table, her footsteps seemed too loud, as if someone large and heavy behind her made the noise. She looked over her shoulder, knowing she was alone. What had happened to her life? To all their lives? To Danny's . . . ?

She pulled out a chair, and its wood legs scraped the floor loudly, filling the room with noise. She stopped, waited for silence, then lifted the chair away from the table so she could sit down.

Suddenly there were footsteps in the hall, just outside the door. The door opened, and Ketti stood framed in the opening, her hair looking darker than usual and more straggled, her face thinner and pale as an old bone bleached in the desert sun.

"Mama!"

Babette rushed toward her, the small room ringing with her footsteps. She threw her arms around Ketti's neck and hugged her. Ketti was just enough taller than Babette that Babette could still rest her head against her mother's shoul-

33

der. She pressed her face for a moment to Ketti's neck, and felt the nervous thumping of a pulse.

Ketti gripped Babette's arms and drew her toward the table. Babette saw her look back at the policewoman, and the woman withdrew, pulling the door quietly shut. There were no footsteps moving away down the hall, so Babette knew she was still outside the door, like a guard.

Ketti pulled a chair to the end of the table and pushed Babette down into the chair beside it. Her voice came low and hissing, her words quick, hurried, almost whispered. Anxiety tightened her face, and there was something in her eyes that Babette realized she had seen before, a lot of times. She was beginning to understand it was fear. Deep, malignant fear. It had rarely let up in Ketti's life, and Babette wondered about it, and remembered: Ketti telling her to be sure to keep all the doors and windows locked, to open the door to no one. No matter how hot the weather, or how much she wanted to take Danny out in the evenings after Ketti had gone to work, Ketti had left orders to never leave the house, or open so much as one window.

She remembered, too, the times she had disobeyed Ketti, keeping it to herself that she had taken Danny for a walk around the block in the cool of the evening or down to the convenience store for one popsicle, which they split. The popsicle was purchased from fifty cents she had found on the sidewalk, and other times from pennies she kept back out of the grocery money. Stolen pennies, in a way. But the one time she had told Ketti that she had taken the baby to the store for a popsicle, Ketti had become so upset that Babette never told her of the trips again. She had known Ketti was afraid, but she had never known why. She had never asked. But the time had come for that question.

"Mama," she wept, interrupting words she hadn't really heard, tears burning her eyes now that Ketti was here. "Why are they doing this to us? Mama, *Danny* is . . . oh, Mama!"

Ketti's hand gripped Babette's arm so tightly she heard the sound of her bones, and Babette's fingers began to grow numb. Ketti gave her a shake.

"Stop! Listen. Listen to me, Babette. I should have told

you this a long time ago, so you wouldn't have let Patrick into the house—''

"I didn't let him in! I thought you did."

For a moment Ketti paused, then she said in words hurried and hushed, "I didn't let him in. He was already there when I got home. Now, listen to me, Babette. I want to know—how did he find us?"

Suddenly Babette knew what caused Ketti's fear. It was Paddy. *Paddy.*

"Mama! Paddy is my brother. It was his birthday last month!"

"You sent him something."

"Mama! Why—why don't you like Paddy? You're afraid of him, aren't you? Why?" Her voice was a cry, confused and hurt. It was as if in feeling this way toward Paddy, Ketti also rejected Babette. "I don't understand you, Mama."

Babette saw her mother's face and body sag, and for a heartbeat she was terrified that Ketti was going to faint, perhaps die too, suddenly and without warning, the way Danny had, and Billy. Ketti leaned against the table. She put her elbows there and supported her head in her hands. When she spoke again, her voice was slower.

"That boy—Patrick—is not Paddy, Babette."

The silence in the room intensified. Something began throbbing in Babette's ears, rushing like a river out of control. She drew in her breath and stared at Ketti, whose eyes were closed now. Babette could see that she was tired, tired almost to the point of collapsing.

"Mama," she said, assuming the parental role, as she had lately when she could see Ketti was younger than she had always thought of her—younger, more vulnerable, and alone, with only herself against the world. "Mama, have you had any rest?" She could not equate this young mother with what Ketti had just said about Paddy, nor with the scratched and bleeding face of her brother. Babette's eyes were drawn to Ketti's hand, and she saw that the nails were broken and jagged.

Ketti raised her head and looked at Babette.

"Please listen to me, Babette. Your life is going to depend on it. You know that Danny is dead, don't you?"

The authority was back in Ketti's voice, and in the way her eyes had come to Babette, and in the steady lift of her chin. She laid her hand on the table, palm flat, the broken nails outlined against the white formica top. Babette said nothing, just nodded.

"What I'm going to tell you is something you must never for one moment doubt, nor ever tell anyone else. This is between you and me—and Patrick. The police are going to keep me here because I don't have the money to pay the bail, or whatever it is. I can't get out for awhile, maybe for a long time, I don't know. They're accusing me of trying to kill Pad—Patrick—with my bare hands." She gave a short, scornful laugh, her eyes glancing away from Babette. "Oh, God, if only they knew how hard I tried to keep us away from him. I thought, I was hoping . . . I don't know what I was hoping, exactly. Maybe that I was wrong. When I took him to Justin, I was hoping for some miracle for my little boy, Paddy. I don't know."

"What are you talking about, Mama?"

Ketti reached out and took Babette's hand in both of hers and held it tightly.

"When you leave here, you go straight to the house and go into my bedroom and look in the corner of the upper right dresser drawer. You'll find a little package of herbs. It's called *Wolfsbane*. I just bought it day before yesterday, and I hadn't used it yet. I think you're supposed to keep it on your person, or sprinkle it at windows and doors, I'm not sure. But—"

"*Wolfsbane?* What for? What's it for?"

"It's a protection against vampires, Babette."

Ketti's voice was so low Babette wasn't sure she had heard correctly. She stared at her mother.

"Vampires?" The word came slowly from Babette's lips. She was puzzled. Vampires existed on the screen, in movies, just for scary fun. Yet her mother was deadly serious. *Sprinkle Wolfsbane at the doors and windows?* "What do you mean, vampires?"

"He's a vampire, Babette. He's not my son, our Paddy, not anymore."

"Mom! That's crazy!"

"Listen, Babette! Something happened when Paddy was five years old that I never told anyone. One night I heard a noise in his room, and I went in there to find something on him. It looked like a big, dark bird, only it wasn't a bird, it was more like a bat. A really huge thing. Like a prehistoric thing. It was sucking his blood, Babette, and as I stood there in the doorway, it was like a nightmare—I couldn't believe what I was seeing—I could hear it sucking. I'll never forget that sound as long as I live. Never. Well, I started screaming, and it turned, and it had the most terrible face I'd ever seen."

"Mom!"

"Babette, listen—your life depends on it. The thing I saw— I *know* what I saw—it was—human—like it had been human, once. It was like a very ancient thing and its eyes were gone, as if part of it had rotted. It had fangs . . . anyway, I guess I fainted, just blacked out. On my feet. The next thing I knew, I was at Paddy's bed, holding him, and he was dead. Just like Billy later, and Danny last night. We were alone. The—vampire—was gone. But I knew I hadn't dreamed it. Or imagined it. I sat there holding him, and then I remembered that I should try mouth-to-mouth resuscitation. I did, for a long time. And he revived, finally. He began to cough, and to cry, but—"

Babette watched her mother in growing horror, hearing words that brought back a vague memory. She had been awakened by a scream one night, and in the dark, with rain pecking at the closed windowpane, she had gone to her mother's room to find the bed empty. She could remember walking down the hall, where the light was dim and ghostly, and coming to the door of Paddy's room. She saw her mother sitting on the bed with Paddy in her arms. She was rocking him back and forth and crying. Paddy was crying, too.

The distant memory was brief and dim, like a dream vaguely remembered. The images were like a puzzle, making no sense. But the coincidence of the sudden deaths of Ketti's sons, which now seemed to include Paddy too, struck her.

"Mama, you got to him in time to revive him! Mama, don't you see? If we had known Bill's and Danny's hearts

37

were stopping like that, we could have revived them, too!''
It helped, somehow, to know. The illogical heart stopping
of the baby boys could at least have been corrected. *Had*
been corrected in Paddy. ''Oh, Mama, if only we had
known! We could have done something, like you did for
Paddy, if only we had known just when it was happening!''

But Ketti was only staring at her, and Babette could see that
she didn't understand what Babette was trying to say. Didn't
she see? It had been a genetic medical problem that could have
been stopped, if only they'd had a monitor on the boys. With
Paddy, Ketti had gotten to him as he was dying, but with
Billy and Danny, Ketti had reached them too late.

''You didn't hear what I said, Babette.''

''Mama—''

''There was a *bat*, Babette—a huge, bat-like creature. A
vampire.'' Ketti leaned across the table toward Babette. ''It
was huge and black, and its wings were hanging down the
side of the bed, almost touching the floor. It had a wrinkled
face as old as time. It had needle-sharp fangs as black as its
wings, and when it turned its face and looked at me, blood
was dripping off those fangs.''

''Mama—''

''Didn't you hear a word I said?'' Ketti made a choked sound.
''It was like Justin—for a minute. A very old, terrible Justin. I don't know why, unless it was because of that gang
he belonged to—The Vampires, they called themselves.''

Ketti put the back of her hand against her forehead as if
feeling for signs of fever. It was an action of weariness.

The scene was drawn against Babette's will. A large bat,
its wings hunched beside a shrunken, terrible face, turned
its face toward her from Paddy's bed. Then it became Paddy's father, a face so distant and dim in her memory that
she wasn't sure she knew anymore what he looked like. He
was standing in the darkened room beside Paddy's bed,
staring at her and at Ketti in the doorway. A very old Justin. But Justin wasn't old. And he had been gone from their
lives ever since Babette could remember. He was Paddy's
father, she knew that, and sometimes he came to the house
and got Paddy and took him for a day or so, back when
Babette was only three or four. Justin was the absent father.

Not dead as her own daddy was, just absent. Then had come the face of another daddy, Ed Graham. His face was more familiar. But Ed had not entered their lives until she was nine years old.

"Babette," Ketti said softly, slowly, leaning once more toward Babette. "After that, Paddy was not the same sometimes. Even the color of his eyes changed. They used to be darker, bluer, before *that* night."

"Was it really Justin," Babette asked, "at Paddy's bedside?"

Ketti seemed for a moment not to know what Babette was talking about, then she said, "The night he died—the night of the vampire. No, it wasn't anybody. When I—when I came to, there was no one there. The doors were locked. It had come through the window. It must have left through the window."

She stared beyond Babette with that haunted, worried look her eyes carried almost all the time. Babette watched her, beginning to realize that her mother was very ill. She was imagining things. She had twisted things around in her mind and tried to make a crazy sort of sense out of them. The tragedies of her baby boys dying with crib death had deranged her. Babette had heard about SID several times, knowing her brother, Billy, had died of it. Now, she was aware of always being afraid of SID where Danny was concerned, too. It was a defect. Her mother had to realize that.

"The window," Ketti said. "That's how he must have gotten into the house last night. He climbed the porch post, and came across the roof—or the tree, he might have climbed the tree and jumped to the porch roof."

"Mama, it wasn't your fault. My brothers all had this defect, see? Something was wrong with their hearts. But you saved Paddy's life."

Did Ketti have a feeling of dislike toward the only one of her three sons who had survived, simply because he had lived and they hadn't? She remembered it was after Billy's death that Ketti had sent Paddy away, never before.

"You haven't been listening to me, Babette!" Ketti hissed in a loud whisper, her hands closing more tightly on Babette's. Giving her a hard shake, as if trying to wake her, she cried, "Your life depends on you going home and getting that *Wolfsbane,* and keeping it on your person somehow. Even that may not help. The important thing, Babette, is *do not let Patrick near you!* Do you understand? Don't let him come near you! If you see him at night near your bed, wherever you are—and now that he's found you, he'll always be near until he kills you—*don't let him near you!"*

"Mama . . ." Tears burned her eyes again. Her heart felt twisted and tortured. Ketti's face blurred, as if Babette were looking through a window flooded with rain.

Ketti's voice came through urgently. "You have to do something you won't like Babette, but it's necessary. Absolutely necessary. You have to kill Patrick, Babette, before he kills you. You have to save what's left of Paddy from the other thing—*you have to kill him."*

Babette stared at her mother in horror, knowing she had gone mad. Her rational, loving mind was gone, replaced by this terrible belief that her firstborn son was a real vampire.

"He was the one who killed Billy and Danny, Babette. It wasn't SID, or anything to do with a heart defect. I found him myself. Sucking their blood. It was the other thing—the vampire—in my son's body. I heard that sucking sound. It was the same thing, the same sound. I found him, Paddy, at least the shell of Paddy, on Billy the night Billy died. And again last night, on Danny. I heard that sound, and that blood was Danny's. It didn't come from Patrick's face, not all that blood, Babette, it was Danny's. It came out of that creature's mouth!"

"Mama!" Babette cried, unable to listen to anymore. "That's crazy, Mama! He couldn't, even if he . . . he couldn't! Paddy doesn't have—*fangs!* His teeth wouldn't—"

"He uses a knife, Babette! Listen. He makes a tiny, deep cut on the throat, or inside the elbow, the way he did on Billy. Someone gave him a knife, or he got it somewhere once when he spent some time with Justin when he was nine years old. I found him with its point on the baby's arm when Billy was just a few months old. I took the knife away from him and threw it away. But he got another knife. He doesn't use his teeth, like the inhuman vampires, he uses that knife!"

Babette could only shake her head. What had happened to her poor mother? She felt so helpless, so trapped, and so alone. She'd never be able to turn to her mother anymore. Her mother had gone mad.

She felt Ketti's broken nails dig into her hand as Ketti shook her again.

"Listen, Babette! If you don't kill him, he'll kill you, and Babette, I couldn't bear that. Please, Baby Babs, listen to me."

Through her own tears Babette saw that Ketti had started to weep. She leaned across the table and put her arms around her mother.

"Don't. Mama please don't cry. Please, it's all right. It's going to be all right."

The door opened and the policewoman stepped into the room.

"Mrs. Graham, your time is up."

Ketti pulled away from Babette and moved toward the policewoman at the door. When she paused to look back at Babette, her tears had stopped, and Babette saw in Ketti's eyes one cold, horrible fact: Ketti herself would kill Paddy as soon as she was released from jail.

Chapter Five

Paddy looked around the room. He was alone in what he guessed was a hospital room. The bed was higher than ordinary beds and had a lot of railings. He felt as if he had awakened in a strange world. He was dressed, but he couldn't remember dressing. There were a lot of things he couldn't remember, just like always. It bothered him a lot, but he had never told anyone. There were the dreamlike impressions of having seen faces he didn't really remember seeing, of doing things he really hadn't done, of tasting things—that sickening taste in his mouth when he came out of his dream-like spells.

He tried not to think of what might have happened during those times he couldn't remember. But sometimes, when he was forced into inactivity, like now, he couldn't help remembering.

A few days ago he had been home. And then the letter from Babette had come, and in a way, it had meant a lot to him, because he hadn't forgotten Babette or his mother. But in another way, in that dreamlike way, it had only given him a kind of horrible satisfaction. *Now he knew*.

He got up and moved about the room. The door was closed. How had he gotten here? He remembered nurses and doctors. There had been policemen, too. And before that, the other house . . . and that taste in his mouth when he woke up and became himself again.

She hadn't wanted him there. She came at him with her fingernails like talons. He could remember that. He saw the fury in her eyes, the madness, the crazy fear. He remembered hearing the banister crack beneath her weight as he pushed her, trying to get her off him. He wanted to cry out and tell her, *it's me, Mama, it's Paddy, your son*. But he hadn't been able to get a word out.

He looked out the window and saw that he was several stories above the street. Down there was a tree, green grass, cars, and people. The bright sunlight hurt his eyes and he drew back.

It had been getting worse lately, this sensitivity to sunlight. Back home the sunlight had been softer, more filtered, it seemed. Why hadn't he stayed home? But he was alone there now. Now that his dad was gone.

He didn't want to think about that.

His dad was part of the dreamlike world that existed within him, too, especially at the last.

He didn't want to think about that.

He heard voices beyond the door, people going down the hall. Pulling the door open, he peered past the opening and ventured out. The hall was brightly lit, and a man and a woman walked past. They were dressed like ordinary people on the street, not nurses and doctors.

Paddy stepped out and looked both ways down the hall. Not far to his right was a nurse's station, a long counter in a half-moon shape. One of the nurses there was talking to a woman dressed in a suit. She carried a briefcase in one hand. The nurse saw Paddy and smiled, and the woman with the briefcase turned and looked at him.

She had short, gray-streaked hair and was neatly dressed. He thought he might have seen her before. Last night, maybe. Or maybe she was part of that dreamlike, misty memory.

"Patrick," the lady said as she and the nurse came toward him. "How are you this morning? How do you feel about going with me?"

"Where to?"

"To a place you'll like very much, if we can get you in there. Boys' Farm. Did you ever hear of it?"

"No."

"You'll love it. It's a beautiful place."

They each got on one side of him and sort of herded him along, not touching him except to flutter a hand against his shoulder once or twice. Together they went down the hall, into an elevator, and downstairs. Then they walked along another hall, meeting men and women in white, and people in street clothes and work clothes.

All the time they were talking about Boys' Farm as if it was paradise, and without even making an effort to listen, Paddy heard most of what they said.

"It has small lakes, or ponds, seven of them, I believe, with walks that go to every one. There are park benches at each pond, and lovely trees. And, of course, animals—goats, sheep, cows, pigs. They even have a young horse they're training to race. Have you ever been there?"

The Child Services lady was looking over his head at the nurse just as they paused near an office door. Through the partly open door Paddy could see a large, polished desk, a tall plant in the corner, soft, dark carpet, and chairs by the desk and against the wall in another corner. It was the kind of room he had never lived in—the rich kind. Closed draperies on the wall behind the desk suggested windows. They must be on the ground floor now, but he heard no outside noises of traffic here any more than he had upstairs.

"On Saturdays and Sundays it's open to the public for picnicking and for children to look at the animals. It's a three-hundred-sixty-acre farm that a wealthy farmer donated several years ago to be used as a home for abused boys."

They gave him a chair in the corner, and the Child Services lady sat in the chair behind the desk and picked up the phone. She continued to talk as she punched out numbers.

"They're almost always full, but I think they try to keep an emergency bed. We like to send our older boys through there, at least, on their way to a more permanent location. We would like to place them all there." A flicker of emotion crossed the lady's face, creating a slight frown, a quick wrinkling of her forehead. Then her face grew smooth again except for the lines at the corners of her eyes and mouth. She wasn't as young as Paddy had first thought. He wished she would keep on talking. Her voice had somehow filled his head so that the fear and the dread were momentarily pushed away. He squirmed on his chair, and the lady looked at him and smiled. "So maybe," she went on, "we can at least get you there for a week's vacation, Patrick, while we locate your father, or some other relative. Do you have anyone you'd prefer to go stay with, Patrick?"

"No," he said quickly. *Not back there. Don't send me back there.* But of course they wouldn't, would they? Because no one was there anymore.

"Hello," she said into the phone, smiling as if she was face to face with the person on the other end of the line. In her next breath, she identified him. "Mister Preston? Martin? This is Mary. Child Services again."

Her voice had softened. Her smile had softened, and Paddy knew the signs. The lady liked the man. But then she seemed to remember she wasn't alone. She glanced toward Paddy and the nurse, who was sitting in a chair by the desk, swinging her white-clad leg back and forth as if she was anxious to go on to something else.

"Mary Bolinger," the lady said into the phone, settling back into the chair. Then almost instantly, she leaned forward again to pick up a pen and pull a note pad toward her. She began to write. "How is everything on the farm? Great. Lovely weather, yes. Not too hot yet. Do you have room for a new boy, Martin? Just for a few nights?"

Paddy watched her and saw that she was doodling, not writing. She was drawing little animals. A horse, or a pig, or something. A dog and a cat. The cat was drawn the way he had learned in art class. A big oval, then a small circle on top, then the tail sweeping to one side. Then she drew a bird in the sky.

Wings. Silent until they pushed onto his face the terrible heat of its arrival, signaling once again that it was not gone, that it was never gone, but more and more was coming to be a part of him. That it was pushing him out of his own head more and more, leaving him only a tiny corner of his own self. Leaving him the days, with the taste in his mouth, and taking from him the nights. Leaving him bits of memory that made him cringe and cry within himself. Making him try to run away. Following him. Becoming . . . him.

"He's thirteen. We're trying to locate his father, so far without success. His mother is in jail. She attacked him and scratched his face horribly, but we feel he's well enough to be released to Boys' Farm. We feel he desperately needs an environment like Boys' Farm."

Stop drawing wings.

Boys' Farm? Something in his head snapped, and he realized what the lady was talking about. A place where animals were kept. Warm-blooded animals. Blood. *No, I don't want to go there.*

He looked toward the door. It was closed now. If he ran, could he make it out of the hospital and into the crowd on the street before they caught him? How could he stay on the loose? He would be easily recognized now, thanks to his mom and her hatred. He put his hand to his face and lightly touched his cheek. It hurt to move his face, to smile or talk or eat. But the pain was the least of it. That didn't bother him. He just wanted to get away. He should have gone when he had the chance. When she was on the floor of the living room, lying still as if she was dead, he should have

45

run away. He should have known everything had gone wrong. Why had he come to them at all? Part of him yearned to be with them. He missed Babette and Mama in that part of him that still belonged to him. But why had he come, when he knew that the other part, the thing with its terrible need, was with him always?

He knew. He was trying to run away. He had thought if only he could get away, if only he could get back to Mama and Babette, everything would be all right again, and he wouldn't have to be afraid anymore. The days would be his, and the nights, too. The nights. Mama and Babette would make everything right again.

Suddenly his dad's voice intruded on his thoughts. *No, no goddamned way am I going to send you there. Forget that. She brought you to me. She didn't want you—doesn't now—*

Paddy moved in the chair, trying to lose the sudden voice in the back of his head, trying to escape the memory. He pulled up one leg and rested his ankle on his knee. His sneakers must have been washed by the hospital while he slept because they were almost white. They didn't even look like his.

I ought to send you back. All you give me is trouble.

"Thank you very much, Preston. We'll bring him right out."

Paddy looked up.

"Well, Patrick," Mary Bolinger said, smiling at him as she hung up the phone. She looked as if this little act of getting him a spot on Boys' Farm had made her day. "You're going to have a lovely place to stay for a few days. Maybe longer, if you wish, if it works out for you."

Martin Preston sat at his desk, looking across the room to the wall that held a picture of his older daughter, Hagar, and the black filly, Star Beauty. They were both beautiful, and he knew it wasn't just his biased eye that realized it. Hagar's long hair was almost as black as the filly, her face as pale and lovely as the star on Star Beauty's face. His thoughts eased pleasantly around to Mary Bolinger.

She was the only woman he'd met during his years of

46

widowhood who he felt he could spend the rest of his life with. But she wasn't available. It wasn't because there was another man, she had told him. It was her job. It claimed her time and her emotions. She was committed to her job. She was willing to go out with him, but so far, a second marriage did not fit into her life. He had an idea she was afraid of marriage. Her first one, from what little he knew about it, had not been good. One faithless man had done a lot of damage, and Preston felt that if he ever got his hands on Mary's ex, he'd give him a good hard shaking, kick the seat of his pants, push his face in the dirt, something.

He pushed away from the desk, smiling at his irrational feelings toward a man whose name he didn't even know. From the family room came the low drone of the television. That would be Gwendolyn, his younger daughter. She had taken more after her mother. Dainty, feminine, fair-haired, she liked to be indoors more than out, and was apt to dream in front of a show or over a book.

He went down the hall to the family room and looked in. Gwen was on her fluffy, white rug, stretched out on her stomach, a book open in front of her. One hand supported her head. The television was on a few feet away, but it wasn't clear whether Gwen was watching a show or reading the book. She said she did both, when pressed by Hagar. But Martin agreed with Hagar. How could she? "I can," she'd say. "I do." She had seemed to prove it by telling them what the show was all about and explaining the storybook, too.

"Got a new boy coming," Martin said from the doorway.

"Oh, yeah?" Gwen tipped her head toward him without moving her support. "Who is he? Where's he coming from? Who tried to kill him?"

"His name is Patrick Skein, he's thirteen years old, and his mother did it. But must you be so cynical?"

Gwen made a face. "Yekk. I don't know about mothers."

"Sure you do." It hurt—a quick, piercing pain right in the middle of his heart—to hear her say that. Had she forgotten hers? Should he have tried harder to find someone

47

to mother Gwen especially? Hagar, who was three years older than Gwen, had a better memory of Celia. "Mothers are the backbone of the world, Gwen. Mothers are everything. Without mothers, where would any of us be? Come on, you know we only see the bad results of a very few poor mothers."

She got to her feet and shut off the television. At eleven years old, she was almost as mature as Hagar was at fourteen, even though Hagar was at least two inches taller—a gap that seemed to be narrowing lately. He wasn't sure he liked it. He was afraid she'd be wanting to enter the adult world before she was mentally ready to handle it. She was his baby, his little girl. She still wore braids, he reminded himself.

"Can I go meet him?"

"Sure, come on. Good for you to get out of the house." He caught the end of one of her long honey-colored braids and gave it a slight tug. "A little sunshine wouldn't freckle you so much that we couldn't still see your eyes."

"Oh, Dad."

She went ahead of him onto the long front porch. He stopped, while Gwen ran on down the wide steps and onto the shady walk. He always stopped here on the porch and looked out over the farm. He had been director of Boys' Farm for ten years, and it seemed like his own home, his own land. He had to remind himself at times that it wasn't, and when his usefulness here ended, he would be moving away. But the farm's beauty always arrested him, held him for a minute or more on the porch. From here he could see ponds one and two, small lakes the size of park swimming pools with clear, reflecting water edged partway by shrublike mesquite. He could see the overflow of pond one and the mouth of the narrow, shallow spring-fed branch that connected all seven ponds. He could see the animal compounds, the barns and the smaller poultry houses, and he had a full view of the gift shop beyond the fenced entrance with its tall gates that were opened only on weekends.

Over from the gates was the long bunkhouse with its long porch across the south side, facing the land. Martin could see that Rufus, the elderly man who was overseer of the

48

boys and more like a grandfather to them than anyone, was on the porch taking time out in his rocking chair. Lying beside him was the farm dog, Lion, and sitting on the edge of the porch, feet swinging, were three boys.

The building at the entrance was vacant today, its wide middle breezeway, the passage for paying customers, shaded and quiet. The gift shops housed there had locked doors. The people who ran the gift shops came only on weekends, when the picnic tables were occupied with families, when people came through the entrance, paying their dollars to keep the farm going for the boys and the animals. None of the animals was ever used for anything but love. They were necessary in the rehabilitation of the boys, to teach them kindness, to show them that they could be loved and accepted. No animal questioned the looks of a boy, or the level of his intelligence. Animals responded to kindness and love, and the boys who came here were in desperate need of this kind of companionship.

"Is Hagar down at the paddock?" Martin asked Gwen as he went down the steps. He could easily guess the answer.

"Sure. Where else?"

"We'll stop by."

They walked around the north end of pond one. Ducks came swimming toward them, looking for food tossed on the water or grass at the edge of the pond. Farther out in the middle of the pond, whose clear, cool waters were brimming from a recent rain, drifted the swans that could be found in any one of the farm's seven ponds. Martin wasn't sure anymore how many swans were on the farm, but they usually went about in pairs, followed by a line of their baby swans. He stopped at the feeding station and put a quarter in the slot. Food for the ducks, geese, and swans spilled out of the bowl into his palm and he tossed it onto the water. The ducks went after it, their voices eager and pleasant.

Ponds one and two each had a device food could be purchased from, and they were the only eyesores on the farm, the only things that didn't look as if they belonged. But Martin had decided, with the help of the board, that it might be worth it for the ducks and other poultry. Also, the people who visited on the weekend seemed to enjoy the feeding process.

Martin and Gwen came to the cool shade by the barns. The ground here was bare. Roots of tall trees reached out toward the pond, rising above the earth, snaking toward the water. The pens at the sides of the barns held goats munching hay from the open manger.

They took a shortcut to the paddock through the barn, walking down a long, dim, musty, hay-smelling corridor, lined with stalls where the animals spent their nights. The horse stalls were on the west side of the barn, and the exercise area, enclosed with a board fence, covered a half acre.

Hagar, with brush in hand, was working beneath the overhanging roof of the shed area of the barn. She had brushed Star Beauty until the horse's coat gleamed. Hagar's own dark, glistening hair was pulled back into a ponytail. Working with her was Orion Smith, the fifty-year-old cook who doubled as the jockey. He was about two inches shorter than Hagar, who was no more than five feet three herself, and he probably weighed about the same. But he could ride as well as he could cook, and the whole farm was hoping that he and Star Beauty would win the Futurity race in the fall.

"How's she doing?" Martin asked.

Star Beauty's ears twitched and she tossed her head back over her shoulder to look at him and Gwendolyn. Gwen went to the horse and put her face against the filly's.

"Great, Dad," Hagar said with enthusiasm. "She's great. Orion's going to take her out for a workout after lunch. Are you going to watch?"

"Sure."

Orion hung his brush on a nail on the wall of the horse stall.

"Better go check on those beans. I left Rex in charge. He's my right arm. Are you going up to the bunkhouse, Mr. Preston?"

Martin had been trying to get Orion to call him by his first name ever since the lively little man came to work at Boys' Farm two years ago, but he persisted in the more formal greeting.

"Yes. We've got a new boy coming in within the next hour or so, and Rose and Rufus have to be notified."

Orion started talking horses. He pointed out the perfection of Star Beauty. Martin stood listening for a few minutes. There were other horses on the farm, a mare and her colt back on one of the pastures. A pony that was sometimes ridden. Four geldings, good saddle horses. A boy had to earn his hour on the pony or saddle horse through hard work and proper care of the animals. The mare also was ridden at times. But Star Beauty was the thoroughbred, the horse that had been purchased last year while she was still a little, gangling, long-legged thing with a short little brush of a tail.

Hagar had taken over the filly immediately with the help and direction of Orion, who also had picked her out. Martin knew Orion had once been a professional jockey, but he didn't know why he had quit. The man's background was a bit vague, and Martin knew little more than the information on his employment record. It hardly mattered. The man was kind, and a good cook. He lived at the farm in one of the private rooms in the bunkhouse. Rufus, who had been with the farm since its inception, lived in the other private room. Rose, the housekeeper, had an apartment— a bedroom and sitting room—on the farm. The other two houses beyond the main residence were occupied by the farm managers and workers, both families of Mexican decent. They were the folks who kept the fences up, the crops planted, and supervised the growing of the vegetables. The boys who lived in the bunkhouse were each assigned certain hours of the day to work with the farm managers in the fruit and vegetable gardens and to help with other work that needed to be done.

Martin felt proud of the self-sufficiency of the farm. It ran like a well-oiled piece of machinery, or a beehive. He walked the walks often, checking it out, seeing that everything was as it was supposed to be. Yet he sometimes felt that even without him, the farm would have gone on beautifully self-sufficient.

They left the paddock through the gate, latching it behind them. Hagar stayed with the horse, but Gwen followed

51

Martin and Orion over the short green grass toward the bunkhouse. It was a park-like area, with large shade trees surrounded by picnic tables and benches. In the wide spaces between sat pieces of antique machinery—combines, tractors with metal wheels, a wooden hay baler—that weekend visitors looked at, and the kids climbed on. Over toward the grassy edge of pond three, to the southwest of the compound, was a modern swing set and slides set in a sandy spot.

Martin didn't know which was more peaceful, the days when the only people here were the boys and the farm workers, or the days when the farm swarmed with visitors—children, old people, and all ages in between. Dogs were allowed if they were kept on leashes. Because dogs like to bark and chase the animals, especially if they weren't used to them, they had to be held back.

"She clocked two furlongs in twenty seconds and three-fifths the last time, and I figure she's getting in real good shape."

"Is that good?" Gwen asked.

"Oh, good! I'll say. I rode a horse once who broke the record on that particular race track, and he didn't do as good as Star Beauty did on her workout last week. When we do the one this afternoon, you want to watch?"

"Oh, sure," Gwen said. "I do."

"We wouldn't miss it."

Rufus came down from the porch, accompanied by the dog and two of the boys. The largest of the boys, Marshal Mayhewn, was also one of the oldest boys on the farm. Now sixteen, he had been on the farm longer than any other boy. He had arrived at age six, brought from a children's hospital, dreadfully abused by his mother and his uncle, perhaps his father, or stepfather, physically and mentally damaged almost to the point of no return. Incapable of ever making it on his own, Marsh had been taken under Rufus's wing, and Martin felt sure that Rufus would see after the boy as long as he lived. But Rufus was seventy-four now, and in the past year he had almost disappeared inside his overalls, looking more skin and bones with each passing season. His cheeks looked cadaverously sunken as he ap-

52

proached them. His thinning whiskers, though recently shaved, still stuck out like tiny briars.

"Howdy. Nice day."

Martin greeted him, the boys, and the dog. Marsh, the mentally deficient boy, hung back as always, never quite comfortable with people even though he seemed always to want to be near. Martin had never heard him speak more than a few words, but he saw the boy give Gwen a wistful little smile before lowering his eyes. The dog, a long-haired collie mixed with some other breed that gave him a wide muzzle, ambled forward and put his nose into Gwen's palm and then Orion's. He headed toward Martin next, greeting them all one by one.

"We've got a new boy coming, Rufus. He's thirteen, name is Patrick."

Marsh clapped his hands. There was a smile on his face. The scar that traced a permanent white line from his scalp to his neck crossed the corner of his mouth and pulled the smile into a twisted grin.

"A new boy," he said. "Happy. He can sleep by me."

Chapter Six

Rufus had sympathy for all the boys who came under his care, but some touched him more than others, he had to admit. Once in a great while, a boy rubbed his fur the wrong way the minute he saw him. But even those boys managed to settle in within a few days and relax and grow easier to be around. Rufus had a lot of anger, too. The anger wasn't directed at the boys, but at those distant and unseen parents—mothers, fathers, stepparents, whoever they were—who had so savagely mistreated these kids. Some of the kids came after months in hospitals. Others, the temporaries, came from their homes or the emergency room and spent a week or two on the farm. They were the least harmed boys, ones who would have a wiser home to return to one day.

Nowadays it was called child abuse. In Rufus's day, it wasn't called much of anything. But he remembered the terror and pain of living with a stepfather who hated him and a mother who pretended not to see the knocks or hear the curses. There had been many times in Rufus's life when his stepfather had made him stand in the corner while he, the old man, ate. Rufus wasn't allowed at the table until the old man had gotten his fill. Then, if anything was left over, Rufus was allowed to share it with the family dog. The dog wasn't treated any better by this vicious man, and Rufus wondered daily why the man stayed around, since he obviously couldn't stand them. Rufus had asked his mother that once, when he was ten years old, and she had slapped him so hard he'd had a headache for weeks.

When he was twelve, he ran away from home. If anyone ever tried to find him, he never heard of it. From then on, he worked wherever he could, mostly on farms. It was back during the depression of the thirties, and a lot of men were on the roads, riding the rails to warm climates, going anywhere they could to pick fruit or work in the vegetable fields. That meant the south. Rufus had joined them, carrying his own little roll of one change of clothes and one blanket.

He went to California and picked prunes and peaches. He went on up into Washington and picked apples. In Idaho he picked apples and prunes, and he went down to Arkansas to pick cotton and strawberries and more apples and peaches. In winter he headed for Arizona and south Texas, and finally he'd found a home for himself at Boys' Farm in Texas. The farm was just opening, and a lot of work was needed to get it ready for abused boys. Rufus was almost fifty years old, but he'd found his first permanent home. He had been here ever since, working his way up from handyman to overseer of the boys. His education had stopped at the seventh grade, and he didn't pretend to be what he wasn't. But he knew boys, he knew how it felt to be slapped around, abused, and he'd always wanted a home and family.

Marsh had been with him longer than any of the others, and seemed like his own boy. He'd seen Marshall the night he came in, a six-year-old waif whose mother and uncle had tried to kill with an ax. The sharp edge of the ax had entered the boy's skull at his forehead and then had glanced off and spit his face open from brow to neck. Someone had stopped the attempted murder. A neighbor who'd heard the boy scream, the record claimed. The child had spent weeks in a hospital, and then was brought to the farm. The record of the attack was vague, with no one taking blame, and no one prosecuted severely enough. Rufus doubted that the boy even knew, or remembered, what happened. He'd been unable to talk when he was found.

He came to the farm a scared, silent little kid. But Rufus could see in his eyes that he wasn't as hopeless as the welfare people feared he was going to be. The farm was a temporary placement, a place where they hoped the boy would find some tranquility before he was sent on somewhere else. But Rufus persuaded them to leave him. "I'll see after him," he'd pleaded. "He's all right. He loves the animals. He'll be fine here. There's room. He's only one little guy. I'll make room."

So Marsh had stayed. Rufus saw him smile for the first time a year later when Marsh was petting, so very gently, the soft coat of a newborn calf.

Other boys had come and gone, but Marsh stayed. Most of the boys who grew up here were taken away at the age of sixteen to be put in school somewhere else. But Marsh was not able to comprehend the alphabet or numbers, and there would be no school for him. He was a big, gentle boy with a square face and hair that couldn't be plastered down even with lady's hairspray. He had grown up to be almost as tall as Rufus and several pounds heavier. If he hadn't been so gentle, Rufus sometimes found himself thinking, Marsh might have been dangerous, considering his background and the things God only knew had happened to him before those people tried to kill him.

But he was gentle, and he not only loved the animals, he loved the other children, especially the younger ones.

Still, Rufus kept an eye on him. He didn't want Marsh hurt, but on the other hand, he didn't want Marsh to hurt anything.

The new boy arrived an hour after Rufus learned he was coming. Rose had been notified, and Orion set another place at the table. Dinner, as they called the noon meal on the farm, was just being put on the table by Chris and Pete, the ten-year-old boys Rufus called his "twins" because they were the same size and age and had come to the farm during the same month a year ago. Rex was going to help with the drinks. Rex liked kitchen work. It gave him a chance to snack.

Mary Bolinger drove through the service gates on the road that bypassed the visitors' entrance. The gates had been opened especially for her. The moment her car passed through, the gates were closed by one of the Mexican farm workers. The boys weren't in jail, but the gates were kept locked for their protection as well as the protection of the animals. Incredibly, some of the abusive parents still wanted to get at their kids, to knock them around some more, for reasons that puzzled and infuriated Rufus. He'd cuss into the privacy of the night sometimes when an angry mother or father tried to get a kid out of the farm. It didn't happen often. Usually they never tried to contact the kid. Occasionally, the parents were in jail or prison. But not often enough, in Rufus's opinion.

They had all gathered on the porch of the bunkhouse to greet the new kid. Mary Bolinger drove her car up onto the grass just off the porch and got out smiling, just as she always did. Rufus didn't miss the way her eyes lingered a flicker longer on Martin than on anyone else. The boy sat still, the car window rolled up. Reflections in the glass hid his face.

Mary came around the car. She was wearing a dark skirt and a white blouse, very neat, very trim. She spoke to everyone at once, nodding, sometimes mentioning a special name. Marsh, who stood in the front of the group, said, "Hi, Mary."

She touched him on the arm, patting him twice. "Hello, Marsh, how are you today?"

Marsh nodded, grinning his crooked grin.

Mary patted the cheeks of the twins, who stood side by side. "Hi, Chris and Pete. Is dinner ready?"

"We set a place for you, too."

They all ate in the bunkhouse when a new boy came. It was a cause for celebration and didn't happen as often as they would have liked, simply because there wasn't room. All the kids had been told that this boy, Patrick Skein, was a temporary who would be using the small bed that was brought out and placed at the end of the bunkhouse beside Marsh's bunk. One of the other boys, Vance Hunter, would be having his sixteenth birthday in a few weeks, and he probably would be going away. If the new boy's father wasn't found, he could be moved into Vance's bunk.

"Hello, Hagar and Gwen and Orion. How's Star Beauty coming?"

They all said their bit at the same time, making it sound like Star Beauty was unmatched in all the racing world.

"Well, everyone, I want you to meet Patrick." Mary opened the car door. "Patrick," she said to the boy within, "I want you to meet the folks who are going to be your new family for awhile. Come on."

She had to get him by the arm before he would come out. He stood up, his hair gleaming dark and light blond in the sunlight, his face striped with pink marks that Rufus already knew had been made by his mother's fingernails. He put his arm up to shield his face from the bright sunlight. His eyes were squinted almost shut and there was a twisted look of pain on his face, as if the sun hurt his eyes or burned the raw scratches.

As always, Marsh stepped forward and touched the new boy in greeting. Jostled suddenly backward against Rufus, Marsh sidestepped the boys who were behind him. Then he turned blindly, like an animal seeking a way out. For a moment Rufus saw his face, and was stunned.

Marsh looked terrified.

* * *

"Can I see my brother?" Babette asked. She'd been told the lady had come to take her to a foster home, and the feeling of desperation was growing within Babette. She felt as if she was on the verge of falling into a nightmare world she'd never known existed. All the security she had ever known had been jerked out from under her.

"Your brother?" the strange lady said, looking at the papers in her hands. She was a young woman who acted a little unsure of herself, as if this was her first case.

They were still at the police station. Earlier someone had come to Babette in the room where she'd done all her interminable waiting, and told her a foster home had been found and she would be temporarily placed.

"My brother, Patrick."

"I think he's already been placed somewhere. Yes, at Boys' Farm." The young woman, who didn't look much older than the girl at the soda fountain near Babette's house, acted as if she didn't know what was going on. She was wearing a gathered skirt that reached within inches of her ankles, and flat shoes. "I don't know—maybe the people you'll be staying with can take you. Or maybe Mrs. Bolinger can take you out there sometime. Just a minute, I'll go see."

So Babette was left waiting again while the girl, whose name Babette didn't remember, went to see about her chances of getting to see Paddy.

Babette sat down. She'd been in the jail two days now, just waiting. She hadn't seen Ketti since yesterday, and she hadn't seen one other face she recognized, except for Sergeant Ford. He was beginning to seem almost like a friend, but even he hadn't come to see her today.

Babette waited. Yesterday she'd been brought three comics, which she read so many times she almost knew them by heart. She could hear phones ringing somewhere in the huge building, but the phone on the desk in this small room was silent. No one sat at the desk most of the time. Once in awhile, a uniformed man or woman would come in, smile at her, get something from the desk drawer or even sit down and do a little work on the typewriter. But more often than not, Babette just sat alone.

The door opened and the youthful social worker came back in, and to Babette's delight, the familiar face of Sergeant Ford appeared too. He came in and sat down on the bench beside Babette and cupped his hand over hers briefly, the way he always did.

"I hear you're ready to go to a new home for awhile."

His concerned face made her want to give in to the tears that had drawn a permanent curtain behind her eyes. She nodded, unable to speak lest she burst out wailing.

"You'll feel better when you're in a home atmosphere. I'm sorry it took so long to do something. That's the way it works sometimes. Miss Thornton tells me you've been asking to see Patrick?"

She nodded, swallowing the knot in her throat. "And my mother?"

He said, "There are only certain times visitors can see the inmates of a facility, so I don't think you'll be able to see your mother before you leave today. And Patrick has been taken to a great place outside town where it's almost like being at camp. But if you want to see your baby brother's body before his natural father has it shipped to his home, you may."

Babette looked at the floor. She didn't want to see Danny dead. But if Danny knew, in any way, that she hadn't come to see him, he wouldn't understand.

"Yes," she said, her voice very low. "All right."

She left the big building that housed the jail as well as the police station for the first time since the night she had been brought there. It seemed like a long time, longer than it actually had been. The sunlight seemed almost alien, and the fear, the deep panic that had started growing in her like a fungus, stayed with her. Even though Sergeant Ford was here, driving her and Miss Thornton to see Danny's body before it was shipped away, she felt as if she was in a strange world among strangers. Her heart cried out for her mother, her brother, for home—for anything familiar and comforting.

"How long will my mother be in jail?"

"I don't know that, Babette."

"Will I be told when she's let out? Can I go home and live with her?"

"I'm sure you will."

I have to know. Mama has to be stopped from killing Paddy.

"Has Mama been told—will she be told—where Paddy's staying?"

"I'll see that she's told, Babette, don't worry," Sergeant Ford said.

Babette stared out the window at the blur of tall, mirrored buildings on the horizon. No, she had wanted to say, please don't tell her.

"Paddy's dad—Justin—won't you be sending Paddy back to him?" That would save Paddy. Get him so far away that Mama couldn't reach him. That was the answer, the only answer. To send him away, far away. And then something disturbing occurred to her. That was what Ketti had done three years ago. She had sent Paddy away to live with his father.

"We haven't been able to locate his father," Sergeant Ford said. "The police there went out to Justin Skein's house and it looks like the place has been deserted. I'm waiting for more information. Of course, as soon as we find him, there's no reason that I know of that Patrick can't go back to him."

Babette crossed her fingers, hidden in her lap. *Find him,* she said in the silence of her mind. *Find him before Mama gets out of jail.* She'd much rather not see Paddy again—and know he was alive—and have her poor, mad mother at home, safe from becoming a murderess.

They parked beneath a tree and went into a quiet funeral home. There were a lot of coffins in the large room, but the man in charge took them to a small one on a stand near the corner. The coffin was blue trimmed in silver. The man silently raised the lid, and Babette saw Danny, his small head on a little pillow trimmed in blue lace. His plump arms had been placed loosely across his body. His long, dark lashes curled against his cheeks just the way they did when he was sleeping.

Babette stood looking down at him, the panic raging in her chest, the need to scream becoming an almost physical pain. Billy . . . Danny . . . they looked so much alike. It was as if Danny had been Billy returned, and now Danny was Billy again, dead, and none of it seemed real. She was living in a nightmare.

She closed her eyes and opened them again, and the panic receded and she was looking at her little brother sleeping in the finest bed he'd ever had in his life.

And then she saw something that stunned her, made her stare and paralyzed her spirt.

On his neck was a tiny pink mark, a mark that could have been made by the point of a very sharp knife.

Chapter Seven

The light hurt his eyes. The strange faces were all mixed up, like a puzzle with faces in the woodwork, in the trees, even in the clouds. The woman who had brought him to this place now took him through the crowd waiting on the shady porch and on the nearby grass. She led him by touching his shoulder, guiding him up the steps and toward a breezeway that separated the long building.

"This is the bunkhouse, Patrick," she said motioning to the left section. "You'll be sleeping in there with the other boys, and eating over here. Something smells good, Orion, as always."

He became aware of noises around him, boys moving and talking. Among the crowd Paddy saw two younger girls, one tall as himself, with black hair and white skin, the other one younger, blond, with braids. There was another woman, too, older, middle-aged, with short, wavy gray hair.

He saw a skinny old man who wore overalls, and a funny big boy who had stumbled away from him when he got out of the car. Somebody called the boy Marsh, and Paddy noticed the boy kept staring at him, and didn't glance away the way most people did when Paddy returned the stare.

He was only partly himself today. He could feel *it*. His mind had been crowded to that side of his head where it didn't go, and he wanted to claw at his head because it felt like the *wings* were there in the other part, hunched, waiting somehow to feed, leaving a part of itself. And sometime, some night, it would take over, and his body would at last belong to it, and he, Paddy, would finally be gone. He was so scared. But there was no one who could help him. His dad couldn't—no one could.

They gave him a place at one side of the long table. He sat near the end, close to the old man, Rufus. His plate was loaded with food—beans, he noted, another vegetable he didn't recognize, as well as fried chicken and mashed potatoes and gravy. On a side dish was a bun and butter.

It seemed they were watching him to see that he would eat, but he could hardly swallow. He felt as if he would be sick. It was almost as bad as the taste in his mouth after . . . after he had been pushed aside on the nights when things happened that he couldn't remember very well. Didn't want to remember. It was almost as sickening.

But then suddenly a thought came to him, and with a happier outlook he watched the faces of the boys and the other people around the table. Maybe here, with all these people, behind the tall fences and locked gates, the winged thing couldn't find him. Maybe here, at last, he was safe.

He slipped his hand into his pocket and felt the bone-like hardness of his small knife.

Babette got out of the car and stood looking at her house. The Child Services lady, Miss Thornton, who was taking her to the foster home, got out on the other side of the car. Babette heard the door slam, but she could have been alone, the sound was so distant in her perception. She stood still, her back to the car, looking up at the house.

She had never noticed how the paint was peeling, or how ratty the old screens on the second floor looked. A corner had somehow come loose on one of the screens and it stuck out, leaving an opening for insects or even burglars if they scaled the side of the house. She saw the window was up, too. All the windows on the second floor were raised to let in the cool night air. She thought of the last night she had stayed here, the last night she had put Danny to bed there, in that room where the screen was torn.

A horrible, unbidden vision entered her mind. She could see a huge, black-winged, bat-like vampire clutching at the window screen, shaded from the street light on the corner by the tree that grew along the driveway. She saw it come silently through the night and reach out its claws to clutch the screen and hover there, wings folded. She saw it peer in at the sleeping baby, and she saw it use its claws to open the screen, to pull it out so it could enter. When at last it stood in the room, it looked like Paddy.

"Babette? Are you ready to go in?"

Babette jumped, her heart racing. She'd forgotten Miss Thornton was anywhere near.

She followed the young woman up the weedy walk and around the house to the backdoor. Her mom's old car sat in the driveway. Miss Thornton produced a key that Babette recognized as the key to their house. Surprised, she watched Miss Thornton open the backdoor. Where had she gotten the key? But then she supposed one of the policemen, or somebody, had locked the house that night when they all were taken away. Or maybe Mama had given it to them.

Babette entered first. The house was hot from the daytime heat outside and there was a fly buzzing somewhere. The house had an unpleasant smell she hadn't noticed when she lived here all the time.

"I'll need to shut the windows," Babette said, asking permission, feeling as if, in a way, like Ketti, she too was in a prison and not allowed out of sight of her guard.

"I'll help."

"I always opened them at night to let in the cool air," Babette explained. "Then in the morning I closed them again."

"I'll close the downstairs windows while you go up and pack your clothes."

Gratefully, Babette left Miss Thornton downstairs. She hadn't wanted to be accompanied into the more personal parts of her home, as if by letting someone go upstairs with her, where the memories of Danny were so sharp, her private thoughts and feelings would be invaded.

She climbed the stairs slowly, feeling the heat increase as she entered the hall. She stood still. The house seemed haunted, the sounds of the streets muted and of a different world. Here, in the heavy, hot stillness, she felt a movement of cold air. Invisible, like a current in a river, it was like death remained. She shivered as the current moved past her, touching her cheeks and arms.

The broken banister was to her right, and on the bare floor of the hall, she saw dark drops of something, and knew it was blood.

Somebody had stepped in the blood, smearing it into a dark brown stripe.

Walking carefully to avoid the blood, she turned left and went into Ketti's room. Here the blinds were still pulled. She hadn't opened her mother's windows that last night, she remembered. Most of the time she didn't because the room was cooler than the rest of the house. Cool, dark, quiet. And empty. So empty. The bed was neat, the bedspread made up the way Ketti always left it when she got up each day.

Babette went to the dresser and pulled out the drawer Ketti had told her about. Down in the righthand corner was a small, clear plastic bag of herbs. The label on the outside said *Wolfsbane*.

Babette put it back and closed the drawer.

She would like to forget that Ketti had ever told her that crazy stuff about Paddy. She had tried, but it only seemed to get worse, until she was seeing and hearing things that weren't there. Last night she'd had a nightmare about a huge bat-like creature coming at her through the dark, and then it had turned into Paddy. Only he hadn't seemed like Paddy at all. His eyes were strange and distant, more like holes than eyes. And when he smiled at her, he had sharp, long fangs, and the smile wasn't a smile, but simply an opening of his mouth. He was coming closer and closer to her when she woke up, her heart pounding hard. At that moment she'd been glad to be in the jail, sleeping in a cell, with guards in the halls.

She didn't want to dream things like that about her brother, and part of her was angry at her mother for telling her crazy things.

Of course, they weren't true. Poor Mama.

And she wasn't going to allow herself to think these thoughts about vampires and things that couldn't be real.

The real, truly frightening thing was that their mother was going to find Paddy and kill him as soon as she was released from jail. Babette knew that in the depths of her heart and in the clearest part of her mind. *Ketti was going to kill Paddy.*

And Babette had to stop her.

She prayed each day they would keep Ketti in jail until Paddy was sent back to his father, a long way off, too far for Ketti to find him.

She went into Danny's small room. His bed was still tousled, the thin blanket that had covered him thrown back and falling partway to the floor, the pillow still holding the impression of his small head.

The bed sat just a few feet from the open window, where the screen had been torn back at the corner. No flies had gotten into the room.

Babette closed the window and locked it, then pulled the blind. When she looked back at Danny's bed it was shadowed and ghostly with the outside light gone.

She carefully made the bed, pulling the blanket up and smoothing it. She lifted the pillow to plump it as she always did after Danny got up each morning. But she paused, her hand gently touching the depression where his head had been. Then she put the pillow down unplumped, the only indication that at least a part of Danny was still here in this room.

She closed the door and left.

In her room, she worked without pause, pulling her clothes out of the chest of drawers and folding them neatly on the bed. From the closet she took one dress, then hung it back. Then she took it out again. The foster home would probably make her go to church, as Ketti sometimes did, and she'd need a dress. It was a pretty dress that Ketti had gotten for her at a garage sale for one dollar. Babette remembered how thrilled she'd felt at the time. It was like new.

Garage sales were where they'd gotten all of Danny's clothes and most of Babette's. On Saturdays they'd had fun going around to sales in the better neighborhoods. Sometimes they even went into the suburbs, and they'd walk until their feet were sore. Those had been good times. Afterward they'd stop at an ice cream place, or a fast food restaurant. At those times Ketti had seemed happy. Her eyes had sparkled and she'd laughed at things Danny did or said. Though he was only two-and-a-half years old, he could talk in complete sentences, and he said some really original things. Babette remembered the time he had called a car bumper a mustache. "That car's mustache has got a scratch on it," he'd said, pointing his little hand, and Babette and Ketti had laughed. The scratch was actually a big dent that had twisted the bumper up at one end.

Babette realized she was standing in her room staring at the pile of clothes on the bed. She took a pillowcase from the drawer and put her things into it and went downstairs.

Miss Thornton was waiting in the living room. She looked at the pillowcase. "Don't you have a suitcase, Babette?"

Babette shrugged. "This is okay." She thought Ketti had a suitcase, but she wasn't sure anymore. Their trip here three years ago was blurred in her memory. She couldn't remember a suitcase, but she did recall carrying things in a bag.

The front door was bolted on the inside, and Miss Thornton had closed the windows and pulled the blinds.

They went back through the house and out the backdoor, which Miss Thornton locked before handing the key to Babette.

"This is yours. You'll be wanting it one of these days soon."

"I'll get to come back home?"

"Yes, of course, as soon as your mother is released, and I think that will be in just a few weeks. Your brother, Patrick, was not seriously injured. He won't be given into your mother's custody, but there's no reason why you won't be. We don't like to keep families separated any longer than is absolutely necessary. We're not really as cruel as children sometimes think we are. We're just here to help out in emergencies."

Babette got into the car, her bundle of clothes between her feet. She watched the house as Miss Thornton backed the car out into the street. It looked lonely and deserted now, all closed and silent.

"Miss Thornton," Babette said impulsively, "what's wrong when a mother thinks terrible things about one of her own children?"

Miss Thornton drove in silence and it seemed she was not going to answer the question, and Babette was beginning to wish she hadn't asked it. What if the authorities began to question her about why she had asked it? Would they make her tell them what Ketti had told her? No, she couldn't. Ever. She didn't want her mother in jail, or locked away in an insane asylum.

Miss Thornton said, "That is one of the puzzles we social workers have to deal with, Babette. Very often it happens that way. A mother, or a father, and sometimes both, will pick one of their children to abuse. We think it's a mystery even to them. But in some unfortunate families, one child is unwanted. Especially one child. Fortunately, on the other hand, most children are even more dearly loved and treasured by their parents than they know."

Babette drew a long sigh of relief. Miss Thornton wasn't going to pursue it any further.

But now Babette knew she not only had to protect Paddy from their mother but Ketti from herself—her own terrible beliefs, her fears, whatever it was in her mind about Paddy. She had to get to Paddy before their mother did.

"Will you do something for me, Miss Thornton?"

"Of course, if I can."

"I want to know the minute my mother is released from jail."

"Certainly. I can do that. In fact, I'm sure that we'll be taking you home to her on that same day."

But that would be too late. By the time Miss Thornton came and said, "Your mother is out of jail, and we're taking you to her," it would be too late. Ketti would have gone down the steps of the jail and headed out to find Paddy.

Babette would have to find out for herself, and be prepared to leave.

Paddy was safe only as long as their mother was behind bars.

Chapter Eight

Rufus had never seen Marsh withdraw from a boy the way he had with the new one, Patrick. The boy hung back after dinner, standing like a lost kid at a new school, his hands behind his back, leaning against the wall, watching the boys who were at home here drift by, intent on their own jobs and plans for the afternoon. Mr. Preston and his daughters left, as did Mary Bolinger.

Rufus called Marsh to him, and the big guy came with his head down like a beaten puppy. Rufus would have liked to see him lift his head and look at life with pride in his eyes, the way most boys did after they'd lived here a year or more. But Marsh would never lose the fear his early life had instilled in him. Today, though, he was meek to the extreme. Rufus would have thought he was angry, if ever Marsh got angry. He put his hand on Marsh's shoulder.

"Marsh, why don't you show our new boy around the farm this afternoon? Take him by the bunkhouse first and show him his bunk, then by the animal pens, and feed the ducks, geese, and swans."

Marsh looked at Patrick without raising his head, his eyes peering out from beneath his brow. He was just enough taller than Patrick that he was able to see the younger boy without lifting his head. Then, to Rufus's utter surprise, Marsh stepped back and shook his head vigorously.

"No," he said. "No! Marsh is busy today."

He turned and walked away hurriedly, his body bent slightly forward, a posture he assumed in times of stress. Rufus could always tell when something bothered Marsh deeply by the way he held himself, doubled up, as if he were trying to draw into himself, like a turtle pulling back into its shell. But Marsh had never refused Rufus in this manner. He had never disobeyed him at all that Rufus could recall, and Rufus stood silently gaping after him.

Marsh disappeared from sight at the end of the breeze-way, and Rufus was left standing alone with Patrick.

Rufus laughed. It was an embarrassed giggle left over from his own childhood, one of the things that had always gotten him into trouble, but he couldn't help the giggle and hadn't been able to stop it even in old age. If anything embarrassed him or put him on the spot, he'd giggle. He hated it, and he cut the giggle short. He at least had that much control over it.

He reached out and put his hand on Patrick's shoulder, giving it a squeeze he hoped was encouraging.

"Well, I guess that's my job anyway. Marsh has got his chores to do, just like the other boys. This may be the day he works in the vegetable patch. Come along, Patrick, and I'll show you your bunk. It's our spare bunk, our emergency space for guys like you who're only stopping over for a week or two, sometimes less. Last month we had a boy who just stayed overnight. He hardly got a chance to look at the animals. He's come back since then with his parents, and they had a nice picnic and a real good day, and he got to look at the animals with his brothers and sister. You got any brothers or sisters?"

"I've got a sister. Say, that guy, Marsh, his elevator doesn't go all the way to the top, does it?"

Rufus was taken aback for a moment. He even forgot what he'd been going to say next, in the down-home spiel he used to make a new boy feel at home. It always seemed to help to talk about boys who had come and left right away, returning happily to their families. But it seemed to go over this boy's head. Furthermore, he'd never had a boy make reference to Marsh's intellect before. Never. The new boys always took Marsh as he was, without comment. But then Marsh had always been friendlier.

"What?" Rufus said, on the verge of stammering. "Marsh? Oh, he's a good kid. He's one of our best. He's real good with the animals."

The dog, Lion, rose from the floor of the bunkhouse porch, wagging his tail. Then he spotted Marsh going off across the grassy area toward the barns, and he took off in a run.

"That's Lion," Rufus said, knowing most boys loved dogs. "He's our only bunkhouse dog at the moment. Last year our old one passed away, and one of these days I reckon we'll go to the animal shelter and pick out a pup for Lion to help raise. It's not only our pleasure to keep animals, but our duty, too. If a place has room, it ought to make a home for one of the animals discarded at the shelters. Our stock and dogs and cats don't have pedigrees, they're just plain individuals, like you and me and Marsh."

Patrick said nothing. Rufus didn't really expect him to. When the boys first arrived they were always subdued. Most were not sure they were going to like the place. All of them were homesick for one thing or another, usually their parents and siblings.

"You got a sister, you say?" Rufus encouraged as he led the way into the shadowed bunkhouse.

"Yes."

"What's her name."

"Babette."

"Older than you? Younger?"

"Older. Just a year."

"Ummhuh. Well, Patrick, these are the bunks. This one right here by the wall, in the corner, is yours. You're right next to Marsh. The bunk across the aisle belongs to Chris. He was the one who helped serve drinks at dinner. That fourth bunk down is Rex's. He was the other boy who helped serve."

"The fat guy."

70

"Well—we don't think of Rex as fat, and neither will you when you get to know him."

Rufus tried not to frown. There was something about this kid that really wasn't likeable. Marsh had sensed it, he guessed. But then he reminded himself that kids did come in sometimes with chips on their shoulders big enough to break a strong man's back.

"What you're expected to do is make up your bunk good and smooth each morning when you get out of bed. Everybody gets up at the same time, no laggers. We eat at seven."

"At seven!"

The boy's eyes glared at Rufus, and Rufus noticed for the first time that from a distance it would appear as if he had no eyes, they were so pale. Even in the shadowed bunkhouse they looked silver rather than the gray Rufus supposed they were. The boy was frowning at a suitcase on the table beside the bunk.

"What's that? Where'd it come from?"

"I reckon that's your things."

Patrick's face smoothed. "I don't have things," he said softly, and Rufus felt his vague dislike drift away.

Poor kid. No home, no things.

"Don't you reckon somebody brought your clothes?" Rufus said, opening the suitcase. In it were two pairs of new jeans, four shirts, socks, and underwear, all still in their packages. Rufus smiled and said, "That's Miss Bolinger for you. She went out and bought you some clothes. Probably from her own pocket."

"How'd she know my size?"

"She knows boys. She ought to, as long as she's been picking them up, putting them back together and bringing them here. She even brought Marsh, and that was ten years ago. Well, are you ready to go out?"

Patrick came slowly, with a look on his face that Rufus recognized on all new boys, a reluctance, a wish to hide. Only rarely did Rufus give in to that desire. A boy usually got used to his surroundings faster if he was among the animals for the first few difficult hours.

When they reached the porch Patrick pulled back, just as

Rufus felt he would. He put his hands up in front of his eyes and grimaced.

"I can't go! The sun hurts my eyes. It burns my face. Please, sir, don't make me go."

He was hunkering back, as if in actual pain, and Rufus could only guess how much of it was fear. It didn't matter. If a boy really pulled back, he was excused for the first few hours.

"All right, Patrick. You can stay on your bunk for awhile. The television room is opened only for the evenings and Saturday mornings. You can stay in the bunkroom, and come on out when you're ready."

Rufus watched the boy go back into the vestibule of the bunkhouse, a small room with hooks on the walls where coats and caps were hung. He watched him turn left into the cool, dim, long bunkhouse. Rufus's own room was behind the cloakroom. A door off the short hallway beyond the bathroom door led to it. Although he kept the door closed, it was never locked. All his worldly goods were in that room, which didn't amount to a whole lot. He hadn't needed to collect anything. He had the farm, the boys, the animals. Marsh. That was all he needed.

He went down the steps and into the warm sunshine. The grass was soft and green beneath his feet, every sprig mowed to a careful two inches. He walked toward the animal compounds and barns, passing beneath big shade trees, past the picnic tables and benches. He went within touching distance of the rusted, old combine. Usually, every time he passed it, he paused to think of the men and boys who had worked alongside this ancient combine. All of them were long gone, and lived only in his imagination. It helped him feel more at ease with his coming old age, his own mortality, as if those people were still around somewhere, and so would he be a hundred years from now when someone else walked his paths here on the farm.

Most of the farm people were over on the south field, at the improvised racetrack, an oval made in the pasture. Rufus joined Martin, his two daughters, all the boys who didn't have specific jobs—and some who did, but had left their chores to come along. The crowd had clustered into the

72

shade of trees that grew along the fence row separating the fields. Lion lay in front, his head up, watching. He never offered to chase any animals except the ones who had gotten out of their pastures. Then he'd try by himself to put them back, and sometimes he succeeded. He knew where all of them belonged, it seemed. Rufus bent and patted his head.

At the edge of the shade, Star Beauty pranced, as if her energy didn't allow her to stand still this close to her race-track. Her black coat glistened in the light, the lines of her body were graceful and beautiful.

"I can almost see wings on her, she's so great," Gwendolyn said. "Can't you, Dad? Except she's black, not white, like Pegasus."

"She's got wings on her heels," said Orion, who was beneath the horse's belly, tightening the tiny saddle. Hagar stood at the horse's head, holding her bridle, patting and rubbing her nose, murmuring to her. The horse steadied and nuzzled Hagar's face.

"I wish I was riding her," Hagar said.

"Someday I'll teach you," Orion said.

"But you do ride her," Gwendolyn said. "I've seen you riding her around the paddock."

"Not often. Mostly I just walk her."

"Are you ready with that watch?"

The crowd stirred. Boys who had been squatting, rose. Boys who had been scuffling around under the deepest part of the shade settled down and came forward. Rex, the heavy-set boy, stepped forward and kissed the white star on Star Beauty's face. Everyone laughed. Some of the boys called out teasing remarks.

"She'll lose today. Rex gave her a hex. Rex's hex."

"Hey, why don't you go out there and race with her, Ross, give her some competition."

Ross was the track star of the group. None of the boys could catch him even when he was jogging.

"What we oughta do is bring Dolphus over here to let Star Beauty know what another horse on the track looks like."

"That's all she'd learn from Dolf. He won't even walk

most of the time. Last time it was my turn to take a ride on him, he wouldn't go anywhere.''

"Quiet!" somebody in the group yelled.

Rufus felt himself grow tense with excitement and anticipation. Orion was getting ready to mount, and it was always a thrill to see the wiry little man climb into the saddle.

"Got a good hold on her, Hagar?" Orion asked. He was dressed in glistening blue satin, racing colors the farm had adopted from Orion's racing days. He was wearing a matching cap, and the blanket beneath the saddle was the same color. To Rufus, one of these workouts was perhaps even more exciting than going to a real race.

"Yeah!"

"Okay, hold her."

Orion was up and into the saddle with one easy leap, which seemed to Rufus an incredible feat considering the size of the man against the size of the horse. Star Beauty responded to the weight by sidestepping suddenly, almost as if she was thinking of bucking him off. But he was like a part of her.

"All right," Orion said gently, reaching down to pat Star Beauty's neck. "Let her go!"

Hagar released the bridle and stepped back just as Orion leaned forward and tapped the horse's flank with his short whip. He used it only to start her, and she leaped forward, her long body glistening under the bright sun, every muscle melting into the next. Her hooves thudded on the grassy track. She stretched out long and smooth, as if she was racing against a thundering herd of horses behind her, as if she had been born for this work. Orion rode standing, leaning forward over her neck, holding himself perfectly level above the long gallops of her run.

Rufus became aware of the cheering behind him. It was deafening. The voices raised even higher as the horse came to her second turn on the makeshift track. By the time she turned the last corner and was racing back toward them, the dog was standing and so was Rufus, his own voice cheering Star Beauty and Orion on, bringing them in.

Hagar stood with her eye on the watch, and when the horse passed her, she was laughing and crying at the same time. She came running to Rufus and hugged him around the neck, then she went running after Star Beauty and Orion.

Star Beauty was slowed to a trot and Orion brought her back to stand in front of the cheering boys. Orion slid off and patted the horse. Rufus, who had walked forward, heard him say, "That's what it feels like to stand in the winner's circle, Star Beauty."

"She did it!" Hagar cried out to Orion. "You did it! You beat last time's speed."

"Let me see."

She gave him the watch and from the look on Orion's face, Rufus knew it was better than good, it was super, as the kids said.

"We'll take her for a workout at a real track one of these days. But I'll have to hold her back a little so she won't tell the world what we've got. This lady is going all the way to Belmont and the Triple Crown. You watch."

The group moved back across the fields to the paths and ponds. Hagar led Star Beauty in front, and let her drink from a pond. Swans on the pond came forward to arch their necks at this intrusion. Shade from the trees darkened the still, clear water and Rufus could feel cool air drifting off the surface of the cold, spring-fed waters. A small stream of water, which he called a branch, ran from one pond to the next, trickling beneath tree roots, over pebbles here and there, its bed mostly hard-packed soil. The ducks sometimes used the branch to swim from one pond to another and sometimes they walked the grassy banks. One of the younger boys took his shoes off and waded the branch, and two more joined him. Rufus watched with pleasure, feeling a happiness of his own from seeing theirs. He thought of the new boy, Patrick, and what he was missing. Tomorrow maybe. There wouldn't be another workout on the racetrack tomorrow, but there would be walks and whatever was needed to make the new boy feel better.

At the paddock Rufus stood with his arms on the stockade fence and watched Hagar and Orion take Star Beauty back to the overhang by her stall. They removed her blanket. Orion had already taken off the saddle and had carried it back along the paths. Hagar began her daily ritual of rubbing the horse, babying her, talking to her. Sometimes Rufus thought the ritual occurred more often than once a day because it seemed to him that no matter when he came out to the barns, Hagar was here, brushing the horse, feeding her, rubbing her until she glistened.

He stayed until Hagar was the only one left. When she removed the bridle, Star Beauty bounded away, free in her paddock. Then she came back to Hagar and put her velvet nose forward and touched Hagar's neck, as if kissing her.

Rufus left, smiling to himself.

The boys had all gone back to their various chores for the day. He could see Rex on the riding lawn mower just west of the main picnic grounds. Another of the boys was sweeping the breezeway between the kitchen, the dining room, the room they called the TV room, and the bunkhouse.

Rufus went quietly into the bunkhouse, passing through the cool dimness of the cloakroom, into the long room that held the bunks.

The new boy, Patrick, lay face down on his bunk crying.

Rufus stood there a moment in indecision. Would this boy respond to comforting from a stranger? He had a feeling he wouldn't. Whatever it was, fear or homesickness, he was probably better off left alone this first day.

Rufus stepped back, and went out to the porch where he sat down in the rocking chair to wait. He pulled out his pipe, tapped tobacco into it, and lit up. He usually didn't light his pipe during the day, but it was a source of comfort that he needed now. The good feelings he'd had earlier were all gone.

Patrick was afraid of night. He was afraid of the day, too, and the light of the sun. In the two different parts of himself, he was afraid of different things. No, not parts of *himself*— but it, the other part that was within him. He had hoped he was free here, that the bad had gone, but he knew it hadn't. He had heard himself saying things that *he* wouldn't have said, that only the bad would have said, and he knew he was not free, never would be free. And the fear was so intense now that he wished sometimes he could go ahead and die and then maybe he would be free. But no, no, he was afraid of the darkness, too.

His eyes hurt today, from tears and the light. The scratches stung his face, and stung his heart, what little was left of his real heart, his real feelings. It hurt knowing his mother, the only person besides his sister who he could turn to for help, wouldn't help him. Only in coming to her it—the bad part—had done something that made her hate him even more. He didn't know for certain what he'd done, and he didn't want to know. Somewhere within him, within the *bad,* he knew. He could still taste the blood in his mouth.

When the boys came into the bunkhouse, he sat up on the side of his bed, his eyes cast down. He didn't want any of them, or anyone, to see him crying like a baby.

A couple of the boys stopped at the end of his bunk, but when he didn't look up or act as if he knew they were there, they went on. The big guy, Marsh, the guy who had seen the *bad* in him and hadn't liked it, paused too, in the doorway. Marsh had stopped upon seeing him, as if he hadn't known Patrick was going to be there. Paddy could see big feet, Marsh's feet. His shoes were scuffed and molded to the shape of his wide feet. He saw the shoes stop, and then move again, going over against the end of the bunk across the aisle, as if giving Patrick as wide a berth as possible. Paddy did not turn to look at Marsh when the shoes went out of sight. But he could hear Marsh moving around at his own bunk just beyond the one Paddy sat on.

Paddy. Patrick. To all the guys around here, he was Patrick. And sometimes, when the bad took over, he was Patrick. Paddy was gone then, pushed away. And Paddy was afraid. He knew the time would come when Paddy would be gone forever. But then too, his fear would be gone. The tears, the times of trying to hide from the—*master*.

"Son."

The voice belonged to another pair of old-looking shoes. It was the old man, Rufus. Paddy looked up.

"You feeling better?"

Paddy stood up. "I'm all right."

Rufus squeezed Paddy's shoulder for just a moment. Part

of Paddy responded, and wanted to come closer to Rufus, but the other part, the deeper part, drew back.

"It's time to wash up and go eat. If you'll come with me, I'll show you the baths."

Paddy followed Rufus to the cloakroom and a short hall beyond. A door to the left led into a bathroom that was like a school's locker room. There were shower stalls and toilets and a row of wash basins. Some of the boys were already at the sinks washing their hands and faces.

"The door you saw across the hall leads to my room, Patrick. If ever you need me at night, for anything, a nightmare, whatever, you come to my room and let me know. The door isn't locked against my boys."

Paddy nodded. But he knew he would never go there. This old man couldn't help him. If his own dad hadn't been able to help, how could Rufus?

Chapter Nine

Ketti lay on the upper bunk, her face to the wall. Lights were out now and the jail had grown fairly quiet. The other inmates who occupied this eight-bunk cell seemed to be sleeping. Ketti could hear the light snores of one.

Ketti ached for the oblivion of sleep, but it rarely came. For a few minutes, it seemed, toward morning, a few restless minutes she didn't have dreams but images flitting through the darkness of her mind, on and on, more frightening than the memories that raged at her during the hours of lying in darkness in her bunk. She kept wondering— when he was dead, when the poor body that had belonged to her son was gone, when the brain was silenced, would they have peace then, she and Paddy? Or would it somehow go on, forever and ever in the darkness of their eternities?

She had to kill him. She had no choice, she knew that now. It was the only way to save others, to save perhaps even Babette. Maybe Babette especially, she was afraid, because the boy who had once been Paddy kept coming back to her and Babette, as if something of him, some old love, remained to draw him back.

The memories left her no rest. When she closed her eyes she saw again the pale bodies of her two baby boys, and she lived in terrible fear that the poison of the vampire would bring them back to live in the world of darkness preying upon the living as they themselves had been preyed upon.

She closed her eyes tightly against those visions, and was cast back to another vision.

She had awakened in the middle of the night, and lay listening. Nervousness was no stranger to her. She lived alone with her two small children, Baby Babs and Paddy, and she often woke in the night sensing something that shouldn't be there. She had sometimes thought the house they lived in was haunted, but it wasn't an old house, the kind one associated with ghosts and strange, cold places where a terrible tragedy had happened. It was a rental, of course, but it was fairly new. A small three-bedroom, with a small kitchen and living room. The paint was new, the sinks unchipped. She paid for it with money she earned as a waitress at a fairly busy restaurant that catered to businessmen who tipped well. It was in a quiet area at the edge of the small town she lived in, only a few miles from where she had been born and raised. Her family had drifted away to other states, both parents were remarried with new families and step-families, but she had stayed. She clung to the familiarity of big trees around her house and snow-capped mountains in the background.

She walked to work. A car was one luxury she hadn't been able to afford since the old one got to the point of needing too many repairs all the time and causing her too much stress. The restaurant where she'd worked for the past three years was only a mile away, and to reach it, she used a shortcut through the woods, a silent place except for the birds, chipmunks and squirrels. She never walked the path with any feeling other than pleasure and security. Not then.

But at night, after she reached home and the babysitter left, after she went to bed and then woke, she heard things. Almost silent movings, it seemed. The nightlights in her children's room made ghostly little paths in the hall as she looked down it from her bed, lying still, listening. Burglars didn't often break into houses in this small town. That was the sort of crime you read about in newspapers. It happened in Seattle, or Walla-Walla, or faraway places that were only names, like Los Angeles and New York. It didn't happen here.

She listened. It wasn't footsteps she heard. The sound blended in with the night, with the wind blowing gently in the treetops. It was part of nature. So many nights it had awakened her, leaving her tense and listening and growing afraid. She tried to remember how many nights, and realized that it wasn't as many as it seemed. One week, maybe two.

She sat up in bed, moving very slowly and quietly, as if her slightest movement could be heard. She looked toward her window where the blind was up and the window open a few inches to catch the summer breeze. And suddenly she knew what the sound was. Something was flying close to the house. She could hear its movements through the air—not the flapping of wings, but an almost silent zipping, a skimming close to the house, the movement of bats. She got out of bed, went to the window and looked out, but the night was dark.

She went through the house.

Windows were open so there would be a cross-circulation of air. She paused in Baby Babs's room. Standing silently in the shadows by the window, she heard the creature touch a screen and grow still. She heard the scraping of talons against metal. But it wasn't on Babette's window.

She went out into the hall and into Paddy's room, and it seemed she might have left the dark blind down, for at first she could not see the window. It had been blacked out. She stood in the doorway, blinking. Suddenly the darkness lifted and the window was revealed. Puzzled, she turned on the bedroom light and saw the curtains had been pushed back on each side of the window and the blind raised almost to the top. Yet something very large and dark had covered the window for a moment.

Either that, or she was seeing things.

She was seeing things, she decided, and went back to bed. Morning would come soon—too soon for her to be up in the middle of the night trying to find something to spook her. Even if something was flying around the outside of the house, the windows had good, solid screens. Bats were small and quick, and caught flying insects at night. She had never been afraid of bats. Little mouse-like creatures with wings, that's all they were, with a fantastic built-in radar for night flying.

But there was another type of bat she had known—and now it came to mind. On the back of a leather jacket Justin had owned had been a furred appliqué of a vampire bat, an unbelievably horrible creature with hideous fangs. "What does it mean?" she had asked when she first saw it. They had been living together all spring and summer and she was pregnant with Paddy. "Nothing," he said. Emblazoned above the soft, black fur of the vampire bat's wings and its naked, bald head, was the word VAMPIRE in white leather letters that had turned gray and cracked with time. Justin had brought out the jacket to shield him against the growing cold of a damp autumn. "It gives me the creeps," she said, shuddering. Justin's frown was impatient and angry. "Forget it. I used to belong to a sort of club. It didn't last long." But there was something about his attitude. "A gang, you mean," she said, knowing she was prodding him. "Okay, a gang! I was young. It's gone now, forget it."

He would never talk about it again, and he wore the jacket only when it was cold.

In recent years she had thought of that vampire bat on the jacket more often than she thought of Justin.

They had split when Paddy was a year old. Justin had gotten restless. Whatever was on his mind, he hadn't told her. One day he just moved out, telling her he'd send child support and he wanted to see his son now and then. But his visits had dwindled, and so had most of the support. She knew where he lived, if she should get in a real financial bind.

She worked from two in the afternoon until ten at night. She didn't mind the walk to work at all, and became only slightly uneasy during the walk home after she began hearing the sounds around the house. On her walk home through the woodland path, her only protection the flashlight she carried, she thought of the nature surrounding her. She had always loved nature. She felt at home with it. And besides that, houses were close by, just beyond the woodland strip on one side of her, a few hundred yards away. If she needed help she could yell.

Men were always joking around with her, coming on to her sometimes. But mostly the men were family men and wanted to stay that way. They flirted and teased her if their wives weren't along. A motel joined the restaurant, a long, two-story building with deep, draped windows and balconies. A lot of strange men came into the restaurant from the motel, so when she saw the dark man who seemed different from the everyday salesman on the road, she thought nothing of it.

But on this night, lying in bed after she had checked out the house and decided the screens were protection enough, she found herself thinking of him.

He had first come into the restaurant two weeks ago. He was thin and dark, not as if from a tan, but from a nationality. He had a beard, and he looked well-dressed and very dignified. She knew instinctively that this was not a customer who would appreciate banter. He probably didn't even want her to mention the weather. She brought him a glass of water and a menu. At the same time, she looked behind her at the clock on the wall. Ten more minutes of work. Ten to ten. These last few minutes always dragged. At this time of night most of the salesmen had gone on into the bar. At least half of them had asked her to come, too, after she got off work, and she'd explained, "I have kids at home."

"Let your husband take care of them," was the most common answer.

She'd smile. "Who's going to take care of him?" She

never told them she didn't have a husband. She'd had one great love, and she'd lived with another man, Paddy's father, and she didn't want to get into that again. With Bab's daddy, everything had been so sweet, the future had looked so good. With Justin, everything had gone sour. She had been thankful daily that she hadn't married him, though she'd wanted to when she found out she was pregnant.

"Would you like to order now, or shall I come back later?" she asked the man with the beard.

His face was shadowed from the light over the counter, and when his eyes raised and met hers, she stared, a strange, cold fear leaping alive in her, almost stopping her heart. On first glance, it looked as if he had no eyes, that holes of nothingness had replaced them. Then she saw that his eyes were very deepset, but quite light, an odd milky color. She thought then he might be blind. Yet he wasn't, she decided, because his eyes moved with her. Still, they were hollow and unnerving. The area around them was darker than the rest of his face. The man looked almost sick, he was cadaverous. The bones in his face stood out prominently, his black beard only partially covering them.

"I'll just have coffee," he said, his voice deep and low.

Feeling more uncomfortable with him than she ever had with a customer, she brought the coffee quickly, and instead of asking him if he wanted cream, she brought it anyway, placing it on the table in front of him. She couldn't help staring at his hands when he put them on the table. The fingers were long and thin, with nails that were long and tapered. The way his hands lay curled on each side of the cup made them look like claws.

She kept her back to him the rest of her shift, cleaning the counter and tables at the other end of the room. She straightened salt and pepper shakers and placed the little bowls with candles precisely in the middle of each table. The night waitress came in. Tying her apron, she greeted Ketti as always, "How's everything?" At this point Ketti usually filled her in on the customers who were still in the restaurant, so she started to tell her about the man in the corner booth. But when she looked toward the booth, she saw he was gone, even though she hadn't heard him leave.

She went to the booth to pick up his cup, and found it still full, the cream untouched. On the table lay a dollar bill. She used it to cover the cost of the coffee, and put the rest with her tips.

That night on the way home, she kept thinking something was following her. And lying awake now, unable to go back to sleep, she knew her feelings were connected with the strange man.

She hadn't expected to see him again. He was probably one of those traveling men who passed this way once in his lifetime.

But three nights later, at a quarter to ten, when the customers had dwindled to a few late talkers and she had started cleaning up the tables and counters, suddenly he was there, sitting in the corner. She felt her heart lurch in fear and surprise. She hadn't seen him come in, and she always saw customers come through the outer door unless it was rush hour. This man had slipped in sometime when she was cleaning the counter, obviously, maybe when she was bent down behind it for a moment seeing that the napkins and other things the night waitress would need were in place.

She took him the menu and a glass of water, and received the same request: coffee. This time she kept an eye on him as she finished cleaning. Yet when the night waitress arrived and said, "How's everything?" the man was gone.

Like the first time, he had left a dollar bill, and if he had touched the coffee, it wasn't noticeable.

"Did you see that weird guy over at the corner booth?" she asked Nadine as she put the cup among the other dirty dishes and removed her apron to leave.

"What guy?"

"He's real dark, with a beard and quite long hair. Not friendly."

"No, I didn't see anyone."

She would have thought she was dreaming on the job if she didn't have the dollar bill in one hand and his cup in the other. She shrugged.

Three nights later the man was back again, and this time she noticed he was watching her. That night she accepted a ride home from one of the men who often asked her if she'd like a lift. She put up with his trying to give her a goodnight kiss in order to avoid the path through the woods.

The next night, when the man didn't show up, she walked home again. The beam of her flashlight seemed pale and narrow, and the trunks of the trees on each side of the path looked like dark figures waiting for her. That night, for the first time, she noticed the flying of the bats—or the bat. She couldn't be sure it was a bat, because her flashlight had only caught the edge of a movement of something dark above the path behind her as she whirled and pointed the light. She had never been afraid of flying things. When she was a child, in the evenings as the sun disappeared between twilight and dark, she and her brothers and sisters had run in the yard, reaching their hands toward the bats that dived at them swiftly, with movements faster than any bird's. She remembered their sound, the almost silent *swiss*.

But bats didn't dive at you in the woods, only out in the open.

A week passed, then ten days, and the man didn't show up. He was gone, thank God. She wasn't really sure now why his presence, his looks, had bothered her so much. Maybe it was his demeanor, his lack of friendliness. She had known immediately, instinctively, that she shouldn't talk to him, that she should talk only if he talked first, and then take her cue from him.

Suddenly she realized why his attitude had bothered her. In the dark, in the middle of the night in the safety of her bed, she realized it was as if he were royalty and she the subject. He had made her feel powerless, as if he were her master.

Well, he was gone.

Thank God.

She turned over on her side, and put her hands beneath her cheek and closed her eyes. It was time to sleep. Tomorrow morning she and the kids had to walk to the grocery store. They always loved those walks. They each got to pick one thing, one treat. It had to cost less than a dollar, so it was candy or ice cream, and sometimes a small toy.

It seemed she had gone to sleep and time had passed, but

the night was still dark, and very quiet—except for one sound.

An almost silent sound.

She opened her eyes widely and stared at the movement of curtains fluttering in the breeze, ghostly pale against the dark wall.

Somebody was sucking on something. With a faint smack of lips, a quiet intake of liquid . . .

With chills radiating up the sides of her head into her hair, with fear so intense she might have been in a nightmare and unable to free herself from it, she managed to get out of bed.

She went into the hall.

She could see through the open door of Paddy's room, and in the dim light, she saw a huge, black blob hovering over the bed. It was like something from another world; it had no definite shape, though she could see the droop of a long wing and at the end of the wing, *claws,* one, or two only, curled, like the *fingers* the dark man had curled beside his coffee cup.

She screamed, and the thing lifted its head to look at her. Its head was small and hunched between the sharp, bony rise of folded wings. It had a wide mouth and teeth that gleamed in the dim light. Two long fangs dripped blood, one drop each. She saw the blood clearly as it fell to the white sheet folded back over the light blanket on Paddy's bed.

She screamed again. Suddenly the winged thing was gone and a man stood at the side of the bed. The man . . . the dark, bearded man with the protruding facial bones, and the hands that she saw now were not claws, but talons.

She rushed toward the bed, toward Paddy. Then she swirled back and turned on the ceiling light. For some reason, it suddenly seemed imperative to have the light on.

When she whirled back toward the bed, the man was gone. The terrible bat-like creature was gone. And Paddy was alone, sprawled and pale, and she realized he was dead.

"No!" she cried out and lifted him. She held his limp body in her arms, his head lolling. She listened for his heart and found nothing. She panicked and carried him into the living room and opened the door to run down the street. But instead of going out, she placed him on the floor, bent over him and began breathing into his mouth, giving him artificial respiration as well as she knew how. He began to cry and she sat on the floor weeping and rocking him back and forth in her arms, her face against his.

Babette was crying when she came into the living room where Ketti and Paddy sat in the dark. Ketti got up at last, locked the door again, and took both children into her bed where she sat frozen until daylight. The next day Paddy was listless and tired, and she saw on his throat the little red marks of a vampire bite.

It couldn't be real, she told herself. Vampires exist only in fiction, and on the back of Justin's jacket—an appliqué in fur, nothing more. Yet, it was that she had seen, as if at night the horror pulled loose from the jacket and went in search of victims.

It couldn't have been real. She hadn't seen what she thought she saw. She convinced herself of that because she had to.

Yet when she got the courage to go back into Paddy's room, she found the two drops of blood on his sheet. And she found the screen had been torn away from the bottom of his window.

She didn't go back to work for two weeks. But then, forced to make a living for her family, she pleaded for a daytime job and got it.

But the horror had started.

She was consoled by one thought now as she lay in her jail cell. She wouldn't be killing Paddy, her baby, she would be saving him from the horror that had come into their lives.

Marsh was afraid to sleep. For hours he had been lying on his side facing the strange new boy. The night was warm, but he'd pulled up his blanket and was holding it against his cheek, making a tent he could peek out of. He hadn't taken his eyes off the bunk three feet away. He couldn't see the boy, but he could see the bulge he made in the bed, the dark shape against the dark corner. Black on black.

The strange boy hadn't moved.

Throughout the bunkhouse, other boys made sounds in their sleep, sometimes turning over, their beds making mouse-like sounds. But the strange boy never moved, so that Marsh began to wonder if he had put a pillow in his bed and covered it with his blanket to make it look like he was there—like that boy Willard did that time. The next day Rufus and Mr. Preston found out that Willard had run away. He had gotten under the big fence somehow and he never came back. If he had stayed longer, he would have liked it here. But he had only just come.

Marsh was afraid of this strange new boy. He was more afraid than he'd been in all the time he had lived here. He was afraid the way he had been when he lived with . . . *them.*

He tried not to think about his mother, or his dad, or uncle.

They were bad people.

This new boy was a bad people, too.

Person. Bad person.

His eyes closed. He wanted to turn. His right arm was hurting because he had laid on it so long. It was the arm he'd had to keep against his body for a long, long time because of the way *they* had hurt it. And now it was hurting again, and he was sleepy, and wanted to turn over. But he was afraid. The night was dark inside the bunkhouse. He longed to get up and go out, but Rufus didn't like for him to go out at night a lot—the way he used to when he couldn't sleep.

He wanted so much to move, but he was afraid to.

Suddenly the dark bulk on the strange boy's bed moved and sat up, and marsh could see through his blanket peephole the shape of the boy's head against the dark wall.

He heard the bed make its little squeak as the strange boy turned and put his feet on the floor, just inches from Marsh.

Marsh held his breath.

The boy rose slowly and stood in the three feet of space between the bunks.

Facing Marsh. Looking down at Marsh.

Marsh felt the whimper of fear rising in his throat, but like the old times, he kept silent, too afraid to make a sound.

Chapter Ten

Marsh trembled with relief when the strange boy turned and went down the aisle at the foot of the beds. Maybe, he thought, the strange boy was going to the bathroom. Maybe he wasn't going to hurt Marsh after all. He eased the blanket off his head when the strange boy turned right and went to the door.

Marsh sat up and listened for Patrick to go into the bathroom, but after a long, tense time of waiting, he heard the board squeak on the porch. The strange boy had stepped on the loose board between the door and the steps, the board that Rufus had tried to fix lots of times before. Finally Rufus had said, "I reckon I'll let it be. It's my watchdog."

Marsh waited, expecting to hear Rufus get up to see who had walked across the porch. He didn't. This was one of those nights when Rufus snored. It seemed Marsh could hear his snoring all the way through the walls.

What was Patrick, this strange boy, going to do?

Was he going to hurt the animals?

Marsh pushed back his blanket, stood up, and in his bare feet went out to the porch. He stopped short of the loose board and looked around. He didn't see anyone except Lion. Lion was rising from his bed on the porch and coming toward him, the starlight turning his tail into a ghost in the shadows of the porch. The dog came to Marsh, but instead of putting his nose in Marsh's hand, he stood looking eastward. Marsh knew. That was the way the boy had gone. Not down toward the barns and the animals, but toward the other buildings.

Marsh walked around the loose board, as he'd learned to do

on those rare nights now when he went out. Rufus didn't like for him to wander about the farm anymore, and Marsh tried to remember that. Even when he couldn't sleep sometimes, he just came onto the porch. Or went no farther than the machinery between the bunkhouse, the barns, and ponds.

But what was the strange boy doing? Was he going to run away?

There was no way he could get out. That one boy had, but he'd dug a hole under the fence, and the hole was all gone now. Covered in. Grass had been planted on it again.

Where was Patrick going?

Marsh was afraid to follow, to find him maybe hiding around the corner where he'd jump out and scare Marsh.

But this was Marsh's home. And Patrick was a bad boy. He knew that. He had known bad people before. They had a way about them, and had to be watched. He had to watch Patrick.

Patrick was at home in the night. His eyes penetrated the shadows and saw the small, warm-blooded animals, who were themselves nocturnal. A chipmunk beneath the limbs of a shrub stopped and stared. High in a tree, a bird roosting on the edge of its nest slept, its young ones quiet and sleeping, too. The home, the bed, the young, the adults. It was a scene repeated the world over, from the smallest animal to the largest and to the one who considered himself the most intelligent, man. From mice to men.

Patrick smiled.

What egotism, what blindness.

If only they knew.

The men were no more immortal than the mice. Nor more intelligent. Instinct was instinct, however you spelled it, or misinterpreted it.

The immortal lived among men, but the men were even more blind to it than the mice.

The immortal had invaded that boy, Paddy, and become Patrick.

Patrick moved in the shadows of the building. He had seen the woman at the dinner tables, both at noon and in the evening. She was round and plump and had a good supply of blood within her heavy body. They had called her the housekeeper—or was it housemother? It hardly mattered. Where did she reside? She surely must have an apartment on the compound. Or did she leave at night?

He was hungry. He was starving. How could he exist on the revolting food that was gobbled up by those skinny boys?

He pressed close to the side of the building and edged toward a window. The starlight was growing brighter, and in the east, a thin moon was rising. Complete darkness suited him better—it was more difficult for the warm-blooded animals to see to escape. Not all of them had night vision that sustained them, and none of them had night vision equal to his.

He found the window and put his fingers on the frame and felt toward the screen. Of course it would be screened. What did humans think they were keeping out with a thin screen? Only the moths, if they knew.

He must work quickly before the boy woke. When the boy woke, when he struggled against him, his work was more difficult. He had grown very old in his former body. His bones had aged and grown stiff, and his will to move about had somehow deteriorated with his body. Finally he had needed a young, new body. It had been a long and difficult process. The boy had a strong will. He came back sometimes during the day and gave up reluctantly at night. He could sense the boy stirring at times in the corners of his poor, feeble brain, just as he could see the little, furry, blood-filled creatures stirring in the leaves. They were safe from him. If he had to resort to animal blood for feeding, he chose the larger animals. But it was human blood that kept him living, and it was that for which he hungered.

The old times had been better. Light lived with the day then, and feeding was easier.

His fingers touched the screen and he put his head closer to the window and looked in. He saw the shape of a bed and on it, uncovered except for her white nightgown, was the fat woman. He saw the back of her head, the rounded shoulder, the hump of the hip. He heard her long, sleeping breaths, the near-snores as air eased in and out of her lungs.

He dug his fingers into the edge of the screen and drew

his lips back in a snarl of frustration. This young body had blunt fingers. His old body had slowly developed over the years long, hard fingers with talon nails that made it easy to enter any screen. It had been less difficult then to change form, to gain access. But he preferred to move about in the physical world of the human being—even if the appendages were such as these.

He felt into the pocket of his jeans and took out the knife. He opened the pointed blade and put it against the screen. It sank into the thin metal wires with a faint snapping sound. The screen ripped.

He heard a growl, and whirled to meet the noise.

At the corner of the building, not twenty feet away, stood the big, retarded boy called Marsh and beside him, the dog. The dog's lips were drawn back, and he could see the glint of light on white fangs. The pale, thin, rising room outlined the big boy's head.

He felt a growl rise in his own throat.

They dared to confront him? They dared to follow him? It would be easy—within moments both would be dead, and he could feed until dawn.

But then he would have to desert this young, supple body he had found and go through the process of finding yet another who would be as physically and mentally unprotected as this one had been. He heard the almost silent stir of wings and looked up to see the *master* slip through the night.

The beckoning.

Paddy stared at the boy and the dog. He could see only their outlines and he began to shake with fear. The knife was in his hand, he could feel the sharp point of the open blade against his finger.

What was he doing here?

With one hand working surreptitiously at his side, he closed the blade and put the knife into his pocket. He was half-dressed, he realized, wearing jeans, the floppy pajama top he had worn to bed, and no shoes.

The growl of the dog had awakened him, and he pressed against the side of the building for protection. His shoulder felt the edge of a window frame. He glanced swiftly into the room, but saw nothing. He stepped forward, easing along the wall away from the window, his eyes on the dog.

The dog stopped growling, and he saw a single wave of its tail, as if the dog wasn't sure if it should be friendly or attack.

The big boy stared at him without moving.

Paddy looked around. The area was unfamiliar. Fear pounded in his throat. He could feel *the other*, as if his consciousness walked only in the shadow of his real self.

He waited, but the boy and the dog didn't move.

"What are you doing at Miss Rose's window?" the boy finally asked. "That's Miss Rose's window."

Paddy's voice came in a rush of silent tears that hurt his throat. "I woke up here. Where am I? I don't know where I am."

The big boy said nothing for a long time, then he turned and walked in the other direction, around the corner of the building. Paddy followed him, twenty feet away. At the corner, he paused. The front of the bunkhouse was long and silver in the pale moonlight, and the posts along the porch looked like teeth.

Paddy felt the urge to turn back, to find release in the lift of a winged flight. But he struggled against the feeling, knowing it was the pull of the *thing,* the internal urging of the one that was gaining strength within him.

He saw the back of the boy, his open, vulnerable neck. He saw the soft, unprotected warm-blooded creatures ahead of him, and felt the deep hunger, the need of the other. It would be so much easier to give in. To just give in, and let go. It was coming. Sometime, sometime soon, he knew, he could feel, he would sleep and never wake.

Rufus heard the crowing of the roosters and opened his eyes to see the pale gray, almost artificial, look of dawn. He stretched and pushed back his light covers, then lay still, his feet at each corner of the foot of the bed, his hands touching each corner at the head. This was his favorite time of day. He had it all to himself. Even the dog was still sleepy and lazy in the early dawn. Only the chickens were rousing, and he heard the sleepy crow of a rooster.

He stretched again, then got up and pulled on his overalls. He went to the bathroom. This was one of the few times when it wasn't full of boys.

He brushed his teeth, washed his face, ran the electric razor over his chin, combed his hair, looked in the mirror to see that his shirt was buttoned straight and his collar flat. When he left the bathroom, he stepped into the open door of the bunkroom and looked down the long rows of bunks. Twenty-five boys. Twenty-four permanent boys. All were in bed, asleep. Marsh, he saw, had his whole head covered in his blanket. Marsh used to sleep that way, even in hottest weather, and Rufus had regularly pulled the blanket off his head to find him wet with sweat. Gradually, as Marsh had become more at ease, more secure, he slept sprawled on top of his blanket. But now, again, his head was covered.

Rufus tiptoed around the end of the bunk and eased the blanket out of the tight grip of Marsh's fingers and off his head. His hair was wringing wet, just like old times, but he was sleeping soundly. Rufus folded the blanket back below his arms.

He looked at the new boy, Patrick. He was turned with his back to the rest of the house, and had drawn himself into a knot that looked uncomfortable. But Rufus didn't bother him. He stood for a moment looking at the boy's face. He looked younger when he was asleep—younger, more abused, the scratches pink furrows that were scabbing over in places. Rufus had stopped wondering why parents did these things to their kids. He guessed now he hadn't wondered much about it in his own childhood. It was just that way in some houses. Not many. None of the kids he knew then were slapped around the way he was. He'd never forget as long as he lived the time he'd gone to visit a boy who'd tried to befriend him. That boy's mother had been so nice. The boy wasn't one bit afraid of her. Then the dad had come home, and he even kissed the boy. Rufus had been astounded, and from that day on, that family was part of the heaven he formed in his own mind.

A loving family. Heaven.

Rufus walked quietly down the long aisle. Each boy had his

own little table and his own locker. On each table were personal items. Most of them were special birthday or Christmas presents each boy had requested. A couple of tables held pictures of a sister or a brother or some other relative. A few held books. Some of the boys liked to read. Others had to be made to read a certain length of time. Rufus smiled. They were all different, but they were all good boys. And they were going to stay that way, if he could help it.

He turned back down the aisle and went onto the porch. He absent mindedly stepped on the loose board and flinched from the long, tortured squeal it made.

The sound woke Lion, who got up reluctantly from his bed of old rugs and came down the porch toward Rufus. Rufus rubbed the dog's ears.

"Mornin', Lion," he said, and went to his rocking chair. Lion followed and sat a few feet away, looking off across the yard toward the barns. One of the peacocks in the barnyard squalled, and Rufus drew in the sound as if it were a breath of cool air. He enjoyed the sounds of the fowl in the mornings. The birds in the trees, the roosters and hens in their enclosure, the peacocks, ducks, and geese.

He filled his pipe and lit it. He didn't often smoke where the boys could see him. His pipe didn't set a good example, he guessed, since tobacco wasn't exactly good for you. When they did catch him puffing on his pipe, he always made sure to tell them he didn't inhale, he only liked to pull the smoke through the pipe stem.

He watched the glow in the east turn to such brightness he couldn't look at it anymore. He could hear the beginning movement of the day. Orion went into the kitchen; a tractor started somewhere in a back field; the farm workers' dogs barked a few times, their voices distant; cars were traveling along the highway in front of the farm.

Rufus got up, stretched and knocked out his pipe ashes against the porch post. It was time to start the day. And today, the new boy had to come on out and get used to his surroundings. One day of hiding was enough.

Chapter Eleven

Hagar sat on a stool in the corner of the stall and watched Star Beauty munch grain from a bucket. The horse's velvet nose was powdered with a residue of grain, a yellow powder that clung to the short hairs on her nose and made them visible. Hagar laughed and reached over to dust the nose of the filly.

"You've got your makeup on crooked, lady," she said. The horse looked at Hagar with big brown eyes and went on eating the grain, reaching her soft nose back into the small pile of cracked corn, wheat, oats, and barley. Star Beauty loved her grain as much as Gwen loved her candy. As much as Hagar loved Star Beauty.

She heard footsteps on the floorboards behind the stall, in the open area where only three boards separated Star Beauty's manger from the interior of the barn. There, in the coolness and perpetual shade of the barn, the hay and grain were kept. Hallways in the barns led to all the stalls and rooms where animals were housed, or farm necessities, such as bridles and harnesses, stored. Hagar looked up. The footsteps weren't her dad, she hoped, coming to tell her she was spending too much time in the barn, too much time with the horse. They had gone through this before. Dad didn't understand. What was there to do at the house? She hated housework. She did what she had to do in a hurry and left. She didn't like television, as Gwen did. She couldn't imagine herself learning needlework, or even art, even though she admired, even lost herself, in good art.

The footsteps became double, then triple. It seemed several people were coming through the barn. A voice reached her. Rufus, not Dad. Hagar relaxed.

At that moment, unexpected, Star Beauty threw her head back and let out a loud cry, not a whinny but a bleat. She backed suddenly, swerved, and threw her rearend into the boards of her gate so hard she went down on her knees and almost fell. She reared up, pawing the air with her front feet, and they came down just inches from Hagar's head. Hagar fell sideways to avoid being struck, and then climbed into the manger. Star Beauty whirled and pawed at the gate, and it gave way, the top board cracking with a sound that reverberated through the barn. The horse leaped over the broken board and went galloping into the enclosed paddock.

Hagar stood up, staring after the horse in stunned disbelief.

"What happened?" Rufus asked. "What's wrong with Star Beauty?"

Rufus stood in the barn just beyond the manger. With him was the new boy, Patrick, and farther back, as if following at a distance, was Marsh. The dog, Lion, was with them. But Star Beauty was used to everyone, especially the dog, who sometimes curled up in the soft hay in the corner of her stall.

She was used to everyone but the new boy.

"I don't know what's wrong," Hagar said, turning back to watch the filly prance wildly around the far end of the paddock. Her head was lifted and her ears up, pointed like a fox's.

Hagar looked into the bucket of grain. Had something weird fallen in? A tarantula or something else with long, hairy legs? Big insects might scare a young horse. Hagar didn't know.

Rufus and the boys went out of sight through the barn and Hagar heard their footsteps on the boards. A door squeaked open and closed, and Rufus came out into the paddock followed by Lion, Patrick, and farther behind, still keeping a distance, Marsh. Rufus came to the broken gate.

"Anything in her feed?"

"Nothing." Hagar set the empty bucket aside. There was only a bit of yellow powder left along the rim of the bucket. The center had been licked clean.

At the end of the paddock, Star Beauty stopped and turned her head toward them, and Hagar saw she was staring at the new boy, Patrick. Her shiny, dark coat trembled and quivered as if she were terrified.

Once before, when she was a lot younger, Star Beauty had gone into this kind of panic. An owl had swooped out of the barn just over her head and Star Beauty had bolted, running to the other end of the paddock. Hagar had to coax her back to her stall with an apple.

Hagar looked up now to see that her dad, Orion, and Gwen had come to the fence and were watching. Rufus said to the boys, "We better get outta here and let Hagar calm her. I guess we surprised her, boys. Come on, Lion, you too. Get out."

They went to the gate and joined the growing group outside the fence. Hagar glimpsed from the corner of her eyes that some of the other boys were now wandering close. Two were climbing the fence to sit on the top rail.

She also saw that Gwen was smiling at the new boy. That was typical. She was getting boy crazy, and Hagar wondered if their dad had noticed. But she didn't have room to worry about it.

She climbed through the manger and into the dim interior of the barn and the long breezeway that ran between the shed and the rooms inside. In the feedroom was a small barrel of apples, and she reached in and felt among them until she touched smooth skin that wasn't puckered with age. Many of the apples had shrunk. They were last year's crop. One of the boys, Bruce, came to the door and looked in.

"Are you going to feed her an apple? Can I give her one?"

"I tell you what—" She didn't want to discourage, or disappoint him, but with Star Beauty in her present state, she was afraid Bruce would make the horse more agitated. "Why don't you take out all the shriveled ones and give them to the pigs? They'd love you for it."

"Okay!"

Hagar smiled at him as she drew back with her choice apple. Bruce was the baby on the farm. Only seven. He had been here a year now, and seemed to have no family beyond the farm folks. Tommy, a veteran of nine, who had been on the farm three years, appeared in the doorway behind Bruce.

"Can I help?"

"Bruce is going to separate the old apples from the good ones and feed them to the pigs."

"Let me."

"I was here first!"

"There's enough for both of you," Hagar said. Arguments among the boys didn't often occur. "You guys get along, okay?"

They kneeled on the floor, one on each side of the barrel. Bruce was a towhead, as Rufus called him, and Tommy looked Hispanic with black hair and tanned skin. Hagar seldom knew the backgrounds of the boys, but she knew that Bruce had come from a variety of foster homes after early years of neglect and abuse in his own home. Tommy's parents were dead, and his abuse had been at the hands of his aunt after his uncle had taken him into their home.

She left the boys sorting out the shrunken apples and went back through Star Beauty's manger. She opened the broken stall gate and crossed the paddock. Orion had already gone to the horse and was stroking her face and talking softly to her. Hagar could see the filly had relaxed considerably, though when Hagar approached, she jerked up her head again and snorted. And Hagar saw her once again stare toward the strange boy who now stood against the trunk of the large tree just beyond the fence. The others were on the fence, or by it. The boy, Patrick, had pulled away from the group to stand alone. Hagar saw he was staring at the horse, and even over the distance of fifty yards or more, she could see the set of his face and his odd, empty-looking eyes. She looked at him, then looked again. At first glance, she had the impression he had no eyes. She saw Gwen leave the fence and go stand by the boy and start talking to him. Patrick gave his attention to Gwen. Hagar saw him smile, and his face, which had seemed hard and angry, now softened and became handsome.

"What spooked her?" Orion asked. "Rufus said he did it, but he never has before."

Hagar offered the apple to Star Beauty. The horse gave her head a single toss, lifted her upper lip and took the apple in. Hagar caressed Star Beauty's face and listened to the apple's juicy crunch.

"I think it was the new boy."

"Oh, yeah? I've never known her to get scared of one of the boys before. Did he do something to scare her?"

Hagar had to admit he hadn't, though she would have liked to have said he jumped out at her, or something as tangible. There was something about the new boy that set her own nerves on edge—or was it that she picked up her filly's feelings? She didn't understand. She just wanted to make Patrick stay away from Star Beauty and she couldn't. The boys had access to all the animals on the farm, within reason.

"It might be because they came in through the barn," Hagar said. But she turned again and looked at the boy. "He's got odd eyes," she said without thinking. The boy had turned and was leaning against the tree, his profile toward her. He was talking and Gwen was laughing.

"They're gray," Orion said, smiling. "You're used to dark eyes, since so many of our boys are dark-eyed."

"I guess." Hagar rubbed the velvet softness of Star Beauty's nose. "I just wish they'd all go now and let her calm down."

"She's calming, but I'll see if I can get them away. Maybe I can talk Rufus and the rest of the boys into showing Patrick the other animals. I think this was his first stop."

"He won't bother the pigs," Hagar said mostly to Star Beauty as Orion went across the paddock to the fence. "They're too busy wallowing in their pond and they'll be eating apples, too."

She took the horse's bridle and began walking her around the fence. By the time she had come to the shade of the big tree, most of the others were walking toward the pens where the hogs were kept, and to the pens of the goats. Three of the sheep were in a smaller enclosure and some were out on pasture with other animals. The animals that were kept in pens were rotated so the boys would have all variety of farm animals to take care of. Hagar watched the group go to the pig pens and stay there a few minutes. Gwen was sticking close to Patrick. From the pig pens they went on to the cool and shady path through the goat and sheep pens and out of Hagar's sight. Orion was crossing the open area to the bunkhouse and kitchen, and Hagar's dad was gone, too.

Hagar drew a sigh of relief. Star Beauty had calmed and was leading as well as always, almost, though she tended to jerk her head up occasionally and stare toward the trees. But when Hagar urged her on she settled back to walking.

Babette asked, "May I look at the newspaper?"

"Of course," Mother Ann answered, "if you're finished."

She was a neat, round-faced lady with brown hair pulled back from her face in a smooth, easy style that ended in a little braided knot at the back. She never wore makeup, but her lips and cheeks were rosy. She looked fairly happy, and she seemed to love the four young foster kids in her care. She had greeted Babette as if Babette were a niece, or some close relative she hadn't seen in a year or two. But Babette did not feel at home here with the younger children, the father of the house, or Mother Ann. Night and day she wished she could leave, but she waited.

"Did you finish folding the laundry?" Mother Ann asked.

"Yes."

"Then go read the paper."

Babette found the newspaper in the den beside the chair that belonged to the father, Dad Harry. When she vacuumed the room, she had put the paper into the wicker basket beside the chair, just as Ann had told her to.

During her stay at the foster home, she had followed instructions carefully, doing up the rooms, vacuuming, dusting, putting things away. "Neaten the rooms, dear," Ann said each morning after breakfast. The younger children went out to play, and Babette cleaned house. She could always hear Ann in the kitchen, preparing food, or running the dishwasher, or talking on the phone. The other kids, Babette had been told by Miss Thornton, were longtime care children, and some of them had been with Mother Ann and Dad Harry for four years now. New babies stayed for a few months, and one had just been taken away and put in his adoptive home.

Ann knew that Babette was temporary, but was willing to take her. Babette knew why—she needed help with the work. But that was all right, Babette didn't mind. She was used to doing housework, and wouldn't have felt right with nothing to do. Sometimes she thought of the way some kids lived, going to the mall, or the park, swimming every day, playing tennis, hanging out with friends. Babette had never gotten to do those things, and in school she was isolated from the other kids because she had nothing in common with them.

She sat down on the floor in front of the window and spread the paper on the floor. Every day she had searched the paper for anything that might indicate Ketti had gotten out of jail. The worst—that there would be a small item in the back of the paper telling of a mother who had gotten into Boys' Farm and killed her son—was the first thing Babette looked for. And not finding it, she read the rest of the paper, searching for news of the jail, or releases, anything. She'd found nothing.

She wanted to use the phone, but hadn't dared ask.

She had thought about writing a letter to Paddy's father asking him to please come and get Paddy, but knew that the police had tried to find him, and perhaps they had by now. She prayed they had. And perhaps Justin had come and taken Paddy away already. Then she and Mom could go home again.

They would have to move, Babette guessed, because they couldn't live in the old house without Danny Boy. Moving would also make Paddy safer. If he didn't know where they were, he would never be able to find them, and Ketti would never see him again.

Babette put the paper away in the basket and wandered from the den to the living room and out into the hall. The house was old, but pretty, with large, cool rooms, deep porches, and nice old furniture. Babette shared a room with two little girls. She slept on a cot in the corner, but it didn't matter, she told herself. She wouldn't be here long.

She went into the kitchen. Ann was preparing vegetables, using a brush to scrub off the thin skins of small, round potatoes. In a bowl in the sink were scrubbed carrots, small onions, and sweet peppers. Babette could smell meat cooking, and knew the vegetables would be put in with it. But the smell of the food turned Babette's stomach—she hadn't had any appetite since the night Danny died.

"Got it read already?" Ann asked. "You must have been looking only for the funnies, or the advice column."

"Would it be all right if I used the phone? I just want to call . . . to see about my mother. It's not long distance."

"Yes, you may. But please don't keep the phone tied up. We just have one line."

"I won't. Could I go to the one in the den?"

"Yes, certainly."

Babette went back to the den, and with shaking hand looked through the telephone book, found the number she thought might be the right precinct, and dialed.

She explained to the voice that answered, "I am . . . Babette Graham . . . and I'm—I want to know about my mother. Is she there? I mean . . . is she in your jail? I want to talk to someone who can tell me when she's going to get out."

She was transferred to another department twice, and then a female voice told her, "Your mother's case had been taken over by a public defender and he'll probably arrange for her release in a few days. Tomorrow, perhaps, or the next day. It takes awhile to do the paperwork."

Babette's mouth turned dry. "Will—will I know?"

"Of course you'll know."

"But—I mean—right away?"

"Ummm—I'm sure your mother will come and see you, and take you home with her. Or—who was it—Miss Thornton? Who handled your case? She'll be in touch with you."

By the time Babette gave up trying to find out any more, her lips were so dry they felt stretched and rough. She went to the bathroom and splashed cold water on her face. Ketti was going to be freed soon. And Babette had to know exactly when.

She went into her bedroom and to the closet. Her things were looped over hangers at one end of the closet. She took down her jeans, blouses and the one dress she had brought along, folded them carefully, then rolled each tightly and pushed them down into the bottom of the pillow case. It was too large a bundle. She didn't need but one change of clothes, so she removed the rest, including the dress, and put them back into the closet. When Ann looked for her, after she'd gone, and found the clothes, she might think Babette had only gone out for a long walk. And she might delay calling the police to report her missing. That delay might mean the difference between Paddy's living and dying.

She had to get to him.

But she had to wait until tonight, or tomorrow night.

Each day she would call the jail.

And she could call Boys' Farm and ask if Paddy was still there, or if his daddy had come for him, or if he had been sent home.

But in the meantime, her clothes were bundled under her cot, ready for her to leave.

Hagar caught up with Gwen on the path around pond one. The sun was sinking, leaving a red, pink, and gold haze in the horizon over the long, straight roof of the bunkhouse.

"Have you been out all afternoon?" Hagar asked.

"Sure. Why not? So have you."

"I always am. You never are. You weren't tagging around after that new boy, were you?"

"So who're you?" Gwen glared briefly at Hagar. "My mother?"

"I saw you. You'd better be careful Dad doesn't see you making a fool of yourself over one of the boys. They're off limits, Gwen, and you know that."

"I wasn't doing anything! I only went around with Rufus while he was showing Patrick the animals and the ponds and things. Marsh was along too, and some of the other boys. What's wrong with that?"

"Hey, Gwen, don't pull that innocent act with me. I know when you're getting a crush on someone, and you know you're not supposed to fall for new boys."

Hagar saw the pout of Gwen's mouth. Gwen stomped ahead, clearly not wanting to walk with Hagar. Hagar drew a long sigh.

She stopped at the gate to the yard and turned back to look at the bunkhouse. Lights were on in the windows now in the dining room and kitchen, and through the windows she could see the movement of people as they sat down to the evening meal.

It was too far away to recognize anyone, even Orion or Rose. The windows were lighted rectangles in the growing shadows, the figures inside, mere shadows.

She heard the front door of her own house slam as Gwen went in. She had made no impression on Gwen, she guessed. It would take Dad to do that. But she hesitated to tattle on Gwen. Her younger sister had started getting crushes on new boys who passed through on temporary stay when she was only nine years old, but it hadn't been anything to worry about. This time though . . . Hagar tried to put a definite reason on her sense of wrongness here, and couldn't.

She looked toward the barns. They were too far away, she thought for the first time. Too far for her to hear Star Beauty if she kicked her stall during the night, or whinnied in fright.

Hagar turned and went up the walk to the porch. Gwen or her dad had turned on the lights in a room beyond the entry way and the hallway picked up the glow. As she passed through the hall, she heard the voices of her family.

Hagar found them in the kitchen. Gwen was washing her hands. Her job was to set the table while Hagar and their dad made supper. He had already put a steak into a pan and it was sizzling, filling the air with the smell of smoke.

"You want me to do that, Dad?" she asked, trying not to show her sense of revulsion at the thought of eating an animal. In the past year she turned to vegetarianism. It was something that had happened gradually, as she grew older and more aware. But her dad was a steak eater. "Did you know," she asked him once, "that the greatest and most deadly predators on earth are men? Humans? Doesn't that tell you something, Dad?" He'd been reading the paper.

"What?" he asked. And she had answered, frowning, never really having thought about it before. "That we're just an extreme form of all the predators. We're not godly. Not until we start acting like God will we be godly." He hadn't lifted his eyes from the paper. "Takes time. We're on our way."

But thereafter, she couldn't bring herself to eat meat. She was willing to cook it for her dad at this point. Maybe later she wouldn't even want to do that.

Tonight, he was ready to let her do the cooking.

"You're better at it than I am," he said.

He stepped away, and Hagar turned down the fire under the pan. She wondered if she should tell him about Gwen getting all hot and bothered about the new boy, and decided not to. Maybe it would go the way of all Gwen's crushes and last only two days.

Chapter Twelve

Paddy struggled under a dream so vivid it might have been a memory. He woke, tossed on his cot, and went back into the dream. His skin was wet and sticky, and he felt he couldn't breathe. Something was over his face, smothering him.

His dad's hands. Justin's hands. And Justin's face, just inches away twisted and tortured, stared into his own. His voice hissed at Paddy.

"What did you do to her? I know you did it. Don't lie to me, you goddamned little bastard. what did you do to her?"

His voice was strange, as unfamiliar as his face. He was cursing at Paddy without opening his teeth.

"You've hurt her before, haven't you? That's why she hasn't been—well. But what have you done to her now?"

Paddy didn't know what Justin was talking about. He could taste the odd, tangy, terrible taste again, but he couldn't remember. He didn't want to remember. He tried

106

to get out from under Justin's hands, away from the deadly anger that had changed his dad into this stranger. But he couldn't. He couldn't breathe. He felt the bulge of his own eyes and the jerking of his body. He felt Justin bear down, his knees on his chest, and thought . . . he's going to kill me. He's actually going to kill me. But at that moment, Paddy didn't care. He wouldn't have to remember, to face whatever it was Justin was talking about . . . *had she died . . . like Billy?* Was that what this was about? And this taste in his mouth that he didn't like, but which Patrick did . . . was it blood?

The scene blacked out for just an instant. His dad's face disappeared, the bitter hatred gone for just an instant, and then he heard a long scream that he recognized was born of panic, of fear beyond human experience, and his eyes opened.

There it was in the room, skimming the ceiling with its black wings. Its legs were lowering, the talons stretched like a hawk reaching for its helpless prey. It came down at Justin, and he rolled off the bed and onto the floor, and Paddy was free. But he didn't want to be free. He tried to move and couldn't as he watched the dark wings, the long, sharp talons, and the face—the terrible, small face with its empty eyes. . . .

The scream was coming from his dad as if Justin had looked into hell.

Paddy woke. He lay trembling on his pillow, hoping he hadn't cried out in his sleep like a scared baby. He felt cold and wet, and his pillow was damp. He moved, pushing back the sheet, turning his head slowly to look at the long room full of boys. In the dark he could barely make out the shape of bunks in the pale light coming through the window. A thin moon must have risen. Its light lay across the foot of the bunk beds nearest the window. Somebody moved in his bed, groaning as he turned over, kicking back his blanket.

The room grew still again.

But Paddy wasn't alone in his wakefulness. He could sense from his innermost self that something was in the room. With his body cold and stiff, he slowly turned his head toward the door into the cloakroom.

Its wings, folded against its body, making sharp spikes beside the shrunken head, were outlined against the dark wall. It was perched on the foot of Paddy's bed, its black body a darker part of the wall.

Paddy lay in rigid terror. Silent, staring, unable to take his eyes away from the black figure in the deep shadow at the foot of his bed.

The wings began to move, their shape undefined in the dark, but reaching into Paddy's awareness as if he needed no eyes to know the shapes and outlines that were important to him.

The wings unfolded, and in silence it lifted and flew with only a slight twitching and turning of wings. Halfway down the aisle it perched on the foot of another cot, and the wings folded. Paddy had risen from his bed, he realized, and followed without knowing how or when. He was standing in the aisle, the floor cool beneath his bare feet. He watched the dark outlines of the wings as it moved, walking the length of the bed.

A memory intruded, and became his reality.

He was small again, so small he had to reach up to grab the doorknob in front of him. With both hands he twisted the knob. It was white, like glass. He felt the cool, smooth surface that was slick in his hands and hard to turn. But there was something in the room behind this door that he had to see. It was the most important thing in the world to him. He had to see what his daddy had put in this room.

The knob turned slowly, and the door came loose from the wall. He saw the streak of darkness on the other side grow wider. It was a closet, a special closet.

The coat was hanging on the wall in front of him. Black, shiny leather. He smiled. This was what he wanted to see, Daddy's leather jacket with the picture on the back.

It was a picture of a big thing with wings, not a bird, but a bat. The bat had a funny little head pulled down between big wings, and it had two sharp teeth that were long like the blades of knives. Above the black bat on the shiny black leather was a word in white leather letters: V A M P I R E.

But it was the picture of the bat he wanted to see. It had real fur on its wings, and he reached up and touched it. The fur was short and soft, very soft, beneath his fingers. He had seen his daddy wearing the coat once, and he thought it was the prettiest coat he had ever seen.

Here, what're you doing, little guy?

A big person's hand came into the shadows of the closet and pulled him out. The door shut. *I want to see Daddy's coat.*

Daddy doesn't want you messing around with his things. Leave it alone or bad things will happen to you. That thing'll come right off of there and eat you up all gone!

The voice was final. It came from a strange woman, her face warning him, terrifying him enough to discourage him from the closet.

Paddy blinked. The scene changed. The face he was looking upon was as unfamiliar to him as the face of that woman in the early years of his life. It was a pale blur of roundness on the pillow. Round and plump.

The fat boy.

Rex.

In Paddy's hand was his knife. The inlaid ivory on the handle had grown warm in his hand. When had he taken the knife from under his pillow?

The wings of the vampire were outlined on the wall in front of him. They moved silently, stretching out again as if to fly, holding that position, shadow upon shadow, burning their image once more upon Paddy's mind.

He was older. He had been sent to live with his dad, and the woman who lived with him. His mother had sent him away. He hadn't seen his dad in a long time. He couldn't even remember how long. Two years? Three? He didn't go to visit his dad. He used to, when he was a lot younger. His dad would come by, sometimes on his motorcycle, and pick him up. He could remember looking forward to those motorcycle rides. But then his dad had gotten a car, and it wasn't so great anymore. Justin had begun to seem like a stranger coming to take him out for a ride and a hamburger and milkshake.

He wandered through the strange house. His dad was asleep, and his stepmother, or Jill, as she'd told him to call her, was in the living room drinking coffee and watching television.

The house was roomy and old, half hidden at the end of the drive, surrounded by a lot of big trees, dripping moisture. There was nothing to do here. He'd been here less than a month, and he'd thought of running away, of going back to the small house, much smaller than this, where he had lived with Mama and Babette . . . and Billy.

It was because of Billy that Mama had made him go live with Justin.

He didn't remember why, exactly, it was so intermingled with a lot of bad dreams. But his mother had never hated him before. Maybe now, now that a month had gone by, she would be glad to see him.

He went up the stairs. The steps felt loose and unsafe, some of them squeaking like bedsprings when he stepped on them. One made a loud groan. He knew that groan. Every night when his dad came home from work, not long after he'd gone to sleep at ten o'clock, that groaning step would wake him up. Then he'd lie there in his strange bed and hear the murmur of voices down the hall, Justin's deep voice, and the woman's voice. The sounds of strangers.

In the mornings when he got up, Justin was always still sleeping. Where did Dad work, he'd asked Jill, because the only times he saw Justin were Saturday and Sunday afternoons. In a factory, she'd told him, an hour's drive away. He worked from three in the afternoon until ten at night, that's why Paddy never saw Justin except on weekends.

Here, he was not called Paddy, but Pat. Not Patrick, Pat. Jill hadn't asked him what she should call him, and Paddy noticed that Justin also called him Pat. So he guessed that was why Jill did. He wished Jill had some kids, that Justin himself had more kids, so it wouldn't be so lonesome at their house.

He wandered the quiet halls of the upstairs and thought of school. Would he be going to school here, too?

He didn't like school much anymore. But it would be better than not having anything to do. Maybe he'd meet some kids.

The hall turned, and became darker. In the dimness he saw a narrow door. He turned the knob and heard a dull, rusty squeak as he pulled the door open.

Musty air spilled out and in the gloom beyond, he saw a set of enclosed steps leading steeply upward. He looked up the staircase and saw a lighter area at the top, and the peak of a roof far above.

An attic.

Paddy pushed the door back so he wouldn't accidentally be locked into this strange old place, and then slowly climbed the steps. The air grew more stale with each step. The walls on each side smothered him, and felt damp against his fingertips. He kept his eyes on the wide beams of the ceiling above.

He came out on the upper floor and stood looking around. It wasn't a big attic, not as big, it seemed, as the house— as if only a part of the area beneath the roof was high enough to make another room. Only this wasn't really a room. There was no floor, only the beams that held up the ceilings. Some boards had been laid across the beams to make a path to a makeshift closet where clothes were hung on a metal rail. The clothes looked old. A raincoat, gray with dust, and some things in a clothes bag that was zipped shut.

Paddy chose his steps carefully, feeling sure that if he misjudged and stepped between the boards, he would crash right through the ceiling below. The loose boards on the walkway rattled beneath his feet as he walked. Dim light came in a small, double window at the front of the attic. There was no light bulb anywhere in the attic, no way to make the place brighter. Whoever had brought these clothes up here didn't have any plans on coming after them unless they brought a flashlight.

Why had they brought clothes up here when there were empty bedrooms downstairs?

Maybe they belonged to the people who used to live here. Or maybe Justin just rented this house, and they belonged to the owner who put them up here because he wanted to keep them, but didn't want to wear them.

Maybe in the modern zipper bag there were old things, really old, like dresses with bustles and old pinstripe suits with long, split tails like he had seen in books. The kind of thing he and Babette would have dressed up in when they were younger and played more games, before Billy was

111

born. He and Babette had played more when she hadn't had to spend so much time taking care of the baby.

He reached the clothes rack and saw the boardwalk ended and there was nothing else in the attic.

He felt in the pockets of the raincoat. They were empty.

Glancing behind him to make sure Jill had not climbed the attic steps without him knowing it, he started to undo the zipper on the bag.

He paused. It was none of his business. The property wasn't his. Mama would tell him to leave it alone.

But what difference did it make?

The clothes were just hanging there, and he didn't have anything else to do.

He pulled the zipper down slowly so it wouldn't make noise.

A slit opened, and something shining and black became visible. Paddy opened the slit wider.

There was just one garment in the big bag.

A black leather jacket on a hanger.

Paddy stood with the sleeve of the jacket in his hand, frowning. Memories stirred, as they often did as he grew older, images like broken pieces of puzzles came from some distant place in his mind. It was as if he were more than one person, and that other person, or maybe many other people, lived far away, and only parts of their thoughts touched him, the front *him*, the boy he knew and thought of as himself. Something stirred and he felt that old fear crawl up the back of his shoulders and neck and into his hair. His arms grew cold.

His fingers rubbed the leather on the sleeve. It was soft, but had a broken feel, as if it was old. The color wasn't as shiny as it had first looked.

He reached into the darkness of the bag and rubbed his hand over the corduroy collar and down the back.

He jerked his hand away.

Something furry was clinging to the back.

He waited, but nothing fell from the coat, or flew out. He pulled the coat through the slit and turned it.

VAMPIRE.

The white letters had cracked and looked old, but still

they were startling against the black background. But the thing that drew his stare was the big bat made of real fur sewn on the back of the coat. Only it wasn't a regular bat, it was a vampire, with long fangs. A very ugly thing. Hideous. Like . . . his nightmares. Those old nightmares that still came to haunt him, waking him in the darkest part of the night, making him cold with terror. In those waking moments there was nothing left of the dreams, but images, sounds, tastes. Tastes, especially, lingered. Metallic, gagging. But now, looking at this coat, the images fluttered— wings zipping silently, large black, furred wings, eyeless heads, tiny and wizened, fangs dripping dark liquids. And the taste.

He clasped his hands to his head, trying to excise the images. They never formed a whole. It was as if the other lives, the other people who had lived far back, were a part of him, and lived in the darkness so that he couldn't see them clearly.

But he remembered now. He had seen this jacket before. It belonged to his dad.

He had never seen Justin wear the jacket . . . and yet, maybe he had. He couldn't remember. But he had seen it, only he hadn't been able to read the word on the back.

Vampire?

Was this where all his nightmares had come from? Just from having seen this thing on the back of this jacket? He could almost hear a woman's voice warning him to leave it alone.

He let it fall back into the garment bag. But he didn't move. He stared at the shoulder of the jacket. Then on sudden impulse, he pulled the jacket out of the bag and put it on.

The lining felt cool against his arms. The sleeves were so long only the tips of his fingers stuck out, and the wide shoulders hung off his own. He ran his fingers down the front of the jacket and into the pockets.

There was something in the right pocket. It was small and slim and hard.

He took it out, and it lay on his palm like an ivory tusk. An ivory fang.

It was a pocketknife.

He pushed the sleeves up so his wrists would be free, and opened the small knife. It had three blades. No, two blades, and a sharp thing like an ice pick. He jerked, feeling a sting of pain, seeing a tiny drop of blood on his thumb.

The blades were sharp. Like razors. As if they had been deliberately sharpened beyond what an ordinary knife would have been. One blade was shorter than the other, and both fit closely against the needle-sharp pick. Paddy closed the knife, opened it, and closed it again.

Reluctantly, he put the knife back into the pocket, took the jacket off and hung it in the clothes bag.

It was several months before he asked Justin about the leather jacket with the furry bat on the back and the word *VAMPIRE*. In those months he had gotten more used to his dad, even though he saw him only on weekends. He even got to where he liked Justin, and didn't feel so lonesome for his mom and Babette anymore—though he often wondered where they had gone, and why they didn't tell him they were leaving.

Once when he cried, Justin had taken him to see his mother. And that was when he learned that someone else had rented the house. And those new people didn't even know who Ketti Graham was. They had looked for and found his stepdad, and he told them that Ketti had gone away, and he didn't know where.

So Paddy had gotten used to living with Justin and Jill, and the word "Dad" came more easily to his lips. He had wanted to ask about the jacket before, but had been afraid Justin would be mad at him for snooping around in the attic. Then when he became less afraid, he asked.

"Ah . . ." Justin said, his head leaning back against the recliner he rested in when he wasn't working. "I wore that years ago. I used to belong to a club. That's what it was. A sort of club. There were about a dozen of us. We were young and wanted to be different from everybody else. It gave us a big charge to wear these jackets we had especially made and see the looks on people's faces. Teenagers do things like that. I was nineteen then."

Paddy liked the idea of the club. It meant getting together

with a bunch of kids, and having secret meetings in a club-house. He'd never belonged to a club, but the kids down the street had, back when he was too young to play with them. He could remember seeing them go into their club-house in one of the kid's backyard. The clubhouse was really just a shed, the garden shed.

"What did you do?" he asked, standing at Justin's arm.

"We gathered on the beach, mostly. Built bonfires, drank a little beer. Smoked a few joints." Justin smiled faintly. "All the kinds of things I'd tan your backside for doing."

The smile faded. Paddy had images of fires reflected in the water, of figures wearing black jackets with furry vam-pires on the backs—a bunch of guys who drank beer and tossed the cans into the tide.

Justin said, "It broke up." His smile was gone, his eyes closed. "After a few years, the fun went out of it. I don't know . . . it wasn't the same anymore. I haven't seen any of the guys for years now."

He paused. "Some of the guys got spooked. Started see-ing and hearing things. Some of them got this bullshit idea that we had kind of brought back something. Anyway, it broke up."

Later, Paddy couldn't remember whether he had gone back for the knife in the jacket or when it came into his possession. It was the same with the first knife he'd had. Justin had given him that one, but he couldn't remember when or where or why.

The furry vampire bat on the back of the jacket had be-come real, more real sometimes than the rest of the world. And Paddy knew, and wondered if Justin knew, that the vampire bat only rested on Justin's jacket during the day, and at night it flew, its wings silent, its eyes empty, its fangs as sharp as the pick in the knife.

The terror Paddy felt lived with him, sleeping sometimes in the back of his mind, like the vampire bat slept on the back of Justin's jacket. But at night when the wings were swift and sure, the terror returned. And Paddy retreated.

Patrick stood at the side of the bed of fat boy and looked down at his face and throat.

Patrick was not afraid.

There were sounds, bad sounds. Someone was having a nightmare. Marsh could hear the groans. It was like a long time ago when he was afraid to go into his mother's bedroom. This time the groans were different, but he was still afraid. Someone was having a nightmare in which he was caught forever like the fly Marsh had seen in the big spider web high up in the corner of the barn. Too high for Marsh to reach. He had watched as the spider came to the fly and stopped its helpless struggling.

There were other sounds. A sucking, deep and long. The groans stopped, like the struggles of the fly had stopped as the spider sucked out its life.

But still Marsh was afraid to look.

The bad boy's bed was empty, Marsh could see under the edge of his blanket.

He had meant to follow the bad boy wherever he went, and protect the animals and people from him. But tonight he was too afraid.

Chapter Thirteen

Rufus went out to sit on the porch while the boys dressed and got ready for the day. He sat down in the chair and automatically reached for the pocket where his pipe nestled in the evening. No smoking, he reminded himself. Not this time of day, when the boys would see him. Besides, he got heartburn if he smoked before breakfast, so why did he always want to reach for that pipe? Hagar told him once when she caught him smoking that it was equivalent to a baby sucking on a pacifier. Rufus smiled. Hagar would be a reformer, if she didn't turn out to be a jockey.

The farm was beautiful early in the morning. Mist rose from the ponds, the animals were stirring, waiting for their breakfast. Some of the boys responsible for the early chores—the ones done before breakfast—were already down at the pens, feeding the animals. He could see David's blondish head bobbing about behind the fences of the pig pen, and hear the distant grunting of the eager animals. Birds in the trees were singing so loud and so lustily they were sure to awaken the biggest sleepyhead on the farm.

The boys began to filter out onto the porch, some of them quiet and sleepy, some already talking, joking, and taking pokes at one another. Rufus saw that the new boy's face was looking better, and his hair was neatly brushed back with water.

Then he heard someone running in the bunkhouse. It was a foreign sound this time of day.

The screen door flew back and Marsh came toward Rufus, his face pale with alarm, his eyes wide and frightened. The scar on his face stood out more noticeably than Rufus had seen it in a long time, a gash of white that made a permanent, wide part in his hair and ended on his jaw.

Rufus half rose from his chair. Marsh halted at his side and bent forward, breathless.

"Rufus . . . *Rufus* . . . something bad. Something bad, Rufus."

Rufus managed to stand up. He could almost look Marsh directly in the eyes, and he saw a terrified little boy—the same boy who had come to the farm ten years ago. Rufus put his hand on Marsh's shoulder to calm him, but a dread was growing. Marsh wasn't the kind to cry wolf. Something was badly wrong.

The other boys stopped gamboling and were still. Marsh's mouth was trembling. He was having more difficulty than usual expressing himself.

"Easy, Marsh. What is it? Tell Rufus."

Marsh pointed back into the bunkhouse. "Rex. Rex not getting up."

117

Some of the boys began to laugh and hoot. "Rex not getting up! Wow! Hey, is that unusual?"

Rufus relaxed. "Did somebody forget to wake Rex?"

Rex not only loved to work in the kitchen so he could snack between meals, he liked to sleep late, too. If any of the boys had to be rousted out of bed ten minutes after the alarm went off, it was Rex. He could sleep when no one else could.

Rufus said, "Marsh, you know Rex. He could sleep through a tornado."

Marsh kept shaking his head, and Rufus saw tears swell and overflow. Marsh blinked rapidly. Rufus thought at that moment if any of the boys teased Marsh for crying, he'd tan their britches. Hastily he moved toward the screen door as a late boy trailed out asking what was wrong. It wasn't Rex, and that feeling of dread came back. Marsh was running along beside Rufus.

"Rufus," he cried. "Rex—dead. Dead."

"Oh no, Marsh, he's just sleeping sounder than usual."

Rufus went down the aisle. Beds on both sides were neatly made, the navy blue blankets smoothed tightly and tucked beneath the mattresses, military style.

About halfway down the aisle was Rex, a still hump in his bed, the blanket covering him head to foot. He looked longer in the bed than he looked in height, somehow, longer and larger. Yet there was a deflated look to the boy's body. His face stared at the ceiling in white stillness, his eyes open, his lips parted.

Rufus stopped at the end of the bunk for one long, disbelieving look. Hoping that Rex was playing a game, or sleeping with his eyes open, he hurried around the foot of the bed. The moment he touched the boy's cheek, he knew Marsh was right. The cheek was cold. It was almost like touching the face of a doll.

Rufus looked toward Marsh. The boy stood halfway down the aisle leading to the door. Filling the aisle behind Marsh were all the other boys, quiet, sober, and staring.

"Run and get Mr. Preston," he said, and all of the boys but Marsh turned and hurried out of the bunkhouse.

Marsh didn't move. His eyes locked on Rex's face for a

long stare and then he turned to Rufus. The tears were gone, but the fear remained. Rufus could almost feel it himself, it was so strong. He had to think about Marsh, get him out of the bunkhouse to get his mind off this unbelievable tragedy.

"Come on, Marsh, we can wait outside," Rufus said, taking Marsh's arm and turning him toward the door. "Rex isn't well, but Mr. Preston will get the doctor for him and he'll be all right."

Marsh shook his head. "No. Rex dead."

Gwen came up to Patrick. He had been drifting idly across the grass toward the rusty old tractor with the metal wheels. Gwen had been watching him from the porch. They were still waiting. Her dad and the doctor and nurse were in the bunkhouse where something was wrong with Rex. The ambulance was parked on the grass by the porch. Hagar stayed on the porch, and Gwen glanced back at her and saw that she was watching. But what difference did it make? It was like Hagar was trying to be her mother sometimes, and Gwen only wanted to talk to Patrick.

"Hello," she said.

He looked at her, and she felt that pleasant excitement she'd been having lately when a strange, good-looking boy's eyes met hers. Ordinary boys—classmates, boys who'd lived here a long time, boys she was used to, didn't make her feel that way. Only a couple had, so far. One a big, older boy she met on the street one day had looked at her as if he thought her attractive, and that was her first experience. She thought maybe this was what they called love. She was in love with Patrick.

"Hi," he said softly, shyly, and smiled.

His smile was slight, as if he were embarrassed, or timid. He hadn't seemed terribly timid yesterday when she talked to him. But still he hadn't told her much, she'd realized in the night last night when she went over their conversation word by word and look by look. Just the memory of his lovely grey eyes looking at her gave her the most fantastic thrill.

119

"It's terrible, isn't it?" she said.

He rubbed his hand over the rust on the tractor wheel. "Well, I guess it's real old and been sitting out in the weather all this time."

"No, I mean about Rex."

The grey eyes glanced toward the bunkhouses. "Oh, yeah. Sure. I wonder what's wrong with him? Did your dad say?"

"No. Rufus sent some of the boys over to the house. Three of them came in. I was still in bed. I couldn't hear what they said. But when I heard Dad leave the house the way he did, I knew it was really something terrible, so I got up and came, too. Is he sick, or what? Nobody told me anything."

Patrick looked at the house again. He had a way of squinting that narrowed his eyes and made him extremely sexy looking. His eyelashes were long and light to dark brown, curling up at the ends, the envy of any girl. They sheltered his eyes like awnings, lacy, filtering, making his eyes luminous. He stared at the bunkhouse, behind her, and she heard a lift in the sounds there, voices murmuring, louder, steps on the porch.

She turned.

Two ambulance attendants were carrying a stretcher and on it was a body covered, head and all, and with a sudden chill, Gwen realized that they would not have covered Rex's head if he were still alive. It looked like they were carrying a bag of something, instead of a human, a boy she had known and liked. They had eaten cookies together by the pond, lots of times. He was her brother, in a way.

"Oh, my God," she cried softly and ran back across the grass to stop again at the outer edge of the group of boys who had gathered to watch the men with the ambulance push the stretcher up into the body of the vehicle.

They closed the doors and got into the front and drove slowly out toward the gates.

Silence had descended upon the waiting group. Gwen heard a sob, and looked to see that Rose was weeping. Her head was down, her hands lifted to cover her face. She turned, stumbling, back toward the bunkhouse. Orion put his arm across her back and walked with her. He was at least three inches shorter, and Gwen thought, her mind disassociated from the events of the moment, that she had never seen Orion touch Rose or walk beside her. They climbed the steps by the breezeway and went out of sight together. A moment later Orion came back and stood in the breezeway.

"Rex won't be coming back," Gwen's dad said to the group. "I'm sorry. We don't know yet what was wrong. The doctor said it looked like he might have had a heart defect that we didn't know about, and maybe . . . well, we might know more later. There's nothing anyone can do. Rex's family will be notified. For the rest of the day, just go on with your plans, if you can."

The group began dispersing, and Gwen found herself standing alone in the warming sun. The boys were going toward the breezeway, and she realized that no one had eaten breakfast. It seemed odd—disrespectful, somehow— that all of them would go on with the day, eat breakfast, then mow the grass, or weed the flower beds or vegetable gardens, just like always. Or maybe they would just wander around today. Still, they would eat, they would go bicycling, they would read, and talk. They would play games, or watch TV. They would play ball on the baseball diamond or football out in the field, or shoot basketball in the dozen or so hoops on the farm grounds. Life would go on. Yet for a moment, life seemed to have stopped as she watched Rex being taken out the farm's service entrance gates for the last time.

"Gwen," said Hagar, who was standing a few feet away, looking at her and waiting.

Gwen followed Hagar onto the faint path in the grass that led to pond one and then angled toward the main house. She ran to catch up.

"Isn't Dad coming?"

"I guess he's got some things to do first."

"He can't be dead, Hagar. Nobody has ever died here before, have they?" Gwen cried in low breathlessness as she hurried to keep up with her fast-walking sister. "What do you think happened?"

"I don't know. The doctor said his heart, maybe."

"But just think . . . any of us could go to sleep and just not wake up. That doesn't seem—sound right. Healthy hearts just don't quit."

"I guess it wasn't healthy. Rex ate a lot. Maybe he had high cholesterol, and nobody knew it. He liked fats—rich food. I've seen him buying candy bars from the dispenser."

"No, lots of people eat candy bars every day. Do you know what I think it might have been?"

"What?"

"I think he might have killed himself."

Hagar stopped and gave Gwen a hard stare. Gwen herself was shocked at the words, yet she suddenly was remembering how she'd seen Rex sitting with his head down, just staring at the ground. Rex had been at the farm for quite a long time, since she was eight, but who knew what had really happened to him before he came, or how homesick he was? "Remember, Hagar, just the other day when we were all at the paddock watching Star Beauty? Rex was sitting on top of the fence, but he was staring at the ground, just staring. He did that a lot. I asked him once what he was thinking about, and he said nothing."

They were on the path at the end of the pond. The ducks swam toward them, quacking softly, and two climbed out onto the grassy bank. From over in the animal compound came the scream of the peacock, and Star Beauty answered with a low whinny.

Hagar said, "I'm not hungry. You go ahead and eat, okay? I'm going back to the barn."

Gwen watched her walk away, long-legged, but graceful. A feeling of awful depression came over Gwen. It had started the moment she expressed her fears that Rex might have killed himself, she realized. Maybe, she thought, he had gotten into the nurse's dispensary and taken a bunch of drugs. Or maybe, somehow, he had just willed himself to die.

She looked toward the bunkhouse. It looked longer than usual. The breezeway that separated it from the living quarters, and the small hospital-like room where the nurse who came once a week kept all her medicines, was like a dark tunnel that had swallowed all the boys and the adults who looked after them.

But as she looked, her dad came out of the breezeway, ran down the steps, and angled across the grass toward her.

Gwen ran to meet him.

She put her hand in his, felt the firm pressure, and the security it gave her. She was a little girl again and Patrick was forgotten.

Hagar entered the cool mustiness of the barn. She stopped at the pen where three goats were munching grain, and rubbed each between their horns. The sight of their little goatees bouncing when they chewed usually amused her, but today she felt little joy in anything. She needed to be with the animals, with Star Beauty. These animals on the farm were sheltered, well cared for, and loved, and there was something about them that made her feel secure, comfortable, at home. Perhaps it was because they had no obvious worries, no memories of bad times in another environment—though it was possible some of them did, for not all were born on the farm.

She moved slowly through the cool, dim shadows of the barn. Chickens pecked among the hay scattered on the dirt floors of the indoor pens. One hen had brought in her little brood of eight chicks. Hagar paused to listen to their contented peeps as their mother searched out goodies under the bits of hay. The mother rarely ate the corn, oats, or occasional bug she found. She always called her babies to get it.

Hagar climbed through the manger into Star Beauty's stall. Star Beauty stood with her head over the outer gate, which someone had repaired, nuzzling her own pet goat, Billy Boy. When she sensed that Hagar had entered the stall, she reared her head, whinnied softly, and looked over her shoulder.

"Hi, Beauty," Hagar said. She took the brush down from the wall. "Ready to get your hair brushed for the day?"

Here, with Star Beauty and the other animals, Rex's death seemed unreal, far away, belonging to another world.

The day moved on, the sun rose, boys passed by, entering the animal compound to feed and take care of the animals in pens. Hagar took Star Beauty out for her walk around the paddock. Orion came to the fence, perched himself on the top rail and watched them in silence. After several minutes he left, saying something about lunch time.

Hagar reluctantly removed Star Beauty's bridle and let her go.

She stood watching as Star Beauty trotted around the fence. Little puffs of dust rose from beneath each hoof. The horse had worn a path inside the fence, creating a dirt track that was as clean as if it had been swept.

Hagar hung up the bridle with a sigh. She knew from past experience that if she didn't go to the house for lunch, her dad would come after her. "You can't eat oats with the horse, Puddin'," he'd say.

Rufus sat on the porch for the second time that day, just as he did every day, and looked at the dark landscape. The moon was beginning to rise and the tops of the trees made black outlines against the sky. The farm was as quiet as it ever got, except in the winter when even the night birds were voiceless. He puffed his pipe, and smelled the smoke as it drifted around his face. On the floor beside him the dog stirred and stretched out, sighing.

It had been a long day, a hushed day, as if the sun were in partial eclipse. Rex's body had been taken to a morgue somewhere, he supposed, for an autopsy, or maybe not. He didn't know what they planned to do with the boy. After he was taken away, Rufus had been told by Martin Preston that Rex's body would be shipped to relatives in another state—paternal grandparents.

At dinner a kind of eulogy had been said for Rex, and each boy told something special he recalled about Rex, except for Patrick.

"What would you like to say, Patrick?" Rose asked, when his turn came. The new boy sat with his eyes cast down, saying nothing, and after a pause, Rose said, "Of course, we know you didn't get to know Rex. We're sorry you didn't. Knowing Rex added joy to all our lives." Outside of that, Rex was gone, his bed was stripped, his locker emptied. Within a month another boy would be given Rex's bed, a permanent placement perhaps, as Rex had been.

Rex had been on Rufus's mind all day. Rex had been a good boy, as all of them were, for the most part. The other kids liked him. Though they sometimes teased him because of his heaviness, none of them had ever called him *fat* except Patrick, the new boy.

Rex had been on the farm three years. His back was marked by a bunch of burns where his father had held cigarettes to punish him for some little something. Neighbors had finally intervened. Rex had a mother somewhere, but she was no more interested in him than the women who'd lived with his father. There were a lot of brothers and sisters, some old enough to take care of him, but they had problems, too. But Rex had seemed happy here, no longer needing a therapist, never wanting to go back to the father who had burned him, or the mother he hardly knew.

Rufus wondered only vaguely why the father, who had been local at one time at least, had not taken the body. Perhaps the father was no longer alive.

Rufus wondered about those shadowy families, only when the boy in question arrived, or left, went home for a visit, or was visited by various family members.

He drew a long breath and said in a low voice, "Well, Lion, it's been a hard day."

He went to the post and tapped the ashes out of his pipe, then turned toward the door and his room.

He had gone to sleep and slept a little while, he knew, when the sound of the squeaky board on the porch woke him. He opened his eyes and looked at the rectangle of pale light at his window. A cool breeze wafted in, bringing layers of air as sweet as a drink of spring water.

Rufus drew a long breath, listening to the squeak of the step, the one that had started making noise a year or two ago. Marsh was going out, he thought, the way he used to—wandering in the moonlight tonight, disturbed by Rex's death, that strange, unexpected death, that *wrong* death that should not have happened.

Rufus had stood on the porch waiting for the doctor to

give an explanation he could accept. With the boys standing around in silence with Gwen and Hagar waiting on the porch too, and Orion and Rose and even some of the Mexican farm workers gathered, the farm's citizens had waited to hear why a thirteen-year-old boy just died in the middle of the night, as if his heart had simply stopped beating while he slept. They had waited, and when the doctor came out shaking his head, they knew they would be given no reason.

Later Rufus had asked Mr. Preston, and he had said it looked like a heart defect that the nurse or pediatrician who gave the boys their regular checkups had never found. Stranger things did happen occasionally, Rufus guessed, but not around here.

In the beginning, Rufus had followed Marsh when he went out at night, talked to the little boy, and urged him back to bed. But Marsh had stopped wandering the farm at night in recent years. Tonight, though, Rufus understood why Marsh couldn't sleep. He thought about getting up too, going out to keep Marsh company, but his bones liked the feel of the bed. He was tired into exhaustion, it seemed, and his eyes were heavy.

He turned over and went back to sleep.

Chapter Fourteen

Marsh waited.

He lay tense, in an awkward position with his head raised, listening. He had kept himself awake tonight, waiting. Last night he had gone to sleep, and this morning when he woke, Rex was dead. When he had touched Rex, there was no answer from him. Rex was cold, and gone. Because Marsh had not been on guard, Rex had died. Tonight, Marsh was on guard. When he had felt himself going to sleep, he had made himself wake up and listen. Always, he lay in his bed facing the strange boy. He knew it was the strange boy.

He heard the step squeak and knew the boy had gone out onto the grass. He was going to the animals! Or around again to Miss Rose's window.

Marsh got up, spread his blanket carefully, and pulled his jeans on over his pajamas. Barefoot, he went silently out of the bunkhouse and paused in the shadows of the porch.

The moon looked like a white wedge in the sky. Its light on the ground was pale, but it made the shadows beneath the trees too dark, almost black.

The boy was standing with his back to him, over by the end of pond one. Marsh watched him, and it seemed that the boy was looking toward the main house. Was he going over there?

Lion came, toenails clicking softly on the boards of the porch. He stood at Marsh's side, his head up, staring at the boy in the moonlight.

Then suddenly, the boy was gone, blending into the shadows of the mesquite trees that bordered the far side of the pond.

Was he following the paths that went by all the ponds? He wasn't going to the barns after all. Where was he going? Rufus wouldn't like for the new boy to be out at night.

Marsh went to the edge of the porch and leaped down, and the dog followed, running down the steps to catch up. Marsh loped across the wide, moonlighted area and went beneath the shadows of the mesquites.

He stopped, scanning the area for a sign of Patrick.

The strange boy had disappeared. He had become part of the darkness, it seemed to Marsh, and could be anywhere beneath the trees dotting the land between the ponds and the farm buildings. He could have gone across to the barns without Marsh seeing him. Lion stood at Marsh's side, his face pointed straight ahead, and Marsh knew he was seeing the boy.

Marsh touched Lion on the head. "Go," he said. "Find him."

Lion trotted along the path, his body blending with the

shadows. Marsh followed, his bare feet as silent on the paths as Lion's. He began to catch glimpses of Patrick. Moonlight touched his head and shoulders and again he disappeared into the shadows of the mesquite. Moonlight, shadows—he was following the paths.

Marsh kept a wide distance. Lion ran on about fifteen feet ahead, silent as a wolf. At times Marsh saw him stop and look back, pausing just long enough to be sure Marsh was coming too—as if the dog was afraid of the strange boy, of this midnight journey.

Marsh thought of the animals in the pastures, but tonight he was on guard.

At the end of pond five, Patrick stepped into the moonlight. Marsh stopped, his heart suddenly beginning to beat very hard so that he had trouble breathing. The strange boy was looking back toward him, and Marsh thought he had been seen, even though the shadows of the mesquite sheltered him, their lacy, willow-like leaves touching his head and shoulders. Lion stood still a few feet away in the shadows of the path.

But then Patrick turned away, going down a slope and stooping beside a dark little bush. Marsh saw something lying in the moonlight beside the bush, and just as he recognized the shape, a calf leaped up, letting out a terrible cry of pain and anguish.

The strange boy was doing something bad to the calf, but Marsh stood rooted, unable to move. He saw the calf struggling to get away, but the boy's arms were around its neck as if he was trying to wrestle it to the ground. Marsh wanted to move, to scream at him to stop, stop hurting the calf, but still he couldn't move.

Lion rushed forward, barking, and the sound of the dog's voice gave Marsh the impetus to move. He followed, stopping in the moonlight halfway between the pond path, the calf, and boy on the slope. Lion rushed on, barking.

Patrick straightened, and Marsh saw the calf stumble to its knees. Something was wrong with it. The boy was hurting it.

"Go, Lion!" Marsh ordered, pointing. *"Get him."*

The dog rushed up to the boy and as he leaped, Patrick

flung up an arm. Marsh saw something flash in the moon-light, and then heard the sound of it striking the dog. Lion whirled, and in a staggering gait, came back toward Marsh.

Marsh ran forward to meet Lion, forgetting everything but the dog. Lion had been hurt, too, and he was coming to Marsh for help.

The dog fell in the moonlight, and Marsh went down on his knees beside him.

The white fur on his neck was dark, and Marsh's fingers touched the wet of gushing blood. The dog's eyes reflected for a moment the light of the moon as Marsh held him in his arms. Then Lion's head fell back.

Marsh bent over the dog, crying, his hands buried in Lion's spongy fur. He shook Lion and shook him, trying to wake him, to bring him back.

"I didn't mean it—Lion—I didn't mean it." He was sorry, sorry Lion had walked with him, hunting the bad person, helping Marsh guard the animals. Now Lion was hurt.

Lion was dead.

In the dim light of the moon, his blood was black against his fur white.

Marsh remembered the calf, and he carefully eased the dog's head down to the ground, tears blurring his vision. The landscape shimmered, not green and blue and bright, but black and grey and frightening. Over the pasture fence a cow started bawling, and Marsh saw the ghostly white of her face looking toward her calf. Somewhere in the trees an owl cried, a terrible *wooooo,* as if its soul was as tormented, as Marsh's.

Something flew from the trees, a swift and silent thing that threw a large, dark shadow on the ground. The boy was gone. Marsh looked and saw him nowhere. Shadows blended into moonlight and blurred, even though Marsh reached up often to wipe his eyes.

In the moonlight, the calf was stretched full-length beside the bush. Marsh went to it slowly, knowing the calf had been killed too.

He bent over the calf and saw its blank stare and the same glass-like reflection in its eyes. The calf's throat was marked by a spot of dark blood, like a tiny bullet hole. The strange, bad boy had stabbed the calf for no reason. The calf had been sleeping, curled at the edge of the bush, having gotten out of the pasture, somehow. Across the fence, a cow was moving restlessly, her voice rising in a plaintive bawl, calling her calf. Other cattle bunched beneath a tree stirred restlessly.

The large, dark, silent bird flew over them and came diving through the air just above Marsh's head. He ducked, feeling the stir of air from its sweeping, black wings.

He watched it rise higher into the air and turn abruptly, its movements sudden, startling, as it reversed its flight, coming back toward him. Its wing span was larger than an eagle's as it swept toward Marsh. He went down onto his knees, his tears drying in cold terror as he watched the bat-like creature.

Fear cloaked his body. The big bat was after him, and the cattle were trying to run from it too, as it flew toward their pasture. It made another abrupt turn and again swept toward Marsh, beginning a dive that would bring it within inches of Marsh's head.

Stumbling on all fours, Marsh headed for the shelter of the mesquite. He could feel the prickly grass beneath his hands as he scrambled toward the small trees. Reaching them, he clung for a moment to a tree trunk, and then he heard the hiss of the air as the bat broke into the mesquite.

Marsh crawled beneath the trees, feeling for just an instant the tangle of sharp talons in his hair. He slid over the bank to the edge of pond. Then he realized the bat was gone again, and he knew if he didn't run now, and keep running, he would never reach the bunkhouse alive.

He pulled himself up, and with his body bent at the waist, he ran. He didn't look back. He kept beneath the shadows of the trees, on the paths by the ponds. When he had to cross the open areas between each pond, he kept running, his body stooped, the pain within him burning his side, stomach, and heart. Tears were flowing again, terror pushing him on. He was a coward. He was afraid. He wanted to hide in his bed. Too ashamed to face Rufus. To ever let him know how Marsh had run, how Marsh was too much a coward to guard and protect the animals. Marsh, coward. Marsh, afraid. The bad boy had killed Lion. He had killed one of the baby calves. He had killed Lion. Lion, his dog. Rufus's dog. Everybody's dog.

He had reached the porch and falling against it, he slid to the ground. Moonlight spilling around him, he looked back toward the barns, the ponds, and the black, jagged line of mesquite that grew on the banks. He looked, but he saw nothing different. The bat was gone. The bad boy, Patrick, was gone.

He became aware that his pajama top was wet and cold. He felt it, and his hands came away with dark palms that were sticky, shiny and black.

Blood.

Lion's blood.

Crying in silence, turning his head first one way, then the other, unable to escape the horror of this day and this night, Marsh got up and stumbled toward the steps, the bunkhouse washroom.

He closed the door and turned on the light.

In the mirror over the nearest wash basin he saw his face, both cheeks smeared with blood—red blood, like the red in the hamburger before it was cooked. Blood. Raw blood. His hands were covered in blood. And the front of his shirt had a large, sticky, wet place.

He pulled off the shirt, looked at it, then wadded it into a ball and dropped it on the floor. He washed his face, hands, and arms, and then wiped his chest until it began to feel raw. Tears kept running down his face. But he kept his head lowered, after his first look in the mirror.

He didn't want to see Marsh cry.

Marsh was afraid.

He was no good as a guard. He had not been able to save the animals, not even Lion. He wanted to go tell Rufus, but Rufus would be sad, his dog lying dead out in the field. Rufus would be sad.

It was better that Rufus not know.

Tomorrow, in the sunlight, Marsh would go back and bury Lion, and the calf, and Rufus would never know.

131

* * *

The light of the moon covered the slope of the low hill in a gauze-like mist. The cattle had stopped lowing and milling about except for the one cow whose head hung over the wire fence, calling for her calf. Her voice was thin and ringing, and it irritated Patrick. He shook his head, but the irritation continued.

He sat on his haunches beside the dead calf. The night was quiet, except for the cow. It was a long way back to the bunkhouse and the other houses where the people were sleeping. He wasn't worried that the call of the cow would wake any of them. But he was watching for that flitting shadow of the running Marsh to return. The landscape stayed still, each shadow stationary except for the movement of leaves in the wind.

Patrick leaned over the calf again, its mother's voice at his back. He carefully removed the eyes of the calf, then got to his feet and went to a tree by the pasture. He took a leaf and wrapped the eyes in it. The cow was silent, her head still, watching him. He returned her stare for a few moments, then he walked past the calf, and went up the slope and through the mesquite to the pond.

He squatted at the edge of the pond and rinsed the blood off his knife, hands, and face. He sat back and looked out across the pond. The night was silent now except for the whisper of leaves and the ripple of the pond as the wind swept its surface. The water reflected the pale light of the moon, creating a long streak across its middle.

He picked up the leaf-wrapped eyes and slipped beneath the mesquite to the path. He stopped again, looking at the dark body of the dog. Right out in plain sight. The calf's body was half hidden by a bush, but the moonlight outlined the dog, making him visible to anyone who might go out early for a walk.

Patrick carefully put the wrapped eyes into his pocket to avoid any trace of blood getting on his clothes, then he pulled the dog into the cover of the mesquite. It was more difficult than he had anticipated. The dog's dead weight, its dragging hindquarters and lolling head made it like pulling a huge sack of sand. And the touch of its feet in his hands, the thin bones, the hair, revolted him. He dropped the dog in the shadows and pulled broken limbs over it.

Jogging in silence, alert for any movement, he cut across the grass that surrounded the ponds. He approached the barns, and heard the whinny of the horse.

He paused, and listened as a goat added its bleating cry to the horse's voice. The moonlight-covered park between the barns and the bunkhouse held blotches of deep shadows where the trees stood, and the old pieces of machinery looked like large, alien insects. Patrick moved toward them, away from the barns. The animals were noisy tonight, and that wasn't good. Someone would be out to see about them, possibly.

And that idiot, Marsh, might have sent someone. Yet Patrick saw nothing and he was counting on Marsh being too scared, too intimidated, to say anything to anyone.

He walked the rest of the way to the bunkhouse, keeping to the shadows as much as he could, seldom pausing. When he came to the porch he was careful to avoid the squeaky board he had stepped on going out.

At the door, he stopped, listening. The bunkhouse was fairly quiet. The loudest snore he heard came from a room on his right, the old man's room. "You can come to me anytime you need me," the old man had said, and showed him the door to his room. Patrick smiled.

He moved in silence into the bunkhouse and stood another moment at the side of his cot. Marsh had come back and gotten into his bed. Patrick could hear his sobs muffled beneath the blanket.

Patrick silently slipped around the foot of Marsh's bed and up the narrow aisle between beds to the locker. He eased the door open, and laid the leaf-wrapped eyes in the back of the locker, on the middle shelf, behind a small stack of clothes. He closed the door.

By his own cot, he looked down at Marsh's long body beneath the blanket. Beneath his breath he said, "That should take care of you, my boy."

* * *

Orion woke and heard the whinnying cry of the horse. Almost instantly came the bleating of the goat. Orion got up, reached for his jeans, and pulled them on. The animals had been restless as hell lately, as if something was prowling around the barns and lots.

He got his flashlight from the drawer of his bedside table, pushed his sockless feet into his shoes, and went to stand for a moment in the breezeway. His room was next to the kitchen and dining room. A hall reaching from the dining room went to the TV room and the room where the farm's housekeeper stayed if she was not married, as in Rose's case. The rooms were dark. The bunkhouse area, located on the opposite end of the breezeway, was dark and quiet, too. He was the only one disturbed by the cries of the animals, he guessed.

He went down the steps, walking in moonlight, the flashlight at his side turned off. He paused once, looking back toward the porch for the dog, who never failed to accompany him when he went out at night on the rare occasions it was necessary. Last winter one of the goats had gotten spooked by an owl and tried to go through the fence, and he'd had to go down and untangle it. The dog had gone with him. That incident had convinced him that most of the other residents of Boys' Farm were heavy sleepers. Maybe it was because he had learned in his early years of living in or near stables to respond to any sound his horses made during the night, on guard constantly so that nobody and nothing bothered them. They were his life, his three horses. He had raced them at tracks across the country and during those years he'd thought he had the best life in the world. When Proud Austin, his seven-year-old horse, became too old for racing, he'd retired him to his dad's farm for stud work and a long life on pasture, and had replaced him with a young filly. But when the filly, Morning Light, fell dead beneath him, his heart went out with her.

Star Beauty reminded him of Morning Light—she had been a great race horse, and her future looked bright. Together they would earn enough to buy a horse ranch with that special pasture where she would retire in peace. But it hadn't worked out that way. Another dream shattered.

Orion stood in the middle of the compound and listened. The animals were quieter now, but he could hear Star Beauty bumping the boards of her gate or kicking her stall. She was still restless. He started on toward the barn, walking faster.

Once more he glanced back toward the porch, but saw nothing of the dog.

It was almost six years now since he had raced a horse. Would he ever be able to forget the last, terrible day at the track with Morning Light? His own leg had been broken in three places from the fall, but that was minor compared to his loss, his broken heart.

He didn't get back on a horse until he rode Star Beauty, and that first time had made him feel torn, pulled to pieces between sadness and happiness. He shouldn't have stopped riding, he guessed now. He shouldn't have sold the rest of his stable and gotten out of the business. Just like his friends had told him, he should have gotten right back in the saddle and gone on with his life. He could see that now. He felt as if he had lost one-third of his life along with Morning Light.

Too late now to worry about that. What mattered was Star Beauty. She had to stay healthy, well, and contented. It was important to him, more important than anyone knew.

He turned on the flashlight when he entered the barn, shining it all around, looking into the corrals beneath the barn roof that held a few goats and a young heifer who was expecting to calve at any time. The heifer was lying down, sleeping with her head resting on one front leg. Orion passed the light over her briefly, not wanting to disturb her, and went on down the corridor to the next pen. The three goats were lying down too. These animals, at least, were not disturbed.

A loud popping noise came from Star Beauty's stall. She had kicked the wall again, or bumped into it forcefully. Orion ducked his head and went through the manger into her stall. She turned and stretched her nose toward him. He rubbed it, aiming his light at all corners of her stall. Nothing, except a healthy spider web, tough as polyester, up in one corner. They were impossible to keep out. Trav-

135

eling through the cracks, the spiders came down from the barn loft where hay was stored, and built their webs. If you cleaned them out one day, they were back the next. He let them go, most of the time. The spiders caught flies and other insects that otherwise would annoy the horse.

He passed by the horse and went out the gate into the paddock. The goat who lived there was standing alert, and bleated softly when it saw Orion.

"I wish one of you guys could talk," Orion said, and shined his light into the trees around the paddock. One big oak tree occupied the center of the paddock, shading the area during the day. To the west and east, smaller trees grew just outside the fence.

The light touched something dark in the tree, and there was a flutter of leaves. Probably a bird. The goat jerked aside, bleating. From Star Beauty's stall came the sound of kicking, as if she was trying to fight her way out. She screamed, a piercing, quick sound, and the goat ran toward her, as if seeking protection from the bird in the tree.

Orion said. "Cripes, girls, it's only an owl."

His light was absorbed by the black body as it moved in sudden flight out of the tree. Instead of taking to the air and flying away, as an owl would have, it seemed to fall, coming down swiftly toward his head, in the manner of a bat. His light touched it briefly, and as he dodged instinctively to avoid being struck by it, he saw it was larger than any bat he had ever seen.

It came by him and then was gone. The goat reared its front feet at the gate of the stall, bleating. Inside the stall, the young filly pounded at the walls, crying out again.

Orion found himself on the ground, one hand behind him, fingers digging into the grass. He got up and aimed the light into the trees around the barns.

In pens across the way, pigs began grunting and moving restlessly. Chickens and pheasants in their coops and pens began clucking softly. Alarmed but blinded by the dark, they soon quieted. Their pens were covered with wire, and no bat or owl of any kind could get in. Orion wasn't worried about the fowl.

He moved around the paddock, keeping his light beam

in the trees. But whatever had been disturbing the animals was either gone or well hidden.

The animals were quiet now. Star Beauty had stopped kicking her stall. The goat was standing quietly against the gate, Star Beauty's head almost resting on its back.

Orion walked the paddock once more, his light reaching into the trees and the overhang of the barn. It was conceivable that bats would nestle in the barn, but that thing had been many times larger than any North American bat Orion had ever seen.

With an odd sense of danger and fear crawling up his back, Orion spent several more minutes watching the animals. When he was certain they were at last at ease, he left the barn and went back to his room.

But sleep didn't come.

When he closed his eyes, the image of the black, winged creature falling out of the tree toward him was engraved on the inside of his eyelids. Yet oddly, he could not see it, could not get a clear picture of it.

It had been large, and very black.

And swift and silent.

Deadly, he felt.

Chapter Fifteen

Rufus dressed in the pre-dawn light, as always. He'd never needed an alarm clock in all his life, and he'd always wondered how any human could sleep past the rising of the sun. He'd learned to get up with the chickens when he was a kid because he had to get out of the house early to avoid being kicked around. He'd never lost the habit, but he reckoned he was the only human on the whole farm who got up that early—except for the farmhands who had to get out at dawn.

He went onto the porch, sat down in the rocking chair, and lit his pipe.

He looked for Lion.

The dog wasn't on the rug where he slept on summer nights, nor anywhere around that Rufus could see. Well, he thought, Lion might be out wandering around.

The chair squeaked softly as Rufus rocked and smoked. The eastern sky turned from rosy red to a lighter pink. Streaks of yellow reached up into a sky that was still dark blue with a few bright stars glowing like Christmas lights on a tree. Roosters down in the chicken pens crowed. One that roamed the farm freely stood on the paddock fence and stretched its neck high, letting out a piercing crow. Still the boys in the bunkhouse slept.

Footsteps on the porch startled Rufus. Unusual sound, this early in the day.

Orion came out of the breezeway. Pulling up one of the straight chairs, he sat down near Rufus. He looked as if he had been awake and dressed for quite awhile.

"You up early, eh?" Rufus said.

"Yeah."

Orion was looking over toward the barns and the paddock, his eyes squinted.

"You seen Lion?" Rufus asked.

Orion glanced past Rufus down the length of the long porch. At the far end was the doghouse, and Rufus followed Orion's gaze.

"Naw," he said. "Lion don't use that except in cold or disagreeable weather. He's always been right here to greet me every morning since he came to live here. He's never failed before. I just thought that since you've been up awhile, you might have seen him. Maybe he heard you and went down the breezeway, or something."

"No." Orion shook his head. "As a matter of fact, I was wondering a few hours ago where he was. Something was disturbing Star Beauty and the goats, and I went down to see about it. That was three-thirty, or maybe a quarter to four this morning. I didn't see Lion then, either."

"What was the disturbance?"

"A bat, I think. I just got a glimpse of it, though it looked damned big for a bat."

"I reckon they got big bats. South America bats, some of them. Maybe one of them found its way up here."

"It came down out of the oak tree. It came so fast, I didn't even get my light on it."

Rufus puffed on his pipe. The smoke fogged up, a miniature cloud in front of his face, and then slowly dispersed. It reminded him of smoke from an old freight train. He thought of Lion, and the bat in the tree. There was something wrong with Orion's story.

"Bats don't roost in trees, though, do they?"

"Not that I ever knew of."

"It wouldn't have been a bat. They keep on the move at night, after bugs in the air. It wouldn't have been in the tree. Under the barn eaves, maybe, but not in the tree. You must have seen a bird, Orion."

Orion said nothing for a few long moments. Finally he said, "Maybe."

Rufus puffed his pipe and thought about the smoke. Smoke was polluting the world. Why didn't he quit adding to the pollution? His little wad of smoke didn't seem like much, but the little wads of smoke that every smoker put out, and all the big wads that the factories put out, were polluting the world, destroying the ozone layer, or some such thing, according to the news. And it was going to cook everyone and everything one of these days, putting an end to humanity. And probably most animal life as well. Vegetable life, too. The world would become another Venus. A barren Venus.

"I've been thinking about quitting this smoking." Rufus said, holding the hot bowl of the pipe in his hand. "If we don't stop messing up our world, there won't be any world left to mess up." He paused for Orion to say something. But Orion simply leaned forward, rested his elbows on his knees, and folded his hands together beneath his chin. He was still squinting toward the barns. Trying to figure out his bird-bat, Rufus guessed.

"Won't be any animal life left after that ozone layer gets

so messed up we all cook ourselves to death. We ain't any less likely to cook than the rest of the animals. None of us immortal in the flesh."

"Nope, I guess not," Orion said, his mind clearly focused on something else.

Rufus got up and knocked his pipe against one of the porch posts. Little sparks drifted to the ground like falling stars as he emptied the pipe's contents.

"I think I'll take a little walk around and see if I can find my dog," Rufus said.

Orion got up. "I'd better get to the kitchen. It's about time to start breakfast."

"What are you cooking this morning?"

"Biscuits, I think. Ham, eggs, oatmeal, maybe rice. Gravy."

Rufus nodded, and went down the steps. Rice and biscuits, that was what he liked—with plenty of cream and sugar on the rice, and melting butter on the biscuits. Orion was the best cook Rufus had ever known. Made his biscuits from scratch, too. It wasn't unusual to see Orion with flour on him somewhere, spotting his chin or shirt.

Lion was always at the door waiting for his own biscuits. He liked as much butter as he could get, too. Of course nowadays it wasn't cow butter, because of the cholesterol. It was margarine, made from corn oil. And it wasn't cream from the cow, either, it was milk. But still, the rice was good, and the biscuits flaky and rich. Yes, Orion was the best cook he'd ever been around.

He carried the pipe as he crossed the grass, angling toward the barns, passing the old combine and the rusty tractor with metal wheels. The grass had been clipped carefully around the wheels, every sprig the mowers missed gotten later by boys with hand clippers. Each boy had to put in a certain length of time at work. During the summer it was usually two hours in the morning, and another one or two hours in the afternoon. Then there was arranged playtime at the tennis court or baseball diamond. Swimming was allowed in pond three, where small springs kept the water clear. And cold. But they didn't care how cold it was. Rufus hadn't either when he was twelve or thirteen.

He stopped by the pens at the barnyard and looked at the pigs and sheep. They weren't eating or sleeping as they usually did. He couldn't pinpoint a problem, but he had a feeling something wasn't right, that something had disturbed all the animals in the night. Maybe it was what Orion had told him. Or maybe it was because Lion was missing.

From the distance he heard a cow lowing. It was the call of a cow who had lost her calf—that sad, empty call that went on and on, hour after hour, day after day. A low, then a pause to give the calf a chance to show itself, then another low. The sound of it gave Rufus a sense of dread and futility that he hadn't felt in years.

Without pausing at another animal enclosure, he headed off toward the sound of the cow. He passed huddled clusters of the sheep that were allowed to roam the farm freely. Different animals were turned loose at varying times. Sometimes it was calves or young horses, along with the sheep. A couple of pigs rooted at the edge of the small stream that connected the ponds. They were the only sight that seemed natural and right this morning.

He reached the north side of the pasture fence and stopped, looking at the animals in the twenty acres of enclosed pasture. At a tree several hundred yards away, three adult horses stood together with their young. Closer to him, grouped beneath another tree, were the cows. Several calves stood or lay near them. Yet the scene was somehow not peaceful. The slant of the light as the sun rose behind a layer of clouds in the east created shadows. Overhead, slow-flying birds circled. Not crows, he thought, buzzards. Which meant something was dead, its still body drawing the attention of the scavengers.

The lowing cow stood alone at the fence, looking toward the pond. It was pond seven, the last in the string. It was one of the smaller ponds, much of its water diverted into the pasture for the animals' drinking pond. None of the ponds in the pasture were counted among the seven meant for human enjoyment and beauty. But Rufus did not feel that beauty this morning.

He was afraid of what he was going to find, he realized.

141

Something was dead, outside the fence, over toward pond seven, and the cow at the fence told him it was her calf.

Rufus started walking toward the pond. The water was not visible from the pasture fence. The banks of the ponds were lined with lacy mesquite, and hid not only the water, but, he was afraid, the body of the calf.

He climbed the slope and went to the mesquite. The cow had grown silent and he looked back at her and saw her head was up, alert. She was watching him.

He ducked and moved under the limbs of the mesquite. At the edge of the pond he paused. The water was placid, hardly a ripple disturbing its surface. Nothing lay at the edge of the pond that he could see. The grass that grew there was an even height, several inches tall, uncut, as undisturbed as the water's surface.

He stepped back into the mesquite, and walked slowly along in the trees, his body stooped beneath the low fall of the branches. He stopped. About ten feet away, something was on the ground beneath the trees. A dark body . . . an ear no longer pert and lifted . . . a blaze of white down a long, wide muzzle. . . .

With a sudden, wild racing in his heart, Rufus rushed forward. *Lion.* What was Lion doing so far from the bunkhouse?

"Lion!"

He fell to his knees. Lion's body was cold and stiffening, and as Rufus leaned over, he saw the blood.

He drew back, horror stiffening his own body.

But he had to know. What had happened to Lion?

Blood soaked Lion's chest and throat. His still, blank eyes stared beyond Rufus. His muzzle was parted, and his tongue lolled out, as if he had been running when he was struck down.

But Lion would never run again, and a terrible rage rose in Rufus's throat and made his heart pound dangerously fast. Tears that could never be shed choked him.

"Lion, old boy, what happened?"

Blood in the matted fur at the dog's neck meant he had been attacked. Coyotes or wolves on the farm? It wasn't possible. They couldn't have gotten through the tall fence.

He knew that in some parts of Texas, coyotes roamed, but he hadn't heard of a wolf since he was a kid—man had almost made those beautiful, wild creatures extinct.

He squatted beside Lion's body and stared in slow shock as he spread the fur to find a long slit at the dog's throat. It had been made by a knife, or some other sharp instrument, made by man, not animal.

Rufus released the dog's body and moved away, going to the water where he slowly and thoughtfully washed his hands.

Somebody on the farm had murdered the dog—someone Lion followed, to have gone this far from the house, for he never had roamed this far by himself. Never. He stayed near the people, trusted the people, following mostly him or Marsh.

The cow lowed again, a plaintive call that burrowed into his heart and increased the horror of the moment.

He got up and went out to the open where he could see the cow. Her call meant her calf was still missing.

In front of him, halfway between the pond and the pasture fence, was a thick, green bush, and beside it, plainly in sight now, lay the red and white body of the Hereford calf. Like Lion it was stretched on its side, its head beneath the bush.

Rufus half slid down the slope, his hands shaking. He could feel the tremor spread up his spine and into his head, a nervousness, a continual shuddering at visions of what he was going to find.

He stooped over the calf's body. His fingers grasped a limb of the bush to move it off the calf's head. Suddenly the limb snapped off in his hand and he stared into the face of the calf.

Its eyes were gone.

They had been cleanly cut out and removed, leaving no trace of blood.

There was no other sign of wounds, no cut throat, as with Lion, no trace of blood.

Rufus stood up and staggered back.

Then he began to run toward the main house, his breath short and burning in his chest. He felt as if something was following him, keeping him within reach, waiting for the right moment to pounce. To keep him from telling what he had seen.

Gwen woke at the sound of pounding on the front door. Her bedroom window was around the corner from the front porch, but when she went to the window to look out, she couldn't see anyone on the porch. There was a doorbell, but the person didn't seem to know that. The pounding continued.

She heard footsteps in the hall, and the pounding stopped. Voices drifted back to her, but the words were muffled and indistinct. One of the voices was talking fast and excitedly, and sounded only vaguely familiar. Rufus? What was he doing here? Had another of the boys died in his sleep?

Gwen grabbed her robe off the chair and ran to the door. Something else had happened. She thought of the new boy, Patrick, and hoped it wasn't about him.

Ashamed of her thoughts, of picking one to favor, she added to herself, I hope it's none of the boys. Nor Orion, nor Rose, nor anyone. She ran halfway down the hall and stopped.

Her dad had opened the closet door and was taking out his hat, the one with the wide brim that he wore when he went out onto the farm. She could see Rufus in the doorway. His face looked thin and long, sunken at the cheeks, the chin more pointed, bonier than usual. His eyes were deepset and darting, looking back toward the way he had come.

She ran farther down the hall. "What's wrong, Dad?"

Martin gave her a quick glance as he put the hat on his head and closed the closet door. "One of the animals . . . go on back to bed."

The two men went out and closed the door, leaving the house thundering with a kind of warning silence. She didn't like the feeling. When she saw that Hagar was standing in her bedroom door, she didn't feel quite so alone.

"What was it?" Hagar asked.

"Something wrong with one of the animals." Hagar, she

saw, was already dressed. Her hair was combed back into its neat ponytail, her blouse buttoned and tucked into her jeans, the collar folded just right. Hagar always got up early and went to the stable to see about Star Beauty. Gwen watched her face lose some of its color.

"What animal?" she asked.

"They didn't say."

"Oh, my God! Not Star Beauty!"

Hagar came running down the hall. Gwen moved over and let her go by, though she had an urge to reach out, grab Hagar, and beg her not to leave her alone.

A moment later the front door slammed again, and Gwen was alone.

She stood in the silence of the house, in the dim hallway, her hands gripping the railing. Through the glass in the front door, she could see pale streaks of sunlight on the porch, making it not much brighter than at night in the moon light. She became intensely aware of the shadows in the hall above.

She couldn't stay in the house alone.

She could follow Hagar, or she could follow her dad and Rufus. But she didn't want to see what was wrong. She didn't even want to know. Just remembering how Rex's covered body had looked when it was taken out of the bunkhouse yesterday had done something to her, taken away from her part of the joy in being alive.

She didn't want to be alone in the house, though. Yet she had to go back into her room and dress.

She turned on the hall light, but it didn't help much.

In her room, she closed the door to the hall, and then quickly got into shorts and a pullover. Her braid was still intact, and would do. She made her bed hastily, then went to the bathroom and dampened the edges of her hair so they would curl.

She left the house, taking with her an apple from the bowl on the livingroom coffee table.

The sun had risen above the clouds on the horizon. Across the compound she could see people, boys doing their chores around the barn and pens, walking, or just standing. Dad's pickup was gone from its usual parking spot near the yard gate.

One group of boys standing in the shade of a tree was looking eastward. She started toward them, then stopped.

The pickup was coming back, coming faster than usual on the narrow trails that led to the various fields and pastures.

It stopped at one end of the closest pond, and Rufus got out and went over to the group of boys. The pickup came on and her dad parked it in the usual spot beneath the trees. When he got out and came toward the house, he was walking fast, and his face looked strained.

Gwen stepped aside, saying nothing. He reached out, without changing facial expression, and gave her a greeting tap on the top of her head.

She followed him back into the house and stood in the open office door as he dialed someone.

"Dr. Mordecal? This is Martin Preston at Boys' Farm. Could you come over right away? We've got some problems with a dead calf, problems that are unusual."

Gwen stepped back. A calf. Somehow it helped knowing it wasn't one of the pets that lived closer to the barns. A calf in the pasture.

Yet when she bit into her apple, she found she had no appetite for it or any food. She laid the apple on the stand in the hallway and waited for her dad to hang up the phone and come back into the hall.

"What happened to the calf?" she asked.

He stopped on his way out the door and stood for a moment, as if wondering what to tell her.

Then he said, "I guess you'll know sooner or later. The dog is dead, too, as well as one calf."

"*Lion?*"

"Yes."

"But why, Daddy? Who did it? Who killed them?"

He looked at her strangely and said, "I'm not sure it was a *who*, baby. It's more like a *what*. You just try to get interested in something here at the house."

He was gone, crossing the porch and running down the steps. She watched him go, her tall, broad-shouldered dad, his hat pulled down to shade his eyes. His dark hair, curling a little beneath the back of the hat, had threads of silver that gleamed in the growing light of the sun. He got into the pickup, and drove back around pond one toward the service gate to wait for the veterinarian.

Gwen went out into the yard and stood by the gate, watching the activities of the few people who were in sight now. The boys had disappeared, except for two carrying buckets of feed into the pig pen on the other side of the paddock. They were so far away she couldn't be sure who they were, but they were younger boys, their arms skinny and rope-like. They were in sight only a moment before they disappeared behind fences and trees.

She looked back at the house. This was her day to clean the kitchen, but she could do it later, when Hagar was in the house, or Dad, just as long as she wasn't alone. Even the cat was gone, off sleeping somewhere, the way it did sometimes. It was one of the farm workers' cats. Coming to the farm when it was a kitten, it had grown up living part of the time with Gwen's family and part of the time with the other people. Gwen wasn't sure if it was a he or a she, but it hadn't had kittens, so she guessed it was a he. They called him Tommy, anyway, and she wished he would show up now to keep her company.

She opened the gate and went out to stand beneath the trees where her dad parked his pickup. No grass grew here. The ground was hard and dry, the tree roots snaking above the ground like the smooth spines of prehistoric animals.

She sat down on one of the roots and began digging a little trail in the dirt with a stick, waiting, she guessed, for the doctor, just as her dad was waiting.

When the van came through the gates and stopped by the pickup, she got to her feet and dusted the rear of her shorts. Her dad talked to the vet for a minute and then they both drove away toward the east pasture.

Gwen watched two of the boys shut the gates. Today the twins, Chris and Pete, were the gatekeepers. One of them was entrusted with the key, and after the visitor left, the key would be returned to Rufus, Orion, or Rose. Her dad, she knew, had one of the gate keys on the big ring that hung in his office. He kept keys to the daily entrance and service gates, to the weekend visitors gates, to all doors and every building on the farm. But duplicates were kept, too, by the people who tended those gates and doors. She had never thought about the keys before, but now, suddenly, she realized she was locked in, just as the boys were, locked in like animals. Protected from the outside world.

But not protected enough to keep a boy from dying, and the dog and a calf from being killed.

She had a bad feeling. A scared feeling.

Something bad had come into the tall, protecting fences of the farm.

Chapter Sixteen

Babette picked up the two-year-old child and carried her toward the house, feeling sobs jerk the small body. "It's all right, Missy, it's all right. It's just a little scratch, see? And Babette will fix it with some very soothing spray, you'll see." She paused. "I used to take care of my baby brother, who was just a little bigger than you, and I made his hurts go away."

Holding the child, not seeing her face or delicate bone structure, Babette could almost believe she was carrying Danny again. Her arms tightened on the weeping child, holding her closer, and she felt the sobs lessen. This little girl hadn't been here long, the mother of the house had told Babette. She was still not at home here, still cried easily, still hung back from the other kids. She also seemed accident prone, always banging up her knees. Added to the older scratches on her knees was this new one, pink and scraped, but shallow. It was like Missy was looking for attention, no matter what she had to do, and Babette was glad to give it to her.

In the kitchen they paused so the foster mother could look at the scratch, then Babette took the little girl into the bathroom.

Missy stood on the floor, interested now in what was going to be done to make her well. Babette sprayed the scratch with antiseptic, and then, at Missy's insistence, put a Band-Aid loosely over it.

"I suppose it will come right off," Babette said, "but that's all right. It's going to get well now."

"Going to get well now," the child said clearly.

Babette took her back out into the yard and stood for a moment at the sandbox.

She hadn't called the jail for two days now, and it was getting easier to just wait, to keep busy with the younger kids and the housework, to make herself get so tired that she didn't want to do anything else in the evening but watch television and then go to bed and sleep without thinking. It was getting easier, yet when she paused, even for a moment, she was aware of the tension of waiting . . . just waiting. . . .

The five-year-old boy, Robert, looked up at Babette from his corner in the sandbox and then looked at the swing. Babette smiled. She knew exactly what he was thinking. Robert was like that. A dark little boy, loaded with energy, he always looked at whatever he planned to get into next before he made his move. Four of the kids were playing in the sandbox. Robert sat with his back against the corner, his legs stretched straight ahead. Two of the others were patting sand on his legs, burying them smoothly. Babette knew he was going to leap up and cause a small sand slide. When he leaped, sand flew, and one of the girls began yelling and screaming and fighting the sand in her eyes. Robert paused to look at her in surprise, as if he'd had nothing to do with her discomfort. Then he ran to the swing set.

"Swing me, Babette!"

The foster mother came out of the house, walking calmly, her arms held out for the still-screaming little girl. The child, Sandra, seemed to see the mother, even though one arm was in front of her face. Babette bent over her, moved her arm and brushed some of the sand off. Sand clung to her eyelashes, and her tears made streaks through the sand on her face.

Mother Ann picked up Sandra. Crooning and patting, she took the child into the house.

Babette went to the swing where Robert was jiggling back and forth impatiently, his feet a couple of inches off the ground. He had picked the largest swing, of course. If he had gotten into one of the smaller swings he wouldn't need Babette.

"See what you did, Robert?" Babette said, pulling the swing toward her and up into the air. Just before she released it she added, "You should think before you act. Think of the consequences of the action."

She had read that somewhere. She thought of it as her 'grandma wisdom.' Since she didn't have a grandma of her own, that she knew of, she had always liked to read the aphorisms in the almanacs. Her 'grandma wisdoms.'

Robert squealed with glee as she released the swing and it swept through the air so high he had to hang on as he leaned back. She could see his knuckles pale with tension on the chain. But she knew he hadn't listened to her at all, probably had no idea what she had said.

He reminded her of Paddy, when he was younger. Yet she wondered why. Paddy had been as blond as this boy was dark, and he hadn't been so energetic, so quick in his movements, so sudden in his decisions. Maybe it was that all the little boys reminded her either of Paddy, or Billy, or Danny.

She heard the faint ring of the doorbell, but gave it no conscious consideration. Yet the moment she saw Mother Ann stick her head out the backdoor, she knew the visitor had some significance for her. The almost happy feeling she'd had swinging Robert was suddenly gone. Dread settled over her. It had something to do with Mama or Paddy, and her chest grew tight.

"Babette," Mother Ann said. "Miss Thornton is here to see you."

Babette let the swing slow down on its own momentum.

She walked away with Robert calling after her, asking who Miss Thornton was.

By the time Babette reached the porch steps, she could hardly keep from running. Mother Ann smiled at her as she entered the house, then her sharp eyes took in each kid and his or her location in the fenced backyard.

"She's in the living room, Babette."

"Yes, ma'am. Thank you."

By the time Babette reached the quiet living room at the front of the house, her emotions had gone from fear and sadness to hope. Maybe something good was going to happen. Maybe Paddy had been sent home to his dad, and Mama was being released from jail. Or maybe . . . this was her deepest dream . . . her most private longing . . . Mama had changed her mind about Paddy, had decided she loved him and wanted him with them, and the Child Services people were going to let all three of them go home together. And everything would work out. Mama would treat Paddy the way she had treated him when he was younger, the way Babette remembered. Babette still had the memory of Paddy on Ketti's knees, and her laughter as she hugged him close. Ketti had always had a way of hugging and laughing at the same time, as if it was such a great delight.

That was Babette's deepest dream. The one she knew, in the front of her mind, could never come true.

Miss Thornton sat on one of two brocaded, straight-backed chairs on each side of the hearth. The fireplace chairs were pretty but uncomfortable. Miss Thornton was dressed in a neat blue and white suit, wearing white nylons and low-heeled shoes. Her short brown hair was swept up and back at the sides, the top fluffed and hanging down in a side bang. The smile she gave Babette was so brief that Babette knew the news wasn't good.

Babette sat in the other brocade chair, leaving the comfortable arrangement of sofa and softer chairs looking like a display in a furniture store. This whole room, Babette thought every day when she made sure it was neat, had always reminded her of a display. The room was never used that she knew of. Except, she guessed, at a time like this.

"How are you today, Babette?"

"Okay. Thanks."

"Are you getting along well here?"

"Yes." This hedging made her nervous. She knew Miss Thornton hadn't come just to ask her how she was getting along. Her patience snapped. She couldn't wait for the conversation to run its course. "Miss Thornton, how is Paddy? And Mama. Is Mama still in jail?"

"That's why I'm here, Babette. Ketti is being released from jail today. But . . ."

Excitement exploded in Babette, creating a mixture of feelings that almost overwhelmed her. The wait was over. She leaned forward, almost sliding off her chair. "You came after me? I'm going home?"

Miss Thornton didn't move. It seemed to Babette that if she moved at all, it was a subtle leaning back, as if to get away from Babette, or the situation, or something.

"No, not just yet, Babs," Miss Thornton said, and lowered her gaze to her hands. She was holding a blue and white clutch bag in her lap, Babette noticed for the first time, and now her fingers began opening and closing the little gold-colored clasp. Snap, snap, echoed in the quiet room.

Babette felt her hopes sink. Her body slumped, as if her backbone had been pulled out through the top of her head. She hadn't realized how much, how very much, she had been waiting, just waiting, to be released from here, her own jail. Though the surroundings were nice, and the food good, and the little kids sweet, and the grownups considerate and kind, it was still her own private jail. She had no freedom to come and go as she pleased. She couldn't get up in the mornings when she wanted to, or fix breakfast for herself and her baby brother whenever she wanted to. Or turn the TV to any channel she wanted or Danny wanted. . . .

Danny wasn't there, she reminded herself. Just as everything else was gone, so was Danny.

"I'm sorry, Babs," Miss Thornton said, her voice soft with sympathy.

That's not good enough, Babette wanted to cry out at her. Give me back my freedom, my home—my mom, at least.

"Why?" Babette asked, hearing the strain in her voice, the sound of tears threatening to burst. "Why can't I go home? If Mama's going?"

"Because, Babette, she felt you would be better off here."

Babette's eyes jerked up. *"What?"*

"Your mother felt you would be better off left in foster care."

"I don't understand!" Babette cried shrilly. "Why is she leaving me here? How long? How long is she going to leave me?"

"We don't know, Babette. At the present it's your mother's request that you stay in foster care. And if you're happy here, there's no reason you can't spend the summer here. You see, Babette, foster homes that qualify are very hard to find. We have so many children to find homes for that we consider ourselves very fortunate indeed to find a home as nice as this one. Most of them aren't as comfortable as this home. Most are overcrowded, just as the state and county homes for children are."

"But I don't need to be in foster care! I can take care of myself! I have taken care of my little brother and our house for a long time, while Mama worked! I can work, too! I can get a job—"

"At age fourteen? Come on, Babette, use common sense. You need to be sixteen to get a work permit. Your job now is to go to school and prepare yourself for getting a job. Do you want to clean houses for a living or work in a low-paying factory job? You have to have training."

Babette's tears were coming hot and painful, burning her eyes, her throat, undermining what little dignity she had left. She hadn't known how desperately she'd wanted things to be better. Instead, they were worse than ever.

A sudden, terrible thought entered her mind. Was Ketti doing this because she knew she was going to kill Paddy, and knew she would go to jail forever then? Or was she going to kill Paddy and then kill herself?

"My brother . . . Miss Thornton—how is my brother? Has he been sent back to his dad?" *Please, God . . . be here . . . help us . . .*

Miss Thornton hesitated, plunging Babette even further

153

into despair. She knew the answer was not going to be good. But Ketti couldn't have found him yet, it was only today that she was being released. So what was wrong?

"No, your brother is still out at the farm. He's really very fortunate, Babette. You must not worry about him."

"But his dad—why haven't they sent Paddy back to his dad?"

"His dad seems to have—uh—disappeared. I don't believe the police have located him. At any rate, Paddy is still at the farm."

Babette didn't understand. Miss Thornton's face had a faint frown on it and she was staring at the wall, as if deep in thought. Babette waited.

"One of our boys," Miss Thornton said. "I might as well tell you. His name was Rex, and he had been at the farm for quite a long time. He died in his sleep a few nights ago." She seemed to rouse herself slightly. "Of course this had nothing to do with you, or with Patrick, except that it opens a permanent place at the farm for some other boy. But it makes us all very sad, those of us who knew Rex."

Babette felt the flicker of a frown on her face. Died in his sleep?

"How old was he?" she asked, thinking of Danny, and Billy.

"He was thirteen."

Babette drew a long breath. Was the danger never over? Was Paddy himself still in danger?

"Both of my baby brothers died in their sleep, in crib death. And my brother, Patrick—we call him Paddy—he did too, only my mother revived him."

Tonight.

Tonight, she'd leave.

"I'm sorry. I didn't know that. I mean, about Patrick. Or the other little brother. When did that happen?"

"Billy died three years ago. Just like Danny did last week. And Mama told me Paddy was five when he died, and she found him, and breathed life into him again."

Miss Thornton was staring at her oddly. It seemed to Babette there was a look of surprise on her face.

"I didn't know that," she said again. "Your mother must

154

have loved your brother very much to have done that for him."

"Oh, yes. Yes, she did." Now Babette knew why Miss Thornton was surprised. If Ketti had worked at bringing Paddy back to life once, why had she begun to abuse him? Babette didn't know the real answer to that either.

"We like to know as much as we can about our—people," Miss Thornton said. "Our parents, and our children. It helps to understand."

Babette wished Miss Thornton would go, so she said nothing. She would pretend to like it here, to want to stay, so Miss Thornton wouldn't change her mind and take her somewhere even more difficult to get away from. Then to-night, when the house was quiet and the parents were asleep, she'd slip away. She'd try to find Ketti and talk her out of what she was going to do to Paddy.

She had to. Tonight.

Sergeant Mark Ford drove up to the closed gates of Boys' Farm and pulled out his identification for the boys waiting at the gate. One of the boys, his hair bleached almost white from a short lifetime in the sun, his skin as brown as if he had been bronzed, looked at the ID with dark brown eyes, taking his time to read it. Mark felt amusement. The other boy, same height, same weight, same body type, a boy with slightly darker hair but lighter skin, stretched his neck to read over the blond boy's shoulder.

"Gosh," the blond boy said. "We've had the press, people from newspapers, and even one from a TV station, but you're the first real detective that's wanted to come through. We had a couple of cops, too, earlier."

"Yes, I know. That's why I'm here."

It wasn't, really. He had heard about this problem at Boys' Farm because the county police had been out here earlier and he had picked up their messages on the radio. He was here entirely on his own volition—the death of the boy had alerted him because of the oddness of it, the coincidence, and similarity to the deaths of Ketti Graham's two baby boys. Even though this boy, Rex Hunter, was years older, the circumstances had caused him to make a note of it in connection with his other case on Babette and Patrick. He felt so damned sorry for all these kids who were deprived of good homes, of a stable family life with at least one parent and siblings. He felt so damned sorry for them that he had kept up on everything that was happening to these two kids. He felt close to them, though he was sure they probably wouldn't even remember his name.

"What's your names?" he asked the boys at the gate. They answered in unison.

"Chris."

"Pete."

ChrisPete or PeteChris. One voice over in concert with the other. It reminded him of his own Sammy and Sarah. When he came home, they fell all over him, talking at the same time. He had learned to listen to both as they talked. Sarah, who was three, had a slightly more shrill voice than Sammy, who was five. He listened to them, heard every word, and managed to understand what his wife was saying, too. It was great, going home, knowing they were going to be waiting to talk to him all at once. On those occasions when they were gone, shopping or playing, the house had such a hollow sound and feeling that he always took his paper and went out to the patio. He couldn't stand the house without them.

"Well, you guys do a good job with this gate, and let me through, okay?"

"Sure."

"Sure."

They ran, each one taking a side of the tall, wide gate. Chris and Pete. He knew their names now, but he didn't know which name belonged to which boy.

He drove through, looking at their beaming faces, and called out, "Thanks, Chris and Pete."

Through the rearview mirror he saw the gates close, the boys running it shut, and at last swinging on it as it ground together. He smiled. Boys could manage to have fun, if they were healthy, no matter what kind of background they had.

Another boy stood on the grass beside the farm trail, a little dirt road with two tracks free of weeds and grass. The road forked ahead of him, the right fork leading toward a group of buildings by the main gate. A long building with a porch running its full length had a few people on it—boys, it appeared from the distance. Ahead of him was a grassy park-like area with big shade trees. He could see a large pond straight ahead, and beyond that, houses, a large one, and three smaller ones. It was beautiful out here. He had almost forgotten how beautiful. He and Janice had brought their kids here when they were toddlers. Why hadn't they come back? It was a great place to visit.

The next boy who came up to his car was older, larger, and less fortunate than Chris and Pete, at least physically. At some point in his life, this boy had been mangled. A bad scar snaked from his scalp to his chin, pulling the corners of one eye and his mouth out of shape.

"Hi there," said.

The boy came up to his window, looking in as if he was searching for something, but he said nothing. Mark saw his eyes were a soft, light brown and there was a youthfulness about his face that didn't match the size of his body.

"I'm a detective," Mark said, showing his ID again, knowing this boy would probably enjoy seeing it as much as Chris and Pete had. But to his surprise, the boy only glanced at it, then fixed his eyes on Mark's face.

"What's your name?" the boy asked.

Mark knew then, from the almost babyish, awkward way the words were spoken, as well as from the question, that this boy had been more that just physically harmed. And now that he was closer, he could see that the white scar reached up through his hair, leaving a wide, white track on which no hair grew. His skull had been split open. He was lucky to be alive and standing here to ask this question.

"My name is Mark and—"

"That's like my name," the boy said, not smiling, yet sounding eager and puppy-like. "My name is Marsh."

Mark put his hand out the window, and Marsh's big paw grasped it and almost crushed it.

"I'm glad to meet you, Marsh. I'm a detective, Marsh. Do you know what that is?" He wondered immediately if he had said the wrong thing. He had never been comfortable around mentally deficient people, never knew exactly how to talk to them. He didn't want to come off sounding condescending. But the boy took no offense. He shook Mark's hand vigorously before releasing it.

"I know," he said. "A detective finds out things about bad people. Have you come to find out?"

"Uh—yes. Could you tell me where this calf is?"

"I can show you. Can I go with you?"

"Certainly. Crawl in." Mark leaned over and opened the passenger door. And the boy rushed awkwardly around the front of the car, his hand reaching once to the hood for balance. He ran as if something was slightly wrong with one foot or leg.

When he got in, he sat primly, his hands on his thighs, looking straight ahead.

"Where do we go from here, Marsh?" Mark asked.

Marsh pointed, indicating the clear-cut little roadway that curved off to the left around the pond. The farm looked peaceful to Mark. A goat in a pen by the barn was chewing something, its little beard bouncing. One of the boys was carrying a bucket into another pen, and several pigs were running behind him squealing and begging. On the grass outside the animal pens, a peacock strutted, its tail feathers spread in fan-like beauty. Nearby, two plain brown peahens were pecking the ground, paying no attention to the peacock's display.

Mark drove slowly around the pond and saw that the little road continued, cutting across a narrow stream that connected the first pond to a second. They were driving through a picnic area that had tables under shade trees, and displays of antique farm machinery. Marsh had said nothing more. His eyes were looking straight ahead, his features fiercely set, it seemed to Mark.

"Did you know Rex, Marsh?" Mark asked.

"Rex is dead," Marsh said after a long pause.

Mark noticed a flicker of a frown on Marsh's face, just a faint lumping of his brow for a moment. Then the set look was back.

"Was he a friend of yours?"

"Yes, he was a friend."

158

Mark wasn't sure why he was asking Marsh these questions. It could be painful for the boy. It was the coincidence of the deaths that disturbed him. Coincidences always made him uneasy because they so seldom were innocent. Something else was usually at work.

"Had Rex been sick?"

"No. Rex just died, that's all. He just died. And he's gone now."

"I'm sorry."

Marsh nodded. "I'm sorry, too."

Mark concentrated on the road. It seemed now he could see recent tracks dug into the hard-packed dirt, though they were now out of sight of the picnic tables, machinery, farm buildings. The road had switched to the right. They had passed five ponds so far. Mark didn't know exactly where he was because he had never been farther back on the farm than the first pond and the main picnic area. The road began to look thinner and less used, and in places, it almost disappeared. But he saw that Marsh was leaning forward now, his neck craning, as if he was trying to spot the location.

Staying on the road was becoming a job. It dipped close to a pasture fence, and he saw cattle and a couple of horses grazing far out in the field. And farther on he saw another, larger group of cattle gathered at the fence, staring at something outside their pasture. Above the sound of his car engine, he could hear a cow bawling.

Marsh pointed suddenly. "There. There's Mister Preston's pickup and Rufus and the rest of them."

It was a couple of seconds before Mark saw what Marsh had seen—his dark glasses were too good at shielding his eyes from the sun. He removed them, and saw the outlines of two vans, maybe more, and one pickup. On another hilly slope he could see people milling about. One or two had what looked to be cameras. Probably the police.

Marsh had settled back into the seat and clasped his hands together. Mark's attention was drawn to him when he uttered a low, keening sound, almost a cry. He saw the boy was wringing his hands, pressing them palm to palm, squeezing them together, turning them.

Mark stopped the car, letting the engine idle. He could see now that he probably should not have brought this vulnerable boy here. Had Marsh ever seen a dead animal before?

"Is something wrong?" he asked.

The boy grew calm suddenly, looking at Mark from the corner of his eyes. Mark began to feel like the boy was sizing him up for something.

"You're going to—to get the bad one?"

"Yes, if there is a bad one, we'll get him if we can."

"I'll tell you," Marsh said, and then looked over his shoulder to the right, toward a clump of bushes near the car. "The bad boy—the new boy—he's a bad boy."

"What do you mean, Marsh? Bad boy?"

The boy suddenly became very agitated. His hands shook violently and his chin jerked as if he was in the first stages of a convulsion. "No—no—Marsh can't tell—Marsh don't tell—they'll hurt Marsh—"

Marsh grasped the door latch with both hands, threw it open and stumbled out. Then he steadied himself, and Mark could see the danger of a convulsion was gone. The large childlike boy was under control, though his eyes jerked right and left as if he were terrified.

"Are you all right?" Mark asked.

"I'm going now—Marsh go now."

Mark leaned over. They must be a quarter of a mile or more from the main area of the farm, and he didn't feel right leaving the boy here.

"Get in, Marsh, and I'll take you back up to the bunkhouse."

Marsh shook his head. "I come here sometimes. I follow the path." He sounded rational now, almost normal.

Marsh pointed toward the pond. When Mark looked back, the boy was gone. Through the rearview mirror, he saw him running in his slightly awkward lope, favoring his right side. Marsh crossed behind the car to the path leading toward the farm buildings, and disappeared from sight where the path dipped into the mesquite.

Mark drove on, though he still felt uneasy. Marsh knew

160

his way around the farm, Mark guessed—a lot better than he ever would. He'd be all right.

Among the vehicles parked in the meadow was a car and a van from the county sheriff's department. On the ground, he saw, was something covered by a canvas. Spread on another canvas nearby was the body of the calf. It was lying in the shade of a tall bush.

A tall, true-Texan type wearing a Stetson approached him, and Mark automatically removed his ID from his pocket and held it out. The man looked at it and put out his hand. The two men shook hands.

"Martin Preston," the man said, introducing himself. "You're with the city police?"

"Yes. I'm not here on official business, but I heard about this, and I decided to come on out. I was on the Skein case."

"Patrick."

"Yes. How's he doing?"

"Great. Blending right in."

"Is he getting along with the other boys?"

"Seems to be."

"How about Marsh? I talked to him awhile ago. He seemed to not much like the new boy who, I suppose, is Patrick?"

"Yes, he's our new boy. It sometimes takes Marsh awhile to trust, but they're doing fine."

"No special problems?"

"None."

Mark nodded. Marsh was different, Mark reminded himself, somewhat retarded. There was no telling what he had meant about "bad boy."

"What's been determined about this?" Mark motioned toward the calf.

"It's a mutilation, the kind that was fairly common a few years ago. That's Dr. Mordecal over there, if you want to talk to him. We're about ready to move the bodies out now. The dog is going to be taken back up to the bunkhouse so the boys can give him a proper burial. None of them would ever forgive me if I just had him dumped in a hole in the ground, the way the calf will be."

Mark heard the sound of a tractor coming nearer and turned to see it rounding the end of the pond. On the front was a blade, that Mark assumed would be used for digging the calf's grave.

At the fence, her head hanging, eyes watching dolefully, the mother of the calf lowed again, a sound that saddened Mark.

Animals cry for loved ones too, he thought.

"The dog was killed too?"

"Yes, though not mutilated, nor drained of blood. Its throat was cut."

Mark walked over to the calf and looked down.

Its head was small with soft ears and a muzzle that was round and pink. But the holes where its eyes had been were dark and deep, and there was no sign of blood.

Chapter Seventeen

Rufus rode back to the gate with Martin, the body of the dog wrapped in canvas in the back of the pickup. The sun was rising high and getting hotter. The burial would have to take place as soon as possible. Behind them the tractor was at work burying the calf. The cow was still at the fence, walking along it, following the tractor as it carried the body of her baby calf to the burial ground below the pasture, a soft, sandy area where all animals were buried. She would stand at the fence and bawl for two or three more days, Rufus knew from having witnessed other cows who lost calves, and she wouldn't eat or drink during that period. Then, like humans, she would gradually move back into the herd, going on with life. And next year, she would have another calf and she would have someone to love again.

"Who do you suppose—or what do you suppose would do a thing like that, Mr. Preston?" Rufus asked, wanting to pound his fists on the dash of the pickup, on anything, to relieve his feelings.

"I have an idea we'll never know for sure. But Doctor Mordecal said that some birds will peck out a dead animal's eyes so cleanly you would think they had been surgically removed, and of course after the animal is dead for some time, there's no blood to run. So it looks like a Class A devil's cult thing, but actually it's something natural instead."

"But he said this calf had no blood in it, not anywhere he could find."

"I know."

"It's them UFOs, Mr. Preston, like it was a few years ago. That's the only thing that could have gotten over our fences."

"No, now that's the kind of thing we don't want to get started, Rufus, so don't say that in front of anyone else, please. We don't want that kind of publicity. And I didn't want the kind we got already. We don't need to be in any newscast."

"Well, there's news people outside the gates. Where did they come from anyway?"

"It happened when the doctor called the sheriff's office. Somebody got the word. But I asked them to please not make anything of it. We'll see."

Rufus saw two more cars were outside the gates wanting in. The gates were still closed, the twins standing guard, looking as if they didn't know quite what to do. A girl on the other side of the gate was talking to them. A card on the windshield of her car read "PRESS," Rufus figured, though he was too near-sighted to be sure.

"More news people?" Martin asked as he got out of the pickup, leaving the door open and the engine running. He went to the gate and said a few words to the girl on the other side. She looked to be about sixteen, though these days, all the young people looked years younger than they really were, Rufus thought. She was probably more like twenty-five. He watched her, saw the disappointment on her face. Her fingers gripped the chain links of the fence. She was still trying to talk to Martin when he came back to the pickup.

Behind them the vans and cars of the veterinarian and police were lined up on the little dirt road, waiting to get out. Martin got into the pickup and parked it at the side of the road. "I want to be very sure that no one sneaks in while this bunch is leaving," he told Rufus.

Rufus got out of the pickup too, and went to stand at the fence, watching as the gates opened and the automobiles left. The gates clanged shut behind them, and the boys fastened the padlock. Martin smiled and waved at the girl on the other side of the fence. In the second car parked near the entrance was one man, fresh-faced, like the girl. She made a face of disappointment as she turned to go to her car. Then she spotted Rufus and came toward him.

"Hi," she said through the bars of the gate. "Do you live here?"

"I do."

She took out a notebook and a pen from her small shoulder bag. "Can I ask you a few questions?"

"I'm sorry, ma'am. There's just nothing to tell. We try to keep a peaceful and happy home here for the boys, and that's about it."

"I know, and that's great, but what about the cattle mutilation?"

"Cattle? We had one calf die, that's all." Rufus pondered his words carefully. Lying was in order here, he figured, because Mr. Preston didn't want publicity, and neither did he. It was like they were about to be invaded by something from outer space. Aliens. Coming to destroy the peace and contentment of the farm. It wouldn't do. It just wouldn't do.

"Calf? But wasn't it more than one dead animal? And weren't the vital organs and sex organs removed, without trace of blood?"

Her questions made his answers more truth than lies, and he spilled it without hesitation. "Vital organs? No, ma'am. And I reckon every living creature has blood in it. This thing has got all twisted and messed up. You just tell your

folks, your paper or whatever—'' She interrupted him to
say the name of her paper, but he didn't quite catch it, and
didn't care. He never read newspapers. Too much war and
crime in them. "You just tell your boss not to allow any
space in his paper for anything like that, because there's
nothing to it. We can't have folks thinking there's something dangerous out here on the farm or they wouldn't come
on weekends. And don't you know that our visitors is what
keeps us going here? They need to come and feel their kids
are safe, and they are, missy, you can be sure of that.''

He walked away, his heart beating too fast with all the
fury he felt. He saw that Martin Preston was waiting in his
pickup, and had probably heard every word he'd said. He
couldn't even remember now what it was.

"Where do you think we ought to put Lion?" Martin
asked.

Rufus let out a long breath. "I reckon maybe down at
the other end of the bunkhouse, by the mimosa tree."

Martin nodded. "You want to ride along?"

"No, I'll walk. Do me good to walk."

Marsh stood with his back against the board siding of the
bunkhouse, his hands behind him, palms and fingers back
so he could feel the roughness and sharp edges of the wood.
A small splinter came off in his fingers and he rolled it,
feeling it.

Vance, Russ, and Lee, the big boys who were getting
ready to go away to school in a few weeks, had built Lion
a coffin. It was made of old boards some of the younger
boys had found. Not Marsh. Marsh had waited on the
porch, sitting close to Lion's old rug, the dogs' favorite
sleeping place. While the other boys had made the coffin,
Marsh had sat there.

The detective with the name so much like his own had
not taken the bad boy away after all. He was here, standing
with the others around the grave dug for Lion.

Mr. Preston hung his head and said, "And now we lay
our good friend to rest, to sleep the eternal sleep—''

The tears came into Marsh's throat, hurting him. His

own head hung low, his chin almost touching his chest. He didn't want to cry. Big boys don't cry. Little boys don't either . . . don't cry . . . not if they don't want to be slapped. Little boys . . . don't . . . cry. . . .

He glanced up and saw the covered box lowered into the hole in the ground. He saw Mr. Preston shovel in the first dirt. He heard it hit the top of the box. Standing near Mr. Preston was Rufus, Gwen and Hagar. Orion was on this side of the grave, with Miss Rose and the boys, all lined up, side by side. Among them was the bad boy.

The grave was covered, shovelful by shovelful. Marsh heard each clod hit the box and gradually just hit other clods. His chest was going to burst. He wanted to cry and scream. But . . . boys . . . don't . . .

He was crawling, he remembered, the scene in front of him fading to something different, something darker, yet more familiar. The floor beneath his hands was rough, and the splinter came loose and pierced his finger. He held it up, wailing, starting to cry in earnest. Then he saw her coming, and he could see on her face that this was a bad time to cry.

He turned and tried to get away. He got to his feet, but he fell, his leg still weak and hurting. He wanted to tell her that he had a long, hurting splinter in his finger, and it was bleeding, but he knew this was a bad time. He felt in his heart the blow before it reached him. He dodged and covered his head with his arms.

The blow never reached him. Not this time. Not yet.

Then he heard her laughing.

His mother was laughing. She wasn't mad at him after all?

But when he looked up at her he saw that she still hated him. But something he had done had made her laugh, and he tried to laugh too.

"Why are you dodging?" she asked, as if it delighted her to see him cover his head.

Why are you dodging . . . ?

Why are you dodging . . .

Marsh was alone, he realized when he became aware of his surroundings again. The grave was a mound of dirt, like a sore in the grass, beneath the fingery shadows of the mimosa tree. And the people, Rufus and the others, were gone. He could hear their voices around the corner of the bunkhouse.

He hurried to follow them. He didn't want to be alone to remember, to *remember*—things that still hurt.

The figure jumped out at him unexpectedly from the corner, and he saw the face he had seen last night. That white oval that looked at him over the body of the dog. It seemed to spring at him, its eyes so pale they were like strange, hating lights. And Marsh knew—he knew—it meant death. And he was afraid. He shrank back, slid around the corner, and waited.

When he dared look around the corner again, Patrick was walking with Gwen.

Marsh stood still, his hand grasping the sharp edge of the boards that sealed the corner.

The bad boy . . . it hadn't helped to tell the detective.

He hadn't heard what Marsh said.

Rufus looked for Marsh. In the early years, Marsh had liked to go into the dirt-floored rooms in the barn where the animals were kept, where the soil was dark and loose and soft, and sit in the corner with his back to the wall. Rufus had found him there a number of times, with the goats accepting him as if he was one of their own. Later, Marsh had taken to roaming the entire barn, with all its rooms, corridors, and openings. And today, after the dog's death and burial, just one day after Rex's death, Rufus was afraid that Marsh had regressed, as Mary Bolinger would have called it. He hadn't seen Marsh since the dog was laid in his grave, and he was getting worried.

He had gone down by the vegetable gardens where the boys were at work again. But Vance, the soon-to-be seventeen-year-old who had been here for three years and who was leaving in late summer for college, did not know where Marsh was. Vance folded his hands on top of his hoe handle. Four boys working nearby stopped their slow, playful weeding to listen.

"I haven't seen him, Rufus," Vance said. "Not all day long that I remember. He was with us when we buried Lion, wasn't he?"

"Yeah, he was," one of the boys offered. He chopped at a weed. "But he didn't come with us."

"You don't know his assignment for this afternoon?" Rufus asked. It was usually Vance who chose the fifteen boys who put in a couple of hours work in the gardens, or mowing the grounds. Mowing was a favorite job of all the boys because they got to ride around on small tractors. There were always plenty of volunteers for that job.

"No. Marsh usually does whatever he wants to. Sometimes he comes with me. Not always. He likes the animals."

Rufus nodded and turned away. As he walked away, he could hear the soft chop, chop of hoes, and the murmurs of the boys' voices. When Vance left, the responsibility of work assignments would pass down to the next oldest boy, excluding Marsh. It probably would be Shawn or Lenny, who were both fifteen.

Both were good boys. Capable. Lenny's school grades weren't quite up to the standard set at Boys' Farm, but Rufus thought it was because Lenny had only come about a year ago. A quiet, pale, nervous kid who didn't smile much, he had been in a detention home off and on for a couple of years. He had tried to live with his folks now and then; both of them had separate homes and different spouses and other families. But Lenny hadn't fit in anywhere, and finally he was judged to have been psychologically abused from the time of birth. It was a fact he had never admitted, but it had gotten him into Boys' Farm. He seemed to be settling down and getting along fine. But how could you tell with such a quiet kid? Maybe the responsibility of work assignments and work completion would be just what Lenny needed. Shawn wouldn't mind. He had been at the farm for five or six years, and was a noisy, playful kid with no problems, at least none that showed on the surface.

But it was Marsh who worried Rufus. He hadn't wanted Marsh to see the dog, or even know about him, but it was impossible to protect him from the death. He had to know. He would have missed Lion as soon as he stepped onto the porch this morning. And of course, he'd been at the burial. Rufus had seen him at the rear of the group, standing with his head bowed.

And Rufus wanted to talk to him, to tell him . . . what? What did you tell a boy like Marsh? Another dog someday, a puppy. Marsh would love any dog, any puppy . . . but it wouldn't be Lion.

The gully seemed dark and damp. The bottom had been cleaned out by flash floods. Roots of trees that grew along the banks reached out into the gully like snakes twisted together in a long nest. The bottom of the gully was still muddy from the last rain, and Rufus jumped over it, feeling some satisfaction that he could still jump without cracking something.

He climbed the other side of the gully and took the short-cut across the grape vineyard and northwest edge of the strawberry patch. Working down at the far end were Rose and two of the smaller boys. They had probably come out to pick berries for tonight's shortcake. He could see Marsh was not with them, and he didn't pause.

Farther on, nearing one of the ponds and the farm path, he stopped to listen, but the mother of the calf was quiet. She had probably gone back to grazing for an hour or so. In the evening she would start calling again and walking the fence nervously. He had seen the pattern enough to know what was likely to happen.

When he reached the barn, he went through the pens that opened out beneath the shed roof, but Marsh was not with the animals. At the paddock, he climbed the fence and crossed the grass to the horse's stall. Both Orion and Hagar were brushing Star Beauty. Rufus stood for a moment watching them.

"Ain't seen Marsh, have you?" Rufus asked.

Hagar shook her head. "He hasn't been here. I've been here for the past two hours, and I haven't seen him."

"Me neither."

Orion hung up the brush he was using, patted Star Beauty on the neck, and let himself out of the stall. He stood beside Rufus with his thumbs hooked in two black belt loops.

Rufus turned to look beyond the paddock. The pigs, in a

pen across from the paddock were all lying together asleep. In the adjoining pen, goats grazed among sheep and two calves that had been brought up from the big pasture. It would have been a picture of contentment, but there were shadows now, and the spaces of sunlight were paler it seemed to Rufus. Something wrong with the total picture. He was worried. It wasn't only Rex's strange and unexpected death, and then the brutal deaths of the dog and calf. It was something more—it was Marsh. Rufus was feeling a dread he hadn't felt before. Everything was getting out of step. He wondered if anyone else felt it. Hagar seemed more quiet, not saying anything, just staying with her horse. Orion wasn't saying much either.

Rufus went toward the gate, feeling tired suddenly, not up to climbing the boards of the fence. He didn't know where else to look except maybe the bunkhouse. He hadn't even thought of looking in the bunkhouse. Marsh had never gone in to his bed during the day since he was a little kid. But he might have regressed, as Mary Bolinger would say.

"I'll walk with you," Orion said.

They went out the gate together. The peacock was scratching in the dirt at the base of a tree, his long tail drooping, feathers dragging in the dirt.

Rufus walked in silence beside Orion. They crossed the picnic areas, past the tractor with the metal wheels, and the old wooden baler.

Orion said, "I sure miss Rex when I go to the kitchen. He was the best kitchen help I ever had."

"Who's taking his place?"

"I don't know who'll be there today. Yesterday it was Lee and Russ." Orion grinned slightly. "Neither one of them can peel a potato, so we decided to bake them."

At the end of the bunkhouse, they separated, Orion going to the steps that led to the breezeway, and Rufus to the steps that led to the bedroom section.

The moment Rufus stepped into the cloakroom, he could feel the difference. The building was too quiet, like an old place that had been abandoned for a century. Once he had gone into a tall, round building on the Snake River in Idaho. It was built of stone, one room atop the other, with the stairway on the outside. Built entirely of stone and mud, the windows and door holes had no framing for glass or doors. It was known locally as "the Castle." But it had a sense of abandonment that he had never found in any other place—until now, here.

His footsteps echoed as he walked through the cloakroom. At the door to the baths and toilets he called, "Marsh?"

He waited, listening, knowing from the feel of the place that Marsh was not here.

He went to the door of the long bunkhouse and looked in at the neat beds, every blanket folded under mattresses military style, every bedside table neatly arranged with books, model airplanes or cars. On Marsh's, there was nothing except a small bowl of flowers. The lockers between the beds stood against the wall, all metal, either brown or green. Marsh's locker was green.

The outward appearance met with his approval. He had been a sergeant in World War II and had come to feel the military had a good idea of how to keep a bunk made and a room clean. Most of the boys kept things in good shape. Yet he sensed a difference. There was a smell too, a vague stink of rot and death.

Something was not in order in the room. At first it only seemed that he sensed it as he walked the aisle between the bunks. Then he saw the edge of something beneath Marsh's bed, where the stink was strongest.

He bent. In the darkness it looked like a rolled bundle, about the size of a football. It might be Marsh's football. Rufus knew he had one, and often took it out after supper to play with. The football was supposed to be kept in Marsh's locker. The bed had to stay neat. That was the rule. Both the top of the bed, and beneath it, had to be clear of everything. Marsh knew the rules.

Rufus stooped and reached under the bed.

It was not a football, but clothing tightly rolled into a small ball. A shirt—a pajama top.

There was something dark staining the blue material. Oil perhaps. Rufus's hands had begun to shake. He unrolled the shirt and held it by the corners. The entire front was stained dark. Blood. Not oil.

Blood.

Rufus looked over his shoulder toward the doorway. He felt like he was being watched. But no one was there.

He dropped the shirt on the floor and opened the locker. The odor of rotting flesh swept out at him, a dark, invisible cloud. Marsh's stacks of clothing were neat on the shelves. Underwear, white as new, was folded on the two top shelves. The third shelf held shirts. The fourth, jeans. The next shelf held socks, and the bottom was the place for shoes. There was a special closet, beyond the cloakroom, where each boy had a dress suit and other dressy clothes. Rufus noticed that one shelf of Marsh's clothing was not as neat as the rest. It looked as if . . . something out of place had been stuffed into the back.

Rufus felt into the rear of the shelf, and his hand touched a small object that crinkled with an odd, familiar sound. He drew it out.

It was a leaf, one that had been picked green, but was now drying, making a sound in his hand like winter leaves beneath his feet.

Something rotten was wrapped in the leaf.

The leaf was stuck to the object it covered, and Rufus peeled it away.

He almost dropped it all.

On the leaf, lying in his shaking hand, were two eyeballs with large, red veins on the white, the dark brown iris dull and lifeless.

He realized he was muttering over and over, "Oh God, oh God, oh God."

He sat down on the cot, his knees too weak to hold him up. At his feet was the bloody shirt; in his hand the eyeballs of the calf. He swallowed the vomit that rose in his throat.

Marsh?

Not once had he connected Marsh with the deaths of the animals.

Marsh?

Oh, God.

What would they do to him if they knew?

If Rufus did what he should—if he took this evidence to Mr. Preston, what would happen? What would Mr. Preston do? He would call the police back, and Mary Bolinger, and the child psychiatrist, and before dark fell, Marsh would be taken away.

For the rest of his life he would be behind bars, in the state hospital for the mentally ill, with the insane, the lunatics. Marsh, away from the green farm, the grass, the flowers and trees. Marsh, away from the animals . . .

The animals he loved?

What had happened to Marsh?

Rufus gathered up the bloody shirt and the calf's eyeballs and rolled it all into a ball. He left the bunkhouse, pausing on the porch to look around, to make sure he wasn't seen.

He went around the backside of the bunkhouse to the incinerator and opened its iron door. There were still coals from recent trash burning, and Rufus dropped the shirt and the horrible evidence of Marsh's act into them. He watched as the fabric of the shirt turned red, the coals eating into the material. A tiny flame rose, eating its way deeper into the fabric, spreading like a forest fire.

With a poker that lay on the ground beside the incinerator, Rufus shoved the burden beneath the coals. Then he closed the door.

He stood looking across the compound, toward the trees, and the animal pens. He couldn't think. All his dreams of retirement on a small farm where he and Marsh could live in peace . . . all the dreams were gone.

Chapter Eighteen

Hagar sat on an upturned bucket and watched Star Beauty. She had been let out into the paddock and was grazing. She loved the horse, so much sometimes it seemed to hurt inside her, and she wondered, did deep, true love always have a painful side to it?

Once, she had been in love. Last summer. It was Vance, the worst boy she could have picked, because her dad had explained to her very carefully that she was coming up, as he called it, growing up, and she would be seeing boys in a different light. And that was fine, he had said, but she should make very sure that when she did fall for a boy, it was someone from school, or from outside. The whole world was "outside." The boys in here were her brothers, in a sense. Her family. She was not to look at them in any other way.

She hadn't noticed until his talk that she had been feeling different about Vance. When they went to church she made a point of sitting next to him. He had started smiling at her in an odd way, and she had felt such a breathlessness.

And she knew, after her dad's talk, that he had noticed something she had not. She was falling for Vance. Her dad knew before she did.

Who else had noticed, she wondered. Had Orion? Rufus? Rose? How about the other boys? Gwen? No, she thought, Gwen was too busy doing her own flirting.

Hagar almost died of embarrassment. What had Vance thought of her? Now she knew why he had smiled at her so oddly. His 'sister' was coming on to him.

She almost died of embarrassment. Vance had a girl-friend at school, she knew that. At school parties they paired off, Vance and Kathy. She hadn't exactly been jealous, just envious. She had wished to be in that girl's place. In her daydreams she had often been caught in private corners, in the barn, at the ponds, caught by Vance, and kissed. Oh, *kissed*. Long and hard. She had felt his arms around her so many times in her dreams.

And she had stepped onto forbidden ground.

Before she was over her embarrassment, Orion and her dad had taken her and Gwen to an auction of young and inexperienced race horses, and Orion had told her to pick out one of the youngest ones. She had chosen Star Beauty, and had fallen into a different kind of love.

But she had learned something. Love hurts.

She sat on the bucket under the overhang of the shed

roof, her arms folded, hands clasping her elbows. Star Beauty's lips wrapped themselves around twigs of grass in a comical way, and Hagar began to smile. She was so pretty, this horse. Had her dad known she needed something to occupy her mind and time?

What about Gwen?

Couldn't he see that she needed a talking to?

She'd have to ask him soon. She knew what he'd say, though. "Gwen is only eleven." He was kind of blind when it came to Gwen. She wondered if this was because Gwen looked a little like their mother, with her blond hair and blue eyes. Hagar didn't feel her dad loved one of them more than the other—he just didn't see Gwen in a true light. She was still his little girl.

Star Beauty reared her head. Her ears snapped up, listening. Her tail lifted.

Hagar stiffened and sat up straight on the bucket. Her eyes swept the trees overhead. Something had spooked Star Beauty.

The filly whirled and went running around the paddock fence going to the far side. Then she stopped and looked past Hagar.

Hagar got to her foot.

The horse threw her head back again and whirled, running, tail up, and Hagar saw her eyes. They had grown wild suddenly. Hagar heard her cry out, a frightened whinny. She whirled again, bumping into the fence.

She was going to hurt herself.

Hagar went running across the paddock, calling in a soothing voice, "Whoa, Star Beauty, slow down. Down, girl."

The horse reared again, her feet reaching high above Hagar's head as Hagar grabbed for her bridle. She suddenly wished for Orion. Orion could handle her better than Hagar. Orion would know more, understand what might be wrong.

She managed to reach the bridle, and the horse allowed herself to be pulled down. With her head over Hagar's shoulder, turned away from the barn, the nervous filly allowed herself to be petted and soothed.

Hagar looked beyond Star Beauty and saw that Gwen and Patrick had come into the horse's stall and were standing there together, watching.

The new boy.

There was something about the new boy that disturbed Star Beauty every time he got near.

She rubbed the horse's nose, feeling her relax, her eyes turned away from the invaders.

Hagar felt suddenly furious. At that moment she could have wrung Gwen's neck. Why had she brought Patrick into the stall in the first place?

She raised her hand and with palm toward them, motioned for them to get out of the stall. But Gwen only waved in return, and even Patrick lifted his hand in a small greeting.

Hagar didn't want to raise her voice for fear of unsettling Star Beauty again, so she led the horse around, turning her so she would be less apt to see the visitors.

She pulled up a handful of grass and offered it to the horse, and Star Beauty began eating again. When Hagar released her bridle, the horse went back to her grazing.

Hagar crossed the paddock to the open gate of the stall.

"What are you doing in there, Gwen? You scared Star Beauty half to death. Get out. And if you come down here again, don't go in her stall!"

Cheeze," Gwen said. "Why are you so cranky?"

"When you want to come to the paddock, just come to the fence like everyone else, can't you?"

"But they don't! Marsh always comes in this way, and you never yell at him."

"Marsh doesn't scare my horse."

"*Your* horse! She's everybody's. We've got as much right here as you have."

Hagar saw Gwen glance sideways at Patrick, as if she suddenly remembered he was there, and was embarrassed for quarreling in front of him. She wouldn't want him to see this side of her. Hagar saw a tiny smile softened the lines of her mouth, which was soft and full anyway. When she was angry, it acquired a slight tucked-in crease at each corner. Now the crease smoothed out and turned into tiny dimples.

But Patrick was looking at Star Beauty, Hagar saw, with an intense expression, almost a frown, as if he was standing in bright sunlight that hurt his eyes. She noticed his eyes, becoming more aware of them than ever before. Now that he wasn't looking at her and she could stare more intently at him, she saw that his eyes were like gray pearls. But they looked oddly empty as he stood in the deeper shadows of the stall. His lightly tanned face looked as if he had no eyes, just spaces, liquid holes for eyes.

She noticed suddenly that his gaze had switched to her. Sometime during her examination of him, his attention had switched, and she hadn't noticed. She took a step backward.

She wanted Patrick out of Star Beauty's stall, away from the barns and the animal pens. She wondered if she dared ask her dad to have Patrick assigned duties away from the barns. In the gardens, maybe, or the orchards or vineyards, or even at the bunkhouse and the kitchen. What was he doing here at this hour? But of course lots of boys were free this time of afternoon. She could hear a bunch of them over at one of the ponds, probably swimming. Boys' voices took on a different sound when they were in a pond playing.

"Why don't you go swimming, Patrick? I can hear some boys in pond two, it sounds like."

He shrugged, but his eyes stayed on her. And her discomfort increased.

"Well, come on out this way, Patrick. Come on, I'll show you where the gate in the fence is. You don't need to be coming here to Star Beauty's stall, either of you. She's not used to strangers."

"I know the way out," Gwen said haughtily, brushing past Patrick and leading the way across the paddock to the gate. Then instead of using the gate, she climbed the fence rails.

Patrick followed her. But he paused at the fence, glanced back at Hagar as if she intimidated him, then opened the gate, passed through, and carefully latched it behind him.

"Hey wait, Gwen. I want to talk to you." Hagar took

her time approaching the fence, where Gwen had stopped on the other side. Patrick stood a few feet beyond the shade.

"What about?" The pucker was at the corners of Gwen's mouth again.

Hagar reached the fence. "You can go on, Patrick. Don't you have some assignment for the afternoon?"

He shrugged again. She had seen boys before who used their shoulders to answer a question, and she thought it was rude. It usually didn't last long after they came to the farm. Always before, the gesture had meant a boy was kind of bashful. She didn't have that feeling about Patrick—there was something different about him.

"No," he said at last.

"Didn't Vance tell you what to do?"

"No."

"Well, go ask him. Or go swimming with the boys. Gwen has other things to do right now. I want to talk to her."

Patrick turned and went out of sight around the corner of the barn. He was going to the pond, she thought, and she visualized him standing on the bank watching the boys swim and splash in the water of pond two. It was about the size of a large, commercial swimming pool, with water ranging from a few inches deep to about eight feet. A diving board had been built at the deep end, among the mesquite and the Southern Lilac.

Anger had come fully back to Gwen's mouth. Her lips pouted, while the corners held tightly, as if bound by rivets.

"You're not my mother," Gwen said. "Why did you have to embarrass me in front of Pat? We only came down to watch you training Star Beauty."

That almost threw Hagar, made her wish she hadn't said anything, or made such a big deal out of it. Training Star Beauty? How flattering. Still, the horse had gotten really scared.

"But you came in through her stall, and you scared her. She could have hurt herself, Gwen. Then she'd never be able to race."

"So?" Gwen shrugged, looking just like Patrick.

"So! Are you some kind of heartless rock?"

"I didn't mean that. I meant, so what if she doesn't race? What's the big deal about that?"

"I—well, she's a race horse. I mean, she's from that kind of stock, and it's her destiny, I guess. Besides, it's something great for the farm. To own a race horse, I mean."

"Is that all you wanted to talk to me about?"

"You're getting me all confused. I wasn't going to talk about Star Beauty, you started that. What I want to know is, hasn't Dad ever talked to you about the boys?"

Gwen frowned. "What do you mean? About sex and stuff like that? Why should he? I'm not having sex with anybody, for gosh sakes. We were only walking through the barn."

"Not sex, Gwen. I mean—yes, maybe that's what it leads up to, I don't know. Why did you have to bring that up? I mean—what I mean—" This was more difficult than she had thought. She almost told Gwen to forget it, to go on and do what she wanted. After all, it was Dad's responsibility, not hers.

"Then what are you talking about? I have to go. I don't want to stand around here all afternoon."

"Dad doesn't want you to—to get crushes on the boys, Gwen. Not our boys. They're our *brothers*. And if you want a boyfriend, to walk with or whatever, you have to choose him from outside. You understand?"

Gwen's face relaxed. She even smiled. She drew a deep breath that heaved her chest, and Hagar saw her pointed little breasts push her blouse out.

"Patrick's not going to be here very long. Then he'll be outside."

"Oh? How do you know?"

"He just said he wasn't. Maybe his dad is going to come get him. He said he used to live with his dad. For the last three years he has lived with his dad. He only came to visit his mother. And do you know what, Hagar?

"What?"

"He only came to visit her, and she tried to kill him. Isn't that sad?"

"Yes. I didn't know that."

"She did. Those scratches and cuts that were on his face, she did it. His mother."

Hagar was ready to reconsider her opinion of Patrick, yet she sensed something wrong. It was like a faint warning in the back of her mind, where she couldn't quite reach it, like a distant bell, a toll of death, fear, and darkness.

"Then—if he was living with his dad and only came to visit his mom, why didn't they send him back to his dad? Instead of bringing him here?"

Gwen opened her mouth, but said nothing. She turned away from Hagar, looking toward the end of the barn where Patrick had gone out of sight. She was already walking in that direction before she answered.

"I don't know."

Hagar stood alone. She could hear the buzzing of bees up in the tree, a soft, summer sound, one that she ordinarily loved. But nothing was the same lately, she realized. The sounds she loved, the way she felt, had changed sometime, without her being aware of it. Was this all happening because of Rex's death? Or did it go back further, to Patrick's arrival?

Was this what it felt like to be depressed? Was that what was happening to her, or was there a real change taking place on the farm—a deepening of shadows in the dark places, the growing nervousness of the animals, a restlessness they'd never had before. Even the sounds of the boys in the pond seemed to have taken on a subtle change of tone, a shrieking as if they were almost hysterically trying to have fun, trying to recapture that illusive thing called fun that was theirs last week.

She heard a soft, fluttery sound in the barn, and her heart leaped. She found that she was looking under the dark spaces beneath the shed with a new fear—as if the barn sheltered more now than just the animals.

She looked for Star Beauty and saw the filly had stopped eating and was also looking toward the barn. The intensity of her stare made Hagar more uneasy. Something alien was in the barn. She had heard it, and so had the filly.

Hagar went cautiously into the shed that joined the stall. It was closed off from the paddock by a railing fence. The shed had individual pens used for cows ready to have calves, or goats or sheep who needed to be separated from the herd for awhile. The dirt in the stalls was soft and black, and had a cool, rich smell that invaded the whole barn.

The stalls were separated by railings, so that when she reached the overhang of the shed, she could see to the far end of the shed. The rafters sloped down from the main barn, exposed and gray in spots with spider webs that were seldom disturbed. A barn swallow's nest, built of mud, nestled beneath the roof, but it seemed to be empty now. She expected to hear the peep of baby birds, and felt disappointed that she didn't. There was an emptiness, a lack of activity that she had never noticed before, as if nothing lived here but the spiders.

She saw nothing.

When she looked back at Star Beauty, the young horse had returned to her grazing. Hagar began to feel less afraid. Maybe it had been an owl, she thought, moving from one roosting place to another, going through the open space between the wall of the main barn and the space between the rafters, a space just large enough for a bird to get through.

She left the paddock, carefully latching the gate behind her.

For a few minutes she stood beneath the shade of the maple tree, looking off over the park toward the bunkhouse. She had always liked the look of the bunkhouse, long and low, with its friendly porch overlooking the farm. She had spent many a pleasant hour there with Rufus, her dad, sister, the boys, Orion, and Rose. The farm workers and their families came too, on special occasions. Sometimes it was a weekday afternoon, or a special Sunday when the gates were closed to the public, and they would make homestyle ice cream in freezers the boys had to crank. They all loved it. Those were easy days, even for the boys who took turns cranking the freezers.

Rufus usually sat on the porch, rocking, with Lion beside him. The two could often be found like that, especially in the early mornings, afternoons and again in the evenings.

But this afternoon Rufus was not there.

Lion was not there.

Rex—he would have been going down the breezeway between the bunkhouse and the main living area and kitchen, usually with something to eat in his hand. She had teased him sometimes about his eating, but he hadn't seemed to mind. She hoped he hadn't minded. She hadn't teased him much, just a few times. *Rex, your fingers are going to turn into popsicle sticks.* Things like that. She had wanted him to get more interested in other things so that when it came time for him to leave the farm, he would fit in better with the outside world. So he wouldn't be fat and discriminated against. But he had lived as if he would never leave the farm, as if he would always be protected behind tall fences, away from competition and criticism.

And he hadn't left the farm. And never would.

Except in his coffin.

Actually, the ambulance.

It might as well have been his coffin.

She wondered about the family that had never come to see him while he was living. Those grandparents, or whoever they were, who were going to bury him. Why hadn't they sent for him while he was still alive?

Maybe if they had, he would still be living.

Hagar put her hand out and rested it on the trunk of the tree. She didn't like the way she was feeling about the farm today. Had she felt this way yesterday, or was this something coming on only now?

She wanted to talk to her dad suddenly. She had to see him, be near him, absorbed in his security. He had made her feel safe when she was a scared little kid after her mother went away and died. And she needed him again now.

The main house was shrouded in the shade trees that grew in the yard and surrounding open area. Beyond the main house, lined up like houses on a town street, were the farm workers' homes, three small, white frame bungalows, each with three bedrooms, and porches. In the backyard of one house a wife of one of the workers was carrying a basket, as if she had dried something on the clothesline, even though all the houses were equipped with dryers. Hagar walked away from the barn quickly, crossing the little road so many cars and vans had gone down this morning to see about the calf. And Lion. There was talk among the boys that Lion had been trying to protect the calf. Why else would he have been down there alone?

There was something strange about the calf's death, Hagar knew, but she wasn't sure what. Some of the boys had told her it had been tortured, maybe, and had its ears and eyes and nose cut off, and maybe its feet, like the Satan worshippers do when they sacrifice an animal. But how could Satanic cults get onto the farm, she had asked them. They had no answer, and she knew they didn't really know anything about it. None of the kids had been allowed to go down to the death site.

At noon she had asked her dad, and he had given her a short, incomplete answer that she felt did not really explain anything. She could still see him, not touching the sandwich she had made, his fingers tapping the side of his coffee cup, his eyes staring out the window. "Well," he had said after a long pause, "the calf was killed by something. And so was Lion. We don't know what. The vet thinks the calf might have died naturally enough, and then was found by the buzzards." That didn't answer anything, so she hadn't pursued it. There was such horror in knowing that any animal on the farm had been killed, and she knew Lion had been, because one of the boys who helped Orion put him in the coffin had told her the dog had blood all over the fur at his throat. She didn't really want to face the truth of it—whatever that was.

She reached the pickup and slid her hand along the hood as she passed. The engine had cooled, the hood was barely warm. Dad was home now, unless he had gone out without the pickup.

She went through the gate and left it unlatched. Her steps thundered, it seemed to her suddenly sensitive ears, as she ran up the wooden steps and across the porch.

The hall was cool and shadowed, the house quiet. She had thought Gwen might have come back to the house, but it was too quiet for Gwen to be here. There was no radio or television playing.

The office door was standing partway open, and Hagar looked in.

Martin sat at his desk, leaning back in his swivel chair so

far that it looked on the verge of tipping over. He had turned so he could see out the double windows that overlooked the ponds, trees, and sloping land. One foot rested on the edge of the desk.

"Dad?"

He jumped, pulled his foot down, and turned. The chair squealed.

Martin grunted. "Sounds like I need to squirt a little oil on my chair. How are you, kitten?"

"Okay, I guess. You busy, Dad?"

"Doesn't look much like it, does it? Come on in. I've always got time for my girls. You look like you've lost your best friend."

She sat down on the black leather sofa. It was long and soft, and she had always felt better when she could come in here and sink down into it, her feet drawn up, and her head leaning into the arm. In past days she had brought her blanket, a thick, soft, small blanket she'd had since she was seven years old. It was too warm today for the blanket, but she almost wished it wasn't, even though she liked summer a lot better than winter.

"What's up?" Martin asked. "How's Star Beauty?"

"She's fine. She was grazing. Have you seen Gwen?"

"No, not since lunch."

"I was wondering . . ." Hagar looked down at her fingernails. They were short, not bitten anymore, but trimmed short because she thought they looked neater that way. There was a smidge of something dark beneath one, and she dug away at it unsuccessfully. She wanted to talk about Gwen's attraction to the new boy, yet she felt reluctant. "I was wondering, Dad, if you'd ever talked to Gwen about—about the boys."

"The boys? Gwen? Why?"

"I mean about the flirting and that sort of thing."

He made a sound that Hagar guessed was meant to be a laugh.

"Gwen? She's only a baby."

Hagar said nothing, and kept picking at the black speck beneath her fingernail. Gwen, a baby. She had known that was what her dad would say. Did he know she had started

184

her periods? That she was needing a bra? No, she didn't think he did. She did most of the grocery shopping and clothes buying. When Gwen started menstruating, six months ago, so young at barely eleven, Hagar had simply bought Kotex for her, just as she did for herself, without informing her dad. When he looked over the receipts from the store, if he did, he wouldn't have thought anything about it.

Whose responsibility was it to tell him? Hers or Gwen's? Or did he even want to know? When her own period started, she had gone to Rose because it was Rose who had talked to her and explained it all, as well, of course, as her teacher and the nurse. But she had also told her dad. She hadn't been embarrassed to talk to him about it. But something held her back from talking about Gwen now.

It was the depression, she guessed. This new thing that had happened to her.

"I think I'm getting depressed, Dad."

"Why, how do you feel?"

"I feel—like everything is going wrong. I feel, sort of dull. No, I feel sort of scared, I think. As if something really terrible is going to happen to us. To the farm. The boys. Star Beauty. Orion, Rose, Rufus, I don't know. I just feel— bad."

"I think that's probably a normal reaction to what has happened these past few days, Kitten. I feel sort of depressed myself. We miss Rex, and we miss Lion. We weren't very well acquainted with the calf, but we miss him, too. The farm and the rest of us are going to be fine. Don't worry." He leaned forward. "I have something I'd like you to do."

"Okay, what?"

"Go tell Rose, or someone, to announce at supper that we'll be holding our own private little memorial service for Rex tonight at the chapel, at seven, instead of Sunday."

Hagar kissed her dad and went out. She stopped outside the gate. The sun was gone, clouds covered the western half of the sky. Off to her right, secluded in a grove of trees, was the tiny chapel, just large enough to seat the people who lived on the farm. It had a peaked roof and a cross reaching above the trees. Inside it was dim, quiet, and peaceful, and the light that came through the stained glass windows was of a different hue. She thought of going there tonight to bow her head in memory of Rex, and tears came to her eyes.

She walked on toward the bunkhouse. The sound of two mowers reached her, buzzing in harmony beyond the slope of the land. Over in the back fields somewhere a tractor was running, but today it could well have meant the digging of a grave as much as the plowing of a field.

She had thought she would feel better after talking to her dad, but she didn't.

Chapter Nineteen

At age five Marsh had gone to school. In the first grade he had learned to read and write words he could no longer remember. When he tried now, when he was shown a page with words on it, he felt the frustration begin. He hadn't forgotten that once he knew, that once his teacher had touched his shoulder and told him she was proud of him. She had even displayed one of his pages of writing on the school wall as an example of what a first grader could do. Then he was in second grade and he was almost seven years old. And it was then, when he came home from school early one day because of a teacher's meeting, that he had found them.

Marsh huddled in the corner among the spiders and the dark, warm spaces where the barn rafters met the floor of the hay loft. He had dug behind the loose hay that had been left in the barn loft for the nesting hens. It had been a long time since Marsh had hidden here, a long time since he had been so afraid that he had to come to the only place where he could feel safe. The barn loft.

In the barn beneath him he could hear the soft sounds made by the animals as they moved about, eating, leaving and entering gates to stalls left open for their freedom. He could hear them, but the soft sounds barely reached his ears.

He was remembering. Sometimes the memories came back too often and he was six again, going to have his seventh birthday in just a little while.

When will I have my birthday, Mama?

In just two or three months, Marshal. Go out and play with the little kids.

That last day at school he had gotten a stomach ache, and his teacher had let him go home earlier than the other kids. He had walked the two blocks, carrying his little lunch box, the one Uncle Tyler had given him. Uncle Tyler was his mother's brother and he was nicer to Marshal and his little brothers and sisters than Daddy Will, the man who had come to take his own daddy's place. He didn't know where his own daddy had gone. He never came to see them anymore.

He went into the backyard first, just as he always did after school, and saw Jimmy, Dale, and Sharon playing together in the little wading pool. He would have liked to play too, for the day was hot, but the walk home in the burning sun had made him feel that he was going to be sick. His sister and brothers didn't see him. He went up to the screened back door and found it hooked on the inside. He looked into the kitchen, but didn't see his mother.

He went around the house, down the dirt driveway. It was then that he saw Uncle Tyler's pickup pulled in under the tree close to the house.

Old tires and weeds littered the front yard, and there was something about this disorder that bothered him. All the houses on this street were like his, small, with screen doors and porches on the front, but their yards didn't have old tires, and their grass was cut. Someday when he was bigger he was going to cut the grass.

He found the front door open, and he entered the living

room, expecting to see Mama and Uncle Tyler sitting there, drinking beer or coffee, just talking and watching television.

Mama?

I've got a stomachache.

The teacher let me come home.

There's going to be a teacher's meeting this afternoon so I got to come home instead of going to the nurse.

He heard sounds that made his stomach knot in pain. Sounds of groaning, of someone . . . hurting? Someone not himself, the groans, the little cries, as if one person was hurting another . . . and he became afraid.

Mama!

She didn't answer. There were other sounds now, of metal, a door squeaking, or bed springs. It was the same sound he often heard at night from his mother's room, after they had all gone to bed, his mother and Daddy Will in her room, he and his brothers and sister in the other bedroom.

At night he knew not to go to her room. Then he knew, but today, he went to the door, turned the knob, and pushed the door open. He crossed the threshold and stopped.

Mama and Uncle Tyler were on the bed. Mama was naked from the waist down and Uncle Tyler was on top of her, between her legs. He was hurting her. He was pounding up and down with his body.

He wanted to help his mother, to stop Uncle Tyler from what he was doing, yet he stood still, riveted to the spot, unable to move, to even turn his eyes away. He had never seen this thing before, but he knew, he knew, he began to *know*, and the pain was his, not hers, not Uncle Tyler's. He *knew*. Something inside him screamed, why? Why, Mama? But his voice was still. He heard the groans and cries of his mother, saw her hands clutching Uncle Tyler's arms, her head thrown back, her neck arched, her hair hanging long off the bed.

Then she was looking at him, her eyes blazing, and he knew he had committed a terrible wrong by opening this door.

She came at him, and the slap was so hard he felt a sharp pain shoot through the other ear. She hit him, and kept hitting him, until Uncle Tyler made her stop.

He was on the floor, huddled in the corner, crying, his head lowered into the protection of his arms.

Don't you try to hide from me.

Mama, I didn't mean it. Mama, I didn't mean to.

He never went to school again. That night when Daddy Will came home, after the little kids were in bed, they locked him into the dark shed in the backyard. He could smell the dirt of the floor, and hear the squirming movements of worms, mice, and spiders. But he wasn't afraid of them, he was only afraid of the door opening. The warm wood at his back comforted him, and he tried to crawl into it. He pressed his face against the rough, warm wood and felt it as he once had felt his mother's arms.

During the day he saw light through the cracks. When it rained he put his tongue through the cracks to suck drops of water into his dry, parched throat.

He would never tell. He wanted to promise his mother he would never tell. But she didn't come to him. Not until the middle of the dark night did the door open, finally, and someone stood there. He wasn't sure who was with his mother. The light from the flashlight blinded him. He could barely make out the outlines of a head and shoulders. Daddy Will, he thought, but he wasn't sure. No, Uncle Tyler. Then he heard his mother's voice, and knew she was there, too. *Do it,* she said. *Hurry.*

He saw the light glinting on something sharp, but it moved into the air and came toward him so swiftly it might have been coming out of the ceiling of the shed.

He felt it cut into his head, and knew they were going to kill him. Kill him and bury him here in the soft dirt of the shed as his mama had buried the kittens after she drowned them. He knew, and he screamed.

He screamed, and screamed.

It echoed through his head for days and weeks after he opened his eyes and found himself in a small bed with railings, in a room with a lot of other children.

He learned it was a hospital.

He never saw his mother again. Or his Uncle Tyler, or Daddy Will.

Sometimes he thought about Sharon and Jimmy and

Dale, and wondered if they were dead, too. Then he remembered he was not dead. But he couldn't remember the words now, or how the letters formed them. Sometimes, when he was alone, when he was sure no one was watching, he would take a book from the table of one of the other boys and he would look at it and try to remember. But something was wrong now, in his head.

He pressed his cheek against the rough, warm boards of the barn loft, and silenced the cries in his throat and heart.

Bad people. They had been bad people.

Now that he was away from his mother he knew she had been bad to him, always. He had seen things. He had seen it before, like a dim and shadowy dream, and he had told his daddy, and that night his daddy had taken his suitcase and left. And after that, his mother hated Marsh.

Why are you dodging?

And she laughed.

She had enjoyed drawing back her hand and making him dodge.

She had enjoyed whipping him with the belt that had the buckle on the end.

And she had liked doing that thing with Uncle Tyler.

Had Daddy Will left, too?

Marsh thought he had.

While he was in the shed those days and nights.

Here, there were no bad people.

Not until the new boy came.

He wanted to tell Rufus, but he didn't want to hurt Rufus's feelings. He hadn't wanted Rufus to know that Lion was dead, but he had found out. Rufus loved all the boys, he knew. The boys were Rufus's family. He had heard Rufus say they were. It would hurt Rufus's feelings to know that one of his boys was a bad person.

Marsh had told the detective, but he hadn't heard.

Marsh couldn't tell Rufus.

Rufus went back to the barn for the third time. It was getting close to the supper hour, and still Marsh hadn't shown up. He tried to control the panic and desperation

190

that were making his chest feel tight, as if a band was around it and being tightened another notch with each breath he took. He couldn't have a heart attack, not now. He had to find Marsh and try to figure out what to do about him, how to keep him safe from his own actions, from the consequences. They couldn't lock Marsh away.

He looked into the horse's stall, and saw she was eating hay that one of the boys had put into her manger. She looked at him with big, curious eyes, her ears on the alert. He reached through the boards of the manger and scratched between her ears.

"It's all right, girl. Didn't mean to disturb you."

At her side was the goat, Isabelle, the one that had lived in the paddock with Star Beauty since she was a cute little kid, no larger than a pup. Every horse, Orion said, needed company, just like people, just like most warm-blooded animals. They needed their own pets, you might say. A dog, a cat, a rooster, a goat, sheep, another horse or a cow. Something alive and friendly. Every creature needed someone to love. Rufus scratched between the ears of the goat, too, and said a few words to her before he went on down the corridor of the barn.

He stopped. It was almost dark in the corridor. The sky had turned overcast during the afternoon, and the barn was darker than ever. There were lights strung through the middle rooms and corridors, but he hadn't turned them on.

In the early years, Marsh had come into the barn. Rufus had found him huddled into corners of the barn many times during that first year especially, his face pressed against the wood as if he was trying to become part of it. Gently he had gotten the little boy up, and holding his hand, had led him away, out into the sunshine, into the animal pens, and had taught him to find solace there, with the animals.

Had he reverted? What was in the boy to cause him to turn on the same animals he had loved, to turn on them and kill them so viciously?

Rufus felt nauseated. Marsh meant more to him than anyone in the world. He couldn't stand what was happening to him.

What had caused it?

Rex's death?

"Marsh!"

His voice echoed in the barn. He heard movement in the stalls, and he heard a chicken squawk as it flew down from a perch. The flutter of wings was soft, and then there was silence for a moment.

But overhead, in the loft, a board squeaked.

"Marsh? You up there?"

There were more movements, the rustling of hay, then footsteps in the loft.

Rufus went down the corridor to the opening into the loft. Built against the wall was a ladder leading up to a hole measuring about four by four.

Footsteps came to the hole, and Marsh looked down.

"I'm here, Rufus," he said.

Rufus felt almost faint with relief. He had spent the afternoon looking for Marsh. He had been through the barn three times, looking into corners that Marsh had gone to ten years ago, that fall when he came to the farm.

"Come on down, Marsh," Rufus said.

Marsh climbed down the ladder, and Rufus waited, watching him, wondering. Would Marsh turn on him now, tonight or tomorrow, and kill him, too? He almost wished he would, and somehow end it for them both. But it wouldn't happen that way. It wouldn't be ended for Marsh.

"It's time to eat, Marsh," Rufus said when the boy stood beside him. "I've been looking for you. Have you been in the loft a long time?"

Marsh's face was hard to see in the dim light. Rufus could only guess at the expression. He had learned to read the expressions on Marsh's face because that was the only way to get any idea of how he was feeling. Marsh seemed unable to express himself in any normal way.

But in all these years, Rufus had never seen violence in that face. He had never seen anything but fear, sadness, and gentleness. He put his hand on Marsh's shoulder.

"What has happened to you, boy?" he asked.

Marsh didn't look at him, and after a moment Rufus gave his shoulder a little pat, guiding him outside.

They walked together in silence across the green park,

toward the bunkhouse. Lightning streaked the sky in the west. The clouds there had darkened. The lightning was silent, like a scar. Rufus was reminded of the scar that had marred Marsh's face. Over the years it had lost the bright red color and turned white. It went jaggedly from his scalp to his chin, like the lightning in the western sky.

Gwen wanted to sit beside Patrick at the chapel, but Hagar had gotten her by the arm and made her go on up to the front where they always sat on the rare occasions when they went to the chapel for service. Always on the front pew, with their backs to the boys. Rose sat here, and Orion, and if someone else gave the talk, their dad sat with them. But tonight Martin was standing at the podium, waiting for everyone to settle down. Gwen had no choice but to slide down beside Rose. She was between Rose and Hagar, Orion was on the other side of Hagar.

Martin began to talk about Rex. He had come to the farm when he was ten, and he had been happy here. He had been a straight-A student in school and had many friends.

Gwen heard her dad speaking in a deep, soft tone, but his words began going over her head, soothing her, but not interfering with her thoughts. Patrick was somewhere in a pew behind her, and she dared finally to turn her head and look around.

In the pew behind her sat Rufus, and beside him, head down, was Marsh. She saw familiar faces, but not Patrick's. She twisted in the seat to look deeper into the small, high-ceilinged room, and saw Vance. He sat tall in the seat, his head higher than the boys on each side. His tanned, thin face was as sober and serious as Rufus's or her dad's. She looked beyond him, trying to locate Patrick.

Just as she found him on the back pew, his oval face handsome, his eyes meeting hers, it seemed, Hagar elbowed her in the stomach.

Gwen straightened, saw the silent glare in Hagar's eyes, and made herself sit still for the rest of the eulogy.

When it was over, she tried to find Patrick in the crowd,

but Hagar had a hold on her arm again. Gwen shrugged it off, but stayed with her sister and Rose, waiting for her dad.

Together, they went out into the twilight deepened by the clouds. She saw lightning, and heard the soft rumble of thunder, and listened to the adults making conversation.

"Think it'll rain?" Rufus asked.

"Probably not," Martin said. "That's a long way off yet."

"It'll go north," Orion said, "like they've been doing lately."

They walked. Ahead of them the boys scattered, some running, two of them throwing something back and forth. Trailing the others as they made their way toward the bunkhouse was Patrick. When he turned and looked back, she knew he was looking at her, in a sense saying good night to her, knowing that she would be taking the path to the left, away from the bunkhouse, with her dad and sister.

It was the greatest feeling, she thought, as she bounced ahead and ran on to the gate to wait for Hagar and Martin. The greatest feeling, knowing that he liked her as well as she liked him. That he would be here tomorrow and the next day, and the next, that she would be seeing him from now on, and they would even go to school together, if he stayed, because he had told her he was in the sixth grade, just as she was.

They might even get to sit together on the school bus.

If he left, if he went home, he would write to her, and she to him.

From her bedroom window later, she thought she saw him on the bunkhouse porch, looking toward her.

She knew in her heart that he was there.

Looking for her.

What have you done to her?

Paddy saw the twisted face of his father, but he couldn't remember what was wrong. The taste was in his mouth again, and that blackness that came, that made him know he had been . . . not there . . . not aware. He tried to think back. What had happened? He had gone into the attic, up those dark, steep stairs, and he had walked across the boards to the plastic clothes holder, and he had reached in and stroked the fur on the back of the jacket. . . .

Listen. . . .

They were under the trees, beside Jill's body.

Justin was looking up at the trees beneath which Jill lay, and Paddy saw the torture in his face. He saw Justin cringe, and he knew why. Something was flying through the air. It was flying . . . it that needed eyes because it had none of its own . . . because long ago when it had been killed, its eyes had rotted away. But the men who had killed it didn't know it could fly by instinct, that its wings knew what its eyes could no longer see.

Then the night was still again.

For a long time they stayed by Jill's body. Paddy saw her in the moonlight, the shadows of the trees no longer covering her, and he saw that like the furry vampire bat on the back of Justin's jacket, Jill had no eyes. She lay dead, her skin white as paper, her eyes as empty as the eyes of the vampire bat.

As dawn lightened the sky and took part of the black shadows from beneath the forest trees, Justin went into the house and came out with a sheet. He spread it on the ground and rolled Jill in it. She lay still, like a plaster doll.

Take her feet . . .

It was an order, and Paddy carried her feet, shrouded in the white sheet from her bed. They went into the forest, on and on, and then Justin laid her down. Stay with her, he had told Paddy, and Paddy sat hunched over as he waited.

Justin came back with a shovel and dug the grave.

When they got back to the house there was nothing but silence.

Justin never spoke to Paddy again.

Light flashed in Paddy's eyes and was gone. He was left in a dark place, as black as the fur of the vampire on his dad's jacket, and he felt smothered in it. He could feel the fur against his face, pressing down. The fur wasn't soft and silky, like the fur of a kitten, it was harsh and rough, as if each tiny hair ended in a stinger of poison. He tried to get away from it, and the light flashed again, and showed him a haunted forest. The light was strange, bluish, unreal. The vampire was hovering over him, and he saw its eyeless face in the unreal light as the blood-red fangs came closer to his throat. He tried to cry out and could not. He twisted over, his face in the black soil of the forest floor, and began to crawl. The black wings stirred the air above him, and the talons gripped him and held him back. His opened mouth was voiceless, his call silent.

Mama . . . Daddy . . .

He woke.

The light flashed again, and he saw it was from the storm still far away. For a moment the room before him was unfamiliar, and the fear that held him in his bed as intense as the fear in his dream. A dream that was not a dream, but a memory. That first night—the night he had learned the vampire could lift itself off the coat and fly at will, that it rested in the dark privacy of closet or garment bag only during the day. He had gone to his dad and told him, and Justin had only stared at him in a horrible way, and tried to laugh. "You're dreaming, kid." *You're dreaming, kid. You're . . .*

The lightning swelled silently into the bunkhouse, an unreal bluish white, and even as he recognized the room in which his bed was only one of many, he also saw the haunted trunks of trees in an endless black forest that reached beyond the walls. He tried to sit up, to call out, to warn those sleeping boys they were in danger. They must run, hurry, escape into the light.

A faint wind stirred the black leaves of the haunted forest.

It came, skimming low over the cots of the sleeping boys, its wingspread like a prehistoric monster, a survivor of distant times and distant worlds, of hell and darkness and a horrible immortality. Paddy tried to scream to the boys to run, to hurry to the light, but it was coming on, its wings sucking the air from the room, and consciousness from the boys. It was coming onward, just as it always had, toward him, toward Paddy.

It pressed him helplessly backward, so he couldn't move

and couldn't speak, and he wondered as the fangs sank for the final time into his throat if the vampire had ever lived at all—or if, as Justin had said, he had only dreamed it.

Patrick sat up in bed.

The dark surrounded him softly. He belonged to the dark, the distant, endlessness of time and space. The child, Paddy, had scarcely struggled at the end, too weak even to cry out for his mama.

Patrick smiled, and rose from the bed.

He moved toward the open door.

The girl-child was waiting for him.

Chapter Twenty

The storm covering still hung in the west, the lightning distant, like blood veins, thin and wandering, the thunder soft moans from a dying god. The west sky was black with clouds, while the eastern sky looked midnight blue, twinkling with the hazy lights of stars and planets. Farther east, the moon was as round and full as the bloody eyeball of a dead calf.

Rufus had lit his pipe, though some of the boys were still on the porch. His hand clutched the warmth of the bowl as if it was sanity itself, as if it was yesterday, last month, last year, when all was well. A man forgot his own peacefulness until it was disrupted. A man got stuck in his own mud of tranquility, only to find out it was quicksand.

Marsh usually sat on the edge of the porch, beside the post in front of Rufus, with his legs swinging. He usually sat there with Lion by his side, Lion's paws drooping off the porch, Marsh's hand caressing the long fur on Lion's neck. They would watch the fireflies—lightning bugs, as Rufus had always thought of them. They would count sometimes, and it was just such a time a few years ago that Rufus had learned Marsh could count. He had marveled at the time Marsh counted to two hundred and forty pointing out fireflies. The next day Rufus had gone to Mr. Preston and asked him about that.

"Last night, Marsh counted lightning bugs, Mr. Preston. And he made it up to two hundred and forty before he quit. I thought Marsh wasn't—uh well—bright enough to learn like that. I'd like to know what his records claim. I was wondering maybe if he ought to go to school. If maybe he's capable of learning a lot more."

It was then he found out that Marsh had been in the second grade, and was in the top ten percent of the students at that school when the brutal attack occurred. But he also was told that the doctors felt the brain damage was such that Marsh would not be able to learn, that he had forgotten what he knew.

Mr. Preston told Rufus to watch him, and if there were any signs that the brain damage was not as extensive as the doctors thought, then they would see to it that Marsh got his chance.

Rufus had gone to a store and carefully chosen one of the little picture books, given it to Marsh and asked him to read the words beneath the pictures. Marsh had looked at them, and his face had begun to grimace as if he was in terrible pain. He tried to speak and was unable to do more than make a sound. He had finally collapsed into a terrible weeping that almost broke Rufus's heart. At that moment Rufus decided this boy was his, to love and keep all his life, and to never pressure into anything he was incapable of handling. Whether it was an inability to learn, he wasn't sure. He thought there might be something psychological about it too. A mental block of some kind. The boy associated learning, or especially reading and writing, with something in his past that was too horrible to remember.

From that time, Rufus became Marsh's guardian—his

grandfather, father, and mother. But it was in heart only, not legally.

The thought of seeing Marsh behind bars, in a mental institution, was more than Rufus could handle. That would happen, he knew. Marsh wouldn't be free to walk in the grass anymore, to sit on a porch like this and swing his legs.

Tonight Marsh was at the wall behind Rufus. Last night he had been at the wall behind Rufus, huddled in the shadows there, the light from the bunkhouse windows spilling out past him, creating a pathway to the edge of the porch where Lion used to sleep.

Rufus puffed on his pipe to keep the bowl warm, almost hot, in his hands. Through the thick skin of his hand, the heat felt comfortingly painful. He had been thinking all day that he had to talk to Marsh. Talking might explain some things to him satisfactorily, so that he would at least halfway understand why Marsh had done this horrible thing. Rufus knew what he should do. He should have gone straight to Mr. Preston with the evidence and asked him for help. But he also knew what Mr. Preston would have done. He would have called in the nurse and the doctor who examined the boys at regular intervals and prescribed medicine for their colds, and the therapist who talked to them when they needed help. And the ball would have started rolling, and it wouldn't have quit until Marsh was in the hospital for the insane—the crazy, the mad and the dangerous.

Rose came onto the porch from the breezeway and said, "Do you boys know it's almost ten o'clock? Time to go to bed, all of you."

Other boys came out of the breezeway behind Rose, and Rufus knew the TV in the main room had been turned off. They filed through the door into the cloakroom, their voices muffled as the bathroom door closed behind them. The few boys who had been sitting quietly on the porch got up and went into the bunkhouse, and Rufus heard Marsh rise. Rose said goodnight and disappeared back into the breezeway. Orion was gone tonight, as he usually was a couple of times a week. His car would return about midnight, and he would use his key to unlock and lock the service gate as he came through. He had told Rufus once that he played poker with some guys now and then, and Rufus supposed he had a girlfriend now and then, too.

"Marsh," Rufus said, and heard Marsh pause just outside the door.

Rufus got up and went to the post where he always knocked the ashes out of his pipe, but he wasn't ready to empty his pipe and leave his hand empty tonight. From the corner of his eye he could see the outline of Marsh's slump-shouldered body in the dim light from the doorway.

"Come and take a walk with me, Marsh."

Marsh hesitated, and Rufus understood this was a precedent to Marsh. Never in all their years had Rufus asked that of Marsh. On all other nights at bedtime, Rufus told Marsh good night, that was all. Good night, Marsh, sleep tight, don't let the bedbugs bite. Marsh always giggled at that because, he had said once, it was so silly. His bed didn't have bugs. Rufus supposed most people didn't know what bedbugs were anymore. He'd only seen a couple himself, when he was a kid and on the bum. Something had started biting him one night when he was rolled in his blanket beneath a bridge where the hobos hung out, and one of the old hobos had told him he had bedbugs. The next day he had examined his blanket and found some odd flat little critters that resembled ticks in shape and size, and he had washed his blanket in the river all day long. He had knelt on the rocky river bank and washed the hell out of that blanket. The older hobos had laughed at him, and laughed and laughed, and the more they laughed, the madder young Rufus got.

But he never had any more bedbugs.

Rufus looked back at Marsh, and at last Marsh moved forward. Rufus understood. To Marsh this was breaking a rule. Bedtime at ten on a weeknight, eleven on the weekend.

"It's all right, Marsh, if you're quiet when you go to bed and don't disturb the other boys. I think we need to talk."

Marsh came wordlessly down the steps. The one board let out its long squeak, and Rufus realized he had stepped in the middle of it. He had learned to walk at the outer edge where the board had more support.

"We got to fix this board, Marsh. We been putting it off too long."

"When, Rufus? Tomorrow?"

"Yes, tomorrow."

"I—I know where there's a board. I'll get it."

"All right, you do that. Bring it up tomorrow morning, and we'll get it put down."

"It's in the barn. Some loose boards."

"Oh. Probably those left over when the horse stall was boxed in."

"Yeah, that."

They walked toward the barns. The shade trees looked black in the moonlight.

"Is it going to rain, Marsh?"

"Yep. Lots of popping. Long way off. Fire in the sky."

"I thought maybe the storm was going to peter out, the way it seems to be stuck back there in the west."

Marsh held up his hand. "No. It's slow, that's all. The damp—air damp."

Sometimes it was almost as if Marsh was normal. His sentences were always short, but sometimes they made perfect sense. Especially about the weather, Marsh seemed to have a sixth sense.

Rufus stopped at the old tractor and turned so that he could see Marsh's face softly illuminated by the moonlight. Marsh's head was lifted, his eyes looking beyond Rufus toward the lower farm.

"I want to talk to you, Marsh," Rufus began, and saw Marsh's eyes focus on him. "About Lion—and the calf. I want to know, Marsh, did you go out of the house last night—"

The change in Marsh came suddenly. He began to act as if he was rooted to the ground, yet trying to escape. His upper body turned, his hands lifted and made jerking, nervous motions. He jerked his head one way, then the other, as if he was being slapped repeatedly. Rufus felt he had unloosed some terrible trauma in the boy's memory, and was sorry he had said anything. But then he remembered that Marsh was guilty, and this was his way of trying to escape it.

201

"Marsh, Marsh!" Rufus stuffed his pipe into his shirt pocket and put both hands on Marsh's shoulders. "Listen to me, Marsh. You can tell me. Talk to me about it. What happened? Why did you kill Lion? Why did you hurt the calf, Marsh? You've never done anything like that before. Why did you do it now?"

"No—no! Bad boy—bad boy—!"

Marsh was crying. Rufus could see the tears flowing down his cheeks, catching the light of the moon and looking like drops of glistening oil. They ran into the twisted corner of Marsh's mouth as he shook his head and motioned wildly with his hands.

"No, no, no . . . bad boy . . . *bad boy* . . ."

Rufus began trying to soothe him. He patted Marsh's shoulder, shook him, and shook him again. "Marsh! There, it's all right, you're with me. Marsh. *Marsh.*"

Marsh's hands reached out for Rufus, grasping his over-all galluses, pulling, jerking back and forth on Rufus. His face had come close, the tears smeared but his eyes taking on a fierceness, a desperation.

"Believe me . . . believe me . . . Rufus . . . bad boy, bad boy . . ."

And then he was only making noises, the words indistinguishable from one another until it was nothing but jabbering. The strength with which Marsh tugged at him made Rufus know that Marsh could kill him now easily if he deteriorated that much into whatever had caused him to kill the animals.

Rufus stopped trying to calm him and merely stood, waiting for the storm within Marsh to subside. He saw the boy slump, his shoulders droop. His head bowed and the jabbering stopped. At last, his hands released Rufus's galluses.

They stood in silence.

After a few minutes, Rufus patted Marsh's shoulder, and turned him back toward the bunkhouse.

"It's time to go to bed, Marsh."

They walked slowly, with Rufus's hand on Marsh's back. What had his accusation done to the boy? What monsters were in this boy that Rufus had never known about, and would never know? Therapy had been no help to Marsh because he couldn't express himself. Rufus had felt it was better to just let the boy forget the attempted murder by people who were supposed to care for him, let him forget and live in peace.

He had never dreamed Marsh would turn on something he loved, and kill.

At the door to the bunkhouse bedroom, Rufus said good night.

Marsh tried to answer, but his throat gave forth only grunts. Then he turned, and almost running, stumbling clumsily in the dark went to his cot.

Rufus waited, listening for Marsh to get into bed. The light from the bathroom, left on tonight, sent a twilight dimness a few feet down the aisle of the bunkhouse bedroom. As Rufus's eyes adjusted to the near-dark he could see that Marsh had gotten into bed and covered himself completely. It looked as if he had even put his head under his pillow.

In the next cot the new boy, Patrick, slept. His head was on his pillow, lying in the dead center, and his arms lay on top of his light summer blanket. He was on his back, and when Rufus first looked at him, it seemed his eyes were open and watching, but as Rufus looked again, the eyes seemed closed.

Rufus glanced down the long rows of beds, and saw boys sprawled in all shapes and positions, some of them on their stomachs, some with legs hanging off their beds, most of them uncovered.

But Marsh was huddled, hiding beneath his blanket, his body facing the end of the room, facing the new boy who lay so precisely in the center of his bed, like a body in its coffin.

He rose slowly. The bunkhouse had been quiet for a long time now, and it was time to go. He could sense the fear of the trembling body in the cot next to his, and stood a moment at the side of the cot just to enjoy the terror of the other, the power he received from a trembling body. He looked down upon the covered hulk, his mouth curled in

203

disgust. Then he turned away, picked up the jeans at the foot of the bed and pulled them on.

Human trappings, so foolish, but so necessary when one had to mingle in a human world.

The boy, Paddy, was gone. He had made a last struggle during the day, but had weakened. He knew, and felt contempt, for the weakling that had been himself just a few hours ago. The sunshine had almost brought the boy back, but the sunshine had weakened, too, as clouds concealed it, as the day drifted onward. Human clocks divided the day into degrees of time, but were unable to influence its passing in any way. And the night came, as surely as the vampires rose.

He needed human blood. Animal blood was a poor second, still being in the lower stages of evolution. Human blood was a step upward, but only a step, a degree, like the degrees of time arranged by the human mind. Did the humans know that any animal could pinpoint a certain time of day without benefit of such devices as clock? In those ways, and in others, they were not inferior, but their blood did not satisfy his need. Their fear did not give him the power lift that human fear gave. Human blood, human fear.

The trembling Marsh had gone to sleep. He moaned, and his body went into a brief spasm. Patrick stood still, looking back at him. It would be so easy . . . pull back the blanket . . . the boy would never know. Just as the fat boy had not known. Except for a long, long moment of silent terror.

But it was the girl he wanted.

The girl he needed.

He went out onto the porch and stood still, looking across the moonlit park toward the main house. Moonlight touched a window there, but it was not the window where the girl was. Her window was on the dark side of the house.

She would be sleeping now, but her window would surely be raised to let in the cool evening air.

He went to the end of the porch and leaped down, and then he was running as if he could lift his arms and fly, silently loping across the grass, from shadow to shadow, the moonlight soft on his head.

He left the yard gate open, and went around to the side

of the house and put his hands on the window screen. It was latched tightly. He took the knife from his pocket and wedged the blade into the corner of the screen. He had forgotten about the screen. Windows had screens, and they always had to be cut.

The knife slipped in, making a thick, metallic cutting sound.

Gwen woke.

She lay blinking, looking at the ceiling fan; its blades were still on this cool night. A night light in the hallway beyond her partly open door showed her the dark outlines of the fan blades, and she could see where the edge of the white ceiling met the blue and pink floral wallpaper.

Something was pecking at her window. No, the sound was louder, steadier, a ripping and scratching, as if something was at the screen. It was like an insect lighting there, its feet like claws that dug at the tiny wires of the screen as it clung there, trying to enter, to get to the light.

But there was no light in her room.

She jerked up in bed, her heart pounding. The sound at the screen was not an insect. It was something else.

She stared at the window, and saw the moonlight shining on the metal posts of the fence. And she saw the outline of a head and shoulders.

His face, for just an instant, seemed pressed to her window screen. Oval, pale, even in the shadows.

"Patrick?"

The sound at the screen stopped, and she knew he could see her in the dimness of her room. She threw back her covers and sat up. It was Patrick at the window, scratching the woven wire of the screen with something sharp, trying to wake her.

It was wild, it was romantic.

She ran to the window and knelt beside it, her face close to the wire.

"Patrick," she whispered.

"Open the screen," he said, returning her whisper. "Unlatch the screen, Gwen."

"Yes, yes," she whispered, stealing a glance over her shoulder at the half open door, as if Hagar or her dad was standing there watching her do this terribly wicked thing. It was wild. Wickedly wild. She could hardly wait for tomorrow so she could call her best friend Stacy and tell her about it. How romantic to have a boy come to your window. It was just like a romance novel of the last century.

Her fingers fumbled with the screen hook. It was so tight she could hardly move it.

"Hurry," Patrick whispered. "Hurry, I need you."

For just an instant the dark outline of his shoulders had the sharp, raised effect of folded wings—as if he wasn't Patrick at all, but a winged creature hunched outside her window.

Chapter Twenty-One

Babette listened to the noises in the neighborhood decrease. She lay so tensely in her bed that her muscles began to ache. She had been waiting, waiting all her life, it seemed today. She could see Ketti leaving the jail, going right away to the Boys' Farm where Paddy lived. They would let her in, wouldn't they? They wouldn't deny a mother access, would they? She would tell them she wanted to see her son. And then . . . and then . . .

Something was wrong with her imagery. She couldn't move it from there.

She could see Ketti at home. She could see her opening the drawer and taking out the *Wolfsbane*.

She could see her getting into the old car and leaving—but—

Going to Paddy? Killing him?

Would she buy a gun first? A handgun at the pawn shop?

Or would she have gone to bed, this first night out of jail, to try to sleep and rest?

Yes, Babette thought. Maybe she had. She prayed her mother had gone to her own bed this first night out of jail.

If Babette hurried, she would be able to catch Ketti before she left home. Maybe. Yes, she had to.

The younger children had been put to bed at eight, and at ten, it was her turn to go. Then she had listened. She heard soft movements of the parents in the house, an occasional murmur of voices. The television had been turned off after the news, and the hall light turned low. The woman had gone to each of the bedrooms to look in, and Babette heard her enter the room where she and two of the little girls slept. She closed her eyes tightly and waited. She heard the soft movement of blankets as Mother Ann covered each little girl, then her soft footsteps carried her to Babette's cot where she hesitated. Babette could feel the scrutiny. Did she know? Did she suspect that Babette was not asleep, that she was waiting to slip out when the night grew quiet?

Miss Thornton would have told her about Ketti. Mother Ann probably had been told more than Babette.

The footsteps left, and the door closed softly.

The night sounds decreased even more. There was no traffic on the street now. Down the block a dog barked a few times, then hushed, and much farther away, another dog barked, his voice sounding like an echo of the first.

The house was quiet, but Babette dared not move. Another fifteen minutes, she told herself. Another ten. . . .

She had no way of telling the time. Her sense of time was distorted, she knew. Seconds seemed like minutes. It had been that way all day, since Miss Thornton had come, bringing the news about Ketti.

She could stand it no longer.

She got out of bed and reached beneath it where she had laid her folded jeans and shirt. She put them on quietly, holding her breath, pausing at the rustle of heavy denim going over her legs and hips. She waited, listening, but the house was quiet.

She wished she had fixed the window so she could climb

out of it—that would have been the safest way. The room was dark now, and she moved carefully through the darkness, hoping that one of the girls hadn't left a toy where she would step on it and create a noise that would bring Mother Ann. Feeling with each bare foot, moving forward an inch at a time, she reached the window at last.

She pushed back the curtains and found the window raised about three inches. With her hands carefully placed beneath it, she applied pressure. The window did not move.

She pushed harder, and the window shrieked upward a fraction of an inch. Horrified at the sound, she drew back and watched the door, expecting it to open. The difficult window was almost like an alarm system, it was so tight in its frame. She blamed herself for not checking it out during the day, for not having raised it when no one was in the house to hear.

The door didn't open. She stood watching it, listening for footsteps for what seemed like an eternity. She didn't dare get caught. If Mother Ann caught her trying to run away, the authorities would be called, and Babette would be moved somewhere else. To a detention home, probably, from the stories she had heard, and from things Miss Thornton had told her. There she would be living behind as much security as the young criminals, the runaways, the incorrigibles. She hadn't done anything, yet she would be treated as if she had.

Mother Ann hadn't heard, she now realized. But in order to get out of the house, she would have to use the backdoor. Never the front—it was too close to the master bedroom.

She went back to her cot, put on her sandals, and pulled her clothes out from under the bed.

When she opened the bedroom door, she prayed that it be silent, and it was, as if God had heard her. A night light in the hall seemed far brighter than it was, making her feel exposed. Eyes were watching her, it seemed. Eyes from the bed behind her, eyes from the master bedroom, eyes looking through the walls.

She had to hurry now and get out. If she waited much longer she would panic, her imagination making her feel as if something was ready to pounce on her. She had a fleeting notion of how small animals felt when they tried to leave their lairs, knowing that predators were all around, in the grass, in the sky.

She decided to go on as if she was headed for the kitchen to get a drink of water. Quietly, but surely. She moved into the hall, saw that the master bedroom at the front end of the hall was closed. Turning left toward the kitchen, she hurried, the bundle pressed against her side.

"Babette."

Babette let out a cry, frightened, desperate, too soft to be heard beyond her own ears. She turned, her heart falling, her hope gone.

Mother Ann stood in the master bedroom doorway in her nightgown. "Go back to bed, Babette."

Babette felt like crying. She swallowed a huge knot that had risen into her throat, and it felt as if the knot expanded, filling her chest, her head.

"You don't understand," she whispered, her voice carrying in the hallway. "I have to get to my brother before my mother does."

Mother Ann's brown eyes became soft with sympathy. She came down the hall and put her arms around Babette for a moment. Then guiding her with one arm still at her shoulders, she said, "Your brother's at Boys' Farm. It is very secure. No one can enter without going through the main gates. Don't worry. We'll work something out. Go back to bed now. You know I can't allow you to leave here without someone coming for you."

Babette was escorted back to her bed, and Mother Ann began helping her undress. She had pulled the jeans on over her pajamas, Babette now realized. She had done it all wrong.

She had done everything wrong and she had failed.

Rufus jerked up his head. He had fallen asleep, without meaning to. He was going to stay awake nights from now on, somehow, and make sure that Marsh did not leave the bunkhouse. But he had fallen asleep.

He got out of his bed and went barefoot down the hall to the bunkroom, flashlight in hand.

He turned the light on, and aimed the beam at Marsh's bed.

He was there, under the blankets, just as he had been when Rufus left him.

Rufus felt himself relax. He snapped off the light. Down the aisle somewhere a couple of boys were snoring. In the wall a small critter moved, rattling paper or leaves or insulation, as if it was making a bed. Chipmunks used the crevices of the buildings as much as mice. And none of them minded the chipmunks. They didn't mind the mice too much either, if they kept on their own side of the wall.

Rufus went back to the bathroom, and got himself a glass of water, then went back to his room, leaving the door open. He propped it back with one of his shoes so the breeze through the open window would not blow it shut. The storm was still in the west. He could hear faint rumbles of thunder, but it seemed closer now than it had at suppertime.

He sat down in his armchair and leaned his head back against the headrest, a cushion he had pinned there some time ago. He was only going to rest his eyes. But he wouldn't sleep.

If Marsh tried to leave the bunkroom, Rufus would hear. The floors were covered in tile, and the porch was plain boards. Footsteps could not be disguised. Rufus would hear, he was sure. But he had a feeling that Marsh was sleeping tonight, that he would not leave his bed.

Gwen discovered the latch was stuck. She couldn't open it. The sharp point of the hook dug into her fingers and made them hurt.

"I can't," she whispered. "It won't open."

"I'll cut it," he said, and she saw that he had a knife. Moonlight touched the blade for just a second, creating a glisten that made her mouth drop in surprise.

"Hey," she whispered shrilly. "You can't! Don't do that."

He stopped, and the glinting blade disappeared. His face

was inches from hers, only the wire was separating them. He would kiss her, she felt, her heart racing with excitement, if only the screen wasn't between them. How romantic, how utterly, wildly romantic. If only her friends could see them now.

"Come on out then," he said.

She nodded. "All right." It wasn't wrong. Not really. The moon was shining, covering the land like a cap of pale light. Everything was so quiet and so perfect for a walk in the night.

"I'll come out the backdoor," she whispered. "Wait right where you are."

She slipped away from the window and went on tiptoes to her door and out into the hall. Hagar's bedroom door was closed. Farther along the hall, she saw the dark rectangle of her dad's bedroom door. It was wide open and she could hear him breathing long, deep inhales and exhales of air, almost snores. He was deeply asleep, he wouldn't wake and hear her.

Feeling as if she was as free as air, she ran barefoot down the hall to the kitchen door. She turned the knob, heard the soft click of the lock releasing. Sometimes, she knew, the door wasn't even locked. In fact, this seemed to be a first, so far as she knew. Was it because of the dog and the calf being killed last night?

She hesitated, the cool night air brushing her legs and arms and raising goosebumps.

She stood on the back porch, remembering, feeling a little scared suddenly. The shadows beneath the trees in the backyard were so dark and black, without form. Behind the black was the dim, fragile light of the moon spread out over the land.

But last night something had killed within these fences. And she wanted to go back inside, to the security of her room, and talk to Patrick through the screen again. That was romantic. This was frightening. The chills on her skin weren't caused by cold.

She turned back to enter the kitchen, and something cold and dry clutched her arm.

Her cry came involuntarily. Her heartbeats were crashing

through her and fear was almost blinding and paralyzing her.

The hand slapped over her mouth and deadened the cry, and she looked over the edge of the hand into the oval face, just a couple of inches above hers, a pale, ghost-like image in the dark.

"Shhh," he cautioned. "You'll get us both in trouble."

Oh God, Patrick. She almost collapsed. His arm supported her. She felt his hand ease up on her face and then slide slowly away.

"I'm sorry if I scared you," he whispered, and it seemed to her there was amusement in his voice. She wished she could see his eyes, but they were lost in the oval of his face, almost as if he had no eyes at all.

"It was what happened last night," she told him. "Not you." Yet it had been him at that moment of terrible fright—the surprise of him taking hold of her arm when she had thought she was alone. A spark of anger made her feel stronger. "I told you to wait for me around there! By the window."

"I was afraid you'd change your mind, and you did, too, didn't you? You were going back into the house."

She gave her head a toss. She could feel her hair swinging over her shoulders and back, soft strands protecting her from the cool air like a cloak. She had taken her hair down from its braids before she went to bed. She had sat at her dressing table brushing it, and brushing it, feeling it with her fingers, and thinking of Patrick.

His hand slid down her arm, and his fingers caught hers, threading with them.

It was the first time a boy had ever held her hand like that.

"Let's walk in the moonlight," he said, his breath cool against her cheek.

She hesitated, thinking again of the killing of the animals. She wanted to talk about it, to ask him if he thought they should, but it would ruin everything. All the romance of the evening would be gone.

"Let's not go far," she said.

"We won't. We'll just walk by the ponds."

"Okay."

They walked in silence through the dark at the side of the house.

The gate was open, and they went through it and toward the first of the ponds. It was then, in the moonlight, that Gwen remembered she was wearing her shorty pajamas. She felt a little rush of embarrassment, then was glad she had put on her newest pair, a lacy top and thin bikini panties. The top covered her to her thighs. Her legs in the moonlight looked long and white to her own eyes. She glanced sideways at Patrick, and saw he was looking straight ahead.

He was walking purposely, not strolling, holding her hand in a tight grip, his fingers entangled with hers. She became aware of the hardness of his fingers, as if they were made only of bone, of fleshless skeleton, binding her to him.

"Why are we walking so fast?" she asked.

"Shh. We have to get out of hearing."

"But . . . Patrick. . . ."

"Shh, come on. I have something to share with you."

"What?"

They had reached the lacy mesquite that bordered the east side of the pond, and Patrick pulled her into the cover it gave so that the moonlight was only darting slivers of light, touching them as they moved along the bank of the pond. Gwen pulled back. The house seemed a long way off now and so did the barns. They were going too close to the ponds, too far away from the house.

"I can't," Gwen protested, pulling back again.

She felt him get a closer grip on her arm, tucking it in beneath his. But he stopped, and she felt his lips touch her cheek lightly, like a brush from the narrow leaves of the tree that drooped over their heads.

"Come with me," he said.

"I'm—I can't go so far away."

"Are you afraid?"

She couldn't admit that yes, she was. "No," she said.

"Then come on. Just a little bit farther, I promise. I have something to show you."

"What?"

"It's a secret. You'll be glad you came."

"Where is it?"

"Down by one of the ponds, farther on."

"Something to show me?"

"Well, I just want to be alone with you, to talk to you without being heard. No one will know we were gone, if we're far enough away. I'll take care of you."

"But . . ." It was so flattering. Such an ego builder, her friends would say. And besides, she didn't really want to go back. Not yet. "But—what about the animals? Something killed them."

"Oh," he said in an offhand manner, his face turned away as if he was looking across the pond. "Don't you know what that was?"

"No, do you?"

"Sure. It was a couple of wild dogs that some people had brought in. I mean, they weren't wild when they brought them in, but they left them here, and they became wild. That's all it was. They've been caught now."

"Really?"

"Sure."

It seemed she could almost hear him laughing. And yet, that didn't seem appropriate at all. Why would he laugh? And there had been no real sound at all, just his voice, the casualness of his words. He wasn't afraid, and maybe he was right about the dogs. People did bring their pets along sometimes and even though they had to be kept on leashes, who could be sure they always were? And maybe Patrick was right, maybe some of them had been left behind. But Dad hadn't said anything about wild dogs.

"It is a big place," she said, walking along with him, beginning to run when he did, her hand in his, her hair bouncing against her shoulders as they ducked beneath the trees and ran into the moonlight between ponds.

"But Dad would have known, wouldn't he?"

"Maybe, maybe not. It was the Mexicans that got the dogs."

"Oh? Really?"

She saw he was laughing now, silently, looking at her with his eyes catching the light of the moon. She laughed

214

with him, feeling free as the wind, as birds in the sky, as the bird that sailed so low above them. She felt her hair touched. She ducked her head and glanced up. Not a bird, a bat.

"That thing dived at me!" she cried, not having to keep her voice down now, yet not really caring. It was only a bat, though it had looked larger than any bat she had ever seen. She had only glimpsed it, a swoop of black wings, a feeling of movement close to the top of her head. But she didn't mind. She wasn't afraid any longer.

They ran past pond two and splashed through the shallow stream that connected the farm's seven ponds. The stream floor was lined with slick rocks and even slicker, hard packed mud. Gwen slipped, one foot going out from under her.

He caught her just before she hit the water so that both of them fell into the icy pond. The water surrounded them, soaking the back of her lacy pajamas.

Patrick pulled her up, and they stood ankle deep in the stream. Gwen was laughing and holding on to his arms. They stepped out of the pond and walked more sedately into the shelter of the mesquites. Patrick's arm was still around her; she was out of breath now and shivering.

Suddenly the moonlight was gone.

Through the cover of the trees she saw the flash of lightning, and heard the rip of thunder. Head tilted back, her eyes traced the fingers of the red streaks in the black clouds overhead.

She started to speak, to tell him she had to go, that they both had to go because the storm had moved upon them suddenly unnoticed while they were having fun.

His face pressed against her neck suddenly, and the unexpectedness of the gesture startled her so that her words came out in a gasp. He was holding her tightly, his arms around her waist, pressing her to the ground. This was the kind of thing she saw sometimes on late movies, before her dad discovered what she was watching and turned the TV off. This was the kind of thing men did to women, and she wasn't ready yet to become a woman. It would ruin so much, she sensed. Sex too early in her life would deprive her of all the romance of getting acquainted with boys, of holding their hands, of first kisses. She hadn't even been kissed on the lips yet.

"Don't," she whispered, putting her hand against his forehead and pushing him away.

His strength seemed superhuman, not the strength of a boy only a couple of inches taller than herself. She felt dizzy suddenly as the events of the few days since she had known Patrick formed broken patterns in her head, creating visions like nightmares. A boy who had smiled at her shyly. She had almost forced him to talk to her. She had asked him as they stood under the shade of the tree by the old tractor what had happened to his face. His answer was so simple and non-condemning she had started to love him at that moment. "My mother tried to kill me," he said, his silver-gray eyes like those of the Persian kitten she used to have— round, pure, and hiding nothing. She had been the first to take his hand. She had felt the pulse in his wrist, and she had wanted him to know that she was holding his hand because she felt something she had never felt before. This boy was going to figure prominently in her life, she knew. She just knew that.

But this Patrick was different. This Patrick was too strong for his age and size, and she now realized, too bold, too aggressive.

This was not the same boy who had stood under the tree with her, it seemed. Something had happened to change him.

She was afraid. The fear had been coming, she now knew, from the moment she heard the scratching on the screen. Now it shrieked like a silent wind, its sound too high-pitched for human ears, but vibrating through her, making her suddenly frantic to get away from him.

With her breath fast and short, she twisted suddenly, throwing herself sideways, trying to roll, to loosen his hold on her. But the effort was useless. She cried out, a hoarse objection, giving in to the terror in her soul.

His face was still at her neck, and in the numbness of her terror, she felt a pain there, as if something very sharp had pierced her skin. The lightning flashed, a long, fractured sliver across the dark clouds above, and she saw in its light the spread of wings above her, dark, furry wings, and bent to her throat was a horrible head with needle fangs.

Chapter Twenty-Two

Orion felt the air in his face, and the swift pace of the horse. She was running like a true champion today, faster and faster under his urging. They rounded the track, leading to the outer side. She was taking her own lead, choosing her own path. Her stride was long and graceful. He could see it as if he was viewing her from afar, and he could feel her swiftness and her strength beneath him. She was a marvelous filly, her coat as black and shining as black satin, her muscles working together, rippling beneath her coat. He stood in the stirrups, murmuring his encouragements, and she ran as if she had wings.

They had come forward from a slow start. It was as if she wanted to gallop easily, taking the rear until she had passed the second call. Ahead of them the horses had grouped, running almost as one down the middle of the track. Then it was time.

She came up on the outside, going around them as if they were sheep.

She was running easily, beautifully. He heard the cheering of the crowd. He felt her increased speed as the cheering urged her on.

She passed the third horse and was coming up to the second. She passed him, a brown gelding, and was within a length of the leader. Half a length now, a head, and a nose.

She passed the leader, and the horses were all left somewhere on the track behind.

He felt the drop of her front quarter, and the drop created a sickening lunge in his belly and his heart. God, no, this couldn't be happening.

She was going down, down.

She was falling.

He heard the snap of bone, the cracking of the front leg that was a death knell.

His filly was down.

Her leg broken.

He fell with his head on her neck, crying, seeing the horrible pain in her eyes, feeling her rear her head up and look toward the goal, the wire, the winner's circle. He felt her try to rear up, to go on with her race. He saw the fear when she couldn't, and felt it in his heart.

He looked at her.

This wasn't *Morning Light.* . . .

It was Star Beauty.

Orion woke, cold but wet with sweat, shaking so hard his teeth chattered. In his dark room, as he reared up in bed. A strange red light outlined for just a moment his chest of drawers across the room and the foot of his bed.

Then darkness came back, blacker than ever.

The nightmares. God, the nightmares. The race had been run all over again, every day of his life since it happened. The nightmares had seemed to let up for awhile, but now they were coming again.

Star Beauty. Morning Light.

It was only a dream, he told himself. It was anxiety, and remembering, always, the fall of his own horse. Of Morning Light going down, her leg broken.

He got up and looked out the window. Rain had started to fall, big drops that sounded like hail. Not heavy, yet, but promising to be. The lightning illuminated the ground outside his window in a weird, whitish light so bright that for an instant it hurt his eyes. Behind the light was the black cover of clouds so low they seemed to hang just over the fence.

Would he ever be able to race Star Beauty?

What if his dream was a warning of what would happen if he did?

Was it only his anxiety?

She had good breeding. They could let her live as a brood mare, raising baby horses, race-horse quality, to sell. The farm could profit from that as much, almost, as if she was a race horse.

On the other hand, she was a born racer. She seemed to enjoy the very act of running. And she might, as his filly had, love the cheering, the prancing into the winner's circle.

Orion stood at the window remembering.

Once Morning Light had not won. It was her first loss in the past three races, and she had lifted her head and nickered at the horse that was led into the winner's circle in her place she felt. She had wanted to go there, too, to be patted, admired, photographed.

Orion hugged her neck and promised her the next time— the next time would be theirs.

And it was the next time that she had fallen.

He would hear the crack of that slender leg for as long as he lived.

His only consolation was that her pain was brief. A downed horse's pain always is brief. It wasn't as if the horse was out in the wild, where if it stepped in a hole and broke its leg, it had no choice but to lie there until the predators found it.

Yet it didn't help to rationalize, to try to convince himself her pain was brief. His was forever.

He didn't know if he could race again, with Star Beauty or any other horse.

He went back to his bed and sat on the edge of it, his hands clasped together between his knees.

The horses had been his life. He had tried a few times to date, and had been fairly successful when he was in high school. Then he had stopped growing. His mother was small, but his dad was average height. His own height stopped at five-one, and the girl he had fallen in love with was five inches taller. The one time he had tried to get serious with her, she had looked at him as if he was mad. They had been friends since they were kids. They went places together because of that friendship, she told him. The memory of that day still haunted him, though the humiliation and pain were dull and distant. Nothing compared to the pain of that fragile, cracking leg.

"Oh, Orey," she had said, putting her hand on his shoulder. They were in his car, parked by the river. Although it was evening, it was still light, and he could see her pretty face clearly, and worst of all, the sympathy in her hazel eyes. "Orey, we've been friends too long. I love you like a brother, Orey, didn't you know that? I can't date you seriously. I'm not in love with you, and I never could be."

It was because he was small, he thought. It turned out his brother, the younger one, six feet tall, dark good looks, and mean as hell to the women in the sense that he loved them and left them, was the man she wanted. She married him, and was left with one child to raise alone. The brother had gone on to fresher stuff, Orion guessed. But then, just as Orion was hoping Beatrice would consider marrying him because she needed someone, Doug returned and she went back to him.

Orion knew they lived in California somewhere. Maybe it had worked out, after Doug matured and settled down. For Bea's sake, he hoped so.

He had put his heart and life into horses and riding. He had owned a small stable of three, but after Morning Light's death, he sold his two geldings and gave it all up. Two years ago he had come to Boys' Farm to cook.

Two years. And still, in his sleep, he wept for Morning Light.

And Star Beauty.

He didn't know whether he could race her. He just didn't know.

At times he felt he had to. Not only for all the folks here at the farm who were looking forward to it, but for Star Beauty herself.

What was in the heart of a horse? He had wondered that a lot of times. They grew lonely, just like everyone. They needed companionship. They needed pets to love, someone to nuzzle and care about, just like everyone who was alone. They liked some of their own kind, and disliked others. Just like people.

They liked to work, to race if that was what they had been bred for.

Maybe. Maybe, he didn't know.

Would she be better off just raising her babies, or would she be happier with her chance at the crown?

He lay down, his arms under his head.

The lightning lit up his room again, and thunder cracked at the same instant.

He couldn't relax. It wasn't the storm. He had always slept good through a storm.

Was it Star Beauty? She wasn't used to storms like this. She was, after all, only two years old, and he could probably count on one hand the number of storms she had known. No animal understood the crashing and lightning that took place in a storm. Most were frightened by it.

Star Beauty was in trouble.

He knew that suddenly, and as surely as if he could see her.

. . . *down on the track, her leg broken* . . .

He got up and hurriedly pulled on his jeans and shoved his feet into his shoes. By the time he reached his door, he was running.

He leaped off the porch into a torrent of rain, the lightning flashing almost continuously now. The slope of the green land between him and the barn was silver with light that came and went, blinking, wavering, spot lighting the old machinery, making it look like brown, rusty skeletons in a graveyard.

He ran, his head down against the rain to protect his eyes. Ahead of him was the outline of the barn, its peaked roof lighted by the weird and dancing silver-white streaks overhead. The thunder clapped like a giant applauding. From somewhere on the farm came the sound of a sheep bleating and a cow bawled.

Then he heard a crash and the sound of wood being struck, and he knew Star Beauty had gone down. Somehow he knew, without knowing why.

He climbed the paddock fence and ran through the sloppy grass and bare ground to Star Beauty's stall. She had fallen partway across the gate, and it was broken beneath her. Her rear was out in the rain, but her head was still in the total blackness of her stall.

Why hadn't he thought to bring his flashlight?

He stepped over the broken gate, and at that instant, the lightning illuminated the world again, and in the strange, half-light he saw something large and dark rise from Star Beauty, its wings lifting silently beneath the pounding thunder. For one second, he saw a small and hideous face without eyes turn his way. Two sharp fangs drooped from a wide mouth that snarled in anger at him. Then the black wings were lifting away, with the swiftness of a bat. The world lost its light and became black, and the flying creature was gone.

It was a continuation of his nightmare. Nothing of the kind he had seen existed. He blinked at the darkness, stunned for a moment, unable to move, and then he felt his way into the center of the stall, his ankles brushing Star Beauty's belly.

With his hands in the air he felt for the string that would turn on the electric bulb installed on a rafter in the middle of the overhang. He felt it, and lost it again. The lightning refused to flash, and the dark he stood in was as black as the depths of a cave.

His hand brushed the string again and it bounced away, as if playing a horrible game with him. The horse lay still— as still as death.

God, what was wrong with her?

What had he seen?

The string touched his fingers again and he grabbed it and pulled.

The light came on, and he found Star Beauty lying full length on the ground.

Chapter Twenty-Three

Babette lay awake in her bed listening as the storm moved east. Mother Ann had come into the bedroom during the height of the storm to see if the little girls slept. And, Babette knew, to see if she was still in her bed.

The thunder still moaned behind the steady fall of rain. Did Mother Ann figure the rain would keep Babette from leaving?

She had to hope that it did.

She was in trouble now, she knew. Tomorrow Mother Ann would call Miss Thornton and they would make other arrangements for her. Because Mother Ann had caught her trying to get out of the house.

It was now, or not at all. She had to go now.

She had to leave her clothes, because the only way out was through the bathroom window. If she got up to go to the bathroom and Mother Ann found her, she could just pretend it was only the bathroom she wanted.

That meant the only way she was going to have any clothes to wear was to roll her jeans, shirt, and sandals into a ball and try to get them outside.

She sat up, her hands trembling. She had to hurry, yet she had to be quiet. She had looked at the city map she'd found in the den, and had her path routed. She had thought she was farther out in a suburb than she really was. If she hurried, she could get home within the hour. She had memorized each street she would take, each turn. She would keep to the shorter, out-of-the-way streets, cutting through residential areas, and across the edge of downtown. Then she would be there, her old neighborhood where the houses had bars at the windows, and the yards were small and mostly bare. But it was home. And at this moment, she was so homesick she could have cried, and so excited about going there, even if it was wrong. Wrong to go home. She had never thought, in all her fantasies, that it would ever be wrong to go home.

To go to her mother.

She rolled her blouse into her jeans, and hooked her fingers in the straps of her sandals. She tucked the clothing roll under her arm.

When she stepped out into the hall the thunder seemed louder, as if it was rising to cover her almost soundless footsteps.

She hurried down the hall to the bathroom, glancing back once toward the master bedroom. She was safe.

She locked the bathroom door behind her, and did not turn on the light. The window flashed like a neon sign, bidding her to come, drawing her to its light as if she were a moth.

The window latch turned easily, and the window went up with a slight push. It was often raised and lowered, and there was no sound except the soft sliding of the metal frame.

She pushed the screen, and it fell out of sight. The opening wasn't large, and she had to push against the toilet seat to wriggle herself into it.

For a hopeless, frantic minute it seemed she wouldn't get out. She could feel the aluminum frame scrape her back, and heard the tear of her nylon pajama top. She began to moan in frustration and anxiety, and then heard herself and bit her lip to make herself stop. Silence, she told herself. Silence is crucial.

Suddenly she was through the window, her head hanging down, only her legs keeping her from falling to the ground. With her arms stretched down for support, she eased herself out the window. Her fall was easy, though when she stood up, rain from the eaves was pouring down upon her, and her hands were coated with mud.

She had dropped her bundle of clothes.

There came the sound of a door closing, a faint but definite sound that could have been the master bedroom door.

Had Mother Ann come out of her bedroom to check on her?

With her heart thudding so hard it seemed that her body was filled with it, she pressed against the wall. Rain poured down from the roof, and her hair dripped water down the back of her neck. Her clothes were somewhere out under that rush of water, and she was wearing only nylon pajamas. She began to shiver, as much from anxiety as from the chill of the rain.

Then a light came on, streaking out across the wet grass and the fence. At first she thought it was from her house, the master bedroom perhaps, but then she saw it was from the house next door. She heard a voice there, and the door closing again.

She almost sank to the ground with relief. The door closing, the light, all of it was coming from the house next door, just across the fence, yards from where she stood.

Then in the faint light that filtered through a nearby shrub, she saw a bundle on the ground.

Her clothes.

Her clothes.

With a soft cry in her throat she lunged for it. Hands shaking, she unrolled her jeans and shirt and pulled them on over her pajamas. The wet clothes felt cold and heavy, yet in a way as safe and warm as a blanket on a cold night. Without her clothes, she would have stood a big chance of being seen and reported just because of the way she was dressed. With her jeans and shirt, even though they were wet, people who might be out on a night like this would at least think she had a right to be out too.

She hoped.

She had to count on it.

She hurried through the backyard gate, keeping to the shadows. The light in the house next door blinked out, a car started, and headlights trailed down the alley behind the houses. But by the time she had closed the gate behind her, the car was moving on.

She began to run down the alley and to the street on her left. At the corner, she turned right. She had spent hours looking at a city map until she had memorized every turn, every shortcut through every alley she could find between streets. Alleys were sometimes safer, especially in the areas of town where alleys were little paved roads connected to garages, mostly residential areas. When she got farther downtown, the alleys would have to be avoided. The lighted streets would be better.

She had no watch. The night seemed endless, yet she knew from her memorized map that she was almost halfway home. By the second hour, her breath was short and burning in her chest, and her legs felt like rubber that would fold up at any moment. But she was afraid to stop. The streets were deserted, and any time she saw the lights of a car, she ducked out of sight in whatever cover she could find—a doorway, a yard with a shrub. At this time of night, any car might be a patrol car, and a cop would be sure to stop and ask what any fool would be doing out on a night like this. Probably even the criminals were holed up somewhere.

She had to stop. She had reached the outer edge of the old downtown part of the city, where the buildings were tall, and the few houses that were squeezed in, mostly boarding houses, had bars on the windows. She was beginning to feel at home. She huddled against a stone wall and felt exposed by the street light on the corner. Its glow spread like a white cone into the rain.

She had planned her route to cut across the edge of downtown. She didn't know the exact distance, but she thought she must be within a few minutes of her home now.

There was something spooky about this part of town at this time of night with the streets empty, the noises of daytime absent. Tonight, in the slackening rain, everything looked dark and glistening; the streets seemed narrow, like deep canyons in the western mountains, filled with the mysteriousness of silence.

She was exhausted, yet she had to move on, hoping, praying that no patrol car came along before she could get back to an area of trees and yards where she could hide. It seemed, at this time and in this place, though, that she was alone in an alien world. Even with her mother and little brother, she had seldom come downtown. There had been no reason to. What little they needed was available within a few blocks of their house.

She began jogging again, her sandals slapping the wet pavement and sounding like small explosions in the canyons created by the buildings.

She let her thoughts drift back. Paddy, clinging to her hand when they had been allowed to go alone for the first time to the ice cream store in the small town where they lived. He had been even more scared than she.

"It's an adventure, Paddy," she'd told him, hoping he wouldn't run back crying to Mama. If he did, she'd have to go too, and they wouldn't get their ice creams. "It's an adventure. Think of it as an adventure." She liked the word. She was six years old and Paddy was five, but she had felt almost grown up, responsible for her little brother. Paddy had not much liked the word, her new word. but he had not run back to Mama, not then. In a little coin purse she carried the change that would buy the ice cream. Mama had counted it out and told her to give it to the man behind the counter. It had looked like a lot of money to her, quarters, dimes. She knew what they were because sometimes Mama's boyfriend, Edward, gave her a dime or a quarter.

They had gotten within sight of the store when something flew out of the trees and came toward them. Paddy screamed, and jerked his hand away from hers before she could think what was happening, before she could reassure him that it was only a bird. Why was he afraid of a bird? It was a big bird, a crow or jay or something, and it was gone, circling out of sight above the tops of trees on the other side of the road. But Paddy was running, still screaming, back down the path toward the house.

Babette stamped her foot in frustration. Oh no! They had been going on a real adventure, and Paddy had gotten scared of a bird, nothing but a bird.

In disgust she had gone back too, down the path at the edge of the forest and to the house, where Ketti had Paddy in her arms, trying to calm him. He was hysterical now, crying and shaking as if it had been something really scary, like a snake. If it had been a snake, she might have run, too. Mama always told her to watch out for snakes when she went out to play, and even though she had seen only one, and it wasn't a bad snake that bit people and animals, it had scared her. Come to think of it, that had been an adventure, too.

But today Paddy had ruined the greatest adventure of their lives.

She stood looking at the back of his head with Ketti's hand on it, his face hidden in the hollow between her neck and shoulders. Over his head, Ketti looked at Babette, and Babette began to feel guilty.

"I didn't do anything," she said.

"What happened?"

"He saw a bird, that was all. It was a crow or something. Maybe a jay."

Ketti began to croon against Paddy's cheek, rocking him, patting him, and her eyes looked puzzled, or maybe worried, it seemed to Babette. Babette didn't understand.

Later, when Paddy had stopped crying, Ketti took them in the car to get the ice cream.

In those days they'd had a different car. Sometimes it ran, and sometimes it didn't, but it was always an adventure to go for a ride. Sitting in the car at the ice cream store, the store where they also bought groceries and once even a little knit shirt for Paddy, he had been unafraid, and she could still see the way he had licked the ice cream cone, turning it carefully to keep it from dripping onto his hand. Ketti had taught them both how to eat a cone without the ice cream dripping.

Chocolate. He had always wanted chocolate ice cream. He never changed the flavor. He never liked the adventure of trying new flavors like she did. On that day she had eaten butter brickle. She remembered it clearly now as she ran along the wet sidewalk; it was as if she was six again and sitting in the back seat of that old car watching Paddy eat his ice cream.

Ketti had been so good to him then, so loving.

And now, tonight, Babette was terrified that Ketti would get to Paddy before she could stop her.

Would it help if she reminded Ketti of those days?

The other—the things Ketti had told her, came like a

dark cloud into her mind. She felt herself frowning. Paddy had run screaming from a bird, a large bird.

Ketti had told her she had seen a bird or a large, bat-like creature on Paddy. . . .

There was no way she could make sense of it. It was like a nightmare that was split into images, a puzzle that didn't fit together. Ketti—Ketti's mind—something had happened to it. And now, in trying to think about the things Ketti had told her, she could find no sense in it—but she felt as if her own mind was fragmented, broken like the puzzle.

She couldn't handle it.

She couldn't start remembering, trying now, she thought, to make sense of what Ketti had told her. Paddy was her brother, she had lived with him until she was eleven years old and he was ten. She knew him.

She knew he was afraid a lot. Maybe more than most little boys. He hadn't been adventuresome. She had never been able to get him out of the house to explore the woods, or even to ride the bicycle with her.

Edward had bought the bicycles when he and Ketti got married. Both of them were used, the paint worn off in places and the metal rusted, but to her, those bicycles were beautiful. Paddy had never learned to ride his, so she had tried to get him to ride with her. He could sit on the seat, she had promised him, and she would stand up and pedal. Or he could sit on the handlebars, or the bar between the seat and handlebars. Once she had gotten him out of the house to try riding the bicycle, and they had wobbled around the house once before they both fell. He had gotten his feet tangled in the spokes of the wheel, she accused, but he had said no, he had just fallen. He couldn't balance on the little seat with her pumping the pedals in front of him. And he refused to try riding any other way. He had wanted to go back into the house. He had a new coloring book, and he liked to have the television on, though when he lay on the floor coloring in his book he hardly ever looked at the TV screen.

After the baby was born, that pink little baby her mama and stepdad had named Billy, Paddy never wanted to leave the house. He loved the baby more than anyone.

She could still see him leaning over Billy when the baby was old enough to smile and coo.

Paddy leaned over Billy, his hand gentle on the baby's stomach, and both of them cooing . . .

Paddy had adored Billy—how could Ketti think—what she—

She had to stop her mother. She was so tired now even a bed beneath a dripping shrub would have looked good, but she had to go on, had to stop her mother somehow.

The night seemed to be turning lighter. A cold, gray look was coming into the air, and the midnight blue sky was brightening in the east. Lights were coming on in houses, and cars began to pass along the streets, the traffic slow and infrequent, as if the drivers were only half awake.

She was within blocks of home. She had been here before, when she walked to school a new way. The houses were small here, the yards mostly bare. Windows were barred in a lot of the houses. She ran down a street where office buildings were still closed and dark, passed across the empty lot of a small shopping center, cut through a muddy back alley, and came at last to her street.

Trees hid her house, and the old buildings next door, garages that were closed now because of bankrupt business.

Then she was running down the muddy driveway of her own home, a driveway seldom used. Weeds grew in the center of it, and ground vines straggled out across one of the old ruts.

The car was still in the driveway, a rusty old lump of shadows and cracked glass.

The house was dark.

She ran into the backyard and up onto the porch, walking now, stumbling to the door. Just as her hand touched the knob, she remembered she had no key. It was in her suitcase, back at the foster home. But Mama had to be here, somewhere, in the house. At this graying hour of dawn, she would be in her room asleep.

Her car was still here. She hadn't gone to the farm yet.

Babette prayed she would be in bed. That she was still here, somewhere in the house, this first night out of jail. She had to be here. Where else would she have gone? Without the car? She couldn't have gotten into the farm tonight. She couldn't have gone to Paddy. Yet. Surely, please, God.

Then another thought came to her. What if Ketti had asked that Paddy be released to her? Would they have let her take him?

How was she going to get into the house?

She knocked on the door and called, "Mama?"

She was answered by silence. Rain dripped from the trees behind the house, and from the eaves. Now that she was under the shelter of the porch, she could feel water from her hair dripping down the back of her neck.

Traffic had increased on the street, car lights sweeping through the early morning. The gray light had turned into a cloudy, overcast morning that would have a dim quality for hours yet. The inside of the house, the kitchen she could see through the glass in the door, was still dark.

Her hand was on the knob, but she hadn't turned it. She had assumed it was locked, and when finally she gave the knob a shake and then a twist and felt the door open, she stood in stunned silence a moment before she could move.

The door unlocked? Ketti would never sleep in the house without the door locked as securely as possible. Nor would she leave the house without locking the door behind her.

Unless she never intended to come back, and didn't care if anyone entered the house.

Babette moved quietly into the kitchen, easing the door shut behind her, not really sure why she was trying to be so quiet. She felt puzzled now, and scared. Something had happened out of her control. Ketti was not in the house, she felt sure, or the door would have been locked.

Or, Ketti had not come home, and a burglar had entered and left the door unlocked behind him.

She preferred thinking it was a burglar.

She remembered to lock the door behind her, then she turned on the kitchen light. The air was stuffy with the stale odors of cooking and lingering smells that seemed to have permeated the walls of the kitchen.

She became aware of her heavy, wet, cold jeans, and she stripped them off, listening for any sound in the rest of the house. Would the kitchen light bring whoever had opened the door? Or were they all gone—whoever or whatever had been in the house?

She left her jeans on the linoleum. Without them, her pajamas seemed even colder, clinging to her skin like plastic wrap.

She went into the front room. The old TV was still there. It was the only thing in the house a burglar might take, which meant a stranger hadn't left the door unlocked.

She climbed the stairs, going into the lighter gray of the hall above. She looked at the broken banister. It seemed so long ago, that night when Ketti had fought with Paddy. Yet in another way, it seemed like it was happening now, or was just about to happen, as if she had been sent back in time.

The doors to her bedroom and her little brother's were open. But the door to Ketti's room was closed.

She went to the closed door and opened it, saying softly, "Mama?"

The bed was made, just as it had been the last day she was here. On that day, she had changed sheets and done the laundry at the launderette down on the corner, in the small shopping center. She and Danny had gone there just as they always did, carrying their basket of dirty clothes. It had always been fun to go to the launderette because they'd been allowed to spend part of their money in the machines dispensing candy and pop. Her mind was filled with the image of Danny sitting in one of the launderette chairs, his short legs sticking straight out, eating his candy bar. The image was imposed, it seemed, over the picture of a young Paddy sitting in the back seat of the car, eating ice cream. So long ago, and yet so close.

"Mama?"

She was not in the room, Babette could see that. Regret stung her heart; loneliness mixed with it, and depression gathered in a dark cloud around her. She had gone, Babette thought, leaving the door carelessly open behind her because she wasn't coming back.

She had gone without the car.

Babette went to her own bedroom, stripped off the wet clothes, and hung them over the iron railing at the foot of her bed. She dressed again in dry things from the closet, putting on a pair of jeans so old they were tight and short and uncomfortable. She covered the gaping waistband with a long shirt, then pulled on socks and put on her school shoes.

She went to the bathroom and turned on the light.

Immediately she saw that Ketti had been here, very recently, and Babette realized the story the scene told her.

Chapter Twenty-Four

Rufus snapped awake. He hadn't meant to fall asleep soundly enough for time to pass without him knowing what was going on. He had meant to doze only as needed to get through the night, catnaps from which he could wake ungroggy and alert. He had listened through the night, he'd thought, for any footsteps coming from the bunkhouse bedroom. But sitting up in his bed with the gray light of dawn coming in the unshaded window, he knew he'd let himself slide into deep sleep.

For only an hour or two, that was all. The last time he'd looked at the clock, it was three-thirty. It wasn't likely Marsh would have gotten up after that.

Rufus dressed hurriedly, pulling on overalls that had one gallus already snapped into place. He didn't bother with buttoning the sides of the overalls or tying his high-topped work shoes. He could hear a soft sliding of rain at the window, and knew they were in for a wet day.

The interior of the bunkhouse was still dark, except for tracks of pale dawn light on the floor beneath the windows. He looked only at Marsh's bed. The boy was there, asleep

233

now. Rufus could see the tanned arms stretched out over the top of the blanket.

His eyes stopped for a glance at the nearest bed, the bed of the new boy, Patrick. He was on his side, facing the wall, legs drawn up. Rufus could see nothing of him except the shape of his body beneath the blanket. He was a smaller, younger, more slender boy than Marsh, with narrow shoulders and thin arms, and curled under the blanket, he looked even smaller.

Rufus drew a long breath and backed out of the bedroom. Pulling his pipe from his pocket he went out onto the porch and sat down in the rocking chair. Before he thought, before he remembered that Lion was gone, he patted his thigh, the way he had always called the dog to come and keep him company.

He sat down feeling lonely, as gray inside as the day outside was shaping up to be.

He poured tobacco into the bowl of his pipe, and unable to see clearly in the half-light, he felt some of the leaves spill onto his hand. He muttered under his breath an old cuss word that he'd never spoken out loud in all his years at the farm. Little pitchers have big ears, he'd heard the old man he once worked for say many a time. "Little pitchers have big ears" meant, he reckoned, that the boys would catch on to any cuss word they heard and use it themselves.

He realized he had just been sitting there, holding his pipe between his teeth, using his finger to pack the tobacco into the bowl, not striking a match, but staring off across the park. Ready to strike the match on the bottom of the cane chair, he stopped.

He had been staring at a light without realizing it—light that was unusual for this time of day.

He put the match back into his pocket and stood up, the pipe stem gripped between his teeth. A light on in the barn?

From here, through the branches of a tree, the glow of the small bulb beneath the overhang of the shed was like a star. He could see no details. And when he moved his head, the star of light disappeared behind the tree limbs. Something was wrong at the barn.

He went down the steps without his hat, forgetting about

the rain until he was in it. He paused, looked back. But the rain was light, more like a heavy mist. He walked faster, aware of an awful new dread, that constant fear, that feeling of standing on the edge of the world about to fall off into the darkness, hopelessness and foreverness of space.

The darkness of death.

He could feel it all around him now.

In his later years, as he had sat on the porch, rocking, smoking, pondering life, he'd come to the conclusion that there is nothing after death. And yet he was afraid there might be—terrible things people only dreamed of in their worst nightmares. That thing called hell by the fundamentalists, the pulpit screamers. He was afraid . . .

By the time he reached the paddock gate, he could see the movement of someone in the lighted shed, in the horse's stall. Someone was with the horse.

Hagar?

At this time of day?

He knew she came early to feed the filly, but this early?

He latched the gate carefully behind him, mindful of the goat that lived in the paddock and whose white coat he could see against the dark, wet boards of the barn just outside Star Beauty's stall. The goat was standing still, awake, quiet.

He walked into the path of light from the stall and saw it was Orion with the horse.

Rufus watched a moment as Orion rubbed the horse's neck and talked to her. He couldn't hear all the words, but the tone of voice was like a mother to her baby.

"Come on girl, you'll be all right. You've got to be all right—get your spirit back. We'll race—we'll run again. We'll go all the way—we'll get that triple crown, I promise you."

Rufus took his pipe from his mouth. "Something the matter?"

Orion jerked his head around, and Rufus knew he had startled the man, but there hadn't been any other way to announce his arrival. "Saw the light," he explained, "and wondered if something was wrong. So I just came on down. I know that Hagar usually feeds her filly right at the break of good light, but this seemed a little early."

Orion said, "I came down a couple of hours ago to find her on the ground, something wrong then. It took me almost all of this time to get her on her feet again. I haven't been able to figure out what it is."

Rufus noticed the difference in the horse then, the way her head hung forward instead of up and alert. Even when she slept, she usually looked more alert than this, her legs locked under her so that you almost had to look at her eyes to see if she was awake. But this, yes, it was different. Her head was hanging, and she was breathing as if it was difficult to find the energy.

"What are you going to do?"

Orion didn't answer for a moment. He was rubbing the horse's neck, and there was a look in his eyes that Rufus had never seen before.

"I saw something here," he said. "But I'm not sure what it was."

"Eh?" Rufus had missed most of the words, Orion's voice had been so low.

"I've looked her over good, and can't see anything wrong with her," Orion said in a louder voice. "I've listened to her heart, and it sounds a little fast. I guess I'll go call the vet, if you'll stay with her a few minutes, Rufus."

"Sure. I don't have anything else to do."

"I guess I'll get Rose to start breakfast this morning. She can get some of the boys in to help. We'll make it a simple one. Cereal, all the boys like cereal. It's better for them than too many eggs, so they tell me."

"Times are changing, Orion. Hens are going out of style."

Rufus heard the latch of the paddock gate as Orion left. He entered the stall and stood at the horse's head, looking into her face. She didn't seem to know he was there. To Rufus, she looked plain tired. But it couldn't be from the workouts for racing, because she hadn't been worked out for several days now. Mostly Hagar took her for long walks, leading her, seldom riding. "Why don't you ride," he had asked her once, and she had looked at him as if he was daft. "She's going to be a race horse," she'd said with pride. "She's not just a riding horse. When someone gets on her back, she's going to know that she will be getting ready to run as fast as she can. I'm not a good enough rider yet to work her out, but one day Orion is going to let me try."

"Hi, Rufus," Hagar's voice said, and at first, it seemed he was just hearing it in the memory of the day they'd first talked about her riding Star Beauty. Then he saw she had come through the dark barn and was looking at him over the manger. Almost immediately she cried, "What's wrong with Star Beauty?"

"Looks a little tired."

Hagar ducked her head and crawled sideways through the manger stall and jumped down onto the dirt floor.

No matter how often Rufus saw the girl, he had to look twice, his gaze lingering a moment longer on her beautiful face. She was one of the prettiest girls he had ever seen, with her skin contrasting with her dark hair, and her eyelashes so long and dark naturally, without the gummy stuff so many girls used. This morning, like most times, she had pulled her hair back into a French braid. The loose, wavy end was tied with a little red bow. The shirt she wore tucked into her jeans was red and white checked. She never wore lipstick, at least not this year. Last year she'd had a spell of putting on lipstick and leaving her hair loose and curly around her face. And she'd also taken to hanging around Vance. But that had ended pretty fast.

The worried look on her face made him feel badly.

"I'm sure she's going to be all right," Rufus said. "Even a horse can wake up feeling out of sorts, I reckon."

"Of course, I know that," Hagar said, the tone of her voice not as certain as her words. "All animals have feelings as intense as people's, they just can't talk to us about them. But Star Beauty is in good health—or was. I've never seen her like this."

"Orion has gone to call the doctor for her."

"Oh, good!"

Rufus watched her caress Star Beauty's face, and he saw the horse's eyes close as blissfully as old Lion's had when he was getting his ears rubbed. But Lion was dead now, and Rufus had a sudden and terrible feeling they were lucky that Star Beauty had managed to get to her feet. If it hadn't been for Orion, he thought, unable to finish the idea running through his mind.

Martin sat at the kitchen table with a cup of coffee. Hagar had grabbed a slice of bread, slapped a little butter on it and hurried out, as she did most mornings. And Gwen wasn't up yet. She never got up until eight or nine. Gwen was his sleepyhead, once she got to sleep. She also liked to stay up late.

There was a knock, and then the door opened. Orion called, "Martin?"

Martin lifted his head and put out effort enough to answer. "Yeah, Orion, come on back. I'm in the kitchen."

He got up as the footsteps came down the hall, and took another cup from the hooks beneath the upper cabinet. Orion would want coffee.

Orion stopped in the doorway, a small but well-built man, capless, which was unusual, his brown hair plastered damply to his head. There was a tense, tight look to his face. Cheekbones that were always prominent looked even sharper today.

"Coffee?" Martin asked, ready to pour. He hesitated, adding, "What's up?"

"I think we ought to call the vet for Star Beauty, Martin. I went down to the stall this morning about three or threethirty and found her on the ground, her head bowed back, her eyes wild. I thought for awhile I wasn't going to get her on her feet again. I finally got her up, but she just doesn't have the energy she usually does."

Martin nodded. "Sure. Call the vet. You can use the phone in the office. Want some coffee?"

"No thanks. I'd better get back."

"I'll go with you."

Martin got his raincoat and hat and went down the hall. He could hear Orion's voice in the office, but by the time he reached the front of the hall, Orion was waiting for him.

As he went out the door, he paused and glanced back toward the bedroom hall. It was softly lighted by a small, light-sensitive night light that probably wouldn't go out all day if the sky didn't clear. Gwen would be all right, he decided. She'd been left sleeping in the house alone many times.

"We'll take the pickup," Martin said, going with Orion down to the gate. "I think the rain is getting heavier."

Orion didn't comment. He didn't even seem to notice that his hair was wet and the shoulders of his shirt were clinging damply.

Babette moved into the bathroom slowly, staring at the things Ketti had left on the counter top. An empty bottle of hair coloring. Scissors. And on the floor, in blond clumps, Ketti's long hair.

Babette stood looking at the mess, seeing in her mind what had happened. Yesterday Ketti had gone to the store right after she came home, and she had bought black hair coloring. Then she had come home and cut off her blond hair, dying what was left black.

She had disguised herself. Why?

Babette backed out of the bathroom, leaving the light on. She couldn't have forced herself to turn out the light. It was as if the house was haunted now, so that if she didn't move in utter silence, she would awaken the ghosts that lived here.

She went to Ketti's bedroom again and turned on the light, hesitating at the threshold, afraid to enter. But she had to look in the drawer to see if that stuff Ketti had told her about was still there. If it wasn't, she knew Ketti had taken it for protection—and gone to Boys' Farm. And in that case, the disguise could only mean that she hoped Paddy wouldn't recognize her. She had been careful that no one recognized her. She had not even taken the car, which she would have had to park where it could be seen. She'd probably had the money, which Babette didn't, to ride the bus to Boys' Farm.

If the Wolfsbane was gone, Ketti might already be at the farm.

And her change in looks meant Paddy might not recognize her. Babette knew Ketti was counting on that.

Paddy hadn't been with their mother since he was ten, so maybe he wouldn't know her with black hair, until she was too close for him to get away.

Babette crossed the floor to the dresser, walking as softly as she could, yet hearing her own steps as if they were foreign, following behind her. The drawer made a noise that echoed in the house when she slid it out.

There was nothing in the drawer but pantyhose and shorter knee socks. Babette dug among the contents, looking for the package of herbs Ketti had told her about, that she had seen in the corner. But it wasn't there.

Of course, Ketti would have taken it. Babette had known that the minute she saw the evidence in the bathroom.

Babette ran out of the bedroom and down the stairs, no longer concerned about the noise she made, only wanting out of the house now, feeling the need to hurry. When she saw the old black telephone, she stopped. If she called the police, they probably wouldn't do anything but come and get her, not Ketti. She could almost hear them saying, "There's no crime in dying her hair."

They wouldn't understand. They thought Paddy was in a safe place, but Babette knew he wasn't.

At the kitchen door, she stopped again. The knife drawer was open a few inches. She hadn't noticed that before. She went to the drawer and pulled it out. That drawer had always held three small paring knives and one long, sharp bread knife.

The bread knife was gone.

Babette left the drawer hanging open and ran out the backdoor. Now she knew how Ketti was going to kill Paddy.

She would come up to him at the farm and stab him before he could escape.

Babette couldn't let it happen—she prayed in silence that she could stop it.

Chapter Twenty-Five

Martin looked at his watch as he drove the pickup back to the house. Eleven-ten. Getting close to noon. The rain hadn't stopped, but it had never gotten very heavy. The veterinarian's van moved off across the area, following the little trail to the main gate where a couple of the boys were waiting to close and lock it. If the rain kept up, Martin found himself thinking, there would be no visitors this Saturday, and their profit for the month would be greatly reduced. Most of the time if they came out even at the end of the year, he considered it a good year. But it looked like so many things were going bad this year that they might be coming out in the red.

He didn't like that. The boys and animals had to eat. They all had to eat. Of course a lot of what they ate came right off the farm—the vegetables, the fruit, everything but meat, grain, and things such as sugar and salt. But clothes had to be bought, too, and a lot of extra cash would be needed with school starting soon.

He drove slowly, his thoughts returning to the horse. If anything happened to that horse, it would hurt Hagar irretrievably, he was afraid. And of course they never wanted anything to happen to their animals. It was always a sad day when one of the young steers had to be sold. If a year came along when the cows had more boy calves than girls, it was inevitable that the young bulls or steers would have to go sometime. Overpopulation—they tried to avoid it so that the animals born on the farm could expect to live their lifetimes on the farm.

Dr. Mordecal hadn't found anything wrong with Star

Beauty. He had spent a couple of hours looking at the horse, and had taken a blood sample to test, saying he would report back if she was showing problems there.

Hagar wouldn't be dragged away from Star Beauty for the next couple of days, Martin was afraid. He'd probably have to take food to her.

He smiled and sat thinking about his oldest daughter for a few minutes after he parked the pickup beneath the trees. Big raindrops, plunked down on the roof of the pickup, sounded like stones dropped from the sky.

He went into the house through the backdoor, leaving his raincoat and hat on a hook in the mud room. The house seemed too quiet for this time of day. Where was the music from Gwen's radio or tape player, or the morning TV shows she sometimes watched.

"Gwen?"

She was not in the kitchen or the family room, and as he walked through the too silent hall toward his office, an urgent need to see his young daughter's face and know she was safe came over him. He turned back to the hall that led to the bedrooms, calling her name. The girls' bathroom door was closed, and he knocked on it and listened for an answer. He heard only a soft drip, drip—the faucet Hagar had told him needed fixing. He'd forgotten.

He opened the door and found the bathroom dark, with only a sliver of light coming in beneath the shade.

He was scared, he realized suddenly. His young daughter—blond, blue-eyed, growing up to look like her mother, her face a perfect picture of girlish youth with a small cleft in the chin and high cheekbones that seemed to tilt the outer corner of her eyes up—who was so important to his life, and at this moment, his peace of mind, where was she?

He crossed the hall to her bedroom in two long steps and threw open the door.

The bed was unmade, covers thrown back as if she had just gotten up.

He felt the sheet and found it cold.

It had been a long time since Gwendolyn left this bed.

* * *

Babette walked as casually as she could, but fast, her head slightly lowered. She had been walking for hours after her sleepless night, but she only slightly felt the strain. At times, if she hurried too much, she got a little pain in her side. Then she'd have to slow down and hold her hand over it for a minute before the pain went away.

In the backyard this morning, in the early dawn with the rain drenching her dry clothes, she had stopped to think, and then had gone back to the kitchen. She didn't know the exact distance to Boys' Farm, how long it would take her to get there, or even where it was for sure. On the map she had studied at the foster home, she had looked at the location again and again to place it in her mind. It was a tiny mark on the map that read Boys' Farm, and it had taken her a long time to even find it. If she spent too much time in the den looking at maps of the city and surrounding counties when she was supposed to be in there vacuuming and dusting, Mother Ann was sure to get suspicious. So after she found the farm on the map, she had tried to place it in her mind. She had already forgotten the highway number, she was sure only that it was east of town.

What would she do, she'd asked herself as she went back into the haunted house and stood in the kitchen light, without proper clothes, food, or money? In a small pitcher on the cabinet was the grocery money, most of it dollar bills and change that customers gave Ketti as tips. It was the bread and butter and milk money, Mama had said. "If you need something when I'm gone, here's the money for it."

Babette looked into the pitcher, and saw only change in the bottom. She could almost see Ketti, pausing on her way out of the house, reaching into the pitcher for the loose bills.

Babette counted the change. Eight quarters and three dimes. She put it in her pocket. It would mean a bag of chips, when she needed food most, or an apple or banana.

From the hall closet she took her windbreaker with the hood. It was waterproof and would protect her to the hips.

She started out again, her hood up, then stopped. Her anxiety to hurry and protect Paddy from their mother, and in turn keep Mama from doing that terrible thing and ruining all their lives forever, had made her lose all common sense. She would need food. She wouldn't dare take a blanket—she'd be spotted right off as a runaway, she knew that, if she wasn't careful.

She wanted to get out of the house. It was as if she was beginning to hear things, like the sound of Danny's fast little footsteps on the floor above. Or the crashing of the banister, as one of the struggling bodies fell through to the floor below. She could hear the sirens coming again, and then realized it was a real siren, and it was coming closer and closer.

Panic rose like hot oil in her throat, nauseating her. Were they coming after her? Had Mother Ann discovered that she wasn't in the house and called the police?

But the siren went on by, and she leaned against the cabinet in a sudden spell of weakness. Then she almost laughed. Why would the police rush after her with a siren on? She was only a runaway. She hadn't committed a real crime.

Unless running away from a foster home was a crime.

And she wasn't really sure that it wasn't.

She began looking frantically for food. She had to get away from here, keep to the alleys and side streets, and head east out of town as fast as she could. What food was there that she could take? She found half a loaf of bread. It was green with mold on one side, but the other side looked all right. She dug a small brown sack out from under the cabinet and stuffed the bread into it. In the refrigerator she found a jar of peanut butter, half empty, and put it into the sack. There was a package of bologna, but it was green too, and slick as vomit beneath her fingers when she touched the open package. Gagging, she backed off, pushing the refrigerator door shut. Wadding the top of the sack down, she pushed it underneath her windbreaker, under the tight grip of her arm, and left the house.

She had walked for an hour through a part of town she'd never seen before, following streets labeled east, and arrows that pointed toward eastward freeways. Finally she stopped in a convenience store and asked the girl behind the cash register where Boys' Farm was. The girl looked at her as if she was from outer space, then shrugged. "Never heard of it."

Babette could have spoken the words in unison with her, because she knew exactly what the girl was going to say.

244

Then she saw the map, and spent three of her quarters to buy it. She didn't dare ask too many people where the farm was. She felt as if everyone who looked at her on the street knew she was a runaway, and in a few minutes, after she had passed by, a policeman would stop and ask that person if he had seen a runaway girl, and the answer would be, "Sure, she was just here asking where Boys' Farm is."

She bought the map, then underneath the warmth and privacy of the restroom light, looked at it, and got clear in her mind the highway and the streets she would have to follow to get to the farm. It was a tiny mark on the map, Boys' Farm, but it was such an important place in her mother's and brother's lives, and in her own.

The rain persisted, cold and steady but light. The clouds were gray and low overhead. Her shoes squished through little puddles of rainwater as she walked alongside the highway out of town. There were no sidewalks part of the time, but a block farther on, she could see the wall behind a housing project, and a sidewalk.

When she realized she was getting too tired, she thought of the food she was carrying and stopped, her back against the wall of the housing project, protected somewhat from oncoming cars by a shrub.

She opened the jar of peanut butter and realized she had not brought anything to get it out of the jar. She looked into the jar for a moment, and then in frustration, closed it again, and took a half-moldy slice of bread out of the bag. She was picking the mold off when the car pulled to the curb. She looked up.

A man leaned over and opened the passenger door, smiling at her. He was middle-aged to old, with a fringe of graying hair he had combed over his bald spot so that it looked like threads had been used to make a cap for the top of his head.

"Wanta ride?"

No, she almost said. It was dangerous to ride with strangers. She had heard that all her life, and she knew from the terrible stories of rape and murder that it was dangerous. This man looked like a kind person, but how could one tell?

"Come on," he said. "It's all right. I'm going several

miles, and you look like you'd be good company." His eyes had already found the bread and the sack, and she wondered now if he had seen her put the peanut butter back.

Did he know she was a runaway?

"I'm only going a few miles," she said, and wished she hadn't. Why would she be out in the rain to go miles? "I mean—blocks."

He nodded, still smiling.

She moved forward, as if her legs, her body, knew better than her mind the punishing distance, and the need to get there faster than she could walk.

She slid into the warmth of the car.

Rufus walked along the pasture fence, hands in his pockets. It was getting on toward evening now, and he had been out searching for the past several hours. As soon as he could get away from the others—Mr. Preston and the police that had answered the call about the missing child—he had started looking.

Every step took him closer to the terror he had started feeling the minute he heard Gwendolyn was missing. With the boys gathered at the bunkhouse, and Mr. Preston and Hagar at their own house, and the police car gone, Rufus walked away, as if he was just strolling. But he had a purpose in mind.

Gwendolyn, a runaway? That was what the police had suggested. "Did she have any reason to run away?" they had asked, and for a moment, there had been stunned silence. No one felt like answering the question. It was too preposterous. Of course she didn't have a reason to run away. What would it have been?

They had looked at the ponds, all of the boys, organized by Vance.

"Five of you go to pond one, and five to pond two . . ."

Rufus had wandered along behind them, following for awhile the boys who had gone to check out the first pond, and then the boys at pond two, on and on, through all seven ponds. There were arguments, too, about that. Why would she go out in the rain to fall into a pond that she would have been able to swim through on any day? Or night. Of course it was possible to drown in one of the ponds, but not Gwen, not here, not in the rain. It didn't make sense.

Finally the boys had given up and gone back to the bunk-house. The day was fading, and they were wet, cold, and confused. Mr. Preston had driven his pickup over the whole place, following each little trail, going into small groves of trees, around each pond, along the pasture fence. Rufus had ridden part of the time with him, and had heard Mr. Pres-ton say, "She's not here. Why would she be out here in the rain? She's got to be here. She wouldn't run away. Why would she run away? The gates haven't been opened. The keys are on the wall in the office."

She could have taken a key. But the keys were still there, except for the ones in the care of the boys who were respon-sible for the gates today.

Where is she?

Rufus had heard the cry from Mr. Preston, and from others, so that as he walked in the silence of the evening, he kept on hearing it.

She was here, somewhere, a terrible premonition told him. She was here, somewhere, and he was afraid that one of the boys knew where she was.

Marsh.

He had watched Marsh during the search, had seen that look on his face, the same look that had been there after the dog's death. He had seen it, and he was sick inside. Where is she, Marsh? He had wanted to ask, but hadn't.

He stopped and looked at the sky. The buzzards would tell him where she was. He knew all he had to do was wait until they started circling.

He saw a crow and heard its caw, caw, and then, sliding silently through the air was one buzzard, then another. They were moving in, large, dark birds, nature's revolting but necessary scavengers.

He watched them circle, their heads lowering, their si-lent, gliding flights bringing them closer to the ground. They were coming down near the edge of the woods, down below the hollow near pond three. So close? No more than a quar-ter of a mile from the main house.

Rufus began to walk fast, going back over his tracks, then

247

turning right, he headed away from the path he had taken, and went toward the small tract of woodland. It was here the boys cut wood for the big old fireplace in the living room of the bunkhouse. The fireplace was used only for special occasions, Thanksgiving, Christmas, a winter birthday.

Shadows filled the hollow, but through the trees, he could see the ground was almost as neat as the mowed area around the buildings. On the other side of the woods, though, nearer the ponds and the paths, was a pile of brush.

Rufus went toward it.

He stopped at the edge of the brush, dreading his next move. She was here. The buzzards had told him. They were still overhead, still circling, waiting for him to go away.

He bent down and began moving the cut limbs and dried leaves. The white hand lay palm up on the dark grass, the fingers curled. She was still wearing the small birthstone ring she had gotten for her last birthday, and which she had shown him so proudly.

Look, Rufus, what my dad gave me. And see the diamonds, one on each side. Look, Rufus.

Her face was turned toward him. Empty holes where her lovely blue eyes had been seemed to stare at him, mutely questioning this horror that had happened to her. Her mouth hung open, her lips pale and white, as if she had been drained of blood.

Rufus fell to his knees. "Oh, God, Gwen, oh Gwendolyn, oh God, Marsh, *Marsh.*" He had hoped, prayed, he was wrong. That he wouldn't find her—that it wasn't Gwendolyn that drew the buzzards. He had prayed, he knew now, without knowing he prayed.

He turned away, tears hot beneath his eyelids. Two thin drops squeezed out. Tears had not come to his eyes in so long, he no longer knew how to cry. He needed the relief, but it didn't come.

Marsh. . . .

He had to protect Marsh.

Marsh didn't know what he was doing. The calf, the dog, and now the girl? The eyes—Rufus didn't understand—why was he removing the eyes? He had to be using a knife. Marsh with a knife? Where had he gotten it? Why? Would the psychiatrist say it had something to do with the ax attack on Marsh when he was hardly more than a baby?

It was his fault for letting Marsh leave the bunkhouse.

He had fallen asleep. He had meant to stay awake and listen to any movement Marsh might make through the night. But he had failed. It was as much his fault as it was Marsh's. Something was haywire in the boy's brain, but it wasn't his fault, not the boy's fault. Blame those faraway parents, blame anybody but Marsh.

Rufus took off his raincoat and put it over the girl's body. When he pushed the brush away he saw she was dressed only in those little shorty things he'd seen in catalogs. So she had come out at night?

It didn't make sense.

Could Marsh have gotten into the house and taken her out? Without anyone knowing?

No, it didn't make sense.

But here she was, and only Rufus knew. And Marsh.

He would have to bury her, somehow. It would be better to let everyone think she had run away. Better than letting Marsh suffer for something he couldn't be blamed for—something he didn't know was wrong?

Yes, he knew. Surely he knew.

Marsh, oh, Marsh, what have you done?

He straightened, leaving her covered with his raincoat. The deed was done. It would have to be hidden. What good would come of having Marsh punished? Taken away and put behind bars?

From now on, he would watch Marsh, every minute through the night. He would spend his nights in the chair. The future . . .

There was no future.

Only tomorrow, and another tomorrow if they were so granted.

And tonight.

Tonight he would bring a shovel from the barn and dig a grave in the soft soil of the woodland, and bury her deeply enough the buzzards would go away. Later tonight.

Lights were coming on in the houses when he approached the barn. Twilight would soon turn to darkness. He walked

249

toward the bunkhouse with a heavy, slow tread, feeling his life and energy draining away step by step.

Babette saw the gates to Boys' Farm. The man had driven slowly, talking, telling her about his family. Three daughters, and four granddaughters and Babette reminded him of them. He had told her about his wife dying, and how far away his daughters lived, all of them married to men who were from other states. "Met them in college," he said. Sometimes he went to visit them, but he didn't feel like intruding on their lives or going to live with them permanently, so he had gotten himself a job selling cameras, and he pointed out the cases in the back seat. The job took up his time, but kept him on the road a lot, and he had gotten tired of listening to the radio. Did she know the kind of music that was being played these days? Well, he supposed she did, but she was young. His music wasn't played much anymore. And he got tired of listening to news. All of it bad, it seemed. Where was she going?

She had finally told him Boys' Farm. Her aunt lived there, she said, worked there, and she was going to see her.

He knew where it was, he had passed it a few times.

On the way he had wanted to eat, and asked if she was hungry. A hamburger, he said, a Coke and fries—fast food. So they had stopped, and it seemed they spent an hour. He was in no hurry, and she had stopped being afraid of him. He was a grandpa, he told her. She was far hungrier than she had realized.

When he stopped on the side street by Boys' Farm, the high, closed gate just yards away, he asked, "Does your aunt know you're coming?"

"Oh, yes," she said. "Thank you for the ride. And everything."

She got out and stood watching him, wanting him to go. Behind her the long buildings just beyond the fence looked weathered and deserted, and she hoped they stayed that way until the man was gone. Lights in the windows at one end of a long building looked like jack-o'-lantern eyes, yellow and hooded, with the blinds drawn.

At this moment she was glad it was still raining. There was no one out, that she could see. Trees beyond the gates hid parts of more buildings, most of them white, like regular houses. She glanced back and then looked again at the grandfather, realizing at that moment that she didn't even know his name.

"Why don't I drive you on up to the house?" he asked through the open passenger window.

She shook her head, and cast a glance over her shoulder. She saw a woman come out onto the narrow porch of the long, low building with the lighted windows.

"There she is," Babette said hurriedly. "There's my aunt."

The man nodded, waved, and drove away. Babette watched the window shut as the car turned and pulled onto the street leading to the highway.

Babette looked toward the woman and saw she was still on the porch of the long building to the right of the entrance building by the big gates. She seemed to be looking north, but Babette couldn't see her features. Was the woman watching her? Dusk had settled beneath the overhang of the roof, and the woman was a shadow without identification except for the round, grandmotherly shape of her body and the dress she wore.

Babette looked around, suddenly frantic for someplace to pretend she had been going to, any place other than those big gates, and those buildings behind the high fences. If the woman went back into the house and told someone there was a visitor, Babette wouldn't stand a chance of getting to Paddy. Someone would come out to see who she was, and the police would be called—and Miss Thornton—and she'd be taken away. And if she told them to please protect Paddy from his mother, and why, they would only think she was being hysterical. She couldn't say, "My mother thinks my brother is a vampire, and she's going to kill him."

She couldn't.

She saw a house across the road, a white farmhouse, at the end of a driveway, sheltered in a grove of trees. She started toward it. The woman would think she had been let

out on this side of the highway, and she was visiting someone at the farmhouse.

She went to the edge of the highway and stood waiting
for traffic to pass. Before she started across, she looked back
at the porch. The woman was gone.

Babette saw to her right, along the tall fence, a row of
mesquite, like a hedge, a green camouflage.

She ran toward the trees along the fence of Boys' Farm.

Rufus sat in his place at the dinner table unable to eat.
The boys were quiet tonight, sharing little of the banter and
joviality that usually went on. Always quiet, Marsh sat on
Rufus's right. Rufus could see his big hands as they tore a
bun in half, then tore each half, and kept tearing the bread
until it was in bits. Then the boy's big, smooth hands, bigger than his own, picked up the bits of bread and wadded
them into a round, hard ball of dough.

Marsh had come to the farm ten years ago with this habit.
But in the years since, he had eaten heartily and grown,
and had seemed to be happy and well.

The authorities had wanted to take him away after a few
months on the farm and institutionalize him. Rufus had
persuaded them not to. "He's all right," he had told Mary
Bolinger. "He's going to be just fine here." He had tried
so hard to persuade them to leave the boy.

He saw now that he had made a terrible mistake.

After dinner he sat on the porch, waiting, his fingers
drumming on the wooden arms of the rocking chair. He
watched the night darken, and then he saw the clouds thin
and the moon come out full and bright.

He waited until all the boys had gone into the bunkhouse
and were in bed. All evening Marsh had sat on the porch,
in front of Rufus, leaning against a post, his legs swinging.
All evening he hadn't spoken a word, and Rufus had said
nothing. A few of the other boys had sat with them awhile,
and a conversation about baseball had come up.

But it was with relief and dread combined that Rufus
waited to be alone. He waited for the sounds of settling in
for the night to cease, and the bunkhouse lights to go out.

Then he went to his room and took his rifle down from the top of the closet. It had been a long time since it was used. A few years ago he had enjoyed keeping it in shape with a little target practice in one of the back fields. But it had been three or four years since the rifle had even been cleaned.

He checked the bore and found it still looked fairly clean. He snapped the barrel in place and loaded it from the little box of bullets tucked in the corner of the top shelf.

When he left his room, the rifle was under his arm, the muzzle pointed toward the ground.

Tonight he had to bury Gwen, the little girl he had rocked on his knee when she was only a baby. He wondered if he could bury her, if he could put her body into a hole and cover it with dirt. He wondered if he could ever go back to that wooded lot.

He had to stop Marsh before he killed again.

He walked across the park-like area between the bunkhouse and the barns. A light from the horse's stall spread like a lacy fan out into the paddock. Shadowed upon it was a long, thin figure standing next to the huge shadow of the horse. Orion. Rufus had watched him cross the yard toward the barn, a small, quick figure going to stay with the horse.

Rufus paused. The shovels were in the barn. Could he take one without Orion knowing? The shed room containing the shovels, rakes, and hoes, was on the side of the barn opposite the horse stall. There should be no problem.

Rufus swung to the left, keeping to the shadows as much as he could, the light of the moon seeming like filtered sun in contrast to the darkness of last night with its clouds and rain.

He passed within reach of the rusted old combine and the picnic table beneath the maple tree. He went toward the barn, under cover of the tall trees.

The shovel. The grave . . .

He wouldn't allow himself to think of it.

It was something he had to do.

And then he had to stop Marsh.

"Rufus."

Rufus almost dropped the rifle. The voice came out of

the darkness and trees to his right. It was a man's voice, but he didn't recognize it.

He blinked and saw the pale outline of a man's face. The the figure moved, separated from a black tree trunk, and became the familiar shape of Mr. Preston.

"I see you've got your rifle, Rufus." Martin said.

"Uh—yeah, I thought I'd best get it out."

Martin Preston stepped into the scattered moonlight at the edge of the tree so that his face, head and shoulders were dotted with light. Rufus watched him lift his head and look off toward the big gate.

"I'll walk along with you, Rufus. Out for a walk, or going down to the cattle pastures?"

"Uh—just thought I'd walk around a bit."

Rufus angled toward the string of ponds, away from the grove of trees where the child's body lay. For a few yards they walked in silence. Rufus started shaking so hard that the rifle rattled against the little stud at the side of his boot. He lifted it, cradling it in his arm, the muzzle pointed forward and slightly downward. With his finger on the safety catch, he snapped it off.

"Her mother ran away too, Rufus," Martin said.

"Eh?" Rufus thought at first he hadn't heard Mr. Preston right.

"I never told you," Martin Preston said, walking at Rufus's side, hands still in his pockets. "I never told anyone. She ran away from me and the babies, said she wanted some excitement out of life. She was a beautiful woman. Gwendolyn took after her. Hagar isn't like that, she's more like me. Daily life was always good enough for me, and seems to be for Hagar, life and animals, and the people around home. But Gwen is different. I could see that, though Gwen didn't know I could. Hagar came to me a short time ago, a few days, and wanted to talk about Gwen—but I wasn't ready to take a real good look at what I felt might be trouble someday."

Rufus didn't know what to say. He could see the little girl, her hand thrown out, palm toward the sky. He could see her face, and the holes where her eyes had been. He felt he was going to collapse, his legs giving out beneath him.

But he had to keep on walking. To keep on listening. Mr. Preston wanted to talk.

Rufus had to listen. And say nothing.

"Her mother had been restless for a long time. After each of the girls was born, she was interested in them for a little while. But maybe she was too young to be a mother. She was twenty-three when Gwen was born. Maybe for her, it was too young."

Rufus nodded. They walked through moonlight, strolling more and more slowly toward the bright surface of the pond. On the grass at the edge of the pond sat the ducks, settled for the night, their heads tucked under their wings. Rufus looked at them without feeling. For the first time in the lives of these fowl he had so enjoyed watching, he wasn't really seeing them. He had a sudden memory of Marsh holding one of the baby ducks in his hands, making a soft, cooing sound of pleasure. He had held the little duck so gently. Those big hands that had turned into killers . . .

"She filed for divorce . . . she had been gone two months. And then one night I was watching the late news and there was a report of a traffic accident. A man and a woman traveling at a high rate of speed had gone off the road, overturned several times, and were both killed. It was my wife."

Rufus had never known that. He knew Mrs. Preston was dead. That was all. He had never even wondered about it much. Lots of folks die when they're still young. There had been too much other stuff to keep his mind occupied over the years since he met Martin Preston and his two little girls.

"So when I saw that Gwen was growing up to look like and act like her mother, I knew the time would come when she would leave, too. I just didn't think it would be so soon. I still saw her as my baby, you know."

"You—uh—you think she ran away then," Rufus said, hearing his voice unfamiliar in its huskiness.

"I have to think that. It *can't* be anything else. If I have to lose her it has to be that, Rufus. At least she's somewhere out there—and I'll find her if I can."

It was better that way, Rufus saw. Burying the girl would

be the most humane thing to do after all. It was better that Mr. Preston think his little girl was still alive somewhere in the world than for him to know the truth.

"We'll go ahead and open the gates tomorrow. The farm has to go on."

He walked on and Martin kept step with him, silent now.

The moon rose higher in the sky. They stopped and looked at its trail across the surface of pond two, and then Rufus turned back toward the bunkhouse.

He had known, in the depths of his heart, that he couldn't bury the child anyway. Not without a casket, not without the protection of at least that. He didn't know what to do.

In the middle of the moonlit compound he separated from Martin and went back to the porch of the bunkhouse.

He climbed the steps, his legs trembling with weariness. He sat down in the rocking chair, leaned back with a sigh, and laid the rifle across his legs.

The chair squeaked softly as he rocked. Tomorrow, as Mr. Preston had said, the gates would be opened, and the Saturday crowd would come in. And none of them would know that within the last week two children had died here, one of them—and perhaps both, he now thought—mysteriously. So too had a dog been violently killed, and a calf mutilated—and one of the children.

There was a pattern, it seemed to Rufus. Something in the back of his mind was trying to get his attention, like a portion of a dream that would mean something if only he could understand. But then it was gone, and he could only lean his head back, close his eyes, and listen to every movement around him.

Tonight he would not sleep. Tonight, but later, he had to make himself attend to the burial. He had to keep thinking that choice was best for them all.

Or tomorrow night—

Tonight he must stay awake.

If Marsh came onto the porch tonight, Rufus would know.

The rocking of his chair stopped. The night grew still, traffic stopped, even the barking of a distant dog silenced. In the deep quiet, Rufus half heard the mooing of the cow far over in her pasture, and the sound reached him like a great moan of despair and loneliness. It ran over his skin like a warning.

He snapped alert. He hadn't gone to sleep, yet he had dozed, sitting upright in the chair, his head back against the wood slats. But behind him there had been a movement. Not a sound, just a feeling.

Someone was behind him.

Just standing there.

He could feel it.

A rush of chills covered his body, and he whirled.

The boy was standing within arm's reach behind his chair. Rufus could see the ghostly outline of his face, and nothing else. He clambered to his feet, and the rifle fell to the floor with a loud clang.

Marsh . . . *not Marsh*.

"Here," Rufus said, a rush of anger flooding into his fear. "Here," he said again. "What are you doing out here?" It was the new boy, he saw. Patrick. He saw the boy stoop and pick up the rifle and hand it toward him, the stock first, as if someone had taught him the proper way to hand a gun to another person. Rufus took it, his hands still shaking, the fury blending with fear, his heart pounding.

"I just got up to go to the bathroom," the boy said.

"Well, go on, it's not out here!"

The boy turned and went back into the hall, and Rufus sat down in the rocking chair, his hands gripping the rifle between his knees. He was already sorry he had barked at the boy. The kid had probably seen him through the open doorway, and had wondered what he was doing on the porch at this hour.

Well, tomorrow he would tell Patrick he was sorry.

Then something popped into his mind. He was seeing the boy again, a shadowy but dimly visible image. The boy hadn't been wearing pajamas. He had been wearing his jeans.

Rufus sat forward in his chair frowning. Then he shook his head and leaned back again.

No, he must have been wrong.

Chapter Twenty-Six

Ketti mingled with the crowd of families entering the open main gates to Boys' Farm. Though she walked behind a family of five—mother, father, and three children—she felt exposed. No one knows I'm here, she told herself for the hundredth time. No one would ever recognize me.

She hardly recognized herself. For the first time in her life, her hair was short. After she had cut and dyed it, she had gone to a beauty parlor several blocks away, where she was certain not to meet anyone she knew, and had it professionally shaped. Her reflection in windows she passed revealed a woman she'd never seen. Thinner from her days in jail, days of terrible trauma and the decision she'd come to accept, days when she had trouble forcing food down to keep up the strength she knew she would need.

It's for Babette, she kept telling herself. It's to make very sure that Babette will live.

She wouldn't allow herself to think about the moment when it would happen. The knife was wrapped in a dish towel and carried in a brown sack at her side. Anyone looking at her would think she carried her lunch.

She paid her entry fee at the window, and went through the small, open gates in the breezeway, past the open door of the gift shop, and the soft drink dispenser.

At the end of the breezeway, porches with benches ran along the sides of the buildings. Ahead of her, families were walking toward picnic tables, children were running toward a pond where ducks and geese and a couple of swans paddled in clear, glassy water. Kids were beginning to climb onto the antique machinery that spotted the grassy park. Some families, she saw, were down at the barns, looking at birds in pens, chickens, pheasants.

She went down the steps, looking toward a long building to her right that had a full-length porch facing the slope of the park, the barn, and the ponds.

She knew, in her heart, he was here somewhere. Or he had been, not long ago. She saw someone sitting on a rocking chair. A man. He was too distant for his features to be clear, but he looked like he might be quite old. As she watched, a boy came out of a door and onto the porch. But it wasn't Paddy.

The boy was watching her, she could see, probably because she was staring at the bunkhouse. She turned away. She must remember to act very casual, like a guest. Someone who had come to spend a pleasant day, that was all.

Clutching her brown bag close, she went back to the porch of the entry building and bought a can of Coke. Sipping as she walked, she followed the families toward the ponds to watch the ducks.

The sun was growing hot. She could see steam rising from somewhere beyond the trees that edged part of the pond, and she went toward it. To her right, she noticed, was a big barn, a sprawling structure that seemed to have a lot of pens and sheds. It was surrounded by big trees. Families were going to the pens, looking at the animals, reaching through the wire to stroke animals' heads or feed them from the bags of packaged grain purchased at the entrance.

Ketti watched, making sure she smiled, so she wouldn't stand out as different. She stood at a fence and looked in at three cute goats.

She walked on around the fences of the barn and looked over a board fence at a beautiful black horse standing in a stall. A young girl with hair almost as dark as the horse's coat was brushing the horse, paying no attention to the people who watched over the fence. She reminded Ketti of Babette. They were enough alike to be sisters.

Ketti pulled away and headed toward the barn, going down a kind of open pathway between fences. In the shadows beneath the overhang of the barn roof, she saw a door.

She was alone for a moment.

She went to the door and turned the wooden latch. The

door swung open and she stepped into a darkened inner hall. Rooms off the corridor were shadowed and dim, the only light coming from the corridor or cracks in the walls. Farm equipment of various kinds filled the rooms, harnesses were on the walls, along with saddles. It was quiet in the middle section of the barn.

She went back out to the corridor and followed it to a lighter area in the center. To her right was an open area of pens with animals eating and resting. It was a roofed area, and no people had come into the pathway between the pens. In one was a cow with a calf so young it was still wobbly on its feet, and Ketti suspected this was an area in which the public was not invited. This was a private part of the barn, and it would be a safe place for her to hide later.

To her left was a room that held loose hay. Beyond the hay, she saw when she looked cautiously around the corner, was a manger and beyond that a horse stall. The beautiful black horse had been taken out now, and beyond the open end of the stall she saw the young girl who reminded her heartbreakingly of Babette as she walked the horse in the half sun of the open area of the paddock.

Ketti moved quickly and quietly back through the barn. She would mingle with the people until time for the gates to close, then she would come back to the barn to hide. She hadn't seen Paddy yet—Patrick, as she must think of him now, because she knew in her heart that Paddy had been gone from her, and from himself, for a long, long time.

She must let him see her, come near her. She must lure him into the barn, where it was quiet and dark. She pulled her paper sack tightly under her arm. A terrible nervousness came up her spine and spread across her shoulders and into her jaws. Her teeth began to click together faintly, and she felt colder than she ever had in her life. It was the cold of Danny, and of Billy—she wondered how many other deaths Patrick must have caused—and the forewarning of her own death, so soon to come now. Of course she must die. She would not be able to live after killing the body that had been her son. She was afraid . . . so afraid, so filled with terror because she knew deep down that she would not succeed.

* * *

Babette came into the outer groups of people, picnickers at a table beneath a big tree not far from one of the ponds. Two little kids were wading in the shallow edge of the pond, and a baby sat on a quilt near the picnic table. Babette paused near another tree, her arm brushing its trunk, and saw the couple on the picnic benches glance at her.

She had safely entered the public area of Boys' Farm.

She went on, walking casually as she felt any visitor would, though her heart beat fast and hard. She felt conspicuous, even though she saw she wasn't the only lone stroller. Many people wandered the paths or sat alone at tables or benches, or stood at the ponds feeding the water fowl.

She was tired, so she sat down, her back against another tree trunk, closer to the gates, to the long bunkhouse she had seen yesterday when she first arrived at the gates of the farm.

She had spent the morning walking the fence that surrounded the farm. and found it tall and barbed at the top, impossible to climb. In a way, it was like a prison fence, she guessed, though she knew the wires were to protect all within. She walked miles, it seemed, with nothing but fields and trees on her left and the tall fence on her right. Through the wires of the fence she could see pastures with cattle, horses, goats, and sheep. She could see pasture fences, all of them miniature in comparison to the big outer fence. She saw ponds like small lakes surrounded by lacy mesquite. She could see open ponds, with paths, and swimming areas in the distance, and people. The people seemed to come out with the sunshine.

Last night she had seen she would not be able to get inside the fence, and she had found a clump of mesquite close to the wire and had huddled there, sleepless most of the night, hearing sounds she'd never heard before. Things moved in the leaves, in the air. Traffic was a comfortable drone, familiar but even that had faded, leaving her in the dark, with the drizzling rain, and finally moonlight. That she had slept at all amazed her when she opened her eyes to see sunlight. She had stood up and looked around, her sense of accomplishment overwhelming, bringing to her face a half-smile.

She had survived.

And she had found a way in. A hole under the fence, back where the fence took a sharp angle to the west. To her surprise, the tall fence ended, and the barbed top was gone. The fence was still higher than her head, six feet tall perhaps, but she could manage the climb. But after she had walked a few hundred yards looking for an easy place to go over, she had found the ravine, and at its bottom, the fence didn't quite reach the ground. Something else had burrowed under there many times in the past, it seemed, so that a bare little tunnel went under the fence. Her body barely fit in it, and without too much strain, she crawled through.

She strolled the grounds. The farm was even more beautiful than it had looked from the outside. Big trees dotted the grassy, rolling land that stretched from the ponds past big barns, sheds and pens to the bunkhouse. Over to her right, she saw a row of white houses with their own little yards. She strolled, trying to look as casual as the others. Kids ran, climbed on the machinery, hung on boards of a stockade fence connected to the barn. Boys that looked as if they might live here went around in twos and threes, sometimes stopping to talk to the families or the kids.

But somewhere around here was her mother. Somewhere among the crowd, a woman with dark, short hair, was carrying a knife.

Where would she have gone?

Had she not arrived yet?

Or had she been here and already gone, leaving Paddy dead somewhere, and no one aware of it.

Babette moved across the sunny park toward the building by the gates. She was thirsty, but not hungry, never hungry. Her package of bread and jar of peanut butter had not been touched. She felt in her pocket for two of the quarters and stood for several minutes near the Coke machine, her fingers tightly clutching the coins. Dads came to the machine with their kids, getting cans of pop. She told herself she was waiting because the machines were in use, though in her heart she knew she was afraid to spend what money she had.

But if she had a can in her hand, wouldn't she look as if

she belonged to the crowd that had paid its way through the gate?

She slipped the quarters into the slot before she could think too much about it. Then, with the opened can of Coke, she sat down on one of the benches and watched the boys, looking for one among them.

Long after the Coke can was empty and had grown warm in her hands, she got up from the bench and went down to the barns and strolled the sandy, hard-packed paths that led from pen to pen. The sun had dropped low in the west, and there were fewer people looking at the animals. Babette had moved among them for hours without seeing a familiar face—not Ketti, not Patrick. At times she felt she had come to an alien world, that neither Paddy nor their mother had ever been here.

She watched a group of boys come with feed for the pigs and wished she dared ask one of them if he knew Paddy.

People were leaving through the breezeway that led to the steps and gates in front. Near the big entrance gate was another gate that opened and let out a red pickup, and then closed behind it. Two boys at the gates looked like Paddy. Both were blond. She went toward them, but stopped beneath a tree. If she went too far out into the open she would be expected to leave with the crowd.

She saw groups of families over beyond the ponds, and she went toward them, walking as if she were going to join one of them. As soon as she was behind the mesquite at the edge of pond two, she ran under cover of the shrub-like trees toward the pastures, where she would not be seen. Where she could safely stay until dark and find her brother.

Ketti positioned herself in the barn so she could see the bunkhouse. She had spent most of the afternoon in the barn, watching. The chores had started, and she remembered from her youth how animal feedings were handled. The boys would be around with buckets of grain or pitchforks of hay. And among them, somewhere, she might find Patrick.

A small boy with dark hair went into a wire pen with a bucket of grain, pulling the door's wooden latch into place.

"Chick, chick, chick," he clucked to the pheasants as they came to him. Ketti watched as he poured the grain into feeders and then went out to a hydrant to get a bucket of water for the waterers. Three little children clung to the wire and watched him, silent and awed. Their parents stood nearby.

Ketti almost didn't see the boy coming down the path. She glanced at him, and then stared. Patrick. Shadows covered his face as he walked beneath the deepening shade of a tree. His eyes looked hollow—lifeless—in that first startled moment of recognition.

Then he was staring at her, and she saw the pale gray, that odd lightness that had replaced the soft blue of Paddy's eyes.

She felt penned by his eyes, trapped against the shadowed door of the corridor in which she knew Patrick had recognized her. He was not fifteen feet away, and other people wandered the path—the two young parents, the children who had watched the feeding of the pheasants, the boy with the feed bucket and others. Yet she felt as if she was in a frightening world alone with this person—this non-person—she must kill.

She had wanted this confrontation, yet now she was terrified.

Then Patrick was moving on, casually going out of sight.

With her back pressed to the rough board wall, she hid. Through the open end of the corridor she had a narrow view of part of the path and the dark trunk of a tree. Two children ran by, in her view for only a second. Maybe she had only thought he recognized her. Maybe he had stopped and stared because she was staring at him. She had planned to call him to her, to get him away from the crowd, to . . .

But she couldn't.

In the end, she couldn't, and hadn't she known, perhaps, that she would never be able to kill him?

Yet if she didn't, he would kill Babette—she had to remember that.

She edged down the central corridor into the darker areas of the barn. She pulled the knife out and let the paper bag fall to her feet. She stood with her back against the wall, around the corner from the corridor, and listened for footsteps on the board floor. Beyond the wall at her back she heard animal sounds, shuffling, eating, and the voices of people. A man called, "Come on, kids, it's time to go."

"Wait just a minute, Daddy, he's going to feed the goats. The little baby goats."

Their voices sounded light and happy, a stark contrast to the truth of her world, her feelings. She wanted to cry. Why couldn't her life have been like that . . . three sons, one daughter . . . Edward . . . a day at a park, or zoo, or farm like this.

He was there, suddenly, his face at the corner by hers.

She had heard no sound, no approaching steps.

Her hand jabbed into her pocket for the small plastic bag of *Wolfsbane,* and found nothing. She had lost it. Dear Lord, where had she lost it? When she rested for a few minutes on the hay? When she leaned down in the corridor to tie her shoe?

She was unprotected. She had to get away.

Escape . . .

Get to Babette—take her away—run once again from this being that had once been her baby boy.

She jerked back and started running, stumbling over the hay, her breath caught in her throat and chest. Something dark and swift flew over her, and she whirled and felt her feet tangle in the hay. She felt his hand grip her wrist and press, and heard the cracking of her own thin bones. The pain shot up her arm and she gasped. Her fingers released the handle of the knife. She twisted away from him and tried to get to her feet, but felt herself being thrown back again, pushed into the hay. His face above hers was a pale and featureless blur, his eyes as empty as holes. She saw . . . wings . . . wings growing from his body, and his mouth had fangs. It was the terrible creature she had seen over his bed that night so long ago . . . when Paddy was only five. . . .

She could no longer separate her son from the winged creature. They became one, and her fear distorted what she saw. She tried to scream, but heard only a gurgle in her throat. And it was then that she realized she had already been slashed, that her throat had been laid open. She could smell the warm, metallic scent of her own blood, and she saw it sprinkle his face like freckles. Then he was opening his mouth and lowering his face.

And she lost sight and feeling.

Mark Ford lay in the recliner on the patio at the back of his house. Light from the kitchen made a slight, almost sickly contrasts to the dwindling light of day, passing over his feet and fading away on the potted plants at the edge of the patio.

The kids were still in the wading pool probably with chattering teeth, he thought, but he was reluctant to tell them to call it a day and come on in. It had been a great day, the kind that came too seldom. He had been off work for two days now, and was just about to get so used to it that he would never want to go back to the dark side of life, the killings, the drugs.

He heard the phone ring, but it was a distant sound that had nothing to do with him. On his days off, he was seldom called back to the station, and their friends and family were always taken care of by Janice.

When she called him, he felt surprise, irritation, and then curiosity.

"For you," she said again, looking out the patio doors, the light creating a halo of brightness around her blond hair. "It must be fairly important. It's someone from the station."

On Saturday evening, the second day of a three-day weekend?

He got up, feeling a little stiff from lounging so long on his spine. "Better come on in, kids," he said, pausing at the door. "You'll be turning blue the next thing you know."

"Aw, Daddy . . ."

"I'll pull the plug on that thing when I get back if you're not out of it."

"Okay, Daddy, just a minute."

Mark gave his wife a light kiss on the cheek as he passed by her. He saw the kitchen phone was dangling at the end of its cord, but he passed it by and went to his office.

"Hey, Ford," said the familiar voice of a fellow detective. "I know you're real glad to hear my voice, but we finally got some news on that guy in Washington that you were interested in a few days ago."

"Justin Skein? The boy's dad?"

"Yeah. They found him. I thought you'd want to know."

"Sure. Where is he?"

"He's dead, that's where. They found him in the woods, behind his house under some brush. But the strange thing is, he was covered by a leather jacket that had a furred vampire bat and the word 'vampire' on the back—like a cult or gang jacket. You know the kind. And there was something else. His eyes had been cut out of his head. He'd been dead about ten days."

Mark frowned at the wall in front of him, seeing again the dead calf, its eyes removed. He didn't realize he hadn't answered Detective Johnson until he heard him ask, "You still there?"

"Yeah, I'm here. Was there anything else?"

"Not much. No one in the area seemed to know anything about a vampire gang or club. They said Skein had lived there for about seven years, and had been a good enough citizen. He had a woman living with him, and until recently, a son. The son had gone to school, with ordinary records. There had never been any trouble."

"What about the woman?"

"Nothing. But I've got a hunch she's hit the road. She probably got mad at him. Pretty damned mad, if you ask me. Killing him wasn't enough."

"You think she's the killer?"

"Well, that, or it's a cult killing. Anyway, I thought you'd want to know. I knew you were wanting to find the kid's dad so you could send him home. But that's it. I guess the boy is a permanent at Boy's Farm, if they've got room for him."

After they hung up, he sat down at his desk and stared at the calendar on the wall.

A calf with its eyes removed. A man with his eyes removed. A leather jacket with a vampire, a cult thing?

A retarded boy calling another a "bad boy."

He leaned forward, dialed the station number, and asked for Detective Johnson.

"You didn't tell me how Skein was killed," Mark said.

"Well, maybe that's because I didn't have anything to tell. The report from there simply said he was found dead. I guess the ordinary way, shot or stabbed. Maybe, if it was done by the woman, he was poisoned."

Mark Ford hung up the phone again. Or no visible means, he thought, just as there had been no visible means on the calf, only a strange lack of blood in the body. And its eyes had been removed.

He looked up Martin Preston's number at Boys' Farm and dialed it, not exactly sure what he was going to talk to the man about. Just before the phone rang, he hung up. He sat frowning at the back of his hand as it rested on the phone.

He would have to talk to the boy, Patrick. The father had been dead for over a week, ten days, so that meant the boy must have some information about it. *He went away,* he remembered the boy saying to him. His old man had gone away. Left.

Yet there was something wrong. And Patrick, was tied to it.

Tomorrow would do. He could drive out tomorrow and talk to the boy.

He started to leave the office, yet a feeling of urgency drew him back to the phone. He felt puzzled, thoughtful, as if the answer was behind a curtain in his mind. One phone call, tonight.

A girl answered on the first ring, and said, "Hello?" Not "Boys' Farm," as he had expected. This had to be one of Martin Preston's daughters.

"This is Detective Mark Ford. Is Martin Preston available?"

"Have you found Gwen?" she asked quickly, her voice anxious and rising.

"Gwen?" Was he supposed to know someone named Gwen? He couldn't place the name.

"My sister," the girl said, her voice dropping, becoming soft and faraway. Then she added, "My dad isn't here. He went to look for her, I think, though he didn't say."

"Your sister was expected home at a certain time and didn't come?"

"My sister ran away, the police think, night before last."

"I hadn't heard about this. Would the county police have the information?"

"Yes, I guess so."

"Tell me about her."

"She was only eleven. But she looked older. She had blond hair and blue eyes. She didn't take anything. Daddy's been looking for her everywhere."

"You don't think she ran away." It was a feeling he had, more of the puzzled blackness in the back of his mind.

"Why would she?" the girl cried, and he could hear a throatiness in her voice, as if she was holding back tears. "Dad thinks she might have, because he said our mother did, and Gwen was a lot like her. And she knew where the keys are. The keys to the gates. But none of them is missing."

He heard the doorbell ring, and his wife went down the hall. A moment later, the two kids were squealing and greeting Grandma and Grandpa, and Janice called, "Company, Mark."

He had to go. His mother and father-in-law had driven from the other side of town to have dinner and spend Saturday evening with them. The case of the missing girl was in the hands of the county police since Boys' Farm was outside the city limits.

"I'm sorry about your sister," he said. "I called to talk to your father about one of the boys. I'll be in touch tomorrow—"he started to say, and then he remembered that tomorrow was Sunday, and he had promised Janice they would go to church, and then on a picnic with friends. One more day, he supposed, would solve nothing that couldn't be solved the day after. "I'll call back Monday."

He hung up the phone, listened for a moment to the voices of the kids, still loud and eager. In the back of his mind the puzzle squirmed, broken pieces fitting together on their own.

And in the middle of it was the missing child, thought to have run away through locked gates.

He knew as he went back to the family room to join the

guests that he would not be waiting until Monday to talk to Martin Preston.

Chapter Twenty-Seven

Babette sat on the bank of the pond looking into the clear water. Beneath the surface she could see the green tops of plants undulating in the still water as though there was a slow current somewhere in the depths. Air from the pond's surface rose to chill her arms, and she put on her wind-breaker. She saw her reflection in the glassy surface of the pond, a triangular face framed by a fringe of dark hair. Her bangs had grown since she had last really looked at herself in a mirror, and now they reached almost to her eyebrows. She put up a hand and pushed them back, but they fell forward again. She thought of Narcissus looking into the water, and falling in love with his image.

She sat still, her small sack of food on the ground beside her. She had finally eaten a slice of bread with peanut butter, using a little stick to dig it out. She had tried her fingers first, and they still felt gummy even though she had washed them in the pond.

The sounds of the day were changing. The voices of the children and other visitors were gone, and in their place she heard frogs beginning to peep from ponds farther away, and the sounds of chickens and ducks clucking and quacking to be fed. She wanted to look for Ketti, and for Paddy, but if she walked across the park now, she would be seen—a guest who hadn't left, they would think, and would escort her to the gates before they closed for the night. Maybe they had closed already. She had heard cars starting and moving away, soft droning sounds in the distance, rising over the sloping land. She heard the put-put of a tractor somewhere back on the farm and then it stopped, and the evening grew more quiet. Twilight was slipping rapidly toward darkness.

In the stillness came the flip of water, not far from where she sat. A fish, she thought. But the soft splashing continued, and then she saw a boy's hands reaching into the water not ten feet away from her, on the other side of the clump of mesquite under which she was hiding.

She leaned forward slowly, cautiously, to catch a glimpse of his face. She saw blond hair as he leaned down to wash. His hands covered his face, and she stared. Paddy? The hair was like his—not light blond, the way it was three years ago, but dark blond, a soft, golden brown frosted with sun-bleached lightness. *Paddy?*

She wanted to call out his name, but didn't dare. It might not be Paddy, it might be any of the other dozen blond young boys she had seen today, boys that she thought at first glance were her brother.

He took his hands away from his face, and she saw the vaguely familiar features, the soft lips, the firm cheeks, the high forehead.

"Paddy!"

His head jerked toward her, and he stared a cold, hard stare that she thought meant only that he was startled at seeing her here. In that first moment his eyes looked oddly empty, as if he had no eyes. The deep chill that moved over her was denied, pushed beneath her delight in finding her brother at last. Not harmed, but well, alive. Safe.

"Oh, Paddy!" She began crawling toward him beneath the mesquite branches. She saw that the front of his shirt was wet from the water he had used to wash his face, arms, and hands.

"Babette," he said, and smiled faintly.

She could see his eyes better now, but there was something odd about them, and against her will, she was remembering what her mother had said. His eyes had changed, at age five. They had been blue, a soft, light blue, but they changed to gray. *He was no longer my son, Paddy. He was the other—thing,* Ketti had said.

She shivered in her windbreaker. It was the cool air off

271

the water, she told herself, and hugged her arms against her stomach, tucking her hands in beneath the jacket.

"I've looked all day for you, Paddy."

He seemed not to hear what she'd said. His eyes were slightly narrowed, as if he was suspicious of her, withdrawn from her. She felt the lack of friendliness, the absence of the brother and sister relationship they used to have. A deep loneliness settled in her. Weren't they going to be close anymore?

"What are you doing here?" he asked.

"I've—I've been trying to find you—I—"

"You're supposed to leave at six o'clock, didn't you know? They locked the gates at six."

"Paddy, I have to talk to you. Did you know our mama came here today? And she was looking for you, too."

He stared at her, and she began to feel that he was scared, as she was. That they needed to stick together. She wanted to reach out and touch him, to reassure herself, but the chills kept her hands beneath her jacket.

"She's—she's—she thinks terrible things about you, Paddy. Her mind just isn't right anymore. I had to come— I've run away from the foster home where I was living, and I can't let anyone see me or they'll take me somewhere and lock me up. They do runaways, you know."

She gave him a chance to answer, to ask about their mother, but he only stared at her. Shadows seemed to be deepening all around him, taking him away from her, his face growing darker, his eyes deep holes. Once again they were looking empty and soulless, and she couldn't bear to look at him. She let her gaze drop to his hands. She saw something dark beneath his fingernails. He seemed to see it too, now, for he began digging at it.

"She even dyed her hair, Paddy, and cut it short. I went home, and I saw where she had. Then I came out here, yesterday evening, but I didn't have the money to come through the gate, so I crawled under the fence at the back of the farm."

He said nothing.

She heard a loud cry from somewhere up by the barns. She shuddered.

"Peacock," he said. "They make that noise."

"Oh. Paddy—what are we going to do? You haven't seen Mama, have you?"

"I haven't seen her."

For a moment he gave his attention to cleaning his fingernails. She watched him dip his hands into the water again and wash away whatever it was that darkened his nails.

"I know she's coming to find you. I just know it."

"If they see you," he said, "they'll make you leave. Or Mr. Preston will call that Child Services lady and they'll take you back, like you said, and put you where you can't get out. So I have to hide you."

"I slept under the mesquite last night. Paddy, I was thinking. We can go together. Why don't we go together? I know where to get out. Come with me, Paddy. Together maybe we can get back to your dad, and he'll let me live with you, too."

"Naw."

"Why not?" She felt frantic with anxiety. She reached over and clutched his sleeve. The thought hadn't really come to her until now, but it seemed the only solution. "Mama doesn't want us now, Paddy. She thinks you—you're—she thinks you killed Danny and Billy. She's gone crazy, Paddy. And if we run away together, it will help her too, because she'll have to go back to work, and maybe in time she'll be better. Come with me, Paddy. There are a lot of farms and woods and places we could hide."

He shrugged slightly, pulling his sleeve away from her hand. "Look," he said. "Maybe you're right. Yeah, we can do that."

"Oh, Paddy! Come on, hurry." She stood up.

"No, we can't do it that way. I tell you what. You wait for me in the barn, and I'll come out after everyone's asleep. If I'm not there for supper, they'll find us before dark. But if we wait until midnight, we'd have hours and hours before they found out I was gone."

She squatted, some of the fear coming back. She wanted to leave now, both of them. "In the barn?"

"Sure. It's dark and safe. It's a big place, with lots of

rooms and passages, and I can take you there. Come on. Wait, let me see if anyone's around.''

He stooped and went out under the hedge of mesquite, calling to her, ''Okay it's safe. Nobody's in sight. They've all gone in for supper now. Hurry. I have to go, too.''

The chills had come back, shaking her whole body, causing her teeth to chatter faintly. She tightened her jaws until her teeth began to ache.

Away from the mesquite, with no guests roaming the area, she felt exposed, as if the dark windows of the houses beyond the trees could see her, and were watching her. Dusk was falling rapidly now. Paddy went ahead of her, walking fast, keeping to the edge of the mesquite. At the end of the pond he glanced back only to see that she was close, then he ran to the shelter of the tall shade trees that grew between the upper end of the second pond and the lower parts of the barn lot.

At the corner of the barn, near a pen built with two sides of board fence, a barn side and a wall, he stopped and took her arm.

''In here,'' he whispered. ''There's a long hall.''

They passed by the pen where three goats munched hay. They raised their pointed faces with the little beards, and looked at them. They looked oddly contented, it seemed to Babette, but a little weird. She wasn't afraid of them . . . yet she was afraid.

She hesitated at the door Paddy opened. Beyond it she saw darkness, and smelled a dusty, musty, hay-like odor, and smothery blackness.

''It's not as dark as it looks,'' he said softly in her ear. ''When you get in there you'll see that light comes through the cracks. You'll be all right. I'll be back at midnight.''

She stepped up into the barn, and the door closed. She stood with her back against the wall, her hands feeling the rough boards.

Midnight was so far away.

Martin stopped the pickup at the gate, got out, and took his keys out of his pocket. A tall light near the gate outlined the hood of his old, red pickup. He could hear a faint buzz from the light as he unlocked the gate.

He had driven into the small town to the east where the kids went to school, and had talked to three girls he had heard Gwendolyn mention. None of them had heard from her.

He had driven the highway, as slowly as he could, pulling over when a car wanted him out of the way, as if he might find his child walking in the grass at the side of the road.

He felt drained with weariness and hopelessness. Where was she? His baby, his little girl.

During the day he had walked the farm, looking. Why did he keep going back to the ponds? It was as if he would see her reflection in the water. His baby, tucked safely into a basket and set to drift on the ponds.

He had gone again to the sheriff, but there was nothing. They had put out a missing child report, the sheriff's people told him, and they were on the alert for the girl, not only here, but everywhere. She had become one of the thousands of missing children.

He drove through the gates, got out and locked them again, and put the keys into his pocket. He drove to his usual parking place under the trees.

Hagar was still up, or else she had left lights on all over the house, it seemed. For the first time, he wondered if she had been afraid of being alone in the house.

But the house was quiet. The hall lights were on, and that was all he saw, even though it had seemed as if every light was burning. He went into the bedroom hall and saw that her door was standing open.

She was asleep, her face softly outlined against her white pillow. He bent and kissed her cheek lightly before he went out into the hall.

Gwen's door was closed. He stood with his hand on the doorknob, hoping that a miracle had happened and Gwen had come home and was safe in her bed.

He opened the door. But the hall light shining across her bed showed it was the way she had left it, covers thrown back, the pillow still bearing her impression.

Empty.

Marsh lay stiff and still in his bed, his eyes glued to the cot against the wall, to the figure that lay on it.

Marsh would not sleep, tonight. Last night he had meant to not sleep, but he had, without knowing. And when he woke, it was turning day, and time to get up. The strange boy, the bad boy, was in his own bed. Then, as now.

Marsh's eyes closed against his will, and he felt as if he was spinning off into a dark, safe, warm tunnel. He pulled his eyes open.

Movement somewhere. He could hear the soft sounds of a blanket, like the sounds of a mouse making its bed. He widened his eyes and stared toward the dark corner.

The boy was moving, at last. He was rising from his bed.

Marsh heard the sounds of his movements, of his bare feet on the floor as he slipped toward the porch.

The sounds made Marsh tremble. Fear held him, kept him safe in his bed.

The boy was gone, onto the porch, toward where?

Marsh moved. He had to follow. He couldn't lie trembling in his bed the way he had trembled in the dark so long ago.

Marsh got up. He had gone to bed with his jeans on, and like the boy, he went barefoot, going out into the cloak-room, instinctively knowing the way through the dark.

For just an instant, the other boy was a dark figure in the doorway. Then he stepped to one side and was gone.

Marsh hurried to the doorway, and saw that Rufus was sitting in the rocking chair, but he was sleeping. Marsh could hear the sounds of his breathing, the snork-snork of his faint snores.

And outside, going toward the barn, was the bad boy.

He was going to hurt Star Beauty.

Marsh followed him.

Rufus jerked awake. For the first moment he was disoriented, his eyes blinking at the moonlight that turned the edge of the porch silver. It seemed brighter than he had ever seen moonlight, as if it was part of the distant dream that had been his world just a moment ago.

Something had awakened him. Now he knew where he was. He had settled on the porch, determined to stay awake, to make sure Marsh did not leave the bunkhouse.

The chair squeaked as he sat forward.

The figure was only a shadow in the moonlight before it slipped beneath the darkness of the trees. *Marsh*. Going toward the barns.

Rufus reached down and lifted the rifle from the floor beside his chair. His finger released the safety catch as he hurried down the steps.

Chapter Twenty-Eight

Mark lay on his side of the bed, his arms under his head, staring at the ceiling. Light from the moon filtered through the trees and spread across his feet like lace. The ceiling light was an object to stare at while he pondered the puzzle of the boy, Patrick Skein; his mother, Ketti Graham; the two little brothers who had died in their sleep; the sister, Babette, that lost, scared fourteen-year-old who had been the main caretaker of the baby boy; the girl, Gwen, who at eleven was younger than she looked and who suddenly was missing; and the calf with its eyes removed; and now the father of the boy, his eyes missing from his body . . . The puzzle kept changing form, like a kaleidoscope. The pieces shifted, yet refused to come together.

Bad boy . . .

Vampire . . .

No, it was crazy.

Insane.

He had to get up. He couldn't lie still in a safe, comfortable bed while something he didn't understand was unfolding among a group of helpless people.

He had to get up and do something about it. Maybe if he took a drive, it would help. Maybe if he talked to Preston, it would help. Maybe he ought to just have a cup of coffee and think more about it. Sometimes a midnight cup of coffee helped him figure things out.

He sat up carefully, trying not to disturb Janice, and found himself reaching for the jeans he had taken off, instead of the robe he had meant to put on. He was pulling the jeans on when his wife turned over.

"Couldn't sleep?" she asked groggily.

"No. There's something I have to do before I can. I may go out for awhile—to Boys' Farm. Something is going on, and I need to talk to Preston." He had told her part of it—the missing girl, the mother who had tried to kill her son, the calf with its eyes removed.

She drew a long breath. "Okay. Be careful."

In the hallway he pulled his keys out of his pocket and began walking faster. Now that he'd made a decision, he felt relief to a certain degree, and something new—an urgency to get on with it, as if suddenly he knew that nothing would wait until tomorrow.

It seemed to Babette that she had stood in one place for hours while around her, strange, faint noises went on—movements beyond the walls, bumps under the boards of the hall floor below her, rattles like leaves or old hay. Once she sneezed, a sound that seemed to echo through the vast darkness of the barn and, as if her own alien sound had frightened others, the barn became very quiet for a few minutes. She heard the pounding of her own heart in the silence, and felt the coldness of her fear throughout her body.

"Babette."

It was a thin whisper, but it was Paddy, calling her, from down the long, dark corridor in the center of the barn.

She started toward him, toward the sound of her name, her hand touching the wall for guidance. "Paddy?" Her call to him was soft, yet it seemed to resonate in the barn. She heard the stirrings again, the bump of an animal against its stall. The horse? She could only guess. She listened intently, and got no answer.

"Paddy? Where are you?"

"Babette."

The whisper again, as if it came from far away, as if he was calling for help.

Thin tracks of moon light came in ahead of her, showing her a more open area, and the edge of something that might have been hay. The light looked like bars across the hay, thin and pale.

She went toward it.

Something silent and swift zipped over her head. She felt its movement, the stir of air. In the thin spots of moonlight she glimpsed its body, and saw a wide span of dark wings.

It was gone, and then suddenly it was returning, coming through the arrows of pale light swiftly, and it seemed she heard it now, a piercing, high-pitched sound, almost inaudible. With a small cry in her throat, she dropped, to her hands and knees.

It skimmed over her head, and she felt the current of air pull against her.

Her fingers touched something small and cool. A pouch. A small plastic bag of something. She could feel the cardboard label at the top. With her breath held, she picked it up. Herbs in the bag crinkled faintly in her fingers as she turned it, feeling, reading from memory.

Wolfsbane.

Protects you from vampires, Babette.

Mama!

She almost cried it aloud. *Mama.* Mama was here. Had been here. She had dropped this little bag of herbs that she bought for protection.

Babette sat still. She slipped the bag into the hip pocket of her jeans and stared through the darkness around her.

He had lied.

He said he hadn't seen Mama.

He had lied.

She had to get away from him, go for help, try to find Mama.

She reared up and ran, her head low, toward the hay and the open area of pale moonlight. She stumbled over something in the hay, and almost fell, catching herself on her hands. When she looked down, she saw a face staring blankly at her.

She rolled sideways, away from the person in the hay, and got to her hands and knees again. It was just a pale face, with dark blank holes for eyes and mouth, the features shadowy and hardly recognizable. Then as she steadied herself, she saw the face more clearly, the moonlight revealing the outline of nose, chin, and shadowed sockets where eyes should have been.

Mama.

Babette slowly pushed herself to her feet, her hand still touching the hay. In the moonlight she could see Ketti's throat—the open, raw wound, red against her white skin.

The shrill scream that echoed through the barn seemed to come from an animal, not herself. She heard the cracking of boards and the pounding of hooves as the horse tried to break out of its stall.

She turned, and turned again, desperately looking for a way out.

Mama . . . Mama had been right . . . it was Paddy . . . Paddy, the killer . . .

Or . . . Patrick, the vampire . . .

Ketti was right. Her mother was right.

Babette whirled toward the horse stall, and the light of the moon beyond, toward safety and away from the horror that her brother had become. But he was there, standing between her and the dim light of outdoors, the horse stall behind him.

She couldn't see his face, only the shape of his head and shoulders. She heard the *whirr* of wings again, an almost silent, swift approach, and saw the winged creature light on Paddy's—Patrick's—shoulder so that in the shadows it now looked as if the boy himself was a winged vampire.

The horse had reared and was hammering at the boards of its stall. Beyond the horse, Babette saw someone else had entered the paddock. Another dark, shadowy figure was running, climbing over the stall gate.

With a cry, she ran toward that person, trying to dodge around Patrick.

She felt herself grabbed by a hand on her arm, and she was flung sideways. She fell, crashing into the stanchions. With her hands out, grasping for anything, she got hold of the boards and tried to pull herself free. If she could only get into the horse's stall, she would be safe . . . safe with that other boy . . . whoever he was.

But the hand that gripped her arm pulled her back slowly, and she saw moonlight glint on the knife blade as it flashed toward her.

Marsh heard a strangled cry somewhere in the dark of the barn, beyond the empty horse stall. Star Beauty was gone. He could hear her hooves pounding the packed soil of her track at the far end of the paddock. The goat had gone with her, a small, quick movement, like a ghost in the shadows of the open paddock. But the bad boy was hurting something—or someone—In the dark of the barn, a voice cried out, hoarse and low.

Marsh went toward it, blinded by the darkness. Smells of hay and manure, old and gone to black dirt now, mixed with the scent of something else—something tangy and sickening. It was a smell he remembered vaguely, a smell that once came from his own flesh. Blood. *Blood.*

He came up against the wood of the manger and stanchions, and crawled through. In the striped moonlight that lay beyond, he saw the dark movement of bodies in the hay. Something large and black with swift and hissing wings came at him and he felt the scrape of talons in his scalp.

He lunged forward, and felt something like the fabric of jeans beneath his hand. He closed on it, and found he had grasped an ankle. He jerked, putting all his strength behind the pull. In the pale streaks of light he saw the oval face turn toward him, teeth barred, a hand raising and a knife catching the light before it plunged into darkness again.

He didn't feel the tearing until the knife was pulled from

his flesh. Blood squirted onto his shirt from the open wound in his shoulder.

With both hands he reached for the arm with the knife and felt slender bone and thin muscle. Pulling hard, he reared back and felt the boards of the stanchion give way as he tumbled out into the horse stall, the burden of the other body grunting over him.

Who had cried out? She was screaming now, her voice raised. *Hagar?*

With a cry of fury and fear in his throat, Marsh dragged the boy out into the stall and jerked him up, his hands around the soft throbbing neck. His eyes caught a glimpse of movement above him as dark wings swept down, the talons coming at his face.

The horse's scream blended with the bleat of goats and the restless stirrings of other animals. The paddock, spotted with moonlight and black shadows, revealed nothing. Rufus heard the sound of the horse's hooves against cracking boards.

He ran, his rifle up.

As he reached the paddock fence, the horse broke free and pounded out into the open. The black body flashed briefly in the moonlight before it passed in front of Rufus, a wild flight from danger.

Beyond the broken stall gates, Rufus saw Marsh, a dark shadow moving at the edge of the moonlight.

He raised his rifle and aimed.

Tears blurred his eyes, and his hand began to shake so badly that he couldn't pull the trigger. There was no way he could save Marsh from the punishments that lay before him. He couldn't kill the boy. Just as he hadn't been able to bury Gwen's body, he now couldn't kill Marsh.

He lowered the rifle. But he had to stand up like a man and do what he had come to do. He had to kill Marsh.

He brought the rifle up again, aimed, and pulled the trigger.

A hand grabbed his arm and shoved it upward, and Rufus heard the bullet whine harmlessly off into space. He looked at the face beyond his shoulder.

The lawman. Ford.

Without a word, the detective ran to the paddock fence and leaped over it.

As Rufus's eyes cleared, he saw that the figure he'd thought was Marsh was actually two people fighting in the horse stall.

He heard footfalls and turned to see Mr. Preston running past him toward the paddock gate.

A girl's scream tore through the air, released, it seemed, from a trance of silent fear.

Hagar?

Rufus dropped the rifle and ran.

Passing him from behind came Orion, and then others. The boys, disturbed and frightened, waited at the paddock fence.

The light in the horse stall came on, and Rufus saw before him a white-faced girl who he at first thought was Hagar. Then he realized Hagar was behind him.

Marsh knelt over someone on the ground. His hands were on the boy's neck. The boy's head hung awkwardly to one side.

EPILOGUE:

Babette sat on the fence watching Hagar ride Star Beauty around the paddock. Orion stood near her, his arms folded across the top board.

Behind her, Babette heard the contented cluck of hens. Tomorrow was visitors' day, and the boys were getting ready, grooming the animals, choosing the chickens and roosters that would be penned for viewing.

Racing season was growing near, and Orion had decided to give Star Beauty her chance. She would be entered in her first race, the Futurity. She was three years old now, and ready to race.

A year had passed since Babette slipped beneath the farm fence, since she had stumbled onto her mother's body. Since Patrick had been killed by Marsh. Since the body of Hagar's little sister, Gwendolyn, had been uncovered by Rufus.

Patrick was known to be the killer, of not only Gwendolyn, but his own mother, father and stepmother—and Babette knew in the dark, secret places of her mind, of Rex, also. But all the things Ketti believed of him were not known by anyone but Babette.

She was finally happy with the Prestons, living on the farm, knowing she had a home and a family again. But at night, she lived the early part of her life over again, when Paddy was her little brother, innocent and sweet, before the other—whatever it was—had come to him.

At night she thought about a lot of things. She thought about Rufus, and Marsh. The knife wounds had not been deep, and Marsh had spent only a few days in the hospital.

At first Rufus had gone to jail for concealing Gwendolyn's death, but then Martin hired a lawyer for him and he was released.

Marsh had not been taken away at all. He was their hero. He had saved Babette's life. She could see the two of them on the bunkhouse porch, Rufus in his chair, Marsh petting the new pup.

At night she thought of everyone who had been a part of her life—even Rex, who had not really been a part of her life. Rex, whose picture hung on the wall of Dad's office.

Sometimes at night Babette saw a dark figure drifting through the moonlight, and she wondered—has Patrick in some way survived to come back to the farm? Was it the winged creature of darkness, the vampire that was part of him?

She had never told.

But she was afraid of the nights.

Between her breasts, in a locket, she carried a tiny portion of *Wolfsbane*. She would carry it all her life.

J.J. MARRIC MYSTERIES

Time passes quickly . . . As *DAY* blends with *NIGHT* and *WEEK* flies into *MONTH*, Gideon must fit together the pieces of death and destruction before time runs out!

GIDEON'S DAY   (2721, $3.95)
The mysterious death of a young police detective is only the beginning of a bizarre series of events which end in the fatal knifing of a seven-year-old girl. But for Commander George Gideon of New Scotland Yard, it is all in a day's work!

GIDEON'S MONTH   (2766, $3.95)
A smudged page on his calendar, Gideon's month is blackened by brazen and bizarre offenses ranging from mischief to murder. Gideon must put a halt to the sinister events which involve the corruption of children and a homicidal housekeeper, before the city drowns in blood!

GIDEON'S NIGHT   (2734, $3.50)
When an unusually virulent pair of psychopaths leaves behind a trail of pain, grief, and blood, Gideon once again is on the move. This time the terror all at once comes to a head and he must stop the deadly duel that is victimizing young women and children — in only one night!

GIDEON'S WEEK   (2722, $3.95)
When battered wife Ruby Benson set up her killer husband for capture by the cops, she never considered the possibility of his escape. Now Commander George Gideon of Scotland Yard must save Ruby from the vengeance of her sadistic spouse . . . or die trying!